SPARROW

SPARROWDANCE

Anne Lewis

HONNO TEENAGE FICTION

Published by Honno
'Ailsa Craig', Heol y Cawl, Dinas Powys,
South Glamorgan, Wales, CF6 4AH

British Library Cataloguing in Publication Data

A catalogue record for this book is available
from the British Library.

ISBN 1 870206 47 9

*Published with the financial support of
the Arts Council of Wales*

Cover design by Debbie Maidment

Typeset and printed in Wales by Gwasg Dinefwr, Llandybïe

Prologue

Be cautious what you dream of – it might come true

It was dark enough out there on the moor, but here in the wood it's blacker than the inside of a coal sack. It even feels like one: dank and musty and airless, and smelling faintly of cat.

If there's a path somewhere, I've missed it. I'm having to grope my way between the solid pitch blackness where the trees are and the very slightly thinner pitch blackness where they aren't. Everything I touch seems to be oozing great dripping globs of slime. Even the ground isn't safe: every so often my feet go straight through a rotten log, and the soggy mess inside gives off a gust of fungus spores that make my nose itch and my eyes swell up. Any minute now I'm going to start sneezing, and when I do, I know I won't be able to stop. It's amazing I haven't broken an ankle . . .

A normal wood shouldn't be like this. Normal woods aren't hot and stuffy and riddled with terminal rot like this one. The air shouldn't feel as though you could stir it with a stick. There should be leaf-mould underfoot, and the fresh green smell of chlorophyll, and gaps overhead through which to see the stars . . .

This is not a normal wood.

I keep thinking I can hear faint stealthy noises some distance behind me but it's hard to be sure because the blood's pounding in my ears loud enough to deafen an army. And this gives me fresh grounds for worry because now I daren't try to turn back . . .

I'm not cut out for this kind of thing. I'm all on my own. I'm sweaty and itchy and filthy dirty and covered in slime and the one thing I want more than anything else in the world is a bath. No, cancel that. What I *really* want, right now, is out of here. And *then* a bath.

I haven't a clue where I'm going, or what to do when I get there. I'm bruised and scratched and aching all over . . . oh, and scared. Don't forget scared. Every few moments I have to stop to let my knees catch up with the rest of me.

Every scrap of common sense I possess keeps telling me that this can't be happening to me. That this is not *real*.

I *know* what real is. Real is suburban Sussex; it's 68 Birtles Road Estate and Beech Lane High. Real is hanging about outside the Plaza with a bunch of my mates and hoping like hell that Alan McBride will appear with a bunch of *his* mates and that he'll maybe stop and smile at me and chat – knowing perfectly well that if he did, I'd be too embarrassed to say a word . . . Real is *safe*: it's fiddling about with make-up and hairstyles and reading the horoscopes and waiting for something to happen and being bored.

This is not real.

On the other hand, it can't be a nightmare. You don't get scratched and bruised and smelly in dreams. Well, not in the ones I normally have, anyway. Terrified, yes. Injured, no. Anway, if it is a dream, why's it taking me so long to wake up?

It's not fantasy, either. In my kind of make-believe I wouldn't be *alone* like this. I wouldn't be jelly-scared the way I am. Somewhere in the picture there'd be a Hero – tough, laconic, devastatingly good-looking – and he and I would be quarrelling like crazy the whole time because I'd be determined not to let on how attracted I was, not realising that he'd already fallen madly in love with me and was desperately trying to pretend he hadn't . . .

The voice of cold logic says, in that particular dream scenario, I wouldn't be *me*.

I'd be . . . oh, dear . . . that other persona. You know the one I mean – the glamorous alter ego at the secret heart of everybody's daydreams: the one with the perfect features and hair like a conditioner ad and legs up to her armpits and cheekbones you could cut your finger on . . .

This is definitely me, though, I can tell.

And I am groping and stumbling through this horrible wood in the pitch dark with all these random idiot thoughts skittering about inside my head because a bloke I don't even *fancy* any more didn't have the sense to recognise Trouble when it stared him in the face. If this were your average romantic fantasy *he* would be trying to rescue *me*, for Heaven's sake, not the other way round . . .

Too real to be fantasy, too fantastic to be real . . . There's only one thing I'm sure of – no amount of disbelief is going to get me off this particular hook.

Please God, my guardian angel if I have one, anybody Who

happens to be out there listening . . . Don't just hang about – *do* something. I'm not asking for miracles, You understand, because I'm well aware that direct intervention is dead against whatever rules operate Up There. All I'm asking is, if there's a booby trap in my immediate vicinity, or if something seriously horrible is about to jump out at me – just *warn me*, okay?

Please?

How did I get into this mess, anyway? I must have been *insane*.

PART ONE

Aurora

1.

Your Stars: CANCER (June 22–July 23)
All aspects of your chart emphasise the need for restraint
at present. Try to avoid direct confrontation with authority
figures. A close friend may be less than supportive in a
crisis, and a cherished dream may seem further away
than ever.

Let's be fair, though: I'm not psychic. So when I woke up that
Wednesday morning in June I couldn't possibly have known in
advance that this particular day would turn out to be the worst
on record bar one.

The day itself started with a row, which in our house is not
unusual. Basically, I didn't see why I had to go to school.

'Nobody else'll bother to turn up, so why do I need to go?
Everybody skives off after their GCSE's – it's *traditional*.'

'Term doesn't end for another four weeks, Foss, you know
that.' But Mum's voice was ever so slightly tinged with sympathy,
so I pushed my luck.

'All the exams are over, we've done the post-mortems . . . it's
just a waste of time going. Even the *staff* don't want us around. I
could be a lot more useful at home.'

Mum made a fatal error of judgement. 'Like how, exactly?'

'Shopping. Cleaning. Picking Geraint and Bridgie up from
school so they don't have to go to the minder's. You can come
straight home from work for once. And I'll cook dinner.' Cooking
is one of the things – no, correction: the *only* thing – I do quite
reasonably well. Okay, can the false modesty: I am a *good* cook.
I even thought about making a career out of it once, before
everybody started pointing out the snags and telling me it was a
mug's game and a feminist issue and that there were far more
worthwhile things to do with my life.

Mum was sorely tempted, I could tell. 'Well . . . I don't know . . .'

And from that point onwards everything could have been utterly different – if Scott hadn't appeared and put the boot in.

Scott is Mum's current (and serious) boyfriend – and we don't get on. I can guess what you're thinking at this point – I read the shrink pages too. I'm obviously the jealous, over-possessive type, probably suppressing anger at my dad for being dead, and outraged at the thought of anyone else trying to take his place . . . Poor old Scott, he hasn't a chance.

Nice theory. Plausible. The kind of thing your local GP comes up with when he or she knows nothing but the bare facts and doesn't actually care much anyway. But it simply isn't true.

I *know* it's not true because I never reacted that way to Martin, who was Scott's predecessor. Martin was lovely. Nothing much to look at, mind you – tall, gangly, all knees and elbows – but so *nice*. He was never sarcastic, never sneered at my school reports and never once made me feel like something the cat threw up – all of which Scott does, all the time. I never found out why Mum and Martin split up, but I was really upset when it happened.

Because, let's face it, my mother isn't the self-sufficient career type. She had a terrible time after Dad died in that car crash. My little brother Geraint was only a few months old, Bridget was four, and at eleven I wasn't a lot of help. There was something dodgy about the insurance, and if my Aunt Oz hadn't stepped in and played hell with the company we'd have been homeless and destitute as well as bereaved. As it was, we just about scraped by.

Mum deserves a slice of the good life, after what she's been through. I just wish she hadn't picked Scott, that's all.

We hadn't heard him approach. His voice just boomed out over our heads and made us both jump as though we'd been wiring up a slab of Semtex instead of contemplating a bit of minor truancy.

'Did I hear someone say that Francesca isn't going to school this morning?'

Mum and I spoke at the same moment: me saying 'Yes!' and Mum saying guiltily 'No, of course not!'. We both flushed scarlet and glanced accusingly at each other.

Scott isn't into Martial Arts: he doesn't have to be. Instead of the Path of the Dragon or whatever, he's developed his own technique. It's called the Eyebrow of Disdain, and it's a cracker. Guaranteed to transform the most confident, assertive, articulate person into a guilt-ridden wreck in a matter of seconds. He used it now.

'I see. And who said you could take the day off? Your Headmaster? The Deputy Head? Was there a note, perhaps, that you forgot to deliver?' He switched focus abruptly to Mum, who flinched. '*Did* you get a note?'

Mum was flustered. 'Well, no . . . but . . .'

'In that case I fail to see the problem. Francesca attends school, and continues to attend, until we are officially informed otherwise. End of story.'

At times like this, just on the perilous slippery verge of a major confrontation, people always urge you to keep calm. Be reasonable, they say. Don't lose your rag. Don't screech, don't give way to emotion: stand up for yourself but be dignified about it.

Which is all very well in theory. But what the agony aunts fail to appreciate is the past history of the row: the hundred similar confrontations in which reasonableness simply didn't work – when assertiveness was put down as rudeness and calm self-control as brass-faced insolence. The moment it starts up, all your good resolutions vanish out of the window and you yell and screech and get hysterical because this row isn't a new one, starting from cold – it's actually an extension of all the other rows: one more skirmish in a continuing war. The last thing it's really about is bunking off school.

It was a short, nasty, noisy row. I stormed out of the house in floods of tears, as usual. Mum caught me on the doorstep.

'Go to school, darling. Please.'

'Why should I?'

She looked drained, and I felt terrible. She handed me my school bag.

'Please, Foss. Your father would have wanted you to.'

I went off down the road choking back a whole new rush of tears. Okay, so perhaps Dad would have taken the same view as Scott on bunking off – he was dead keen on education, was Dad. But for Mum to imply that Dad and Scott had anything at all in common apart from being male was unbelievably hurtful.

On the way my mental videotape rewound itself and started treating me to an action replay of the whole incident, including

11

a running commentary on what I ought to have said and done if only I'd had the bottle. I was so absorbed I didn't realise that someone was trying to overtake me on the footpath past the roadworks at the end of our street. The first thing I noticed was a shadow on the wall beside me, and a sharp, faint chill. Someone in a hurry was very close behind me. I moved back against the tapes to let him/her pass.

There was no-one there. The shadow had vanished. The only person in sight was an ancient, decrepit baglady stumbling along twenty yards behind me.

I suppressed a shiver. I'd been so *certain*. I'd *felt* that urgent presence at my shoulder. Stress, I told myself firmly, and hurried on to join my friend Kirsty at the bus stop.

I'd been right about school. More than half the class hadn't bothered to turn up. End-of-term exams meant that our usual classroom wasn't free. We wandered about feeling spare until somebody directed us to the biology lab.

Mrs McAllister was tackling a mountain of paperwork and looking harassed.

'Amuse yourselves, people. Catch up on your reading, or something. Anything, as long as it's quiet.'

Jacquie and Leanne and the boys got out the lab TV set and began to watch cricket. The rest of us bunched around Kirsty who was reading the horoscopes in one of the magazines she'd brought.

'Gemini. Who's a Gemini?'

'Me!' said Carol, and shoved past me so as to read over Kirsty's shoulder. The lab stool I was sitting on rocked wildly. I grabbed at the bench to steady myself and knocked Kirsty's pile of unopened magazines onto the floor.

'Oh, for chrissake, Carol,' I said, and climbed down to pick them all up again.

That was when I saw the advert. It had spilled out along with all the other bumph they slip into magazines: the mail-order ads, the holiday brochures, the special offers on make-up and heirloom china and patio geraniums. But this was different.

It wasn't glossy or upmarket or even in colour. Just a single sheet of cheap paper smudgily printed in black-and-white. It caught the eye simply because it didn't seem to belong inside that kind of magazine.

At the top, a huge, tabloid-type headline urged:

12

GIRLS!!! DO YOU HATE THE WAY YOU LOOK???

An attention-gripper if ever there was one. I eased myself back onto the stool, and while Kirsty at my elbow went droning on about planetary influences on Carol's as far as I knew non-existent love-life, I gave the blurb a cursory scan.

CHANGE YOURSELF NOW!
*Doctor Dawson's Secret Formula Can Give You
The Beauty You've Always Wanted!!!*

It crossed my mind that any product using that many exclamation marks to sell itself had got to be a scam. But I read on anyway.

There was a whole paragraph in small, blurred print about how generations of women in Eastern harems had used a secret recipe to make themselves beautiful and desirable. And how Dr Dawson had rediscovered the recipe and refined the formula to make it available to all women, everywhere.

The clincher was a pair of grainy photographs side by side. One was of a miserable-looking skinny type with frizzy, darkish hair, sticking-out teeth and acne. The other was of a glitzy blonde bulging spectacularly out of a minuscule bikini top.

Jane (25) was plain and unloved. Until she tried a course of **Doctor Dawson's Secret Formula**. *But just look at her now!!!*

'What are you looking at?' said Gemma, and snatched the ad out of my hand. She spread it out on the bench, and five heads crowded together to look.

'Yuk, it's *disgusting*,' said Fiona.

'Wow!' said Carol, bug-eyed and believing every word of it.

Kirsty came to the same conclusion I had. 'It's a scam. It's not the same girl.'

'It is, though! See that mole? It's the same in both photos.'

'Felt pen,' I said.

'Aw, c'mon, Carol,' Kirsty said. 'You don't seriously believe a course of pills can do all that, do you?'

'It *could* be the same girl,' Joanne said dubiously.

'Yeah, after plastic surgery and a bleach job. But *not* as a result of dodgy old Doctor Dawson's so-called secret formula. Where did you get this, Foss? It's obscene.'

Carol still wasn't convinced. 'It's only fifty quid for a whole three months.'

'Fifty quid? You're off your head!'
Fiona was reading the last few lines aloud.

We hadn't noticed the lab door opening. Suddenly a slender, immaculately manicured hand was reaching over Kirsty's bent head. It picked up the ad. Sniggers and suggestive remarks froze in mid-flow.

'Interesting,' Xenia said in a tone of voice that conveyed the exact opposite. 'Haven't you anything better to do? Though I suppose drooling over this type of thing is normal for your age.'

Most people's mouths are automatically wired up to some kind of caution circuit. Mine is not.

'Tell us about it,' I heard myself say. 'You were this age two years ago. Perhaps you could give us some useful tips on sleaze in general.'

I could feel the people around me stiffen and lean surreptitiously away. Everybody knows Xenia is bad news.

She just smiled. 'I was never your age, Fishcake.' She surveyed us from her slender height. The gleaming ash-blonde hair swung briefly out and back again like one undivided swathe of silk. The delicate nose wrinkled just a little as she sniffed the air. Even her *nostrils* were immaculate.

'I don't quite know how to put this . . . but did someone forget to shower this morning? There's a certain odour hanging around you lot. Rotting seafood, perhaps? Definitely – well – fishy.'

Carol and Gemma giggled, and Kirsty aimed a glare in my direction which meant *Shutupshutupdon'tmakethingsworse*. I subsided, seething.

Foss, as you've probably gathered, is short for Francesca, which I couldn't pronounce when I was little. And given the range of options and the random nature of baby-talk, it was an amazingly lucky accident. (Think about it.) For once in my life I'd done something right by instinct and come up with a nickname most people can live with. Until the day I moved up to High School, and Xenia marked me out for a victim. I don't know why she decided to pick on me. I was going through a bad time at home, and perhaps it showed. Whatever the reason, for two whole years she made my life hell on a daily basis without leaving a single mark. Give me sticks and stones any day. Names can make you *suicidal*.

Xenia let the ad flutter back onto the bench, and dusted her fingers fastidiously with a tissue from Kirsty's box.

'Where did you find this thing? In a magazine? Heavens. You'd think the advertising standards people would have banned something as obvious as this, wouldn't you?' She bent down to peer at the photographs.

'Mind you,' she added, thoughtfully, 'The girl in the first picture does look an awful lot like little Fanny Fish.'

Having dropped her bombshell she smiled radiantly and was gone. Everyone suddenly sagged with relief and began to talk.

'She does, you know,' said Carol. 'Just a bit.'

'Does what?'

'Look like Fish . . . I mean Foss. The girl in Picture A.'

Everybody's eyes swivelled in my direction, and then down in unison to look at the photograph. I could feel myself going red.

'She does, too. She's got the same shaped face, for a start.'

'Don't be silly, Joanne,' Kirsty said sharply. 'Foss isn't *spotty*.'

'She's got freckles, though.'

'The hair's the same,' Gemma said with a hint of malice.

Fiona tittered. 'Blue-rinse Betty's Bargain Perms.' I winced. Everybody else but me gets their hair done at Maxim's, in town. I go to the hairdressers round the corner, to save money. My big mistake had been telling people so.

Joanne gave a saw-edged giggle. 'And the figure . . . Mind you, you're probably just a late developer, aren't you, Foss?' This time everybody sniggered.

'Well,' Kirsty said, glancing smugly down at her D-cup bosom, 'it's better to be small-busted than built the way I am. Buying bras is an absolute nightmare, you've no idea.'

The conversation drifted away into the arcane of underwires and cleavage and silicone implants and how you actually measure your bust in the first place. I just sat there and felt numb.

I didn't much mind the cracks about my figure. I know I'm thin, and 32A. It goes with being five foot nothing and small-boned and the youngest in my year: something I just have to live with. If I had Kirsty's figure I'd fall over frontwards. But what gutted me was the way they'd all taken Xenia's catty remarks on board with only a token protest from my best friend.

Perhaps my ego was feeling extra fragile after that row with Scott. Or perhaps all the thoughtlessly cruel little jibes I'd been trying to ignore over the past few years had finally gone critical. Whatever the reason, I suddenly felt as though a shadow had come between me and the sun. It chilled me and darkened me, like the shadow I'd glimpsed on the wall. Did I *really* look like that Jane woman? Even a little bit like that?

I tried to tell myself that it was just Xenia's influence at work. Xenia has an amazing talent for poisoning the atmosphere. Even after she's gone, malice condenses out of the air like fog.

Even so . . . I'm not *that* ugly, surely? Round-shouldered, sour-faced, gawky, with a perceptible moustache? Do my teeth stick out like that?

The rational, logical part of my mind said, Of course not – they're just being thoughtlessly catty out of boredom and because Xenia put the idea into their heads. Nothing personal intended. While the emotional side of me – the fearful, self-destructive, dark side – whispered, *How do you know? They could be right.*

I did a quick audit from memory. Okay, there are quite a few things I'd change if I had the chance, my hair being one of them. It's the kind of drab gingery-mousy colour you associate with parcel string, and so fine and frizzy it's unmanageable, even in braids. (I'd give *anything* for genuine black African hair like Gemma's, or failing that, just the normal, glossy European sort.) My specs, of course. My skin, which is dead-white and has so many freckles I look diseased. And yes, in a perfect world I'd be taller and better developed, no use denying it.

But suddenly it wasn't a case of *when I get that Saturday job I'll be able to afford contact lenses without having to bother Mum,* or *one day I'll get my hair professionally straightened and go properly red,* or even *one day I'll start filling out a bit here and there* . . . Suddenly these individual whinges weren't an issue any more. It was the whole package my so-called friends had been sniggering at. They'd been sniping at *me.*

I *can't* be that hideous. Can I?

And the sour, destructive side of me, like a dark shadow inside my head, whispered, *You're always the last to know.*

When break came, Kirsty and I wandered outside.

'Kirsty . . . look, be honest, will you? Am I really . . .?'

She wasn't listening. She was gazing speculatively across the quad to where a bunch of Sixth Formers were chatting to Jacquie and Gemma. Amongst them were Nick Davidson, Kirsty's current heart-throb, and Alan McBride whom I'd fancied for a whole year without having the courage to do anything about it.

'See you later,' she said, and sashayed across to join the group. Bosom out, tail in, head tilted provocatively to one side: confident, sexy, inviting. I watched the circle open to receive her, the smiles broaden and the wisecracks start.

I stood there, and once again felt numb. 'See you later,' she'd said: dismissive. As though I didn't count. Kirsty of all people knew how I felt about Alan McBride, just as I'd known about her crush on Nick. And now an opportunity had arisen and she'd dropped me like a used Kleenex. Because I wasn't in her league, and never would be. Because she was afraid that being seen with me would mess up her chances with Nick . . .

But it wasn't Nick who was chatting her up – it was Alan.

All at once I'd had as much as I could take. I wanted to go home. Crying my eyes out when I got there was a distinct option. I picked up my bag from the biology prep room and sneaked out of school. The bus came. I sat on the back seat grappling with a rush of totally illogical rage, thinking *Why did I have to be me?*

Why couldn't I have been Kirsty, or even Carol who, dim as she was, had only to ask her parents for fifty quid and got it counted out into her pudgy little hand? Why did I have to be poor, and ugly, and pathetic? Why was I *me*?

I didn't even register where the bus was going. It must have been a good ten minutes before I came out of my stupor and realised with a shock of recognition that I was on the wrong route. I'd been operating on automatic. I'd got on the bus that went past our old house in Victoria Avenue – the house which we'd sold three years ago but which I still thought of as home.

I got off at the familiar stop, letting a rather smelly old lady with a bunch of clinking carrier bags climb out in front of me.

The Avenue hadn't changed much: the trees overhung the road a little more and the hedges were a bit taller, but that was all. Until I reached our house.

The new owners had done it up since I'd seen it last, and converted it into flats. I didn't like the colour. Or the tacky plastic conservatory. Or the new gravel drive, or the fat-bottomed Porsche squatting in front of the new row of garages, or the shaved lawn where the old orchard used to be. They'd have tarted up the inside, too, I knew: divided the rooms, lowered the ceilings, stripped out all the big old fireplaces in favour of central heating, laid down fitted carpets everywhere . . .

I'd known this kind of thing was likely to happen – of course I had. But I wasn't prepared for the shock-wave of grief and loss that went through me on seeing the reality. I suppose deep down I'd been cherishing a wistful fantasy that perhaps one day we'd buy it back again. Now I knew different. There was no going back. The lovely shabby Victorian semi I'd grown up in had gone forever. The only place my old home existed now was inside my own head.

It was nearly two o'clock when I got back to our new house in Birtles Road. I let myself in quietly, out of habit. (Scott had played hell about latchkey kids at first, but even he had been forced to accept the inevitable.) I went upstairs, changed into jeans and a cotton top and was on my way down again to raid the fridge when I heard Scott's voice in the sitting-room. He was on the phone.

It was a horrible shock. He should have been at work. I froze on the halfway landing, expecting the door to open any moment and the roof to fall in.

Nothing happened. He just went on talking. Slowly it dawned on me that he hadn't heard me come in. He still thought he was alone in the house.

The sitting-room door was slightly ajar. As I backed cautiously up the stairs his voice got suddenly louder: he was pacing around the room with the phone. What had been an indistinct vocal drone suddenly gelled into real words, with terrifying implications.

'May I just point out that you haven't seen the child for five years? How can you possibly know what's been going on? . . . What? . . . I tell you that girl is driving Mairhi up the wall. I'm doing my best, but even so . . . Oh, yes. The other two are perfectly reasonable . . .'

Whoever it was that said eavesdroppers hear nothing but ill of themselves, was spot on correct. I went cold inside. Who was he talking to? Social Services? A shrink?

'She's rude, insolent, disobedient . . . What? Perhaps I haven't made myself clear. As a detached observer, I'd say she was verging on delinquency . . . Sorry? . . . No, I am not exaggerating . . . We both feel that a good boarding school . . .'

They're sending me away? All at once my knees collapsed. I sat down on the stairs, feeling sick and wobbly.

Inside the sitting room, the fractured conversation went on.

'I simply don't understand your attitude . . . What? . . . I can assure you, Mairhi thinks as I do . . . It's not as though the child is a blood relation, after all . . . Yes, I'm perfectly aware of the circumstances . . . But, when all's said and done, not her own child . . .'

I couldn't move. Black speckles were whizzing about in front of my eyes and joining up into blotches the size of jackdaws; I had to duck my head between my knees to stop myself passing out.

I heard the sharp angry clunk as Scott slammed the phone down. He marched out into the hall without looking up. The front door banged shut behind him.

I don't know how long I sat there. Emotions were roiling around inside me like time-lapsed thunderclouds. But the dominant one, the one that stayed, was fear. Gut-wrenching, paralysing fear.

Why hadn't anybody told me I was adopted?

Was that why I never seemed to do anything right? Why I didn't seem to fit in any more? Why Mum wanted to get shot of me . . .?

Verging on delinquency . . . The difficult one. The one who caused all the rows and the tears and the bad feelings. Of course they didn't want me around any more. Scott, Mum, Bridgie, Geraint – they were a unit which didn't include me. I was the outsider – the bossy little git who acted as though she had *rights* . . . I could feel myself going hot with shame and humiliation.

Why hadn't they told me?

Suddenly I was desperate to run – anywhere, as long as it was away from here, so I wouldn't have to face the family coming home and the horrible stinking sham we'd been living all these years. I raced upstairs and started cramming things into a backpack at random: clothes, underwear, toilet things, tampons. My hands were shaking and I couldn't see properly for tears. I took my savings book out of its drawer and the cash Oz had sent me in advance for my birthday, and stuffed them into my wallet.

There was something else in the drawer: the antique silver pendant Dad had given me for my eleventh birthday (*Dad-who-was-not-my-Dad*, an inner voice chanted sadly). I held it in my hand for a long moment, tracing the design of intricately twined leaves and long-legged birds with the tip of one finger. It was the single most precious thing I owned, and suddenly I couldn't bear to leave it behind. I fastened the clasp round my neck; the little silver talisman lay heavy and shining and oddly warm in the hollow of my throat. It felt *right*, somehow, and gave me one solitary grain of comfort in a day that in all other respects had been as barren as the moon.

Then I left, praying I wouldn't meet anyone I knew.

2.

Your Stars: CANCER (June 22–July 23)
You are facing difficult decisions which could have far-
reaching effects. Consider the options carefully before
making your choice. A significant encounter with a
stranger will have unexpected results.

First stop was the café in the park, where I bought coffee and a sandwich. Irrespective of the emotional crises currently ravaging my higher centres, my stomach was insisting it wanted filling, and was threatening to kick up quite a fuss if I didn't comply.

I found a quiet corner by the window and tried to work out what to do next.

The obvious place to run to was Kirsty's house – but I didn't know if I could trust Kirsty any more. She'd given my ego a vicious backhander and the bruises were still smarting.

Where else was there? Youth Hostels? The Salvation Army? London? Where do you go when you're ten days off your sixteenth birthday, and look younger, and don't have a home any more?

I couldn't think straight. My head was operating on two levels. The everyday sensible part of me was busily considering the options as above and automatically planning for survival, but a deeper, darker level kept surfacing and obliterating its progress. The darkness was whispering things like, *Why bother? Who needs you, anyway?* And it was right. I was nothing and nobody – just a scummy scrap of garbage chucked into the bin.

I'd been fingering my pendant idly in my right hand as I pondered. I glanced up in despair – and noticed a baglady sitting on the bench outside the café. Nothing remarkable in that. Except that today, for some reason, smelly old ladies with bulging carrier bags seemed to be *everywhere*. But this time, there was something disturbing about the squat figure hunched over that huge greasy shopping bag. It was double-focussed, somehow . . . like one of those holograms they put on credit cards. At one angle, you saw a perfectly ordinary baglady. Tilt your head a little the other way and you saw . . . a man-shaped shadow. Dark, not quite solid, and completely featureless. The two images swam in and out of focus, occupying the same space.

I let the pendant drop – and the effect vanished. Perhaps I was hallucinating – going nuts . . . It didn't bear thinking about.

I dragged my wandering wits together, and had a flash of inspiration. Kirsty's house might be out of bounds, but her brother Kieran lived in London. I'd known Kieran since I was six. Kirsty and I had stayed in his flat for a weekend just before Christmas. He wouldn't mind if I kipped on his floor – not for a few days, anyway, while I sorted myself out. And afterwards . . . Afterwards could wait.

I made my way to the station and got on the London train. I was half expecting the ominous baglady/shadow to be there on the platform, but there was no sign of her.

In London I took the tube to save money, and ended up half a mile from the street I wanted. The whole area was a lot seedier than I remembered: half-demolished houses, boarded-up windows covered in peeling posters and obscene graffiti, sinister-looking loiterers in grimy doorways. When I finally located the house and rang the doorbell, nobody answered. Kieran and his flatmates were out.

The next few hours were dire. It was a scorching hot day. I just wandered around, trying to avoid the stares of the loiterers and feeling acutely vulnerable. Kieran didn't appear. As evening drew on I began to get hungry, but I dared not go off in search of a decent place to eat in case I missed him again. In the end I bought a cup of greasy coffee in a neon-lit dive with dead bluebottles on the windowsills. Even hunger didn't tempt me to sample the cuisine.

At around ten-thirty I spotted a light in the flat's front room. By now the street lights were on and there were drunks about.

I rang the doorbell again.

A woman's voice drawled 'Yerss?' through the intercom. The voice sounded old, scratchy-hoarse. Not a girlfriend, then. The landlady? Somebody's mum?

I said, 'Is Kieran there, please?'

'Who?'

'Kieran. Kieran Leigh.'

'What d'you want *him* for?' It had to be the landlady. Poor Kieran.

'Um . . . I'm a friend of his sister's. Foss Ewins. I want to talk to him urgently.'

The mike went dead.

Eventually, lights went on somewhere down the hallway. Then the hall light itself. Finally the door opened an inch or two, still secured on its chain. I could hear heavy, wheezy breathing somewhere in the vicinity of the crack. The chain clinked and the door swung open.

Hall light and street-lamp shone full on her as she stood in the doorway. There was absolutely no mistaking that squat, hunched figure. It was the baglady.

And behind her, the doppelgänger. Only now it was huge and ink-dark, like thick black smoke from a tyre dump. It reached out towards me over the baglady's head – and an answering darkness inside me responded. I could feel it urging me to *Let go . . . Give in . . .*

I backed down the steps. Somewhere in the innermost crevices of my brain neurones were screaming at me to run, run – but I couldn't move. The dark fog enveloped and flowed through me, and part of me hugged it eagerly to myself. The darkness was warm and safe, it promised merciful oblivion: no more worries, no more pain or loss or humiliation. It was clogging my blood, paralysing my muscles, seeping through my bones. My hand went up to my mouth and I heard myself give a terrified whimper.

Above me, baglady and Shadow advanced onto the top step.

My hand dropped to my throat, where it touched something warm and metallic: the pendant round my neck. I felt a distinct *click!* somewhere inside my head, as though a switch had been thrown – and a millisecond later, a blessed surge of energy which kick-started me into what I swear was the fastest 100-metre dash outside the Olympics. And the Shadow followed.

I sprinted down the street and around the corner, past the café, the lurching drunks, the neon-lit pub and the shuttered shops, thinking *People . . . Lights . . . The Tube . . .* Ahead of me was the subway, under a big road junction. I risked a backward glance. The Shadow-thing was gaining on me, flowing along, moving in a way nothing with two legs has ever moved . . . Terrorstruck, I dived down the steps and raced along the tunnel.

Suddenly the subway branched. I couldn't remember which exit to take, and could barely read the signs in that dim greenish light. I chose one branch at random and forced my aching legs up the stairs two at a time, my backpack bouncing against my shoulder-blades.

It was the wrong exit. Not the busy shopping area I'd been aiming for, but a wide street lined with offices and banks, all closed, all dark. Cars streamed past on the road, but the pavements were deserted. No help here.

I forced my legs up a gear and went on running. Out of the tail of my eye I was aware of the Shadow emerging from the subway exit and giving chase.

I dared not turn my head or slow down. But as I ran I was keeping a lookout for a gap in the traffic. When it finally appeared I launched myself into the road and across the centre reservation. Cars swerved and hooted, but somehow I made it to the far side. I dashed down a side street and under a railway bridge. This last manoeuvre brought me out onto a major road.

By now I had a stitch in my side and every step was hot agony. The straps of my backpack had worn a sore strip across my shoulder. Away in the distance I could see lights and the blessed logo of London Underground. I glanced behind me as I ran, and saw the Shadow emerging from under the bridge.

At first I didn't notice the car pulling up alongside. After a moment or two I realised that the driver was keeping pace with me. Fresh panic surfaced. Having a run-in with a kerb-crawler was the last thing I needed.

The driver sounded the horn at me. I ignored it. And still the car kept pace. Something about it was vaguely familiar – it was an old Morris Minor – but I was too frantic to wonder why. Then I heard the passenger window being wound down and a voice shouting 'Foss! Foss!'

I turned my head without slackening speed. The car pulled ahead of me, stopped. Somebody stretched across and flung the passenger door open. 'Foss! Get in! Now!'

In the driver's seat, craning anxiously up at me, was the prim silver-haired figure of Miss Adeled Ossian Ewins. My great-aunt Oz.

My jaw dropped. I clung to the open door for support and gasped out the first thing that popped into my head.

'I'm not going home! You can't make me! I won't!'

'Don't be *silly*, Foss, of course you're not going home. Get in!'

I glanced back. The Shadow was less than twenty yards away, and accelerating. Terror overrode principle. I hauled the pack off my shoulder, fell into the passenger seat and slammed the door. Oz was moving up the gears while I was still fumbling with the seat belt.

A gust of total blackness enveloped us from behind. The car juddered. Next moment, G-force slammed me against the back of my seat. Maybe I was hallucinating as an after-effect of that incredible dash – but for a moment the little Morris seemed to take off as though it was reinventing space-flight. I got a confused impression of blinding whiteness obliterating the black, and a faint diminishing yowl of pain and rage. Above us and on either side the lights of the city streaked into a tunnel of multicoloured streamers. I yelled at Oz above the noise.

'What have you got in that tank? Rocket fuel?'

She gave me a brief, tight grin and concentrated on steering. The streamers condensed into individual globules of light and suddenly, without any sensation of braking, the Morris was moving sedately along in the middle of a normal flow of traffic. I guessed we were somewhere on the M25. As to how we'd got there – well, I must have passed out for a few minutes. No other explanation made any sense.

But the Shadow-thing had been real. Hadn't it?

Somewhere along the line, I'd stopped breathing. Now I started again. In, out. In, out. It felt wonderful. I leaned back and felt my aching legs throb as they relaxed. Gradually I got a grip on my fuddled wits. 'Who told you?'

'Mairhi phoned. She was hysterical.'

'Oh, God . . .' I went cold. That was something I hadn't considered. Mum in tears on the phone, sobbing, accusing . . . I hadn't even left a note . . .

'Why did she ring *you*?'

Oz said bitterly, 'Last resort, I suppose.' After Dad died, Mum had cut Oz out of all our lives. I'd never understood why.

'How did you know where I was?'

She shrugged. 'Lucky guess. Where does a person head for when they're running away from home? London. Who do you know in London? Kirsty's brother. I was on my way to his flat when you showed up.'

Put like that, my grand gesture of defiance seemed pretty infantile, after all. Embarrassingly predictable, in fact. I could feel myself blushing.

'I didn't know where else to go,' I mumbled.

The Morris purred along in the inside lane. The billion-dollar question was trembling on the tip of my tongue. Finally it burst out of me.

'Why didn't anybody tell me I was adopted?'

'*What?*'

'Oh, right,' I said bitterly. 'You too. It's a conspiracy, isn't it? All of you stringing me along . . .'

'Foss, what the hell are you talking about? . . .' She broke off and groaned. 'It was Scott, wasn't it? On the phone this afternoon. You overheard.'

It was my turn to gawp. 'What? How . . .?'

'I could *throttle* that man,' Oz said angrily. 'He really is the most complete *pillock*.' She saw my bewildered expression and explained. 'It was me on the other end.'

Light dawned. 'But he said . . . he said . . .'

'Cast your mind back, lovey. What exactly did he say?'

I tried to remember the precise words. It wasn't easy – they'd got lost in a fog of emotions. 'Something about me not being Mum's flesh and blood . . .'

'Correction. What he actually said was "*it's not as though she's a blood relation.*" Meaning *mine*. I was your father's guardian, remember?'

I was stunned. I'd always known that Oz had adopted my dad after his parents had died . . . it simply hadn't occurred to me to make the link. I'd shot off on my own trajectory, like a rogue rocket in self-destruct mode. And imagined all that stuff about bagladies and Shadows on the way? None of it made sense otherwise. Stress can do weird things to people . . .

'Oh . . . Oz . . . But he said, "*not her own child*" . . .'

'I suspect you weren't hearing too clearly at that point, my love. Not her, *your*. If I remember correctly, he was telling me I couldn't possibly know you because your father wasn't my own child.'

Sheer relief opened the floodgates. I started to cry. Oz handed me a packet of Kleenex and let me get on with it.

We'd left the motorway now, and were on a substantial and very busy link road. Oz began to indicate left.

'All-night caff,' she said. My stomach griped: I'd forgotten how hungry I was.

The Morris pulled up in the car park. Oz switched off the engine and just sat there, looking thoughtful. 'If you had been adopted – would it have made that much difference to you?'

I wanted to say yes – mainly to justify the pain, and running away. But Oz is one of those people who won't accept convenient lies.

26

'I . . . No, probably not. Of course not.' She'd done a good job on Dad, after all – no traumas there.

'But it upset you at the time?'

'It was a shock, that's all. On top of everything else . . . after all those things Scott said about me . . .'

'You don't think your mother had anything to do with that, do you? Scott was lying through his teeth. That boarding-school scheme . . . '

'Did you believe him?'

Her snort of contempt was manna in the wilderness. 'Don't be ridiculous. I *know* you!'

I couldn't help it, I started to cry again. This time the tears wouldn't stop, however hard I tried to contain them. Oz put both arms round me and hugged me hard. I wept into her shoulder, wept and wept until her cardigan was soaked through. Eventually the flow diminished and I pulled away.

'Oh, Oz . . . I'm sorry . . .'

She handed me the Kleenex again. Her voice was grim.

'Now you're going to tell me exactly what's been going on.'

I told her, in between sniffs and hiccups and more tears. Things I'd never said to another living soul. Mum's depression attacks after Dad died. Bunking off school over and over again in the first and second years to look after Geraint and Bridgie because Mum couldn't cope. Lying awake night after night listening to her crying. Being worried sick in case she took an overdose. All those awful holidays with the Irish aunts in Dublin – gruesome people with a graveyard fixation which made Mum worse . . . Xenia and her non-stop needling at school. Being afraid to ask for money, and missing out socially because of it. The thoughtless little jokes at my expense. All the rows with Scott . . .

Oz's face got stonier and stonier.

'I can't go back there,' I said at last. 'I know I ought to. But I can't. Not right away.'

'No reason why you should. Nothing happening at school right now, is there?'

I shook my head. 'Only Work Experience in July.'

'Then give yourself a break, love. First we eat, then I phone Mairhi to say I've found you – then I suggest you come back to Triddon with me.'

Relief glowed a little brighter in the bleakness – relief, and a familiar ache of loss.

'Triddon?'

She shrugged. 'Up to you. Not what you'd call the hub of the universe, but Jo'll be there, and he has a fairly active social life from all I hear, so it can't be too dire.'

My conscience kicked in, all the harder for having gone AWOL. 'But Mum . . . the kids . . . Scott . . .'

'You can't go on fighting your mother's battles for her, Foss. She has to sort out her relationships for herself. Good God, where has Mairhi *been* these last five years? I knew things were bad, but . . . If only she'd come to me . . . I could have helped.' She made a helpless gesture and looked very sad. 'We can't intervene unless we're invited. You understand that, don't you?'

'Why doesn't Mum like you, Oz?'

'It's a long story, love. Come on. Food. You'll feel a lot better.'

'I look such a mess,' I wailed. Oz assessed the damage.

'Actually, it's not too bad. Most of the mascara came off in the first round.' She took my glasses off and dabbed around my eyes with a tissue. 'There. Perfectly respectable, if a bit shiny. Nobody'll notice. You weren't counting on meeting a talent-spotter for *Blind Date*, were you?'

I had to giggle.

It was a *good* caff. Freshly-made pizzas, real coffee. Oz went to phone Mum while I ate. She came back looking grimly pleased with herself.

'If it's any satisfaction to you, my dear, you seem to have scared the living daylights out of Scott. Round One to Foss, I'd say.'

I fell asleep within minutes of getting back in the car. It was warm, relaxed sleep, but very shallow. Every now and again I surfaced briefly and was aware of motorway lights sweeping past and around us like a giant carousel with the car humming and vibrating in the middle. Later, I woke to a dark road with no other traffic about.

'Hate motorways,' said Oz. 'Go back to sleep.'

I relaxed back into a doze, thinking, *Triddon. Triddon Magna.* And Tan-y-Fedwen, Oz's home. Before Dad died, we'd stayed there every summer. I'd had friends in Triddon, too: Jo, three and a half years older, from Meini Hirion, the farm next door, and Anwen and Enlli from the village. I'd lost touch with the two girls, but I still sent birthday cards to Jo. It occurred to me that I'd missed him more than anyone: Jo, the kind, big-brother figure who hadn't minded an adoring little girl tagging along wherever he went. I'd loved his parents, too: Emlyn and Bess had been like an uncle and aunt to me in those days . . .

Triddon had been my second home. A small, secure, sunshiny world which had vanished out of my life the day Dad died. It had meant so much to me, and contained so many memories, I wasn't sure if I could handle it.

I must have drifted off to sleep again, because the next thing I became aware of was Oz's voice talking to someone. The car was still moving.

'. . . keep an eye on the situation for me? Thanks. Yes . . . She's fine . . . No harm done, thank God . . .' I must have stirred slightly, because she said, 'Uh-oh. Can't talk now. Good-bye, Magnus. Take care.'

There was a click. I opened my eyes. 'Who's Magnus?'

'Just a colleague.'

'You ring colleagues up in the middle of the night?'

'It's not the middle of the night where he is.'

Oz as an international executive was a startling development. I said slyly, 'Is he nice?'

'Very nice. But far too old for you, my girl.'

'I wasn't thinking of me.'

She laughed, and wouldn't say any more.

Outside, the darkness was greying towards dawn. I sat up and stretched. 'Where are we?'

'About an hour away. Are you awake now?'

'M-hm.'

'Good. Because there's been a slight change of plan. Really, *not* a problem, okay?'

My heart sank. 'What?'

'Remember that conference I wrote to you about? The one in Philadelphia?'

It all came crashing in on me. She'd retired from her job with Social Services two years ago and, typical workaholic Oz, had immediately registered to do research for a doctorate. In the letter she'd told me how she'd been invited to present a paper at this high-powered conference in Philadelphia, and how excited she was.

I felt terrible. I hadn't answered the letter; I'd been so absorbed in my own problems I hadn't even sent her a good luck card. 'And it's soon?'

'The conference starts tomorrow, but my bit's not until the next day. I'm booked on a flight late tonight.'

I was appalled. 'Oh, Oz – I'm so sorry! I've kept you up all night . . . Trust me to muck things up for people . . .'

'Don't be silly. I can sleep when we get home. The thing is . . . It's not a good idea for you to stay at my house all on your own. I rang Bess at Meini Hirion and she'll be delighted to put you up for a week or so, until I get back.'

I must have looked dubious, because she added gently, 'She's missed you, you know. We all have.'

3.

Your Stars: CANCER (June 21–July 22)
You would be wise to await developments before taking
any action which might affect others. Friends and colleagues
give a welcome boost to your ego. Financially, you can
expect a pleasant surprise.

By the time the sun came up, England was behind and below us
and Wales was piling up, grey-blue and starkly beautiful, in
front.

Bess was waiting on the doorstep of Meini Hirion in her
dressing-gown. She greeted me with a hug that would have
triggered off another rush of tears if I hadn't been so drained
already. I wasn't in a fit state to notice much – all dopey and
gummed-up with interrupted sleep – but she didn't seem to
have changed a bit in five years.

Neither had Jo. If I'd allowed myself a fleeting wistful vision
of a Jo grown tall and dark and smouldering-looking, it didn't
survive the reality. Apart from the No. 4 haircut and the earring
and the black leather jacket, he was just a bigger version of the
fourteen-year-old I remembered from last time. Shortish, stocky,
brown hair, brown eyes, all-over ordinary-looking except when
he smiled. In a way, I was relieved. One less complication.

He was fully dressed and shovelling down a hurried breakfast at this unholy hour of the morning because he had to drive
his girlfriend to Manchester airport. I was too dazed to ask why.
Within ten minutes I was being packed off to bed.

I slept for a solid thirteen hours and dreamt vivid, disturbing
dreams. I was being pursued by huge, malignant shadows, by
Scott and Mum and the teachers at school. I was running,
hiding, running again. At one point Dad appeared, but when I
pleaded with him to help me he turned his back and vanished.
In another dream I was searching desperately for Oz's house,
which had unaccountably shifted to the far end of Birtles Road
Estate. When I opened the front door the whole house was
silent and derelict and full of snowdrifts and blown rubbish. Oz
and Bridgie and Geraint were lying dead, and there was blood
on the snow.

I woke up feeling raw and fragile and somehow convinced that whatever was happening to me, it wasn't over yet.

When I got downstairs Bess was alone in the kitchen.

'Oz rang from the airport,' she told me cheerfully. 'She's on her way.'

'Is she okay?'

'Chirpy as a cricket,' said Bess. 'She sent you her love.'

There was cold meat and salad on the table, and fresh bread rolls, with strawberries and cream for afters. Over the meal I tried, a bit awkwardly, to apologise for all the melodrama.

'I'm sorry, Bess. I honestly don't know what came over me. I just overreacted to every single thing that happened . . . Not like me at all.' Which is broadly true. Okay, so Scott blows my fuses on a regular basis – but by and large, in our house I'm the *sensible* one. The one who makes sure there's toilet paper in the loo and the kids have clean socks and lunch money every morning, you know the sort of thing. All of which I'd abandoned yesterday to run away. The worm of guilt flashed a fang.

'I know, *cariad*.' She gave me a hug. 'Don't blame yourself. You've had a tough time these last few years. Sooner or later something had to give.'

I stiffened up. 'Oz *told* you?'

'Only the broad outline. I was worried, so I nagged her.'

'Oh.' I relaxed a bit. If you can't trust Bess, you can't trust anybody.

'You'd be amazed at how many teenagers find themselves in your position, Foss. Young carers that nobody knows about . . .'

'*What?*' I wanted to laugh. 'Mum didn't have ME, or Altzheimer's, or anything like that . . .'

She held up a stern finger. 'You supported your mother through a major emotional trauma. You took on adult responsibilities that no young adolescent should have to cope with. Give yourself some credit, girl.'

Oddly enough, hearing her say that made me feel a bit better. It didn't solve any of the immediate problems, but at least somebody was telling me I wasn't crazy. Temporarily stressed out of my head, perhaps. But not crazy.

'Your mother phoned while you were asleep,' Bess added. 'I told her to try again around seven-thirty.'

Sure enough, at seven-twenty-nine the phone rang. When

Bess called me into the hall my heart started thumping and my hands shook. I'd been dreading this moment.

Mum was distraught. A sly, treacherous thought that popped up out of nowhere, like a gleeful demon, said *When did she ever not sound as if the sky was about to fall in? Even before Dad died?*

'Foss darling, come home.' She was in tears. 'Please, darling. We'll drive down and fetch you tomorrow.'

Panic jammed my mental gears. I said the first thing that popped into my head. 'It's up.'

'What?'

'Up, not down. It's North and about eight hundred feet higher than you are.'

'Foss, I can't cope with this. Listen to me, please. I want you here, back home with us, where you belong. It's your birthday on the 30th. We're coming to fetch you.'

'You and Scott? I don't *want* Scott here, Mum.' The very idea of Scott in Triddon made my neck hair stand on end.

'He's terribly upset. I don't know what you thought he said, darling, but none of it's true . . .'

'Mum, don't cry, please! I'm sorry I disappeared like that without telling you, but . . . It's no big deal, honestly. I'm perfectly okay. I just need a break, that's all. A bit of time to myself.'

'You can have that at home!'

'Mum . . . please . . . I'll be back by the 30th. I just want to stay here on my own for a few days . . .'

Scott came on the line.

'You've caused your mother a great deal of unnecessary anxiety, Francesca. She's very upset. The very least you can do is . . .'

I held the receiver away from my ear in despair. Bess put her arm round my shoulders. We exchanged wordless signals while Scott's tiny voice went on gabbling at the end of the line. She took the phone from my limp grasp.

'Let me talk to him . . . Hallo? This is Mrs Morgan. I can assure you that Foss is being well looked after here. Now, if you don't mind, I'd like to speak to Mairhi.'

I hovered, my hand half-out to take the receiver, but Bess just scowled at me and made shooing gestures. I left her to it and sat in the kitchen with the door shut. The effort of calming Mum down had left me practically catatonic.

Bess came in five minutes later.

'Are they coming to fetch me?'

She shook her head. 'I think I managed to convince your mother that you were perfectly all right with me until Oz gets back.'

'Parents,' I said weakly. 'Who'd have 'em?' – and Bess laughed.

'Wait till you have children! Parents are all the same. You should have heard Emlyn when Jo bought that big motorbike of his. He hit the *roof*!'

'*Emlyn* did?' Emlyn, who never said a word when a grunt would do?

'I know. Amazing, isn't it? You live with them all these years and they still manage to surprise you. Talking of surprises . . .' She winked at me and stood up. 'Got something to show you. It's through here.' She flung open a connecting door with a flamboyant gesture. 'Da-daaahhh!'

I gawped in genuine shock. Five years ago the disused dairy leading off the kitchen had been a cold, damp repository for junk. Not any more. Now it was a fully-equipped caterer's kitchen with stainless steel worktops, a huge double oven and fridges and freezers you could have camped out in.

Bess was giggling delightedly at my reaction. I found my voice. 'Bess, it's *fabulous*! But why . . .? what . . .?'

'Diversification,' she explained. 'Small farms like ours aren't doing that well any more, so . . . We've got holiday accommodation in what used to be the old stone barn – and this. I cook,' she added unnecessarily. 'Private parties, weddings, dinners, you name it.'

'And there's a market for that sort of thing? In *Triddon*?' Triddon village itself is minuscule. Five cottages, a post office and a pub: blink on the way through and you've missed it. Count the various farms and scattered clusters of cottages in the Triddon postal district and you've got around three hundred people all told. Given that there aren't any grand houses around either, whoever christened the place Triddon Magna must have been either joking or seriously out of touch with current events.

Bess shook her head ruefully. 'Not just Triddon. I hate to say it, but we're commuter country now. Conference centres, big houses, weekend guests . . . People like to entertain their business contacts in private, and they want high-class cuisine. I'm expensive,' she added candidly, 'but I *am* the best.'

She would be, too. Bess is absolutely the most gifted cook I know.

She was catering for a wedding buffet at a big country house the next day. She gave me a sly look. 'D'you want to scrub up and blind-bake some tartlets while I start on the tiramisu?'

That evening the years melted away. Suddenly I was eleven again, cooking under Bess's tuition and loving every milli-second. We gossiped and told each other silly stories and laughed a lot and it struck me that I hadn't had *fun* like this since the last time I was at Triddon, five years ago.

Out of the blue I found myself saying, 'Dad always thought cooking was a joke. He wanted me to go for a degree, get a job in a lab somewhere.'

Bess shrugged. 'You haven't lost your touch with pastry.'

Next morning Jo and I got up early to help her pack the banquet into her van. There was a small suitcase as well, because she wasn't planning on getting back until the following day. The wedding venue was half an hour's drive from the house of a friend she hadn't seen for years, so she'd arranged to call in on her way home, and spend the night there. 'Open up a bottle of plonk and have a good goss,' was how she put it.

Jo was uncharacteristically glum. I wondered what had upset him, and hoped it wasn't me.

'Your mum's like a robin,' I said, as the van disappeared down the lane. 'Quick and sudden and chirpy.'

He managed a grin. 'Nah. Robins are nasty little buggers. I reckon she's more like a blackbird. And you're a sparrow, remember?'

I remembered. Jo's nickname for me when I was little. A Cockney sparrer, because I'd been born in Islington. The description didn't exactly thrill me.

'Yeah, small and brown and boring,' I said bitterly.

'C'mon. Sparrows are great. Tons of personality.' He made a visible effort to shake off the blues. 'Want to come down and help me feed the pigs?'

It had rained in the night, and the early morning sunshine made everything dazzle like a chandelier. Jo squinted up at the sky as we trudged across the yard. 'More rain on its way. Hope it clears up by tomorrow.'

'What's tomorrow?'

'Midsummer Church Fête. They hold it in that big field of ours, down by the river. You can help with Jeffrey, if you want. We're giving kids rides in the cart.'

'Isn't he a bit old for that now?' Jeffrey the cob had been a fixture at Meini Hirion for as long as I could remember.

'Nah . . . he loves it.'

'What about your girlfriend?'

'Caren? She went back to Sweden yesterday.' Which explained at least some of Jo's moroseness.

The piglets greeted us with shrill ecstatic squeals and wildly gyrating tails.

'They're new, aren't they? You didn't keep pigs before.'

'M-hm. I had a year out on a farm in Denmark, learning the business.'

'So you'll just stay here and be a pig man?'

Jo snorted. 'Not if I can help it. I'm starting an Agri degree in September.'

A lump composed of sheer envy rose in my throat. First Bess and now Jo – busy, fulfilled, going places, doing things they wanted to do. Whereas I . . . From the perspective of Birtles Road, my future looked bleak whichever way I turned.

As we walked back to the house Jo said suddenly, 'Why don't you go red? I reckon it'd suit you. I mean, you're nearly red as it is.'

I blinked. The shock was considerable. Jo, in his pig-spattered overalls and wellies, doling out beauty advice?

'Never really thought about it,' I lied. 'Anyway, Dad was dead against dyed hair.' I was surprised at the easy way it slipped out. It was true, and it was the real reason I hadn't experimented with rinses years ago. Dad wouldn't have liked it.

Jo stopped and glared at me. 'You know something, sparrow? Dads are dead against all sorts of things that don't matter. You should've heard my dad when I bought that bike.'

'Bess said he hit the roof.'

'He went *ballistic*. But – and this is the funny part – last week I gave him a lift down to the pub. When we roared into the car park all his mates turned round and almost dropped their pints in shock, and Dad went swaggering in grinning from ear to ear. Just for a moment there, he felt like a million dollars, and it showed.'

It was a lovely picture, and it made my eyes fill with tears, soppy idiot that I am.

'What I'm saying, Foss,' he went on awkwardly, 'is . . . don't let your dad stand in your way. You're not ten years old any more. Everything's moved on. You've changed. And your dad would have changed, too, if he was still here.' He grinned. 'If you ask me, that's what teenagers are for. To stop parents fossilising in their tracks.'

By mid-morning the rain had started again. Jo and Emlyn were off in the truck to inspect the fences. 'You can come with us, if you like,' Jo offered. 'It's a pretty manky sort of a day, though, and to be honest there's not a lot you can do to help.'

I thought about it. The prospect of hanging about wet, cold and bored while the men hammered stakes and stretched fencing wire didn't appeal one bit. Anyway, I had unfinished business to attend to.

'I think I'll go up to Tan-y-Fedwen for a bit. Oz wouldn't mind, would she?' It wasn't just the horror of yesterday's dream that needed exorcising. Somehow I had to come to terms with all those other memories, too. And the sooner the better, before I lost my nerve.

Jo understood, and looked dubious. 'On your own?'

'If it gets too much, I can always come back.'

He nodded. 'I'll have the mobile in the truck all day. Give me a bell if you want a lift.'

I trudged up the lane, splashing through the puddles, and reached Tan-y-Fedwen just as the rain eased off. I had to stop at the gate for a few moments to let the jolt of recognition subside. Meini Hirion had changed and moved on – but Oz's little house was like a time warp. Everything about it was painfully familiar: the ancient watchtower with the long, low farmhouse tacked on to it, the garden, the feel of the gate under my hand, the dip in the worn stone step . . .

My heart was thumping as I walked up the path to the front door. Roses dripped petals on my head, and wet lavender bushes brushed against me releasing great damp gusts of scent. I opened up the outer half-door and stood in the porch. It took me a moment to pluck up enough courage to fit the key in the lock and walk in.

Of course there was no snow, no blood, no dead bodies. Oz's cluttered, homey sitting-room was exactly as it had always been. Same pictures, same photographs, the same slightly faded William Morris chintz at the windows and covering the armchairs.

Now the room was slightly chilly, and had that indefinable air of wary expectancy all houses have when their owners are away. I set a match to the fire she'd laid. The flames leapt and the chilled room began to warm as if in gratitude. I pulled her chair close to the fire and sat there for a long time, remembering my father.

At first I cried a storm, but when it passed a calmness fell, soothing raw places I hadn't even known about. It struck me suddenly that I'd never really cried like this after Dad died. There hadn't been time. I'd gone around with a permanent headache and a lump in my throat like a huge cactus ball – but I'd been too busy looking after Geraint and Bridgie and worrying about Mum to cry.

Eventually I got up and began to prowl around the lovely higgledy-piggledy little house. It was centuries old. Each successive generation had added a bit more onto it. I remembered all the steps up and steps down, the unexpected rooms and funny little corridors everywhere. Finally, I wandered up the stone steps and into the topmost room of the old tower where I'd slept as a child. Books I'd left behind were still on the shelves: ballet books, horsey books, annuals. Animal ornaments, a doll, a forgotten hairbrush. Oz hadn't thrown anything away.

She'd made changes, though. Freshly-painted white walls, black-stained beams, a Chinese rug in delicate blues and greens on the newly sanded and varnished floor. The duvet cover was new – pale apple-green with tiny flowers, to match the new curtains. On the low table beside the bed was a lamp I didn't recognise, and a new clock-radio. In one corner was a pine staircase that hadn't been there before. I followed it down to the next floor and found myself in a tiny shower-room with green and blue towels and scented soap. When I sauntered into the middle room of the tower I had another shock – the junk had been cleared out and it was now a little girl's bedroom, all pink and white and frilly: Bridgie's room, which she'd never seen.

It hit me then like a wet sock just how much Oz must have grieved, too – not only for Dad, but for all of us. Up until five years ago, she'd had a family: Dad, me, Bridgie as a toddler, occasionally Mum. And then, out of the blue, the visits had stopped. Summer after summer, an empty house. But still the little improvements: the new shower, Bridgie's new room, a more sophisticated look for mine . . . Just in case, someday, we all came back again . . .

38

Downstairs, the doorbell rang, and I jumped.

The visitor wasn't Jo. It was a tweed-hatted, raincoated lady with cheery teeth and a blonde rinse. She was carrying a couple of baskets and a collection box. When she saw me the bright tombstone smile faded into an expression of guarded suspicion.

'Oh. Is Miss Ewins in?' Her voice was English, and forceful. One of the recent incomers, I guessed. I told her I was Miss Ewins's niece.

'Ah. From Birmingham, I understand?'

'No,' I said, and told her where. Her face cleared. I'd passed the Neighbourhood Watch test and all was well.

'Oh. Hello. I'm Pam Fosdike. I'm collecting for the church restoration fund, you know?' We shook hands, a bit more vigorously than was strictly necessary. The rain had started again, so I asked her in. She went straight into her sales pitch.

'Of course, normally one would hold jumble sales and coffee mornings and so on, but in a scattered community like this, nobody ever seems to turn up. So once a month I do the rounds. There's a discount warehouse which sells to charities, and it's all good, useful stuff.' She plonked the baskets on the table, and eyed me hopefully. 'Miss Ewins usually buys something. There's a jar on the mantelpiece,' she added helpfully. 'I'm sure she won't mind.'

The jar contained a few pounds' worth of small change; the kind of thing you keep for the milkman. 'Er . . . how much . . .?'

'Oh, a couple of quid, usually,' Mrs Fosdike assured me.

I rummaged through the baskets and selected a pack of scrubbing-pads and a bottle of environmentally-friendly washing-up liquid, on the principle that you can't go far wrong with basic cleaning materials. I dug into my jeans pocket and found a fiver with which I bought a bottle of cologne for Bess.

'Tell you what,' Mrs Fosdike said, 'Why don't you get the talc as well? They came as a pack originally, but I find people tend to steer clear of packs unless it's Christmas. I can let you have both for five pounds. It's quite good stuff, actually. They make it for Boots, I believe.'

Remembering my country manners, I saw her to the gate. It wasn't until I'd gone back inside that I noticed the mistake. The round box she'd left with the cologne wasn't talc. It was too small; the packaging was completely different and when I picked it up it rattled. I snatched it up and rushed outside again.

'Hey! Mrs Fosdike! Excuse me!'

She'd parked her car on the only bit of flattish verge, twenty yards further down the lane. She was stowing her baskets in the boot, and had her back to me. I dashed down the path.

'Mrs Fosdike! You've given me the wrong box!'

She'd got into the driver's seat now, and was slamming the door shut. The Volvo's engine roared, drowning my voice. She beamed brightly at me, waved and drove off.

For the first time, I took a good look at the box I was clutching – and started to laugh. The tacky black-and-white label, the tabloid print, the blurb beneath were all horribly familiar. I slit the label with my fingernail and opened the lid. Inside were four little plastic phials of brown liquid, and an instruction leaflet. It was Doctor Dawson's Secret Formula – one course of which was supposed to change your life. Fifty quid's worth by mail order – and I'd got it from a charity lady for a pound.

In the afternoon the clouds cleared away and the sun came out. I strolled around the glittering, fragrant garden. Tensions I hadn't been aware of were draining out of every muscle. I hadn't felt so relaxed and at peace for years. It crossed my mind that I ought to ring Jo and offer to help around the farm – but I didn't want to break the mood. Not just yet. Instead I picked a fistful of clove-pinks for my room and a big bunch of roses for the sitting-room windowsill.

As I was arranging the roses in their vase I suddenly caught sight of my reflection in a little dark mirror, half-hidden behind the curtain. The mirror was very old. The frame was black, and slightly worm-eaten at one side, the glass brownish and uneven. I'd never seen it before – one of Oz's junk-shop finds, I guessed – but why would she tuck it away out of sight like this?

Normally the scrutiny of my reflection would have lasted three seconds at the outside – just long enough to make a sour face at myself and beat a hasty retreat. But in this glass I looked . . . different. My hair was in its usual back-plait (I'd grown it long in the mistaken assumption that the weight would mitigate the frizz, but of course it hadn't), but the front bits had sprung loose, as usual. In the dim stained glass of the mirror it looked cut short, like a curly halo, and where the sun shone through it the colour wasn't the familiar drab not-quite-brown but true fiery red. I was wearing a green top with a scoop neck – but the

40

mirror gave the impression of a low-necked velvet gown. The silver pendant shone brilliantly in the hollow of my throat. It was me, all right – but at the same time, it wasn't. I stared, intrigued and oddly uneasy. The girl in the mirror stared back. Something crucial was missing – but I couldn't quite pin it down.

Just then the phone rang. It was Jo. He sounded tense.

'Foss? Listen. Scott just phoned. They're on their way. Now.'

4.

Your Stars: CANCER (June 22–July 23)
All aspects of your life are improving this week. You'll
have a few tough decisions to make before the upswing
really takes off, but trust your instincts. Romance is a
distinct possibility around the 21st.

My heart gave a thump that all but knocked me over. I sat down
hard on the bench by the phone.

'Foss? Foss, are you okay?'

'I . . . yeah. Yeah. What did you tell him?'

'Dad said you were out. He kind of hinted you'd gone off
with Mum, and wouldn't be back till tomorrow.'

Thank God for Emlyn. The rush of relief made me feel giddy.
'So it's okay, then?'

'Not exactly, no. I'm sorry, Foss. We're in the book, you see.'

'Book? What book?'

'The Farmhouse Bed-and-Breakfast book the Tourist Board put
out.' He explained. Earlier that afternoon, the tourist information
office had phoned and made a booking for tonight. 'Which is
okay because the B-and-B thing's more or less self-contained.
Mum always makes sure everything's ready before she rushes
off anywhere, and Catrin Ty'n Llan comes in to do the breakfasts.'

What the Tourist Board lady hadn't made clear was that Scott
had made the booking. He and Mum would be staying at Meini
Hirion overnight.

I panicked. 'I can't face them, Jo. Not tonight! Not right now.'
Why couldn't they leave me *alone*? Just for a few days? I felt
hunted, just as I had in my dream, and the same irrational panic
was threatening to swamp me. The fragile inner peace I'd begun
to acquire at Tan-y-Fedwen was crumbling like dry playdough.

Jo was contrite. 'I'm sorry, sparrow, I really am. Trouble is, we
can't cancel. It's the Season and Mum's got a contract with these
guys . . .'

And they needed the income. I felt terrible. Once again I had
the feeling of hovering on the edges of other people's busy lives
and of getting in the way and being a pain. I pulled myself

together with an effort. 'Jo, don't worry, it's okay. Listen. They think I'm with Bess, right? So I'll stay here tonight. Can you bring all my gear down before they arrive?'

I experienced a twinge of apprehension as I put the phone down. I'd be alone in the house, all night . . . But Jo'd be at the end of the phone if I needed him. Jo was a rock.

Jo arrived ten minutes later with my backpack. He hadn't forgotten anything – not even my toothbrush. He was still concerned.

'You're sure you'll be okay on your own?'

'I can hack it. If I get hysterical I'll phone you and you can come and rescue me.'

'Fine. Do that.'

He wouldn't stay for a meal. 'I'll pop in later and give you an update after they've settled in. Scott said something about having dinner at the Blossoms.' Yes, I thought. Snapping his fingers at waiters, complaining about the food, the service . . . I shuddered in empathy.

The day was spoilt. After Jo left I couldn't settle. I prowled around, fidgeting and fretting. What if Mum brought Scott round to look at Oz's house? What if they bumped into Mrs Fosdike? And oh, God, how could I face tomorrow? Being dragged off in Scott's car like a condemned prisoner . . . Mum hurt, bewildered, reproachful; Scott coldly furious; both of them going on at me non-stop for the entire journey. *Why, Foss? What were you trying to prove? What did you think you'd achieve? Why . . . why . . . why . . .?*

Jo arrived at ten-thirty with a progress report. Mum and Scott were watching telly in the converted barn. They seemed fairly satisfied with the accommodation – though, being townies to the core, they'd complained about the quietness, the lack of street lights and the mud in the yard. Discovering that Bess wouldn't be back until tomorrow evening, they'd decided to stay for a second night, and drive back to London on Sunday. They planned to spend tomorrow on a sightseeing tour of Malvern and Hay on Wye and the Elan Valley.

'It'll take them all day,' Jo said with immense satisfaction. 'So you can come to the Fête after all.' I tried not to think about what would happen afterwards.

As I was climbing into bed it suddenly dawned on me why the reflection in Oz's ancient smoky looking-glass had been so disturbing. The girl in the mirror – that unexpectedly pretty girl with the wide grey eyes and the halo of red hair – *that* girl hadn't been wearing glasses. A thought sprang up unbidden, and made me shiver. Was she really me, or was she . . . someone else?

As I snuggled down beneath the duvet I remembered that tonight was Midsummer's Eve.

Outside, the sky cleared and the moon rose. I lay awake for a while, watching the criss-cross pane-patterns the moonlight made on the walls and the floor. I'd opened the biggest of the three sash windows and familiar country scents wafted through: wet mown grass, roses, a fragrant hint of cow. There was no traffic noise. I could hear distant owls whooing and whickering in the vast silence outside. The tower room could almost have been afloat between earth and sky: moonlight above and the fathomless dark beneath.

Eventually, I fell asleep. Then, a long time later, in that hazily-drifting state between sleeping and waking, I seemed to hear a voice saying 'Princess! Princess!'

'Princess!' A man's voice, quite young, sounding breathless and ever so slightly scared. It echoed in the silence, rolled around and around inside my head.

I woke up, suddenly and completely. Someone was tapping on the open window, thirty feet above the ground.

Startled is not how I felt. I was *terrified*. My heart jumped into my throat and stuck there, hammering to be let out. Every muscle became instant jelly. Lurid possibilities flashed through my brain like headlines on ticker-tape: a burglar? A rapist? A serial killer with a bloodstained machete under his shirt?

The tapping continued. Discreet, but conveying a sense of urgency. 'Princess? Are you there? Please wake up!'

He was making no attempt to climb in. After a minute or two my heart slid back into its usual place. Arms and legs began responding to central control. I took a few deep breaths to keep panic at bay and surveyed the available options. There weren't many. Screaming for help wasn't a viable one. Lying frozen with terror in the dark didn't appeal much either – nor did being chased around the house by a nutter with an axe. My best bet, I decided, was to tiptoe across, slam the window shut and call (*a*) Meini Hirion and (*b*) the police.

Luckily my bed was in the one dark corner of the room, and not visible from the window. I slithered cautiously out from under the duvet and unplugged the bedside lamp. The weight of the ceramic base was reassuring: capable of inflicting a substantial amount of damage should the need arise. As an afterthought, I prudently removed the bulb. Lamp in hand, I padded silently to the side of the window and peeped out from behind the curtain.

He was young – probably around twenty. He was also quite incredibly good-looking. Even with the stark and treacherous moonlight making dark caverns along the planes of his face, he was still the handsomest man I'd ever seen in real life.

He hadn't seen me. He was still rapping the pane with the knuckle of his right hand. 'Princess? I say, Princess, do wake up!'

The plaintive note in his voice was hardening into desperation. It was a nice voice, I couldn't help noticing. Public school, but minus the clenched jaw and the gulped vowels. As though he'd had elocution lessons from someone at the BBC. This Princess fixation was a bit disturbing, though.

He was standing on a rope ladder with hooks at the business end, which indicated a certain amount of forward planning on his part. Not a spontaneous impulse, then. He hadn't staggered out of a drunken party and succumbed to a sudden urge to scale the nearest tall building. The assault on the tower had been premeditated.

What kind of a bloke wanders around the countryside in the dead of night with a rope ladder slung across his shoulders? I was beginning to discount the burglar/rapist/murderer hypothesis. In my admittedly limited experience (i.e. TV, crime novels and movies) people of that ilk tended not to tap politely on windows beforehand.

So . . . a student, perhaps? – freaking out the natives for a bet?

'Oh, gosh,' he muttered, and this time I caught a distinct quiver of panic. Now was the moment to slam the sash down. But just as I was reaching for the catch I hesitated. His balance on the ladder didn't seem all that secure. And much as I resented being woken up and scared witless at three in the morning, I didn't really want him to end up as a mangled corpse at the foot of the tower. As I've said, he really was very attractive.

Gripping the lamp base hard, I said, 'Who are you? What d'you want?' The way I'd rehearsed it, I should have sounded stern and at least forty-five. What actually emerged was a wobbly kind of squeak.

'Don't be afraid, Princess. I've come to rescue you.'

Uh?

'Look,' I said, 'I don't know who you are or what the hell you think you're doing climbing up to people's windows in the middle of the night – but if you don't start climbing down again right away, this sash is slamming down on both hands. I'm warning you.'

He gave a yelp of horror. 'No! Don't do that, please!'

I liked that yelp. It made me feel quite brave. But not quite rash enough to move out into the moonlight. I stayed where I was, in deep shadow at the side of the window.

'Starting a count of three,' I said, stretching one arm up to the catch with the lamp base poised. 'One . . .'

'Don't! No, stop! I can explain!'

'Don't bother,' I said coldly. 'Look, you're a student, right? Well, you've won your bet, or whatever it was. Just go away and leave me alone, okay?'

'*Bet?*'

'Yes, you know. Rag Week? Custard pies, sponsored shop-lifting, kidnapping Vice Chancellors, that kind of thing.'

There was a long, tense pause. I forgot to count.

'You . . . you *are* the Princess Aurora, aren't you?' he said, as though at last he was beginning to doubt it.

He was a nutter. It was the only explanation that fitted the facts. Poor guy. Confused and a bit pathetic (and unbelievably good-looking, my traitor brain added). Not dangerous, though . . . at least, not yet. Humour him, that was the thing. And *then* slam the window shut.

'Actually,' I said gently, 'I'm not your princess. You've got the wrong address.'

'B—but I can't have! She must be here somewhere!' His voice sharpened, and took on a note of disdain. 'Who are *you*, any-way? Are you a servant?'

'Absolutely not,' I assured him.

'You're the daughter of the house?'

'Niece, actually,' I said.

He glared suspiciously in my direction. 'You're not . . . you're not the *witch*?'

Oh, Lor, I thought, first princesses and now witches. Perhaps he had been frightened by a pop-up book when he was three.

'No,' I said as soothingly as I could. 'I'm not a witch and I'm not your princess. So would you mind just going quietly back down the ladder . . .?'

'Are you sure she's not disguised as a kitchen maid, or something? Because if she isn't here, you see, then something must have gone very badly wrong.'

Humour him. Okay. Right. 'Er . . . suppose you tell me what she looks like? I might know her. What was her name again?'

His face went all soppy. 'Aurora,' he said dreamily. 'Princess Aurora Fossombronia Matilda of Arborea. Lovely name, don't you think? Like a symphony, or something.'

I almost dropped the lamp. Because one of the reasons 'Foss' stuck as a nickname was that Dad used to be an agri-botanist before he went into computing, and Fossombronia is apparently some sort of moss all botanists have to learn about, don't ask me why.

And my second name is Matilda, after my great-grandmother.

Goose-flesh crawled all over me. This *had* to be the corniest dream of my entire life. I found myself asking, 'Wh . . . what does she look like?'

'Tall,' he said raptly, 'Very slim. Extremely beautiful. Dark hair, green eyes. Marvellous legs . . .'

Ah. Fine. Okay. Just forget it.

'Nobody of that description here,' I said truthfully.

The message had finally got through. He sighed. His broad shoulders sagged. 'Well, thank you anyway. You've been very patient. I'm sorry to have disturbed you.'

'It's okay,' I told him. 'By the way, who told you to try this house?' Oz used to work in the psychiatric service; maybe she'd have a file on him somewhere.

'An old crone,' he said loftily. *Right*, I thought. *Of course*.

'I've searched the Zones from one end to the other,' he went on dispiritedly. 'I have to find her, you see. It's my Quest.'

'Zones?'

There was a touch of impatience in his voice. 'You know. Alternative worlds, linked by Gates. The problem is, one can't be sure of catching the right time line. I may have missed her by a hundred years or so somewhere. Time moves differently in each Zone, you see. It's all very frustrating . . . Then, this evening, an old crone showed me *this* Gate, and said my Quest was at an end. So when it opened just now, I rode through . . .'

'I'm sorry,' I said, and meant it.

He made a determined attempt to cheer up. 'Oh, well. Can't be helped, I suppose . . . What's your name, by the way?'

'Francesca,' I said sadly.

'Oh. Hallo. I'm Ferdinand. Prince Ferdinand of Boronia, actually. M'father's King Theodore.'

'That's nice,' I said.

'I don't suppose you know anyone at Court, do you . . .?'

'No,' I said. I was suddenly aware of being desperately sleepy. My eyelids were getting heavy, and his voice had begun to fade in and out like a badly tuned radio. Dream or reality, I simply couldn't cope with any more.

'Right,' he said. 'Well. I suppose I'd better be off, then.'

'Yes.'

'Well, thanks again,' he said. 'Good-night.'

There was a brief scuffling noise in the ivy-plant and his fabulous torso and handsome head began, rather jerkily, to disappear bit by bit below the level of the sill. Bemused, I waited until the hands grasping the sill had also vanished, then I leaned out to look. When he reached the window-sill below mine he stepped onto the ivy-branches (which were much thicker at this point), and glanced up.

'I say, would you mind . . .?'

I pulled out the hooks and tossed the ladder down to him. He nodded and waved and climbed down out of sight.

I closed the window, slipped the catch firmly into its socket, secured the other two windows in case he was tempted to start all over again, and reeled back to bed. I was asleep in seconds.

Next morning, of course, I overslept. I woke up groggily to the sound of someone knocking and calling my name and for a horrible confused moment I thought it was the dream all over again. But the noise wasn't at my window – and it wasn't a polite tapping, it was a hefty no-nonsense hammering at the front door.

'Foss! Foss, wake up!'

I staggered out of bed and went down in my bathrobe to open the door.

'About time, too,' said Jo. 'D'you know it's nearly eleven o'clock? Your mum and Scott went off hours ago.'

The Fête. Jeffrey. 'Oh, Jo, I'm sorry . . . I just couldn't wake up.'

'You look a bit iffy,' Jo conceded gallantly. 'Bad night?'

'Weird,' I said. 'Peculiar dreams.'

'Well, get yourself dressed and whatever it is you girls do . . . I'll make some coffee.'

It was a beautiful morning. I showered and got dressed, and while the coffee was brewing I sneaked outside and checked out the base of the tower. It had rained earlier on, so there were no crush-marks in the thick grass. And no visible scars on the massive ivy-plant, either. Verdict: not proven.

Another weird dream? It had to be. I could feel myself blushing. How corny can you get? And what on earth had possessed my sleeping mind to christen my dream hero Ferdinand? *Ferd the Nerd*, I told myself in disgust.

Jo was bellowing through the kitchen window. 'Stop mooching about, woman, your coffee's getting cold.'

The Church Fête got under way at two o'clock. It was a lot bigger and busier than I'd anticipated and I felt a bit guilty for not having been around early enough to help set it up.

It was a gloriously hot day. By three-thirty crowds of people in summer casuals were milling about clutching balloons and licking ice-creams. As Jeffrey trotted past you could hear a lot of laughter and good-natured shouting mixed up with jangling scraps of music from the various stalls and rides.

Jeffrey and the cart did a brisk trade in ferrying families from the car park and the village to the fair itself – the cart decorated with streamers and balloons, and Jeffrey looking suitably festive with leis of paper flowers round his neck and a rose tucked rakishly behind one ear. Jo drove, and I collected the money. It was nice to have something to do – on my own, I'd have felt a bit spare.

I'd have enjoyed myself a whole lot more if I hadn't been haunted by the knowledge that Mum and Scott were due to return from their day's outing this evening and that tomorrow I'd be on my way back to Birtles Road. I tried to push the panic and the despair to the back of my mind. After all, I'd had two days . . .

As an added complication, the memory of last night's crazy dream kept surfacing and distracting me. My subconscious

49

might have chosen a naff name for my hero, but there was nothing naff about the bloke himself. He'd been, quite frankly, gorgeous. I couldn't stop thinking about him.

At four-thirty Jo called a halt. 'Jeff needs a drink and a rest. What d'you fancy – hot dog? Candyfloss? Toffee-apple?'

I settled for an ice-cream. We found a quiet place in the field just above the fair, where Jeffrey could drink from the stream and graze in the shade. The cart, unhitched, lay tilted against its backboard, with the shafts pointing at the sky.

Jo went off to investigate the stalls while I kept an eye on the cart. As I sprawled on the grass with both hands behind my head, I suddenly became aware of something I'd never noticed before. In front of me the field sloped upwards and flattened to form a shallow valley, with hills behind and on both sides. Above and to my right was Oz's house, Tan-y-Fedwen, on its hilltop, with its tower just visible above the trees . . . and on my left was the church, with its tower, sited in exactly the same way on an almost identical hill-crest. The trees around Tan-y-Fedwen were ash and birch and oak: dappled and fluid in the slight breeze, whereas the trees crowding around the church were a solid mass of blackish-green: yew and cedar, rigid and immutable – and that was the only real difference. It was almost as though they'd been set there on guard . . . the church to the East and Tan-y-Fedwen to the West.

My eyes moved involuntarily to the point of focus in the valley between. And there they were, the *meini hirion* which gave Jo's farm its name and its identity. The long, shaped stones. The menhirs.

As kids, Jo and I had barely given them a second thought: they were just *there* – four tall thin lumps of rock sticking up out of a field, nothing magical about them at all. We'd known all the old stories, of course – like the one about William Llewelyn Williams who'd left his house at breakfast-time in 1503 after a row with his wife . . . and strolled back in time for tea exactly a hundred years later. His tombstone was in the churchyard, dated 1637. All he'd been able to tell anybody was that he'd wandered in amongst the stones and found himself in another world, where, presumably, Time moved differently.

I found myself thinking . . . *The Zones* . . .

Today, a faint blueish heat-haze brought all four spikes into sharp relief. They leaned together, two and two, so that from this spot they looked like a single gateway.

A gateway through which someone was riding a horse.

I sat up hurriedly and rubbed my glasses. I could see the figure clearly: a tall young man with wind-tousled fair hair, and broad shoulders under a full-sleeved, open-necked shirt which made you think of TV costume dramas. And wasn't that a *sword* dangling from his left hip? A scabbard, certainly.

I'd never seen the horse before – it was a magnificent grey – but the rider was all too familiar. It was the young student/ escaped nutter/dream hero who'd called himself Ferdinand, Prince of Boronia.

Horse and rider walked sedately between the clustered stones . . . and vanished.

I got to my feet and started running up the field towards the stones. Why, I've no idea. I just ran. I arrived at the outermost pair of stones panting for breath. The space inside the cluster was hazy-blue and empty.

For a long moment, nothing happened. I could hear a thin wind hissing faintly like sand over the surface of the stones. I could hear the blood pounding in my ears. Very distantly, on the far edge of hearing, there was the tiny insect buzz and twitter of the fête.

The blue haze thickened. When it cleared again, I was looking into a place I didn't know.

Between the stones, where a few moments ago there'd been nothing but rough grass, there was now a green lawn bordered by a hedge of red roses. In the centre of the lawn a single rose tree stood impossibly thick and tall, its long weeping sprays of creamy-white flowers drooping almost to the ground. The horse was tethered to the white rose tree. Ferdinand himself was standing a few yards away. His shoulders were sagging, his hands were stuck in his pockets, and he was moodily kicking a hole in the grass. Obviously, he hadn't found his princess.

Thinking back, that must have been the moment when I began to *believe*. Last night's incident hadn't been a dream. Ferdinand wasn't a well-meaning nutter. He really was what he'd told me he was: a prince, from that mysterious other dimension he'd called the Zones. He was real, and the landscape he was standing in was real – although it would never figure on any local map.

I took one step forwards, between the gateway stones – and bumped my specs on a barrier as invisible and every bit as hard as plate glass.

51

Ferdinand saw the movement out of the corner of his eye, and spun like a cat: lithe and dangerous, with one hand on his sword hilt. His eyes flashed cold disdain.

'Who are *you*?' His glance flickered over me for a moment. Then he shrugged dismissively, and turned his back.

The expression on his face seared me where I stood. It was Alan McBride all over again – only ten times worse. That brief, disgusted glance had said it all. I was gutted.

Okay, so the rose-strewn Paradise on the far side of this eldrich gateway clearly wasn't intended for people like me. Ferdinand himself was all too obviously way out of my league. I could accept that: it was a fact of life. The girl who broke through that invisible barrier would have all the beauty and grace and glamour I'd never possess in a million years.

But that contemptuous dismissal of his cut me to the heart. Last night, in the deceptive moonlight, he'd been polite, pleasant, even chatty. And now, seeing me for the first time in broad daylight, he hadn't even rated me highly enough to say hello. He'd given me the look most people reserve for something slimy in the salad.

An unexpected rush of utter misery and helpless rage swept through me. Suddenly I seemed to be looking into a long, bleak future in which romance of any kind wasn't even an option – a future in which none of the men I fell in love with would ever feel that way about me. And why should they? I was the ugly girl. The one you can't bear to look at. The one you make jokes about. *Death warmed up . . . Face like the back of a bus . . .* I was the girl in Picture A. Short, thin, frizzy hair, glasses, freckles, squashed-in face – *everyone* I knew was better looking than me . . . It wasn't *fair*.

I gazed at Ferdinand's superbly-muscled back and wanted to die.

'*But you could be beautiful . . .*'

I jumped. The voice was in my head – persuasive, encouraging, barely above a whisper.

'What?' I said silently.

'*If you wanted, you could be the most beautiful creature in the world. This is the entrance to the Zones . . . An alternative reality. Here, you can be anything you want to be.*'

I stepped back a pace, and looked round wildly. But no-one was there.

'Wish and believe,' the voice purred. 'Wish and believe!'

It was surprisingly – even suspiciously – easy. The image came into my mind almost as though it had been planted there, fully formed, by someone else. Tall. Very slim. Extremely beautiful. Dark hair (long, glossy, straight), green eyes (huge, with long black lashes); perfect features, creamy skin, perfect figure, marvellous legs . . . Except that she wasn't *me* – she was Princess Aurora Fossombronia Matilda, and standing in front of me was the Prince she was destined to marry.

I admit I wasn't thinking too clearly at this point: it didn't occur to me how desperately *corny* the whole thing was. Beautiful princesses and handsome princes . . . who has dreams like that nowadays? Except, perhaps, the plainest kid on the block, with a head full of romance and nothing to lose. The fact that there might be a hidden agenda here didn't occur to me at all. The words *'why me?'* didn't spring to mind until much, much later.

'*The potion,*' the voice urged. '*Take the potion now! It's in your pocket!*'

My hand moved to my jeans pocket, groped . . . and closed on a small round bottle. I pulled it out and stared at it. The Secret Formula. How it had got there I'd no idea. I prised off the stopper. Inside my head the whispering voice seemed to be chortling with glee. I hesitated. And then . . .

'No!' Another point of contact struck into my mind. Another voice, firm and clear. My Aunt Oz.

'Foss, you don't have to do this! There's no need!'

'*If you don't, you'll regret it all your life,*' the whisperer said.

'Your life's fine as it is,' Oz insisted. 'All he's offering you is an illusion! You've got a future in *this* world, Foss . . . don't throw it away!'

'*Some future,*' her opponent sneered.

'Why are you *doing* this?' Oz was addressing the other voice directly. 'Are you trying to get at me through her?'

'*Of course not,*' the voice whispered. '*It's got nothing to do with you. She's been inviting us in for years. She hates herself and her life and her future. I'm simply in a position to give her what she wants.*'

'Not what *she* wants – what *you* want!' Oz cried.

'*It comes to the same thing, doesn't it?*'

'No!' said Oz, and the force of her anger was like an explosion inside my head. 'Foss, listen to me!'

'*Face facts, kid,*' the whisperer advised. '*What future have you got, looking the way you do? You know I'm right. Stuck in grimy, boring suburbia for the rest of your life. A nine-to-five job in some dreary industrial lab somewhere. Saving and scraping to give your kid sister and brother a better time than you had. Holding your Mum's hand all her life. They wouldn't even let you have a holiday on your own . . . What kind of future's that?'*

He was right. Wave after wave of black despair crashed over me and scoured through me. *You're nothing . . . You're nobody the way you are . . . Go for it. Escape. Be a princess instead. It's an offer you can't refuse. Give in . . . Let go . . .*

'Don't listen to him, Foss,' Oz cried.

I found my own mental voice at last. The pent-up bitterness of years suddenly burst through. 'Why not? It's all true, isn't it?' I tilted the little bottle defiantly, and drank.

The barrier melted away and I stumbled into the glade. Everything seemed to be breaking up into separate, fractured images. I caught a freeze-frame glimpse of Ferdinand staring at me bug-eyed and open-mouthed. He and everything else began to spin round, slowly at first but gathering speed. I had the most awful sensation of being tugged apart limb from limb. I staggered like a drunk, and almost fell.

I was dimly aware of a sudden, confused noise like broken thunder behind me. I had just enough control left to turn around. I saw Jeffrey galloping at full pelt through the gap in the stones, the cart plunging and bouncing behind him – and Jo crouching on the box like a charioteer, shouting something I couldn't hear . . .

It was the last thing I saw before I blacked out.

54

5.

Your Stars: CANCER (June 22–July 23)
A career change is likely, and you'll find yourself
moving up the social ladder. Make the most of these new
opportunities, but expect a few surprises along the way.

I was floating in a vast blackness. No feeling anywhere, nothing to see, nothing to hear. It was like being dead. I was beginning to panic when the voices began again.

'*Her decision,*' the shadow voice pointed out smugly.

'Not an informed decision, therefore not valid.' Oz's voice was crisp and chilly, the way a barrister might sound in Court.

'*Emotional decisions carry equal weight,*' the other voice reminded her. '*She invited me in.*' I was beginning to dislike that voice. Too oily-smooth, far too pleased with itself.

'Point taken,' Oz said. 'But under the circumstances I demand an escape clause.'

There was an alert pause. '*It's not usual.*'

'Agreed. Nevertheless, the contingency *is* in the rules.'

The voices began to recede into the void.

'*Oh, very well. If you insist.*'

'Good.' The voices were diminishing rapidly now, fading out of range. I had to strain my ears to catch the last few words. I heard Oz say, 'I fried your colleague, by the way.'

'*The Shadow? He was stupid. He tried coercion. Persuasion is more effective.*'

'Who *are* you working for these days?'

'*You don't seriously expect me to tell you?*'

They were gone at last, and I was left alone in the dark.

The sick whirling sensation took hold of me again and tugged me down like a spider into a plughole . . . down and down into a spinning greyness which slowly brightened into a kaleidoscope of brilliant colours flashing in front of my eyes like strobe lighting. I groaned and retched feebly, but didn't actually throw up.

Which was just as well, because when the world slowed and steadied I found myself lying with my head on Ferdinand's lap.

'Aurora . . .' he breathed. 'Aurora, speak to me. Are you all right?'

Aurora . . .?

I blinked and tried to move. I felt as limp as wet washing. I looked down, and saw *(a)* a creamy cleavage, *(b)* a low silver-edged neckline and *(c)* a green velvet dress lying decoratively in faintly-gleaming folds and heaps. When I moved, they moved too.

I sat up and glanced wildly round the glade. There was no sign of Jo, or the cart, or Jeffrey. Before I could panic any further, I was distracted by the waist-length dark hair which swung and fell like heavy satin curtains on either side of my face. There was something on my head; I lifted my hands to touch it and felt a thin circlet with some sort of jewel in the centre . . .

And no glasses on my nose. Twenty-twenty vision, for the first time in my life.

I said feebly, 'Where . . .? What . . .?'

Ferdinand slipped his arm round me and helped me to my feet. He was gazing at me in undisguised awe.

'My princess,' he breathed. 'Oh, my God, you're exactly as I imagined. You're *beautiful* . . .'

He seemed to have shrunk a lot, which puzzled me until I realised with a lurch of joy that I had grown. I was tall, slim, long-legged . . .

Against all the laws of biology, against logic, against common sense – the potion had *worked*. Or something had.

It couldn't be real. It was a dream, an illusion.

'You can be anything you want to be . . .' A place where dreams come true. And a chilly little thought at the back of my mind said, *Whose dreams?* Mine? Ferdinand's? That mysterious whisperer's with his even more mysterious boss?

'Gosh,' Ferdinand said boyishly, 'Wait till I tell them about *this!*'

At this point the Foss I'd left behind would have babbled like a brook. Who are *they*, she'd have wanted to know, and what, exactly, happened just now, and where's Jo, and did you hear the voices out there, and how do you know this is Aurora anyway? Don't you need a birth certificate, or something?

But suddenly none of this mattered any more. I wasn't Foss; I was Aurora. All the nasty spiky little doubts and fears which belonged to Foss were just a faint insect scrabble in the remotest corners of a mind full of pink fluffy clouds.

I lifted my eyes trustingly to Ferdinand's face. Even my eyelids moved slowly: I was conscious of the weight of long lashes which I could just see flickering at the top edge of vision. Ferdinand's face was very close to mine; my heart was rattling like a drum and my knees were going weak with anticipation. I expected a long, passionate kiss at the very least . . .

It didn't happen. Instead, he got all brisk and businesslike.

'Can you ride, do you think?'

Aurora's soft voice said, 'Where are we going?'

'To Arborea, of course.' There was triumph in his smile. 'I have to deliver you safely to the King and Queen. Your parents.' And even this didn't trigger off any feelings of panic, as in *how will they know who you are?* It was enough to know that I was with Ferdinand, and nothing could possibly go wrong.

He had to help me across the grass. I was clumsy, and kept stumbling over my own feet. Then the truth dawned: I wasn't used to my new body. It was longer and heavier than my old one, and slower. At five-foot-nothing, you zip about. At five-foot-eight, you glide. The Jack Russell had become a Great Dane; the sparrow had turned into a swan. My heart swelled with triumph. If only my so-called friends could see me now . . .

A white mare was tethered to the other side of the rose tree. Ferdinand had obviously come well prepared to find his princess. The mare lifted her aristocratic head as we approached, and glowered at me with an expression of extreme suspicion.

'Bianca,' Ferdinand said cheerfully. 'The grey is Tarquin.'

He bustled about saddling up both horses. The thought of helping didn't even cross Aurora's mind; I just watched adoringly.

I'd never ridden side-saddle before. Ferdinand had to help me up and show me how to sit and hold the reins. He was quite patient about it, but something told me that if I wanted to impress him, I'd better shape up fast and learn to ride *well*. Perhaps he'd omitted to include horsemanship in his original specifications *re* Aurora, but it was important to him, all the same.

We rode away, side by side, down the sun-dappled glade and into the Zone.

The landscape was magical: red-rose hedges, fields full of flowers basking in the misty golden afternoon, a fairytale castle in the distance and spiky blue mountains on the horizon. I was in a daze of happiness. I cast covert glances at Ferdinand's perfect profile and broad shoulders and well-muscled body beside me; I watched the competent way he rode: relaxed and alert at the same time, effortlessly balanced as though he and Tarquin were plugged into the same neural circuits, and I let amazed adoration and profound thankfulness take over.

In the evening we arrived at a large country-house set amongst lawns and gardens. Servants came scurrying out to help us dismount. Ferdinand lifted me down tenderly, handed me over the care of a trio of older women and strode off in the direction of the stables to supervise the arrangements for Tarquin and Bianca.

As soon as his back was turned, my legs gave way. Illusion or not, I'd spent four hours in the saddle and the price was hot agony all the way up my spine. The pink clouds dissolved for a moment and Foss loomed like an uncharted crag, spiky with outrage. This was not in the script.

I was helped indoors. A hot bath eased most of the pain. Maidservants dressed me as though I was a doll who couldn't lift a finger to help herself. Blissful serenity flooded back. I gazed in awe at my reflection in the mirror while my hair was being brushed. Aurora's beauty was flawless. You couldn't imagine a zit on that creamy-rose skin or dandruff in that heavy glossy hair, or specs in front of those huge green eyes . . . I thought of all the love-poetry I'd ever read, all the romantic films I'd ever seen, all the novels, all the fairy-tales. And I thought, *Yes.*

The only remaining link I had with Foss was the pendant round my neck.

Ferdinand and I had dinner together on the terrace. 'You're so beautiful,' he kept saying. 'So perfect . . . Exactly as I'd thought you'd be.'

When we'd finished our meal he saw me to the foot of the stairs, kissed my hand and bade me a tender good-night. As he left I heard him ask someone where the billiard-room was. I felt ever so slightly cheated. Ferdinand the delivery man seemed to be taking his responsibilities a bit too seriously . . .

He was waiting, just a tad impatiently, when I appeared in the hall next morning. He gave my hand a brief squeeze. 'You look marvellous,' he said. 'Sleep well?'

Through the open doorway I could see Tarquin and Bianca being led round to the foot of the steps. It hadn't occurred to me that we'd be leaving so soon after breakfast. Suddenly the thought of getting back into that saddle for another day of torment made me feel physically ill. Just a few more hours' rest, I thought despairingly – a few hours' walking about to ease sore muscles. Give me a *break*, Ferdinand . . .

'Ferdinand,' I said pleadingly, 'Couldn't we . . .?'

But he'd spotted Tarquin. 'Ah!' he said. 'D'you mind? I won't be a moment . . .' And strode off to have words with the groom. Something to do with the girths, I gathered, and the loading of the saddlebags. His voice drifted back to me through the open door, issuing crisp imperious orders.

So *masterful*, Aurora thought adoringly. After all, what did backs matter, or sore bottoms, set against the inexpressible joy of riding away into the wide blue yonder with the man of your dreams? I'd escaped. I'd broken my chains. There was a marvellous new world out there, and an important place in it, created specially for me. I wasn't Foss any more: I was Aurora, and I was free.

There was something in the pocket of my gown. I fished it out. It was a small glass vial, like those tiny bottles of cheap scent they sell in discount stores. Stuck to it with sellotape was a note in Oz's handwriting.

'*Foss darling – if you should ever need to change back into your former shape*' – tactful of her to put it like that, I thought – '*drink the contents of this bottle. Good luck. Oz.*'

I considered the implications of this for all of three milli-seconds before dropping the bottle in the nearest wastepaper bin. My mind simply refused to speculate on exactly how it had got into my pocket. My aunt Oz, sixtyish, ex-social worker, pillar of the church and the absolute epitome of total respectability . . . no. No way could she have become tangled up in this weird situation.

Except that it *had* been her voice, in the blackness inside my head . . .

Change back? She had to be joking.

The road was as empty as it had been yesterday, the journey just as dreamy and unreal, and the countryside just as sun-drenched and idyllic. Slowly but surely, the mountains were getting nearer.

Ferdinand was more talkative today. It didn't take much prompting to get him to describe the various adventures he'd had while he was searching the Zones for his lost Princess. Even

59

to Aurora they sounded a bit – well – improbable: enchanted castles, wicked witches, an ogre – but who was I to judge?

After a while the flow dried up and I asked tentatively, 'Do you know anything about Arborea?'

For a moment he looked puzzled, as though the question had nudged his train of thought off the main track and onto a siding he hadn't anticipated.

'Arborea? Well, it's quite a small kingdom, on an island . . . about thirty leagues by fifty . . . what did you want to know, exactly?'

'I thought you might be able to tell me about my parents, and so on.'

'Oh. Well.' It hadn't occurred to him that I mightn't already know. 'Your father's King Eldoric, of course, and your mother's Queen Serena. Arborea itself's a bit rural, really. Arboresca's the only major town. Of course, the family's very old.'

'The royal family?'

His eyebrows rose. 'Naturally. The line goes back unbroken for a thousand years or more. One of *the* best families – everyone agrees on that point. But Arborea itself . . . really, there's not much one can say about it.'

'It's not like Boronia, then?' I was quite proud of myself for remembering that.

'Good Lord, no. Boronia's much larger. We have five major cities as well as the offshore islands. We have the best surfing beaches in the Zones. Marvellous hunting in the forests, of course – and ski resorts in the mountains . . .'

He told me about the night clubs and the wild parties and freaking out the plebs; about windsurfing and paragliding; about hunting boar, stag, bear and anything else with enough bottle to stand and fight; about racing thoroughbred horses on the most testing courses in the Zones . . . I was dazzled, and more than a bit intimidated. This was the world of the glitterati, of wealth and sophistication and tough competition to stay at the top. My heart sank. I had the nasty feeling that even Aurora might have problems fitting in.

He must have seen the flash of panic in my eyes, because he said reassuringly, 'Don't worry, darling. The crowd are going to love you. I can't wait to show you off to them all.'

At mid-day we stopped to rest the horses and have a picnic lunch. Halfway through lunch I felt a hard lump in my pocket. I dug it out. The little glass phial was back. I dropped it into the nearest stream.

As we rode on Ferdinand began to tell me about his family: his father, King Theodore, and his mother Queen Aurelia. About his eldest brother Siegfried who was a champion pentathlete, his other brother Peregrine (Perry), who was the clever one of the family (*'parties every single night for three years at University and he walked away with a First . . .'*). After a while I stopped listening and drifted away into daydreams of being married and living in a palace with servants at my beck and call every moment of every day, and having Ferdinand all to myself . . . I didn't get any more information about Arborea.

Evening drew on, and suddenly there was another stately country-house alongside the road. Or was it the same one?

'Ferdinand,' I murmured, as the silent servants scurried out to help us dismount, 'Isn't this the same house as last night?'

He gave me an odd look. 'No. How can it be? We have been riding all day, you know.'

I didn't argue. My memories of last night's hostelry were extremely hazy. It was an effort to recall anything at all clearly – an effort Aurora wasn't prepared to make.

Ferdinand kissed me lightly on the cheek. 'You're tired. Just leave everything to me, darling. Don't worry about a thing.'

He was absolutely right, of course. I smiled back gratefully.

As the journey went on the days merged into one another, each one a golden blur. We rode on and on without seeing a soul. Ferdinand told me about his talented friends, his boarding school and more about his family. Perry had married a million-airess with a most impressive dowry. His younger sister Berenice was the wild one of the family, who rode like a demon to hounds and was engaged to the Earl of Plome, whose immense wealth apparently made up for the fact that he wasn't of royal descent. The Earl adored his young bride-to-be and had purchased a string of racehorses for her as an engagement present.

'How old is he, then?' I asked.

Ferdinand's brow creased. 'Oh . . . fiftyish, I suppose.'

It didn't sound like the perfect match to me – more like a recipe for a soap-opera disaster, but I didn't say so. I knew nothing about these people, after all.

The antics his friends got up to were equally baffling. One favourite sport was to tear around the countryside on horseback after an all-night party, firing shotguns in the air and letting all the stock loose from field and farmyard. It was, I gathered, a fearfully good jape.

'But don't they object?'

He frowned. 'Sorry?'

'The farmers.'

He looked blank. 'Why should they? They're just . . . farmers.'

'Oh,' I said.

Each night we stayed in a comfortable, well-appointed house, and each evening after dinner I stood around looking decorative and admiring while Ferdinand played billiards (never anything as vulgar as snooker or pool). There were always well-dressed people about, but they seemed shadowy, somehow, and not entirely real: they never spoke to either of us. Anonymous servants slid in and out of focus. We never met a host or a hostess. It was like being insulated from the world behind layers of candyfloss.

One evening I plucked up courage and asked Ferdinand if he would teach me to play billiards. He raised his eyebrows and gave me a cold disbelieving look which reminded me forcibly of Scott.

'I don't think so,' he said.

'Why not?'

Another faintly puzzled stare. 'They don't allow novices to use the tables. The cloth, you see.'

'Oh,' I said, and felt about six inches high.

At the end of each evening Ferdinand saw me to the foot of the stairs, kissed my hand gallantly and went off back to the bar . . .

As the days went by I began to feel, not lonely, exactly, but more and more like a parcel on special delivery. Ferdinand wasn't ignoring me – far from it. He was gallant, considerate, his eyes glowed with possessive pride whenever he looked at me, and as we rode each day he talked incessantly about the wonderful experiences in store for me when we got to Boronia and met his friends . . . But none of it was *personal*, somehow.

Vague worries began to ruffle the placid surface of Aurora's alleged mind. Was Ferdinand gay, perhaps? No – I honestly didn't think so. So why couldn't he let that shrink-wrapped self-control of his loosen up once in a while? Was it my fault? Was I giving out the wrong messages? If only he'd allow himself to *smoulder* a little now and again, I thought despairingly. Would he ever thaw out and act normally?

I told myself not to be a fool. Against impossible odds, I'd got exactly what I'd always wanted, hadn't I? Whingeing at this stage of the deal was just plain greedy.

On the eighth day or thereabouts (I'd lost track of time by now) we reached the mountains: a country of deep-blue lakes and snow-tipped peaks, breathtakingly beautiful. The air was chill and crisp and went to my head like a dose of champagne. I began to feel *real* for the first time since entering the Zones. All at once I wanted to get shot of all that stifling demureness and decorum. The impulse was so strong I urged Bianca into a glorious gallop down a long incline. My hair whipped my face and streamed out behind me, and I could feel every nerve in my body responding to the exhilarating rush of cold air.

Ferdinand came pounding along behind me. He caught up with me at the lakeside and tugged Bianca to a halt. He was furious.

'Don't ever do that again! D'you understand? Never!'

'B—but I was only . . .'

'You're a complete novice, you don't know the road; you could have injured yourself and the mare. And where could I have gone for help?'

He was absolutely right, of course. I'd learnt enough about riding in the last week or so to stay in the saddle and keep Bianca moving – but there was no rapport between us. She tolerated me on her back, but that was all.

He was right – but it didn't stop me feeling resentful. As I rode sedately along behind him (Tarquin's massive rump and flicking tail had never seemed so enormous, or so pompously silly), it occurred to me that in all this long and – yes, say it, Foss – tedious journey, I had never once laughed out loud, or done anything on impulse, or even spoken very much. Ferdinand had done the talking and deciding; I'd just listened and complied.

I got a grip on myself. Aurora was Ferdinand's dream princess. Whatever the mechanics of the transformation (and I didn't believe Ferdinand had the least hand in that;) whoever else was involved, Aurora had sprung from Ferdinand's imagination. She was submissive and sweet-tempered because that was the way Ferdinand had wanted her to be. If I wanted to stay with

Ferdinand, I'd have to go along with that. He was the most wonderful man in the world, and I was going to marry him. If anything went wrong now, it would be Foss's fault. Foss had to be squashed.

Next day the only unscheduled incident was the reappearance of the little phial in my pocket. I tossed it over the edge of a cliff.

'How much further is it to Arborea?' I asked, as we plodded along.

Ferdinand frowned. 'Oh, another two or three weeks. Why, is it important?'

'No,' I lied – but I was shocked at my reaction. Three more weeks of travelling like this, with mind-numbing slowness, seeing no-one, meeting no-one . . .

Oh, for a motorbike. Or even a bus.

We'd climbed down out of the pass and into a country of high rolling hills and steep valleys. It was very green down here, every tiny stone-walled field thickly dotted with sheep; tiny whitewashed cottages snuggled amongst orchards of old apple trees and fuchsia hedges in full glowing bloom.

'Wouldn't you like to live in a place like this?' I joked shyly. 'We could buy that little white farmhouse down there, and keep chickens, and ducks . . . go to market once a week . . . and rule Arborea *in absentia*. I'm sure they'd get on perfectly well without us.'

Ferdinand's smile switched off. He gave me what I believe is sometimes described as an old-fashioned look.

'I hardly think your father would approve,' he said. 'I imagine he'd call it evading responsibility.' And rode stiffly ahead, every muscle of his back registering extreme disapproval.

Okay, I thought, as I urged Bianca forwards. So. One doesn't joke about ruling a country. Fine. Next time I'll know.

As I pulled alongside he added, 'It's terribly picturesque, of course, but personally I can't imagine why anyone should want to *live* here. You'd be bored to death, darling.'

'Ba-aed to death first, I imagine,' I said, as the endless chorus of the sheep swelled and faltered and swelled again all around us.

He frowned. 'Sorry?'

I blinked at him. 'What?'

'I'm sorry, I don't understand. Barred to death? What does that mean, exactly?'

64

I could feel Aurora blushing. 'Just a joke,' I mumbled. 'A rather feeble pun, that's all. Ba-aed to death. The sheep. The noise. You know.'

'Oh, I *see*,' he said, and his brow cleared. 'Ha, ha.'

We rode on. He began to tell me, in great detail, about the training unit he'd joined while he was at school, and how they'd spent three weeks on a combat exercise in the mountains, and how his unit had completed all the challenges ahead of everybody else and how the other chaps had been as sick as parrots . . .

Aurora said 'Yes?' and 'Really?' and 'Good Heavens,' and behaved immaculately.

By late afternoon we were riding through the outskirts of a neat, prosperous little town. The sky had clouded over, and mist was descending in a fine mizzle of rain.

'Couldn't we stay here tonight?' I suggested tentatively. 'I'm sure there's a decent inn somewhere.'

Ferdinand gave the matter all of two seconds' worth of serious thought. 'I don't think so,' he said.

The crowds surged around us as we neared the central market square. People glanced curiously at us as we rode through, but nobody bowed, or gave way any more than they had to. I could see this nettled Ferdinand quite a lot: his expression got haughtier by the minute, he sat up straighter in the saddle and looked down his aristocratic nose as though breathing the same air as these people offended his sensibilities. He began to make cutting remarks about the town and its seething populace. I imagine what he said was meant to be private, but the remarks were uttered in such a penetrating voice that I cringed with embarrassment.

The market place was full of stalls selling a fascinating array of goods from trinkets to cheeses. I dared not suggest we stop for a nose round.

On the far side of the square four roads led out of the town in different directions, none of them signposted. We reined in.

'Tedious,' Ferdinand remarked, looking cross.

'Let's ask somebody,' I suggested.

'Good idea . . . I say! You there!'

The little knot of country people he was addressing unwound itself and stared at us. Each face said clearer than words: *Who, me?*

'You,' Ferdinand said, pointing at the man in the middle. 'Would you mind telling me which of these roads goes South?' The words themselves weren't particularly offensive, but his tone and manner set my teeth on edge.

The men glanced at one another, and then back at us, taking in every detail. We must have looked extraordinary, by anyone's standards – two spectacularly handsome young people, richly dressed in silks and velvets and mounted on horses worth more than any of these men would earn in a lifetime's hard work. They stared . . . and weren't in the least impressed.

'Well?' Ferdinand prompted irritably.

The man in the middle went poker-faced. 'Waal, neaw, young mas'r,' he drawled, 'Oi dun' roightly kneaw thut there Sewth Rudd you'm axin' abeawt . . .'

All the other faces went perfectly rigid. They were desperately trying not to laugh.

'Ferdinand,' I said tactfully, and laid a hand on his sleeve. He shook it off like a stray wasp.

A second man spoke up. 'Neaw, you'm don' warrer tek no notice of Ole Jarge 'ere. 'E dunno nuthin, im. Touched in't 'ead, loike, 'ee be . . .'

Their fortitude was beginning to desert them. Shoulders were quivering convulsively. One or two of them had turned their heads away and were giggling audibly.

'Ferdinand,' I said, 'This is no good. Ask somebody else. Please.' A grocer, a lawyer, a doctor – anybody middle-class enough not to mind an aristocrat treating him like dirt . . .

Just then an older man pushed his way to the front. 'I'll tell you where to go, young man,' he said pleasantly. 'Take the right-hand fork, and after you pass the church, turn left. That's your road.'

The group went very quiet. I stared hard at each face in turn – but this time they weren't giving anything away.

'Thank you,' Ferdinand said, and tossed the man a coin, which he caught deftly. Ferdinand urged Tarquin into a walk and I followed in their wake. I looked back. The group had surrounded the man with the coin, and every single one of them was laughing fit to rupture himself.

I manoeuvred Bianca alongside Tarquin and made one last appeal.

'Ferdinand – listen to me, please! It's a joke. They've sent us off in the wrong direction.'

Ferdinand gave me one of his sweet, reassuring smiles. 'Dear one, you're being neurotic. Why on earth should they?'

I wanted to say, because you can't talk to country people like that, and get away with it. But when it came to the point, I simply didn't have the courage to speak up. Ferdinand was so sure of himself. Perhaps I was being neurotic. Perhaps people don't play tricks on the high-and-mighty, however much they'd like to.

I was going to marry this man, I reminded myself. I had to learn to trust his judgement. I followed him meekly out of town.

As we left the last houses behind us the mist thickened, blotting out the fields and making the hedges and solitary trees look ghostly in the fading light. We rode on and on. The drizzle became a downpour. I pulled my hood over my face and hoped we'd reach our destination soon: my fur-lined cloak was designed for warmth and for decoration rather than for keeping the rain out.

An hour went by. A cottage loomed out of the mist at the roadside: lamps were lit inside, and I could see the flicker of a fire.

'Couldn't we shelter here for the night?' I pleaded.

'A little rain won't hurt you,' Ferdinand said tolerantly. 'Don't worry. It can't be far now.'

The road began to climb more steeply. The horses snorted and shook rain out of their eyes. We toiled on, up and up. The only sounds were the squelching of hooves in the mud, the horses' heavy breathing, and the rain rustling down.

'I say, the road's bad, isn't it?' Ferdinand said at last.

Bad? It was practically nonexistent. Great chunks of the surface had been washed out at some time and never been repaired. The horses were delicately picking their way between flooded potholes deep enough to swim in, and the steep incline was slippery enough to make even Tarquin falter.

'This can't be the South Road, surely,' I said. 'Didn't you say it was a busy highway? '

'Er . . .' said Ferdinand. It was the first uncertain noise I'd heard him utter. 'I expect it's a short cut. We should be joining the highway soon. Come on.'

Dusk was creeping up on us, and the rain poured down harder than ever. The trees alongside the road were all pines now, sparse and windswept. Then they, too disappeared and all

I could see in the rapidly darkening mist were tall crags looming up on our right. On the left there was nothing – just a sea of shadowy fog. The road had dwindled to a faint track between huge boulders.

I reined in and pulled Bianca to a halt.

'We're lost, aren't we?'

'Well . . .' he said.

'*Aren't we?*'

'Um . . . I rather think we are, yes. We must have turned off the road somewhere, in the mist . . .'

I was suddenly too cold and wet and angry to be supportive.

'Garbage! Those lads sent us on a wild-goose chase. I told you they had, but you wouldn't listen, would you?'

It was his turn to be angry. 'How was I to know they'd do such a thing? In my country, no-one would dare. They'd be horsewhipped.'

'This is not your country,' I snapped. 'And if you'd been as rude to me as you were to those men, I'd have done the same as they did.' He was wet and cold and bedraggled too, or I wouldn't have dared.

He stared at me as though he wanted to hit me. Then he went all stiff and regal.

'I don't expect to have to waste time on elaborate courtesies with yokels.'

'I'm not talking about elaborate courtesies, I'm talking about a basic minimum of politeness. You were thoroughly obnoxious. Didn't your nanny ever teach you any manners?'

'Leave my nanny out of this!'

'We were lucky,' I went on. (Aurora was horrified, but for once Foss was out of her box – and once she'd started, I didn't seem to be able to stop.) 'Just as well they were respectable country people. If you'd picked a bunch of drunks to insult we'd probably be lying in a ditch right now with our throats cut.'

'Yes, I suppose with your background you'd know all about drunks and their habits, wouldn't you?'

'Oh, for Heaven's sake,' I said, exasperated. All this bickering was getting us nowhere except wetter. I slid off Bianca's back, grabbed the bridle and led her off the track in the direction of the nearest rock outcrop.

'Wh—where are you going?'

'Somewhere dry,' I said, and marched off into the mist.

6.

Your Stars: CANCER (June 22–July 23)
Romance is still high on the agenda, but don't expect the
course of true love to run smoothly: events may take an
unexpected turn.

Ferdinand hesitated for perhaps twenty seconds; then I heard him dismount and come after me.

I skirted the crags and after a few minutes I found what I was looking for: a deep gully winding in between them. The gully didn't possess a cave – that would have been too much to expect – but where it narrowed at the far end a big gnarled hawthorn tree was growing up against the cliff face. By itself, the overhang wouldn't have sheltered us; but with the dense canopy of the tree in front, it was just about adequate, and there was room for the horses.

Ferdinand came squelching up the gully, leading Tarquin, who was looking extremely annoyed.

'All we need now is a fire,' I said. 'Have you got any matches?'

What he had, predictably, was a tinder-box. Very ornate, with lots of gold curly bits surrounding a discreet little coronet in the centre of the lid.

'Leave it to me,' he said confidently, and began crumpling up sandwich wrappers.

Twenty minutes later the fire was still unlit. I watched him fumble with damp sticks and charred paper, swearing under his breath and getting soot on his cuffs, until I couldn't stand it any longer.

'Just get out of the way, will you?' I said, and elbowed him aside.

I like lighting fires: I suppose it goes with cooking. Emlyn once taught me the shepherds' way with fires out of doors, and I've never forgotten. The pile of bone-dry lichen and dead grass and small dry twigs from under the tree lit at the second attempt. A few bigger twigs and then some larger fallen branches, and we had a blaze going.

Ferdinand regarded me with something approaching awe.

'That was marvellous,' he said generously.

We hung our sodden cloaks on the tree to dry, and huddled within the overhang, stretching out numb hands to the warmth. To my astonishment, Ferdinand put his arm round me. 'You're full of surprises, aren't you?'

'Am I?'

I leant my head against his shoulder, and we sat for a while in a comfortable silence while the flames leapt and rustled and the twigs cracked.

'Your face is filthy,' he said.

'So's yours.'

'Is it? Good Heavens.'

'Never mind. We'll find a stream in the morning.'

Beyond the circle of firelight, rain pattered down. The horses shifted and snuffled on the far side of the tree-trunk. I felt happier than I had all week. Ferdinand taken down a peg or two, and with a dirty face, was suddenly a much nicer person than before.

After a while he yawned. 'Sorry. My eyes simply won't stay open any longer.' He withdrew his arm and like the perfect gentleman he was, he moved away and propped himself against the rock wall to sleep. In a moment he opened one eye.

'Er . . . my cloak. Is it dry, d'you think?'

'Possibly,' I said, and waited. He was about to say, 'Fetch it for me, will you?' I'll swear the words were on the tip of his tongue. My face was dirty, my hair was a mess, I'd snapped at him, lit his fire for him, broken a nail – and fallen off my princess pedestal in the process. Ferdinand's world view of women was very simple. You were either an object of adoration, remote and doll-like and not expected to lift a finger on any-body's behalf – or you rushed around ministering to his every whim. Nothing in between. I stared straight back at him and didn't move.

His handsome face hardened a bit, then he got stiffly to his feet and unhooked his cloak from its branch. Mine, too, which was nice of him.

'Well, goodnight, then,' he said coldly. He folded the hood into a pillow, wrapped the rest of the cloak around him and closed his eyes.

I was tired too, but I sat there hugging my knees beside the fire for a long time, feeding bits of stick to the flames and

70

chasing doubts out into the open. I faced a truth which had been nagging at me for days: Ferdinand wasn't actually in love with Aurora. Proud, possessive, amazed at his luck – but not in love. She was his dream princess – every detail as per specification – but that mysterious, essential ingredient was missing.

Why? Was it because love's real, and romance isn't? It was becoming obvious to me that as far as Ferdinand was concerned Aurora wasn't, and never had been, a real person. She was a romantic ideal, a symbol of his prowess, a glittering prize on the way to a throne and a kingdom. Love didn't enter into that kind of equation at all. It was a chilling thought.

I faced some hard facts on my own account, keenly aware that Foss was doing most of the thinking. Ferdinand was all I'd ever dreamed of: stunning to look at, brave, athletic, considerate, commanding (a tiny subversive voice inside me said 'bossy' but I ignored it) – but perhaps . . . well . . . not terribly bright?

Do you really want to marry a man to whom simple jokes have to be *explained*? Can you bear to spend the rest of your life with someone who takes everything literally? – whose sense of humour is practically non-existent? Who's so hooked on duty and responsibility and Doing the Right Thing that he never ever does anything on impulse?

Do you want to marry somebody like *Scott*?

When at last I did drop off to sleep it turned out to be a bad mistake. I dreamed non-stop all night. Every dream was about hiding and running away from some unseen enemy. Sometimes I was in places I knew, and racing from room to room trying to close windows and lock doors which kept springing open again. Sometimes I was alone, and sometimes Ferdinand was with me, and never doing as he was told . . .

I woke up with a mouth like the Gobi desert and my heart pounding as though I'd run the hundred-metre dash six times in a row.

The fire was out. Beyond the hawthorn tree it was daylight – a grey, sullen sort of day without warmth. Ferdinand was still fast asleep, and what I could see of his face above the fur cloak looked untroubled and very young. I got up stiffly and hobbled out into the gully.

Above me a sickly-looking sun was struggling to assert its authority over a sulky and obstreperous sky. Its chances of succeeding seemed remote. I felt sorry for that sun – it looked exactly as I felt: pale and washed-out and wobbly, and all too obviously feeling that getting out of bed had been a lousy idea.

After a wash in an icy stream, I felt a lot better. Ferdinand was sitting up and groaning when I got back to the overhang.

'I feel terrible. I didn't sleep a wink all night. I think I'm going down with flu.'

My heart sank. Ferdinand ill was a complication I hadn't bargained for.

'Well, don't. Wait till we get back to civilisation, and you can be as ill as you like.'

'You really are the most unsympathetic person,' he grumbled.

'I'm not, honestly. Just realistic. If you're ill here, you'll probably catch pneumonia.'

He groaned again, but this time I could tell his heart wasn't in it. Nobody likes being ill in extreme discomfort. He sat up gingerly, and rubbed the back of his neck.

'How are the horses?'

'Fine. Not too impressed with the night's accommodation, though. Judging from the expression on Tarquin's face this morning, you've got a lot of explaining to do.'

His brow furrowed. 'Sorry?'

'Have a wash,' I said, handing him the soap and towels. 'The water's sub-zero but it's wonderful when you stop.'

Half an hour later we'd saddled up and were leading the horses out of the gully.

I don't know about you, but whenever I arrive somewhere in thick mist or in the dark, my imagination roves about picking up all sorts of tiny clues and before you can say Miss Marple it's presented me with a convincing and completely false picture of what the place should look like in broad daylight.

Last night my mind's eye had insisted that we were back in the high moorland country we'd left behind the day before. So it was quite a shock to find ourselves near the top of a single rocky hill which was standing like an island in the middle of an immense flat expanse of forest.

'Good grief,' Ferdinand muttered. 'I don't remember any of this, do you?'

There was no sign of a town or a village or a building of any kind. The forest stretched unbroken to the horizon. Even the track had disappeared.

'We had the crags on our right on the way up,' I said, 'So if we circle the hill with them on our left . . .'

'Good idea,' he said, and urged Tarquin forwards.

As we worked our way anticlockwise round the hill I found myself casting apprehensive glances at the forest looming below us on our right. Those massed and crowding trees seemed to have some sinister connection with last night's bad dreams; some crucial link that I'd forgotten on waking. The feeling of being relentlessly pursued began to hang over me again like a bad smell.

My jitters communicated themselves to Bianca. Every time I tried to pull her uphill, away from the tree-line, she danced and sidestepped and ended up a few feet further down, where the going was easier. I wasn't a complete novice in the saddle any more, but I still had difficulty convincing her I was boss.

Suddenly there was a loud crashing noise in the underbrush – and a snow-white stag came plunging through the brambles only a couple of metres in front of Tarquin's nose. When it saw the big grey it reared, swerved and pelted off along the fringe of the forest before disappearing into the trees again.

Ferdinand let out a yell of delight and went galloping off in pursuit. I hadn't a hope of controlling Bianca: she shot away after her stablemate with me clinging on like grim death.

We found Ferdinand and Tarquin gazing speculatively (and I mean *both* of them, not just Ferdinand) into a long green glade which led between the trees. I reined Bianca to a halt. Every nerve in my body was telling me that this place was bad news.

Ferdinand turned round as I approached.

'Oh, there you are.' His face was radiant, his voice rapt, like a little boy who's just discovered fifty different varieties of ice-cream in the corner shop. 'Listen! It's a hunt!'

I listened. In the distance, I could faintly hear the sound of horns and the excited baying of hounds.

'They're on to him! Huntsman's telling them to hold back.' Ferdinand was reading the horn calls like a VDU.

Personally, I've never understood the hunting ethos. Obviously, if you eat meat, you have to kill it first, but making a carnival out of the process has always struck me as a bit obscene. Ferdinand clearly didn't share my sentiments; he couldn't wait to get involved, you could tell.

And the danger I could sense was increasing every second.

'Ferdinand,' I reminded him tactfully, 'We really don't have time for this. We have to get back to the South Road, remember?'

'Sssshhh!' he said. 'Listen!'

The hound and horn noises were getting closer. Ferdinand and Tarquin could scarcely contain their excitement. Ferdinand kept standing up in his stirrups in an attempt to see something.

'Careful,' he was muttering, 'Slow now . . . slow . . . They're almost on top of him . . .'

The noises reached a crescendo: a melee of barks and frantic horn commands and human shouts clearly audible through it all.

'They've got him!' Ferdinand shouted. 'Oh, well done! Come on, Aurora, now's our chance.'

I grabbed his rein. 'Ferdinand – *please* don't go in there!' The sense of danger – of crouching, anticipatory evil – had become so strong I could hardly bear it. It flowed out of the glade like an almost visible fog.

He stared at me. 'Why ever not?'

'Because it's dangerous. I can *feel* it. Please, Ferdinand.'

He and Tarquin gazed coldly down their nostrils at me, their expressions identical. 'You're crazy. Does it look dangerous?'

I had to concede that it didn't. Just a wide grassy ride, with bracken at the edges and clumps of rosebay beginning to fluff into seed. Perfectly innocuous . . . except that the emanation of evil was stronger than ever. I was vaguely conscious of a prickling sensation at my throat, where the pendant lay, and a faint stinging feeling like static electricity on my skin.

'If it *were* dangerous,' Ferdinand added, 'Don't you think the horses would know?'

He had a very telling point there. Both Tarquin and Bianca were behaving beautifully and exhibiting no nerves at all.

I didn't know what else to say. How can you convince somebody that you know better than he does when all you've got to argue with is an overwhelming presentiment of doom? I tried again. 'What about the South Road? We have to be on it by nightfall . . . do you want to spend another night in the open with no food?'

'Oh, *damn* the bloody Road,' he said. 'This is a *hunt*. Don't you understand what that means? It means civilised people. It means hot baths and a decent meal and somewhere to spend the night. It means good company and interesting conversation.'

The endearing boyish charm had vanished, and in its place was the worldly-wise, patronising young aristocrat who could make every word sound like a calculated insult. I wanted to hit him.

'I don't know what's got into you over the last couple of days,' he went on. 'All you seem to be capable of is nagging a chap.'

'That's not fair!'

'Isn't it? Well, try seeing this from my point of view for once. I've been on this damn Quest for over a year. How long d'you think it's been since I hunted with a halfway decent pack?'

So it was all my fault. I'd had a nasty feeling it might be.

'You can hunt any time you like,' I said wildly. 'You can spend the rest of your life hunting, if that's what you want. Just let's get away from this place and back on the right road. Please, Ferdinand. Something awful is going to happen if we go in there.'

When I was little I had a book called *Tales From Greek Mythology*, and there was this poor simp, I remember, called Cassandra, who kept trying to tell people that disasters were about to strike, but nobody took any notice. I knew, now, exactly how she must have felt.

Ferdinand glared sulkily down at me. 'You're not much of a sport, are you? Come to think of it, you haven't been much fun from the start.'

This was too much. Foss flared.

'*Me?* What about you? All those mind-numbing stories about your boring family and your boring friends . . .'

He went rigid, as though I'd slapped his face. '*How dare you?*'

I went cold. 'I'm sorry . . . I'm sorry. I didn't mean it like that . . .'

'Didn't you?'

'Oh, please, Ferdinand, let's forget the whole thing. Let's find the right road!'

It was too late. As we'd been quarrelling, I'd been dimly aware of the sound of voices approaching – and now, right on cue, a crowd of people came into view at the far end of the glade. There were hounds milling happily about, and foot-servants with wicker picnic-baskets and huntsmen in green cloaks, like Robin Hood. Behind them there appeared a group of riders: tall, handsome young men, and beautiful girls. Their rich clothes glowed like jewels against the sombre backdrop of the pines. They waved to us, and called out. 'Hallo there! Would you care to join us?'

'Thank you so much,' Ferdinand shouted. He urged Tarquin forwards and cantered briskly up the glade without a single glance at me.

Bianca was fidgeting, and tugging at the bit: I knew I wouldn't be able to hold her back much longer. Every instinct I possessed was screaming at me to get out, fast, while I still had a choice. On the other hand, there was Ferdinand, trotting up the glade like a lamb skipping innocently to the slaughter . . .

I took a deep breath and allowed Bianca to trot sedately after the grey.

As we crossed the forest edge I felt a prickling sensation all over my skin, like ants crawling. When the prickling faded I found myself going numb and blank. I could feel my will and my ability to think seeping away into nothingness. I hardly noticed that Bianca had stopped moving. We stood there as though paralysed.

Ferdinand came to a halt and dismounted. A single rider moved forward to greet him. She was young and blonde and beautiful and wore a golden crown on her head. She was also the source of all the power I'd sensed: all the evil. It streamed out of her almost visibly, the way cold air pours out of an open freezer.

No-one in that glittering throng so much as glanced my way. It was as though I had suddenly become invisible.

Ferdinand dropped to one knee and bowed his head. 'My Queen,' he said reverently. She smiled gloriously, and extended her hand. As he rose his eyes never left her face for a millisecond. He'd forgotten I existed.

He mounted Tarquin and the company began to move off. As they reached the far end of the glade their shapes and colours broke up into a whirl of fractured brilliance. I shut my eyes against the brightness. When I opened them again, Bianca and I were alone.

How long we stood there motionless, I've no idea. Eventually, my numb brain began to unfreeze. I looked round. There was no sign of the sunlit glade; Bianca and I were surrounded by dark and tangled trees whose twisted branches gave you the unpleasant impression that any moment they'd start groping for your face.

Bianca came to life under me and started to tremble. I turned her round and urged her into a trot – and she was only too happy to oblige. She didn't like this place any more than I did.

We'd gone less than fifty yards when something huge and black and snarling came leaping out at us from between the trees. I didn't get a chance to see what it was – Bianca took off like a rocket. It was all I could do to hang on and not get thrown. Tree-trunks whizzed past in a blur, twigs whipped my face and tore out strands of my hair while I crouched almost flat against her neck gripping her mane like grim death.

Her sense of direction was infinitely better than mine. Suddenly the trees parted in front of us – and there, rising above the outermost hedge of thorns, was the smooth green hillside and the blue sky overhead.

Bianca cleared the final thorn barrier in one gigantic, soaring leap. I hadn't a hope of staying on her back. I lost rein, saddle, stirrups and all. The next thing I remember is the turf rushing up to meet me with the speed of a 747.

The impact jarred every bone in my body. I rolled over, retching for breath. When I staggered to my feet again, Bianca was gone.

But I was on the open hillside and out of that deadly wood. I limped to the shoulder of the hill. Far below me, the track gleamed white between the trees, which reared away from it like the parting of the Red Sea. And there, in plain view, was a lone Israelite in the shape of Bianca, scudding away down the road as fast as her slender legs would carry her.

At this point in the original drama the Pharaoh, watching from his own hilltop, probably uttered a single unprintable expletive. I know Foss did. Apart from the clothes I was wearing, everything I possessed in the world had gone off in the saddle-bag on Bianca's rapidly diminishing rump. I had no money for lodging, transport or food. I hadn't eaten for twenty hours and I was feeling sick and faint with hunger. Aurora collapsed into helpless misery, wailing *Ferdinand's gone . . . What'll I do without Ferdinand?* while Foss raged and swore.

After a while both of us began to climb down towards the distant road.

I'd almost reached the point where the track started – I could see it ahead of me, winding off between unbroken walls of trees – when out of the corner of my eye I caught a glimpse of something pale and twitching. I blinked and stared. A moment later a fat skewbald horse ambled out of a coppice of brambles. It was swishing its tail as it grazed, and dragging a long rope behind it.

Gypsies? Cautiously, I crept closer.

The camp was in a small quarry at the base of the hill, screened by bushes. At first all I could see was a washing line strung between two trees. It was flaunting an extraordinary collection of underwear – fishnet tights, minuscule satin panties in lurid shades of lime, hot pink and electric blue with black lace trimming, and a few very substantial bras to match. On another section of the line, decorously apart from all that feminine frippery, were two pairs of awesomely vast and very dingy cotton combinations, the kind of thing elderly cow-hands wear in low-budget Westerns to provide comic relief. As I watched, the line began to bounce: somebody was unpegging the washing.

I reached the screen of bushes and looked through.

A few yards away a girl was washing up in a plastic bowl on a small folding table. Another girl with her mouth full of pegs was folding the dry clothes into a basket. Both girls were wearing skin-tight jeans, and check shirts (one pink, one blue) knotted under the bust to expose tanned midriffs. Both had white-blonde hair fluffed up in front and tied in a cute little pony-tail at the back. A large and very ugly mongrel was sniffing at the saucepans.

At the back of the quarry stood a wagon with a tarpaulin cover stretched over hoops. Both wagon and tarpaulin were lavishly ornamented with orange, scarlet and crimson flames, above which were painted the words REPENT YE in letters a metre high. Against the wagon, sitting on a folding chair in the sun, was the undisputed owner of the combinations – the tallest, broadest, fattest man I'd ever seen in my life. He was dressed in a baggy black suit and a broad-brimmed hat. A heavy gold watch-chain lay at full stretch across his immense waistcoat. He looked extremely formidable, and not at all the kind of man who gives lifts to hitch-hikers.

I dithered. Hunger and desperation were telling me to get on in there and beg; cowardice kept pointing out that (a) they didn't look particularly friendly and (b) they had a dog. I'd almost decided to sneak away unseen when the dog scented me and started to snarl.

Three heads swivelled round in my direction. I parted the bushes and stepped out into the clearing. 'Hi,' I said nervously.

The dog went berserk. One of the girls shouted at it, and it lay down, still growling, with fangs bared. Four pairs of eyes watched intently as I walked out from between the bushes. Apart from the dog, who was obviously psychotic, they didn't look particularly startled, or even hostile – just wary.

'I'm—I'm sorry to bother you,' I said. 'But . . . you couldn't give me a lift into the nearest town, could you? If you're going that way?'

The stares broke up in confusion. The girl in the blue shirt glanced over her shoulder and said, 'Paw?'

The man lumbered to his feet. Standing, he was even bigger than I'd thought: at least six foot six and weighing in at considerably more than thirty stone. When he was younger he might have been quite good-looking in a craggy sort of way, but now the eyes were glittering pinholes deeply sunk in fat, and the jawline had almost disappeared beneath roll upon roll of stubbled chin. He stared down at me, taking in every detail.

'Why, honey,' he said in a rich deep rumble of disapproval, 'Ain't you a little young to be headin' into town without your Ma?'

'She ain't country folks, Paw,' the pink-shirted one said sharply. She was the shorter of the two, and the more lively. 'Ever seen a farm kid dressed like that?'

The big man lowered his heavy eyebrows at me. 'Well, honey? Your folks live around here someplace?'

The questioning was the last straw. Aurora burst into tears. There was a moment's stunned silence – then the two girls surged round me, clucking maternally. I was presented with a cup of instant chicken soup and a slice of bread. They stared in fascinated dismay as I wolfed it all down in milliseconds flat.

'Hungry, huh?' the blue one said solicitously. I nodded. My mouth was too full to answer. Under stress, even Aurora behaved like a pig.

The big man stood over me while I ate: uncomfortably close, and so loomingly massive he blocked out the light. At close quarters he reeked of stale tobacco and sweat, and there were dribbles of congealed egg down the front of his waistcoat.

I finished the bread and looked up. All three faces were suddenly shrewd and speculative. They wanted explanations.

Foss did some frantic censoring and restructuring of the script. I told them I'd been travelling to Arborea with my family, that we'd taken the wrong road in yesterday's thick mist and wandered into the forest by mistake. That something had attacked us, and that the horses had bolted in different directions. That my mare had thrown me and galloped off. I was quite surprised at the easy way it all came out: the whole story was a nicely balanced mixture of the believable and the truth.

'You may have seen her,' I added, 'A white mare, with a saddlebag. She went off down the road.'

They exchanged glances and nodded. The man extended a pudgy hand. Large regular tombstone teeth flashed briefly in a smile. 'Guess we'd better introduce ourselves. Hezekiah Frame,' he rumbled.

'The *Reverend* Hezekiah Frame,' the blue girl added importantly. I shook hands.

'My two gals,' he added. 'Mercy-Lou,' – indicating the pink-shirted one – 'and Purity-Jean.'

'Hi,' I said, trying to smile. 'I'm . . . I'm Aurora.'

'Pleased to meet you, Aurora,' they chorused.

'Well, Paw?' Purity-Jean was anxious for a policy statement.

The Rev. Frame looked solemn. 'Well, I guess the good Lord in His infinite mercy has brought this poor li'l lost lamb right here to the fold.'

'You can ride along as far as Ashwood, okay?' said Mercy-Lou. 'Can you pay your way?'

I touched my hair, but the jewelled coronet had gone. My heart sank. 'There's money in that saddlebag.'

'Huh,' said Purity-Jean, and shrugged, implying that the chances of finding Bianca with an intact saddlebag were remote.

Hezekiah patted me kindly on the shoulder. It was like being slapped with a side of beef. 'The Lord will provide, honey. He'll move your heart to service when the time comes.' His fat fingers slid under my jaw and tilted my head up. 'Purty li'l thing,' he rumbled. 'Yeah, I guess there'll be a place for our daughter in the gathering of the faithful.'

He heaved his mountainous bulk in the direction of the tethered horse, belching resonantly as he went.

As we climbed into the wagon half an hour later Foss was communicating jitters. I squashed them. It was a lift, wasn't it?

It was still only mid-morning. Hezekiah drove, with the dog on the seat beside him, and the girls and I sat on the steps at the back. We made desultory conversation while the wagon trundled down the track. Hezekiah, they explained, was a travelling preacher. The girls' job was to entertain the crowds before and after the sermons, and pull the punters in.

'Ain't no-one like Paw for preachin',' Purity-Jean assured me earnestly.

After a while silence fell. I watched the road unrolling like an endless strip of parcel tape from under the wagon's wheels and felt panic and gloom descend. Ferdinand spirited away by enchantment. Myself adrift in a world I knew nothing about, helpless to rescue him. Ifs and buts and maybes of the bleakest possible sort strewing the immediate future . . .

Both Foss and Aurora were quite clear about one thing, however: the moment we got to Ashwood I'd lose no time in putting as much distance between myself and the Rev. Frame as was humanly possible. He scared me in ways I didn't want to think about.

We arrived at Ashwood just after mid-day. Hezekiah drove the wagon into the market-place. We set up trestles to form a stage, then the two girls disappeared inside to change. I offered to help, but they refused. Instead, Hezekiah sent me out front with a leather bag to collect the money once the show got under way – my chance to pay back what I owed him for the lift.

A small crowd was already beginning to gather when Mercy-Lou and Purity-Jean came out onto the stage.

They were wearing identical satin mini-skirts with fishnet tights and high-heeled white cowboy boots, satin shirts with a lot of ruthlessly jacked-up cleavage in evidence, fringed and sequinned waistcoats and white ten-gallon cowboy hats. Fake hair tumbled in improbable curls over their shoulders, and they'd put on full stage make-up which didn't match the colour of their necks. Their false eyelashes were so long it was a wonder their lids stayed open.

As they tottered onto the trestles they got scattered applause and a few wolf-whistles: then they started to sing. Their first number was a catchy little song about S.A.L.V.A.T.I.O.N. Their voices were okay, if a bit shrill, and Mercy-Lou did a bit of fancy banjo-picking which went down well with the crowd. When they'd finished they got a round of perfectly genuine applause, at which point I remembered the leather bag and scurried round shaking it under people's noses.

The girls disappeared, and Hezekiah strode forwards to preach.

Mercifully (or I'd still be having nightmares), I don't remember a word of what he said. All I remember is that his stage presence was horribly impressive. His sonorous voice rolled across the square and every other sound seemed to fade away into insignificance. Within ten seconds he had the audience in the palm of his podgy hand. Nobody moved, nobody fidgeted or whispered; every eye was fixed on his face. This wasn't a sermon – this was mass hypnosis, and sweet susceptible Aurora succumbed to it with the rest, and without a flicker of protest.

What saved me was Foss. Foss was wide-awake, and scared, and desperately urging Aurora out of her stupor. I fought the paralysis and cautiously edged my way to the stage. I put the leather bag down at Hezekiah's feet and slipped quietly away.

As I emerged from the crowd I saw something that froze me in my tracks. From an archway beneath a shabby inn-sign there emerged a horse and cart which were mind-bogglingly familiar. Even more so was the bloke in the driving seat: a shortish, stocky individual with spiky dark hair in a No. 4 cut and wearing a scuffed leather jacket . . .

I started to run. The cart turned sharp right and made off down the street at a brisk trot. Crowds of marketgoers surged between. By the time I reached the end of the street the cart had vanished.

I dashed back up the street to the inn. In the courtyard a couple of farmers were chatting in a corner. A carpet-slippered man was smoking a pipe in the doorway, and an elderly woman was sweeping the steps.

'Excuse me,' I said, still breathless. 'That young feller . . .'

'Eh?' the woman said, leaning on her broom and glaring suspiciously at me. The farmers gave me a cursory glance and turned back to their chat.

I took a deep breath and started again. 'That young man who just left here, with a pony and cart . . . Was his name Jo Morgan? Did he say where he was g—?'

The rest of the sentence vanished in a gasp of pain. A large fat hand had caught my wrist in a grip of iron and twisted my arm in an expert half-nelson behind my back. A voice like muted thunder breathed in my ear.

'Gotcha,' said the Reverend Hezekiah triumphantly.

I turned my head and gaped at him, utterly gobsmacked. How could a grossly overweight man of his age move so *fast*? Less than two minutes ago he'd been right in the middle of delivering the most powerfully impassioned stage act I'd ever seen. I'd heard his voice in the background as I'd hared across the square after Jo. I was still out of breath. And here he was, cool and collected and not even wheezing.

A second, more disquieting thought was, *Why*?

'Let me go!' I yelled, struggling. 'That was Jo, d'you understand? I've got to catch up with him!'

Every eye in the yard was riveted on us by now. The two farmers – middle-aged, respectable-looking men, probably with daughters of their own – took a couple of steps towards us as if preparing to intervene.

Hezekiah's big white teeth bared themselves in a feral grin.

'Purty li'l thing, ain't she?' he said apologetically to the onlookers. 'My own sister's gal. Wouldn't think a sweet-faced kid like this'd run off with her uncle's takings, would you?'

My blood ran suddenly cold. 'B—but I didn't! I left the bag on the stage!'

'Whaddya call this, then, huh? Moonshine?' He dipped his hand inside my pocket and drew out the leather bag. For the second time my jaw dropped open in stunned disbelief. I *knew* I'd put the bag on the stage. I *knew* the pocket had been empty when I'd reached the inn yard. If the coins had been there I'd have felt the weight, and heard them jingle as I ran.

The farmers looked at one another and shrugged.

'You're a crook!' I screamed. 'Let me go! You planted the stuff on me . . . He's kidnapping me! Help! . . .'

The yard began to empty. Nobody wanted to get involved in a nasty little scene between travelling people.

I went ballistic with sheer terror – but Hezekiah immobilised me as easily as if I'd been a kitten. Both my wrists were clamped in one colossal fist and jammed into the small of my back. The other hand came down over my face, squeezing my jaw shut so I couldn't yell or bite and could barely breathe. He propelled me out under the arch and across the market square so fast that half the time my feet didn't even touch the ground.

Mercy-Lou and Purity-Jean were waiting in the square. The trestles and scaffolding and stage-cloths had been stowed away and the horse was harnessed between the shafts. They tied my wrists and ankles with rope, shoved a gag in my mouth and hurled me into the wagon. Nobody paid any attention to them.

Hezekiah bent down and rumbled in my ear. 'Dunno who y'are, li'l girl, or how you got away – but one thing's for sure: you ain't gonna slip ya tethers this time. The Queen's gonna want a word with you.'

I felt the springs sag sharply as he climbed onto the driver's perch. The back screen was pulled down. A moment later the wagon began to trundle away over the cobbles.

7.

Your Stars CANCER (June 22–July 23)
Forces beyond your control are governing your life at the
moment, and a personal dream has shattered. Don't reject
an offer of help, however unexpected. This is a situation
you can't tackle on your own.

As the wagon bumped and swung, so did I, rolling from side to side on the filthy floor, helpless to stop myself.

One particularly bad jolt sent me skidding backwards. But instead of slamming into the side bench, my head hit something which yielded slightly on impact. It was a human foot in a buckled leather shoe.

I hooked my bound ankles under the bench, twisted awkwardly round and looked up through blurred eyes. I saw a muscular leg clad in woollen stockings and knee-breeches. The leg's owner was sitting on the side-bench, his feet firmly planted on the floor. I nudged him with my head and made urgent gurgling noises through the gag. The figure didn't even twitch.

Using the immobile leg as a brace, I wriggled myself into a sitting position. It was then I realised that the young man wasn't the only other occupant of the wagon. Two very pretty girls were sitting on the bench opposite. Not one of them was looking at me. All three pairs of eyes were glassily focussed on infinity. Their bodies were swaying with the movement of the wagon but their minds were somewhere else. Their faces were as blank as waxwork dummies.

I'd been scared before, but never as badly as now. I was almost glad when the wagon bounced and forced me to concentrate on keeping my balance.

At least I was sitting up now. I edged cautiously round until my back was against the bench, then I shuffled along on my bottom until I reached front corner. A bit of judicious wriggling brought me hard up against the canvas screen and my eyes to the gap between the ties.

Hezekiah and the dog were inches away but neither of them

85

noticed me – all their attention was on the road. I guessed the sisters must be on the steps, behind the screen at the back.

I gazed – and for the first time realised that we were travelling *fast*. The horse galloped and the wagon swung – but the road was zipping by like a runway on takeoff. Hedges and trees and scattered buildings were passing in a blur. What was *happening* here?

Eventually the wagon slowed to normal speed. We seemed to be entering a town. My heart lifted. There'd be people, other traffic – Hezekiah might be forced to stop, in which case I'd thump loudly and maybe inspire somebody to investigate . . .

As we went on, that faint hope died. We were travelling through what looked like a war zone. Roofless houses, shop-fronts boarded up, heaps of rubble in the streets. I caught glimpses of a few filthy, ragged shapes, more like animated sticks than people, picking through what seemed to be piles of garbage. The stench of the place made me want to retch.

The wagon began to climb a steep incline and the smell receded. Finally we came to a stop on level ground. The back screen was rolled up. My zombie companions climbed out. The sisters appeared, untied my ankles and wrists, jerked the gag out of my mouth and set me ungently on my feet.

We were in a courtyard, with high walls and a gate manned by tough-looking guards in greasy uniforms. In front of us was a castle, ruined and roofless, with a flight of steps leading up to a huge iron-bound wooden door.

Hezekiah loomed up behind me and gripped my arm in case I had any silly ideas about running away again. As it happened, I hadn't – my ankles were so stiff and swollen that I doubt if I could have hobbled more than three steps before falling over. Hezekiah must have known this as well as I did, but he wasn't taking any chances. He frog-marched me up the steps, kicked the door open and pushed me inside. Then he backed out and slammed and locked the door behind me.

I'd prepared myself for just about anything: rats, chains, a snake-pit, you name it. What I actually saw was a large, wood-panelled hall hung with pictures and lit by candelabra. My throbbing feet sank into rose-red carpeting six inches deep and my nose identified the scents of wax polish and pot-pourri.

I stared, utterly flummoxed. My brain felt as numb as my ankles and I couldn't think straight. This couldn't be real. I had to be dreaming.

An older woman appeared on the landing above me, and came swiftly down the stairs to greet me. She was wearing evening dress with a diamond tiara on her immaculately groomed hair. She held out both hands to me like a shepherdess reclaiming a lost lamb.

'My dear *child!* We were so *worried!* You poor thing, you must be utterly exhausted! . . . Agatha! Emmeline!'

Two maids in mob-caps appeared at a side door.

'Take this poor child up to her room and make her comfortable, will you?' She turned gracefully towards me. 'Dinner is at eight, dear. Agatha will show you the way.'

My brain gave up. A lovely warm feeling of being *safe* flooded right through me. This was where I was supposed to be, the feeling assured me, and from now on everything was going to be absolutely fine. I relaxed in sheer gratitude.

Later, dressed in a gown of pale turquoise silk, my hair piled elaborately on the top of my head, I was ushered into the dining-room.

There were about twenty people at the long table. All of them were outstandingly good-looking and beautifully dressed, and all around my age except for our host and hostess, who were grey-haired and gracious. I registered, dimly, that Ferdinand wasn't there, but it didn't seem to matter.

The food was sumptuous and the conversation sparkled. Aurora was positively dazzling. Delicate witticisms delivered in her soft voice made the whole table rock with laughter, but I had no idea what I was going to say before it came tripping gracefully out of my mouth, nor could I remember it afterwards.

At one point I found myself talking brightly to a young man who looked a bit like Ferdinand. 'You do ride to hounds, of course,' he was saying.

'Oh, yes,' Aurora said. 'I adore hunting, it's my favourite sport.' And somewhere in the deep recesses of my bemused and befuddled brain, faint alarm bells began to ring.

After a while the conversation at our end of the table seemed to languish. Everybody's attention switched to a threesome in the middle: a vivacious blonde girl and two lively, intelligent-looking men. Suddenly Aurora didn't have anything to say: it was as though all that sparkle had been switched off and diverted elsewhere. I leant back in my chair, and my hand strayed quite naturally to the pendant round my neck.

As I touched it, I felt a distinct prickling sensation in my fingertips – and then, for a couple of seconds, no more – everything seemed to swirl and change. I got a startling vision of a vast ruined hall lit by a few stumps of candle; of straw on the floor and filthy pallets against the wall; and of all these people dressed in rags and chewing dry bread and hunks of cheese off a filthy board set on trestles in the centre.

It was only a flicker, and it disappeared as quickly as it had come. A moment later the dining-room with its snowy linen and glittering silver and glass, its gracious hosts and well-dressed guests, was exactly as before.

I tried to control the thumping of my heart. This was all an illusion. I had a flash of intuition: that dream-like numbness wasn't tiredness or delayed shock or bewilderment after all – it was the sign of a mind being taken over and manipulated by somebody else.

Dinner was over – and suddenly, everything went blank.

The next thing I remember is waving with the other girls from a balcony while the men rode away to go hunting. No connection, nothing in between.

Another blank space. I was downstairs again, dressed in a magnificent white satin crinoline with bare shoulders and roses in my hair and long white gloves. It was night; chandeliers blazed and music was playing for a grand ball . . .

Time seemed to freeze and start up and freeze again. There were episodes full of colour and laughter and genteel Victorian country-house activities during which all of us behaved as though we knew exactly what we were doing, interspersed with those peculiar blank periods when everything went dark. It was like being employed as an extra in a costume movie: everything out of sequence and nobody off-camera to let you in on the plot. Except that here, there were no opportunities for private conversation, no time to get to know any of the other players.

One night I woke up in the dark. My mind was perfectly clear. The enchantment – mind-hold, possession, call it what you like – had lifted away for the moment. I was lying on a heap of dirty straw in the same huge, ruined hall I'd glimpsed that first evening. The other prisoners – for that's exactly what we all were – lay sprawled about nearby; I could make out the humped shapes of sleeping bodies in the faint starlight, and hear their breathing. In one lucid instant I suddenly understood what was going on.

We were being played with, like dolls.

The idea was so simple it took my breath away. It explained everything – the blank spaces, when whoever was doing the manipulating got bored, or went off to play somewhere else; the hectic activity, the lack of any plot. We were living, breathing puppets. Whenever the manipulator needed us the stage was set and we performed. We'd perform, and go on performing, until we died. I felt sick with outrage.

As to who was responsible for it all – who had that much power? Who could be so *evil*, so totally switched-off to any normal human scruples? Who but Ferdinand's dazzling blonde Queen? Ferdinand was probably in another of her dolls' houses this very minute, acting in yet another of her plays . . .

So why hadn't she nabbed us both, when she had the chance? A moment's reflection worked that one out too. Ferdinand was being cast in a starring role. I was a bit-player, surplus to requirements. She'd left Hezekiah to pick me up later – if I survived.

An even more frightening thought struck me. So far, the whole thing had been fairly innocuous: a soppy little girl playing TV costume drama. But this Queen wasn't a little girl: she was an adult. My blood ran cold as I realised that a person with so much power and no moral code whatsoever could make us do absolutely *anything*. Ferdinand could be starring in a video nasty this very minute. It could be our turn tomorrow . . .

The warning came as a faint tingling feeling all over my skin. I pushed subversion aside and willed myself to think about painting my fingernails. The mind-hold swept over again; everything went peaceful and warm and hazy. The brief moment of clarity was over and once again I was drifting mindless in the dark.

It was bright daylight. We girls were chattering excitedly. Our dresses were frilly and silky and all the same colour: pale yellow . . . or was it pink? We were carrying bouquets of flowers that seemed to waver between yellow roses and pink carnations. Aurora babbled and giggled along with everybody else, while Foss kept tabs on everything in a state of unusual alertness. Evidently, our manipulator was finding it hard to make up her mind. She was dithering. People who dither make mistakes . . .

Suddenly we were surging down the steps and into the

courtyard, which was decked with flowers. From the other side of the high wall there came a noise like a huge crowd cheering. The big gates opened (I saw guards there in splendid uniforms, and wondered if they were real) – and under the arch came a golden coach pulled by six snow-white horses. It stopped in front of the castle door, and Ferdinand and his Queen got out.

He didn't see me. He wouldn't have recognised me if he had.

We sang songs of welcome, and threw flowers at the happy couple while bells rang in unseen belfries. A white carpet appeared on the steps; Ferdinand offered his arm to his radiantly beautiful bride and together they walked into the castle, waving and smiling to the welcoming crowd, and laughing as the flower-petals showered down all round them.

While the rest of her dolls began to follow them up the steps and into the castle, I dropped my bouquet and loitered behind to pick it up. Nobody noticed.

As the Queen crossed the threshold, the illusions within the courtyard began to fade. The coach started to turn around: its gold paint was suddenly patchy and flaking. The horses plodded straight through a flickering yew hedge and an elaborate piece of statuary. Illusions only act on the human mind; the horses were real, the statuary was not.

Something twanged and snapped in the air. An inner voice screamed at me 'Run! Now!'

I bunched up my skirts and darted across the courtyard. The coach was backing up – a tricky manoeuvre in such a restricted space. Everyone's attention was riveted on it, and for five precious seconds nobody noticed me – by which time I'd dodged through the open gate and was pelting away down the hill.

Behind me, startled horses whinnied and there was a splintering crunch as the coach hit something it shouldn't. People were shouting and swearing. I dared not look back. A bullet whistled past my shoulder. I dived into the shrubbery alongside the carriage drive, tripped over something painfully solid and nearly fell. I grabbed the pendant, and my sight cleared. The shrubbery had been an illusion too. The road was lined with heaps of rubble sloping away towards the backs of derelict terrace houses further down the hill.

The illusion was flickering in and out like strobe lighting as I dodged between the rubble-heaps. When I dashed down an entry between the terraces, it stopped altogether.

The illusion had vanished, but not the hold on my mind. I could feel it thickening the air around me, numbing my senses, making my legs ache as though I was running ankle-deep in quicksand. I kept going.

I came to a big thoroughfare at the bottom of the hill, crossed it in one panic-stricken dash and launched myself into the maze of narrower streets beyond. Garbage was heaped up all round me, rats flowed away like a grey sea as I approached, the streets were slick with filth and the stench made me want to throw up. Suddenly, not far behind me, I heard a fresh burst of shouting and the ominous yelping and baying of a pack of dogs. The hunt was on.

My breath was coming in huge sobbing gasps now; the stitch in my side was crippling me and my legs were jelly. I couldn't run much further.

I turned into another street and almost collided with a big group of black-robed figures. They were chanting what sounded like a funeral hymn, and in their hands they carried banners bearing the word 'Repent'.

I dodged into a narrow alley. Too late: a volley of excited shouts confirmed that I'd been seen and identified. I began to hear the noise of pounding boots in the street I'd just left, and renewed enthusiasm on the part of the hounds. They'd got my scent now, and wouldn't lose it.

The alley opened out into what must once have been a posh residential square. To my left a flight of steps led up to the open doorway of a half-demolished house. I turned sharply, skidded on garbage, made it to the steps on momentum alone, and fell heavily to the ground.

I lay there, winded and helpless. Mind-hold descended in a fog of weariness. Then my hand moved of its own volition and closed on something hard in my pocket. I pulled it out. It was Oz's little phial of change-back potion.

My brain was yammering in panic but right at the back of all the uproar a small, sane voice was trying to make itself heard. It was saying, *The dogs have Aurora's scent, not Foss's. Change back.*

Yes, but what if Foss's scent isn't any different?

What have you got to lose?

Everything! Being beautiful, being desirable, my Prince, my future . . .

Right now the only future you can look forward to involves being savaged by a pack of dogs. Change back!

No!

You really want to die in this hole? You want that bitch to win?

Shouts were echoing inside the alley now, and the barking was loud and eager. I prised the stopper out with my teeth, tilted the phial and swallowed the contents in one gulp.

The ruins spun. Brightly-coloured lights flashed in front of my eyes. My whole body seemed to be buzzing like a chain saw. With the last of my strength I crawled up the steps. I made it to the doorway and saw the dogs come pouring out of the alley in an agitated, tawny flood. Then, mercifully, I blacked out.

There was an arm around my shoulders: a firm, friendly sort of arm. I leant against it gratefully: it was the one thing in the entire universe that wasn't spinning and bucking and doing its best to tip me over the edge into nothingness. I was dimly aware of a lot of barking and shouting going on nearby, and heavy hobnailed boots stomping the pavements, but none of it seemed to concern me.

The nausea ebbed and the world steadied. I was sitting propped up behind a pillar in the doorway of the ruined house. A couple of dirty sacks had been thrown round me, and somebody was crouching protectively beside me, shielding me from the street. A girl's voice spoke in my ear.

'You're okay,' she said. 'They didn't see you. They've gone now.'

I leaned back against the supporting arm and let thankfulness wash all over me. I'd escaped. More importantly, my head was clear. That horrible blank apathy had gone, and with it the sensation of struggling to think my way through treacle. I was conscious of a million neural circuits winking awake, powering up and popping gleefully on line like a town coming back to life after a power cut.

I glanced down. Two hands were lying on my lap: small squarish hands, densely freckled on the backs. There was the split nail; there was the thin white scar where a chisel had slipped years ago, the funny little bump on the index finger . . .

My hands. *Mine.* There was an unaccustomed weight on the bridge of my nose: my glasses. Welcome back, Foss.

I burst into tears and cried as though my heart would break.

The grip on my shoulders tightened reassuringly. 'You're okay. Take it easy.'

My protector was a tall girl of around my own age. Like everybody else in this cesspit she was skeletally thin and so filthy that it was impossible even to tell what colour her hair was. She was dressed in an assortment of rags which had gone stiff and shiny with grease, and she stank to high Heaven. One of her eyes was half closed by an ugly-looking bruise. The other eye gleamed at me: clear and honest and cornflower-blue.

'Hi,' she said. 'I'm Margaret. Mags to my friends.'

'Foss,' I said. 'Short for Francesca.' And then, very inadequately, 'Thanks.'

'You're welcome.' She got to her feet and extended a bony hand. 'C'mon. Got to get you somewhere safe. Can you walk?'

Good question. Brain was fully functional, but the rest of me felt as wobbly as one of those rubber monsters kids put on pencil-ends. Clinging together like a couple of drunks, we lurched along an entry and down a steep flight of steps leading below street-level to a low iron door. As Margaret unlocked it chill blackness came flooding out to meet us. We ducked inside.

We were in a coal cellar piled high with the biggest assortment of junk I'd ever seen outside a Council skip. There was a narrow track through the middle of the stash. A small grating high up near the roof shed a wan light. Against the far wall a fire was burning in a small brick hearth.

Margaret tossed lumps of coal into the grate. 'It'll get warmer in a minute.' She pushed a decrepit armchair close to the blaze, and I huddled into it gladly. The place was as cold as a morgue, and I had begun to shiver uncontrollably in my thin summer top.

'You'll need some clothes,' she said, and began to rummage in a cardboard box. 'Here . . .' She tossed me a couple of moth-eaten jumpers and a thick ravelled cardigan. 'There's a skirt in here somewhere.' A filthy, torn skirt of some coarse material like hessian landed in my lap.

I looked up at her and didn't know what to say. She'd taken a huge risk in hiding me. Explanations were in order, but I didn't know where to start or how much to tell her.

I said the first thing that came into my head.

'Your eye . . . Did somebody hit you?'

She shrugged. 'No more than usual. Sometimes I don't duck fast enough.' All at once she took a deep breath and whirled to face me. 'Look – let's cut the small-talk, okay? What happened out there was—oh—' She shuddered. 'Horrible. I have never, ever, seen anything like that before and I hope to God I never will again.'

I looked at her with respect. 'I changed.'

'Yes! One minute you were running out of the alley, you were tall and dark-haired and wearing the most gorgeous dress . . . and the next – Yuk.'

'I bet,' I murmured.

'And now you look normal again. Different, but normal. I just want to know what I'm dealing with, that's all. Because if you're one of *them* . . .'

I felt an enormous sense of relief. This was not how one of the Queen's minions would behave.

'No,' I said. 'I come from somewhere else. I got snatched on the way here . . .'

Her gasp told me she'd understood. 'By the Black-coats?'

'Black-coats? Preacher types in big hats?'

She went white. 'And you *escaped*?'

I told her as much as I dared. I *wanted* to trust her – but my experience with Hezekiah had shaken me badly. 'Does it happen a lot? Kidnapping, I mean?'

She shrugged. 'All the time. Anybody young, good-looking, anybody with anything going for them . . .' Her face was troubled. 'It's not just the Black-coats, either. When I worked in the coal yards, six or seven years ago, the older girls started having dreams. A beautiful lady would appear – always the same lady. Golden hair and gorgeous clothes and a crown. She'd tell them she was their fairy godmother and that she'd make all their wishes come true – and then she'd wave her wand, and they'd find themselves in a palace, where there was plenty to eat and lovely clothes to wear – just like the place you described. They'd wake up and come to work all dopey-eyed and weepy and tell each other what they'd done in their dream the night before.'

One day they disappeared. She never saw any of them again.

'But you never dreamed like that.'

'No. After the girls vanished I got scared. And very, very careful.' She gestured dismissively at her filthy clothes and made a face.

At last I understood. *Anybody with anything going for them . . .* Margaret's filth wasn't apathy, or self-disgust, or even poverty. It was self-protection.

94

'How did it all start, anyway? Was there a war?'

'No.' She seemed relieved to change the subject. 'It's a mining town, this, on the edge of the Badlands – nothing for hundreds of miles. A century ago there was nothing here either – just that old Castle on the hill.' Then prospectors had discovered the wealth underground. 'My dad always said the geology of this place is practically unique: coal and iron on one side of the ridge, gold on the other.'

While the bonanza lasted the town had mushroomed: splendid public buildings, elegant residential squares, slum terraces, shanties. In all the frenzy of tunnelling and getting rich nobody cared that whole districts were showing signs of subsidence. Then, one winter, torrential rains and flash floods had washed out the diggings and half the town had collapsed. Fires from wrecked foundries had spread. Hundreds of people had died, and thousands more were homeless in one of the worst winters in living memory. Inevitably, a cholera epidemic had broken out.

The Black-coats had arrived as the emergency relief squad. They'd brought food, tents, blankets, medical supplies. People had welcomed them at first – until they called in their troops and took control. Sick and starving as they were, the survivors were forced underground at gunpoint to reopen the mines. Nobody got paid. More houses were torn down. Rations were cut.

'And nobody protested? Nobody told them where to stuff themselves?'

'How could they? The Specials had guns. A lot of people were shot trying to escape. The Black-coats told us the disaster was God's judgement for wickedness, and we had to be punished.' While Hezekiah and his hoods pocketed the profits and the Queen swanned around in a fantasy world of her own creation, playing with living dolls . . . I was so furious I wanted to spit.

'And later – people stopped caring. Didn't seem to have the energy for anything. Went around like zombies.'

'But not you?'

'No. What did you say it was? – mind-hold? Maybe I'm immune for some reason.'

And so am I, I thought. I'm Foss now, I'm real and I'm immune. And all that's got to count for something.

Eight-year-old Margaret had found herself orphaned and homeless. She'd slept rough. She'd worked in the coal yards, and pushed trucks underground. At thirteen she'd got a job scrubbing floors in the barracks, and now she was skivvy, drudge and general maid-of-all-work to the grisly old harridan upstairs. She told her story very simply, without a trace of self-pity.

I was horrified. 'But that's *terrible.*'

'Where you come from, perhaps. Here, I'm one of the lucky ones.'

'Lucky?'

'Sure. I eat. I've got somewhere warm to sleep.' She added shyly, 'There are loads of old books upstairs. *Nobody* in this town reads books any more. Sometimes I take a candle up there and read all night.'

I gazed at her in awe. Courage and brains and a head the Queen had failed to get into . . . I marvelled at my luck in stumbling across her. If it *was* luck.

A querulous voice was shrieking somewhere within the house, accompanied by an irregular thumping noise. Margaret got up hurriedly.

'I've got to go. Stay here. When it gets dark I'll bring you something to eat.'

I huddled there in the gritty dust and the chill firelit gloom. The thoughts which crowded in on me were equally gloomy. Aurora was gone forever. No man would ever gaze at me again in that awed, worshipful way. Heads would never again turn to look at me as I passed. The dazzling future I'd imagined for myself was not going to happen. I'd had my chance to be someone other than Foss – and somebody else had blown the whistle before I'd even got started. It wasn't *fair* . . .

'*All right, Foss, that's enough!*' I jumped. The voice was clear and crisp – and inside my head.

'Oz?' The pendant tingled in my fingers – I'd been fidgeting with it while I was thinking.

'*Are you all right?*'

'Yes, I'm fine. Where are you? What's going on?'

'*No time. Listen carefully. Ask about the dark of the moon. Got that?*'

'What? Oz, come back . . . How are you doing this? Oz?' But she'd gone.

I was dead tired. After a while I fell asleep in the chair. I woke up hours later in the dark to find a heavy quilt tucked round me. The fire was out.

The chair had lumps you wouldn't believe. As I eased myself up and shifted cramped muscles I became aware that the cellar wasn't completely dark. A faint blueish glow was coming from somewhere. I sat up cautiously – and saw ghosts.

They came floating through the walls – frail phantoms dressed like courtiers at a ball, and dancing a stately, silent minuet. Their faces were infinitely weary, inexpressibly sad – but still they danced on and on, graceful and courtly, without a moment's pause. The dance drifted past me and through me and out into the street, leaving a faint chill in its wake.

I was trembling all over. Was this what happened to the Queen's prisoners in the end? Is that what mind-hold did to you – leached away your life-force until all that was left was a feeble spirit still chained to the enchantress's will? The woman was a *vampire*.

Getting Ferdinand out of her clutches was becoming an urgent priority – but exactly how I was going to accomplish *that* little coup was anybody's guess.

Dawn came at last, and with it Margaret, carrying a plate of cold boiled potatoes and a scrap of cabbage for my breakfast.

'What happens at the dark of the moon?' I asked.

She went chalk-white under the grime. Her hands shook. 'Who – who told you?'

'I saw the ghosts,' I said. 'They were real people once, weren't they?'

She nodded, shuddering.

'So what about the dark of the moon?'

She gulped. 'All I actually *know* is that on the darkest night of every month, the guards open the gates of the town. The castle where you were lights up – and other places, too – and suddenly the ghosts start leaving in droves. They say that if you're not careful you get swept off with them . . . Nobody dares look – we just hide until it's over. Even the gate-guards get drunk so they don't have to watch.'

'Where do they go?'

'I don't know. Somewhere out in the wasteland.'

'Wait a minute.' What she'd said didn't make sense. 'They open the gates – for *ghosts*?'

Her eyes went wide. 'Of course! I never thought of that. They must be taking people with them.'

Prisoners? We stared at one another, hardly daring to voice that wild hope. All the prisoners, zonked out of their skulls, making their way across country with only ghosts to guard them . . . There *had* to be a snag. Nothing could be that easy.

'And it's tonight?'

Margaret nodded reluctantly. 'But it's much too dangerous, Foss . . .'

'Doesn't matter. I'm going out there whatever it costs. I don't care *what* that evil cow's got going for her, she's *not having Ferdinand.*'

Brave words, Foss Ewins. Ten out of ten for bravado. Zilch for credibility. I reflected dismally that many a fly must have made the same boast concerning the neighbourhood spider.

'Okay. In that case, I'm coming with you.'

'What?' I was horrified. 'You can't! What if the ghosts take us both?'

'You think you can get out of this town without me? Eat your breakfast and go play in the coal hole for half an hour.'

'Margaret – I'm serious!'

'So'm I. It'll be a long day, you'll need to eat – and you'll need camouflage. Even in those old clothes, you're still too pretty. And much too clean.'

'There's no shifting you, is there?' I grumbled, tackling the potatoes.

'Not a snowball's,' she agreed.

I hadn't wanted her to risk herself on my behalf – but within five minutes of setting off I was thanking my lucky stars she was with me. Margaret knew the maze of ruined streets like the back of her own hand. We dodged patrolling Specials, and roaming gangs of the gaunt, black-robed Brotherhood with their banners. We took short-cuts through back alleys. We climbed walls reduced to rubble and crossed bramble-choked stretches of waste ground. By noon we'd reached the outer limits of the town.

The perimeter was guarded. Tall concrete towers stuck up at intervals along a high wall and a double fence of barbed wire. In places the wall consisted of derelict houses with the gaps between sealed and fortified.

Margaret chuckled at the dismay on my face. 'I was a kid round here, remember.'

We climbed a wall into an overgrown shrubbery, teetered across the roof-ridge of a lone surviving shed half hidden in giant laurels and crawled in through a small window of what must once have been the loo of an office block. A brief scramble up a half-demolished wall to the next floor, and we were in a corridor with a row of doors on both sides.

'Watch out,' Margaret warned. 'The floor's a bit dodgy.'

Dodgy was an understatement. Many of the floorboards had rotted, leaving gaping holes. We were making our way to the right-angle at the end of the corridor when I heard a faint noise. Margaret sniffed. Her good eye went round with dismay. 'Tobacco,' she whispered.

We peered past the corner. Only a few feet away a large hole had been knocked out of the brickwork. A single guard was sitting on the other side with his back to us, smoking a rollup. We retreated silently back down the corridor.

'They must've started a new section of the wall,' Margaret breathed. 'I didn't know.'

'Are we stuck?'

'Not yet.' She turned the handle of the nearest door. It opened quietly enough – but then something on the other side fell over with a heart-stopping clatter. Margaret pushed me inside, slammed the door shut and pushed a couple of slender brass bolts across at top and bottom. A moment later heavy footsteps thumped along the corridor: the guard was coming to investigate.

'Anybody there?' We could hear him trying the door-handles.

This room had no floor at all. All that was left were the joists beneath, and huge holes in the crumbling plaster of the down-stairs ceiling. The roof overhead had caved in and the whole room was littered with rubble and broken beams.

A heavy hand jiggled the doorknob. 'Hey, you, whoever you are. Come out here!'

Margaret bent down and hefted up a substantial length of roofing timber, just as a fist struck the door and made the bolts creak.

'Through the window,' she hissed. 'There's a sloping roof. Get down into the yard.' Then, as I hesitated, her eyes blazed. 'Go, Foss! Now!'

I hopped across the joists to the small window and climbed onto the sill. A heavy weight hit the door from the outside: the man was using his shoulder. Thump. Thump. The top bolt burst. I wriggled out feet-first, carefully avoiding the slivers of glass sticking to the frame – and caught the back of my sweater on a projecting nail.

I was stuck. I tugged and twisted, my head still visible above the window sill. I heard the kick which splintered the bottom bolt away from the wood, saw the door burst open and the guard's bulky figure stumble through.

Everything went into slow-motion. I had time to register the fact that he was a big man, with a red unshaven face and a beer-gut bulging above his belt. I saw Margaret behind the door with the heavy timber poised in her hands. I saw the guard tug the gun out of his belt and take a step in my direction.

'What the hell d'you think you're doing, you stupid bitch? Come here!'

'Bog off,' I spat, still tugging at the tangled wool.

His face went tight and ugly with fury. He strode forwards – and didn't notice where he was putting his feet. One leg went straight through the lath-and-plaster ceiling beneath, and the other knee thumped painfully on a joist. He sprawled there at full-length, glaring across at me and panting with rage.

'I'll *get* you for this, you little cow!' He was aiming the gun when Margaret brought the timber down heavily on his head.

He made a horrible bubbling noise and slumped. His limbs jerked a few times. Then he lay perfectly still, sprawled across the joists.

Margaret and I stared at one another, and down at the immobile guard. I'd freed my sweater at last, and I scrambled back into the room.

'Mags? Mags!' Her face was white and appalled. Slowly, she bent down and lifted the piece of timber away from his head to reveal the mess underneath.

'Oh, my God!' I felt sick.

'I didn't know there were *nails* in it . . .'

I grabbed her, and propelled her across to the window. She didn't resist, but she didn't seem to be able to get her wits into gear either. She was in deep shock, and no wonder. I had to push her out onto the slates and steady her as we slid recklessly groundwards. There was a brief heart-stopping moment of free-fall and then we hit a cushioning patch of brambles and sagged to the ground.

The drop seemed to have brought Margaret to her senses. She got up, breathing hard. 'It's this way. Hurry.'

The yard led into a dump of broken coal trucks and rusty machinery. It was surrounded by an eight-foot fence of iron stakes six inches apart, with barbed-wire lavishly garlanded along the top. My heart sank, but Margaret ignored the barrier completely. Instead, she headed for a corrugated iron shed in the corner. Once inside, she shifted stacked junk away from the wall and revealed a child-sized gap in the sheeting. Behind it, predictably, was the one loose stake in the fence, rusted at the base and capable of being lifted just far enough for someone small to crawl through.

Being skinny, we both just managed it.

We were outside the town walls. A parched, dusty wasteland stretched out in front of us, littered with spoil heaps and smoking slag. Without saying a word to one another, we each found a bramble bush and threw up in discreet privacy.

8.

Your Stars: CANCER (June 22–July 23)
Be prepared to tackle troublesome issues as they arise.
Delaying a crucial decision could prove serious in the
long term. Prospects will improve if you keep your wits
about you.

The day dragged on at a snail's pace. As we waited, crouched amongst thorn-bushes beside an oily, refuse-choked pool, the last few rags of my courage started to work loose and flutter away one by one, leaving me scared and shivering. What we were planning was insane. There had to be guards. Not just ghosts: real, solid human guards with guns and dogs. One mean-minded dog was more than a match for both of us. And Ferdinand might not even be included in this little excursion anyway . . .

Margaret shivered beside me, and I knew she was going through a nasty little hell of her own.

Suddenly she said, 'This Ferdinand . . . are you in love with him?'

The question startled me. I could feel myself going red. 'I—I don't know.' And I honestly didn't any more. I tried to explain. 'In lots of ways he's the ultimate heart-throb, I suppose. Fabulous to look at. Makes you go weak at the knees. Sometimes he's sweet – and other times he's so boneheaded I want to strangle him.' *Ferd the nerd*, I thought sourly. 'Anyway, it doesn't matter what I think. I'm not Aurora any more, am I?'

'That shouldn't matter.'

'It does, though. That's what love's all about, isn't it? Being beautiful, desirable?'

'Depends on whether you mean love or romance, I suppose,' she said thoughtfully. She gave a wry smile. '*Filios, eros, agapë.*'

'What?'

She went pink. 'Just something I read once. The Greeks used to say there were three kinds of love. *Filios* – brotherly love – that's the kind of love you have for your family, your close friends. And it's very strong – people make all sorts of sacrifices for the sake of *filios. Eros* . . .'

102

'That's the little guy with the arrows.'

'Right. Sexual love. Unpredictable. And as far as I understand it, *agapë* translates as worship – the love of God.'

'I suppose the trick is to know which is which.'

'Yes.' She shrugged. 'Maybe romance is different again. Not real love at all. Just pre-programmed *eros* with ego-trip.' She grinned ruefully. 'But don't ask me. I just read books and dream dreams.'

'Yes,' I said, recognising a kindred spirit, and we both laughed.

'I wish I could have gone on being Aurora, though,' I said wistfully. 'I wouldn't have needed Ferdinand. I could have let Foss take over . . . become somebody in my own right. Somebody with a *future* . . .

Margaret was reading my thoughts in my face. 'It wouldn't have worked out.'

'Why not?'

'Because . . . she wasn't real, was she? Somebody would always be pulling your strings. Anyway, I think the important thing is to be yourself. Nothing else works.'

'I suppose so.' I wasn't convinced.

Dusk began to fall. A bitterly cold wind started to whisper along the spoil heaps, blowing grit and sulphur fumes into our faces.

Margaret nudged me. 'They're opening the gates.'

In the gloom we could just make out uniformed shapes tugging at the huge iron gates and pushing them wide. The guards withdrew into the watchtowers, taking their dogs with them. One by one the lights along the perimeter fence began to go out.

The town lay in total darkness. Nothing moved or made a sound except the wind. Suddenly an eerie blue glow sprang up in the sky above the rooftops. It spread and intensified until it was too bright to look at. I turned away, blinking, and saw an even brighter light shine out from miles away across the wasteland, like an answering beacon.

Margaret was trembling. 'They're on their way.'

A glimmer of blue light was approaching the gates from within the town. The procession flowed through the opening and into the road in front of us – scores of young prisoners, blank-faced as sleepwalkers, being borne along by hundreds and hundreds of shimmering ghosts.

We scrambled to our feet and ran to intercept them. They'd

appeared too quickly, and were moving too fast. I caught a glimpse of Ferdinand and lost him again. We groped and clutched in vain. The deathly chill swept through us both as the ghosts drifted past and out of our reach. And then they were gone. All we could see was a quivering line of blue light vanishing into the distance.

Margaret and I were left on our own in the middle of the road.

'How could they move so *fast*?' Margaret wailed.

I swore. Our one chance – and we'd blown it. Because we hadn't been prepared. Because we hadn't known what to expect. If the Queen knew about this, she'd be laughing her socks off.

My fuses blew. 'Right. That settles it. I have had *enough*. Who does that tarted-up blonde cow think she is, anyway? What *right* has she got to do all this? How *dare* she?' Kidnapping, mind-hold, murder . . . the tally was rising by the minute. 'I don't care *what* it takes. I am *not* going to let her get away with this! She's got to be *stopped*! . . . What are you staring at?'

'Your pendant. It's shining!'

I glanced down. It wasn't just shining – it was incandescent. That's how I had been able to see Margaret's face – but I'd been too steamed up to notice.

I didn't give myself time for second thoughts: I just turned on my heel and stormed off into the gloom. Scurrying feet caught up with me.

'You don't have to come, Mags . . .'

'Oh, yes I do! I've got a grudge, too, you know!'

An hour later we'd reached the edge of a dense, tangled wood of dead trees. From somewhere deep inside, a single shaft of intense blue light fanned upwards into the black sky.

That initial adrenalin surge had had plenty of time to dissipate by now, and apprehension was rushing in to fill the vacuum. What could we do, against the Queen? Nothing. She'd make mincemeat of us both. And yet, something – call, it sheer bloody-mindedness if you like – was telling me that if I chickened out now, I wouldn't be able to live with myself. I'd come too far to pull back. I had to find out what was happening in there . . .

The glow from my pendant had faded to a faint gleam.

'Listen, Mags – this is where you opt out. Understand? There must be villages out there – decent people who'll take you in . . .'

She gave me a quick hug. 'Take care, huh?'

I hurried away from her and before cowardice could get the better of bravado, I plunged in amongst the trees.

Within thirty seconds I'd lost all sense of direction. The blue beacon vanished. The wood itself was darker than the inside of a coal sack. I could just about tell the difference between the solid pitch blackness where the trees were, and the slightly thinner pitch blackness where they weren't. Everything I touched seemed to ooze slime. The ground was a deathtrap of rotten logs which imploded like empty eggshells under my weight. Random, panicky thoughts started skittering across the surface of my brain: thoughts like, *What am I doing here? This can't be happening to me . . . This is not real. I know what real is, and this is not it . . .*

Please God, my guardian angel if I have one . . . if something seriously horrible is about to jump out at me – just *warn me*, okay?

Wait a minute. I've said all this before. This is the point where we came in.

At last I began to see a faint blue glow filtering between the tree-trunks. I began to hurry. The cold jittery feeling in my guts was beginning to subside. So far there'd been nothing to suggest that the place was guarded. And why should it be? Who needs elaborate defences when terror works just as well? Why bother with guards, when every human soul for miles around is cowering under the blankets, scared witless by the ghosts?

I'd just reached this comforting conclusion when a black flapping Thing landed heavily on a branch a yard away from my face. My heart missed a beat.

The Thing extended a long rubbery neck and hissed through a miniature forest of needle-sharp fangs. Its eyes shone red. I froze.

Then it spoke. '*You are entering a prohibited area! Go no further!*' The voice was robotic. Perhaps once, a long time ago, it had been programmed to convey the kind of psychotic menace you associate with Daleks. Not any more, though. Essential maintenance had been skipped in the interim and now the voice emerging from that computerised larynx was that of a sick sheep with overtones of distant donkey. I let out a single hysterical giggle before I could stop myself. The Thing quivered on its perch, and backed nervously away.

'This is a prohibited area! You have been warned!'

I ignored it and strode past. All it did was bleat a feeble protest.

Suddenly the darkness was full of twinned red points of light. A whole flock of similar Things were descending out of the air and settling all round me. But not too close. I raised a fist experimentally, and they shrank back, chittering and hissing. Not programmed to attack, then.

Their leader was on the wing again now, and flapping alongside me in a desperate attempt to catch up. *'Go no . . .'* – hop – *'further! This is a . . .'* – flap, scrabble, hop – *'prohibited area! Go no . . .'*

I stopped and glared at it eye to eye.

'For Heaven's sake, shut up. Push off before I wring your neck, okay?'

The Thing blinked. *'Name?'* it brayed. *'Rank? Number?'*

I was stumped. 'I'm . . . er . . . a figment of your imagination?'

'Uh?' The cohort chittered nervously.

'I'm . . . I'm Nobody, right? Got that? Go and tell your boss that Nobody's coming.'

The flock conferred in agitated whispers, and then took off. I heard them begin to screech *'Alert! Alert! Nobody's here!'*

I sobered up fast. So there *were* guards. Or something.

The blue glow got brighter, and in a few minutes I found myself on the edge of an enormous clearing. In the centre stood a glittering, shimmering palace, out-Disneying Disney by a factor of ten. The overall effect was slightly spoiled by a modern glazed aluminium porch flanked by a wagon wheel on one side and an old gas lamp standard on the other. (Oddly enough, the plaster dwarfs in humorous attitudes on the front lawn seemed to fit right in, don't ask me why.) From the topmost turret the cone of blue light stabbed upwards to pierce the sky.

The porch had an occupant. Another of those semi-robotic creatures, I guessed. This one stood about eleven feet high and was garbed (you can't use the word 'dressed' in a context like this) in chain mail. It had four heads and eight arms, each of which was gripping a most unforgiving-looking axe.

I melted back into the trees. Something told me that where this creature was concerned, I wouldn't get very far with back chat.

I circled the clearing, keeping to the shadows. I caught glimpses of shambling, non-human movement amongst the trees on the far side of the palace, but my side seemed deserted. The Nobody trick seemed to have worked. So far. I crossed all my fingers and kept going.

Eventually I found a door at the back which led into a conservatory (cheese-plants and plastic begonias). From there French windows opened into a deserted sitting-room done out completely in purple and gold. The biggest TV screen I'd ever seen in my life occupied one end wall. On it, Daffy Duck was engaged in doing something brutal with a chain saw. The sound was turned down but I noticed with some satisfaction that the reception wasn't all that good.

At the far end another door stood very slightly ajar. Light blazed through the crack. I edged it open another cautious inch or so and peeped through.

I was looking into an enormous, cathedral-sized hall. As my eyes adjusted to the glare I could see that every single object, surface or fitting was covered in gold, or diamonds, or both. Gold tiles on the floor (surely not very *practical*?); gold columns twisting upwards like snakes to support a ceiling covered with gold leaf. The golden chandeliers glittered with the blue-white fire of real diamonds. Along the walls, huge diamond-framed mirrors endlessly reflected and re-reflected the dazzle.

At the end nearest me stood a golden throne on a high dais. The throne itself was encrusted with diamonds the way people slap pebbledash on walls. Sitting on it was a stoutish middle-aged woman with straggly blonde hair badly in need of a touch-up at the roots. She was wearing strapless gold lamé which frankly didn't do a thing for her complexion or her sagging figure. She'd stretched out her left hand and was gazing at it in a detached, businesslike sort of way which I thought was extremely odd until she started fixing artificial fingernails on top of her real ones. Her expression was sulky and bored.

A slightly lower throne to her left barely managed to contain the overflow of a horribly familiar figure: Hezekiah, now minus the black suit and wearing a purple robe like a Byzantine emperor. At least a dozen empty champagne bottles lay around the floor of the dais. His face was red and glistening, his eyes unfocussed: he was very drunk.

Neither one of this unlovely couple was paying the slightest attention to the ceremony which was being enacted at their feet.

The young men and girls were standing facing the thrones. The throng of ghosts formed a half-circle behind them. One after another, the living prisoners came forwards, knelt humbly before the dais and placed his or her forehead on a squarish block of something which looked like rough glass set into a hollow in the lowest step. As each victim rose to move away, the faint greenish glow inside the block became a little brighter, while the prisoner seemed even more empty-eyed and zombie-like than before.

Ferdinand was in the back row. With him were people I recognised: the pretty blonde girl, the two intelligent men, a red-haired girl with a beautiful smile. I remembered how they'd laughed and sparkled that first evening at the dinner party. There was no trace of animation on their faces now. They were as blank as so many porcelain dolls.

The purpose of the ritual escaped me until the woman got stiffly to her feet, reached down absent-mindedly and touched the glass brick. White light enveloped her arm like a glove and spread all over her body. When she stood up again she was looking slimmer, fitter and a good twenty years younger.

At last I recognised her. Ferdinand's dazzling young Queen – thirty or forty years older than she'd been yesterday, but getting younger by the minute.

Suddenly everything clicked into place and I understood what was going on. I knew the reason behind the takeover, the kidnappings, the prisons – everything. It wasn't simply because she was bored and wanted real people to play with. That was just a bonus. The real reason was that she was *old*.

She was old – I had no way of guessing just how ancient she really was. And she'd become hooked on looking young and beautiful: addicted to such an extent that she didn't care what she did to satisfy the craving. Plastic surgery wasn't good enough. She wanted real youth, real beauty. And she was rejuvenating herself by tapping off the life-force of her young prisoners, somehow via that glass brick.

All that once-in-a-lifetime energy that older people complain of not having any more and accuse the younger generation of having too much of – all that fitness and enthusiasm and wild behaviour that should have gone towards all-night raves and kicking over the traces and changing the world – it was all being leached out of her victims in order to give an ancient megalomaniac a face-lift.

I forgot about caution, and all about being decently scared. I watched the dreadful old harridan calmly painting her finger-nails and I could feel savagery building up inside me like steam in a pressure-cooker.

The valve flipped. And then, just as my fury exploded, something utterly unexpected happened. A whole new dimension of anger came flooding into me from somewhere else. It went far beyond any emotion I'd ever been capable of before: as though my own inept, human rage had somehow made a connection with something infinitely more powerful.

And the unmistakable *flavour* of that anger – was my Aunt Oz.

My pendant blazed. I flung the door open and stormed to the foot of the throne.

'Right!' I (or that other) snapped. 'That's *enough*! Gloriana, Zekar,' – where the names came from, I've no idea – 'As from this moment, I'm closing you down.'

Everybody froze. I elbowed the waiting victim out of the way and snatched up the brick. It came out of its hollow with a slight click. The surge of power that shot up my arms gave me such a shock I nearly dropped it. The brick wasn't draining me as I'd expected it would – it was *feeding* me. My pendant went nova. Supercharged energy hotwired through my body. The feeling of power was incredible. With that brick in my hands I could have defeated *armies*.

There was a long moment of stunned silence. The Queen was staring at me with her mouth open. Red nail-varnish dribbled out of her bottle and dripped onto the floor. The metaphorical pin was dropped by Hezekiah in the form of a resounding belch. He was blinking owlishly and obviously hadn't yet got around to noticing that anything was wrong.

The Queen's mouth snapped shut. Her right hand stretched out towards me, three blood-red fingernails (she hadn't had time to fix the others yet) extended like claws.

'*Who the hell are you?*' she demanded. Her voice was silken or seductive any more – it was pure alley-cat, and saw-edged with outrage.

'Nobody *you* know,' I said with loathing.

'Then drop that thing and get out of here, you puke-faced midget, before I fry you for breakfast!'

Bad mistake. If she'd said something along the lines of *That thing's dangerous, dear, drop it before it goes terminal* I might have obeyed. But personal insults from an ageing tart with appalling dress sense? No way. For the first time in my life I became aware of the infinitesimally thin line between being righteously angry and hopping mad. I crossed it.

'*Fry me?*' I yelled. 'A lazy fat cow like you couldn't even fry chips!'

'*Fat?!*' All unknowing, I'd hit a raw nerve. You could have heard the screech from Brighton to Aberdeen.

'Yeah, fat,' I snapped. 'And tarted up like last week's custard. How dare you put my friends through all this? Who the hell d'you think you are?'

The claws stabbed, and a bolt of lightning arced across the space between us. I flinched – but it didn't hit me. It seemed to screech to a halt in the vicinity of the brick and fly outwards in a shower of sparks.

Her face went livid. She sprang to her feet, and in an instant she'd grown to a height of at least three metres. She towered above me like a caricature of the Statue of Liberty. Another torrent of lightning poured in my direction. This time I dodged. It shot past me and burnt a neat round hole in the far wall.

'How *dare* you?' she spat. 'I am the Queen! I am *young*! I am *beautiful*! How *dare you?!!*' Each sentence was punctuated by a fresh burst of electric fury – and none of it struck me. Brick and pendant together were protecting me like armour.

'Oh, yeah?' I jeered. 'Looked in a mirror lately? All those choccies had to go somewhere, didn't they? All that yukky flab oozing over the top of that dress, your backside down to your knees . . .'

She went green. I have *never* seen anybody so angry.

'You festering little pustule!' she yelled. 'I'll shrivel you! You'll wish you'd never been born! How *dare* you insult *me*?'

I clutched the glass brick to my chest and ducked and dodged as bolts of energy exploded out of her hands and came zipping past me like submachine bullets. Every bolt deflected away from me – and wherever it hit, the gold and the diamonds vanished. Holes were appearing like Gruyere cheese in the fabric of the palace, but she was simply too spitting mad to notice.

'It's not cellulite so much,' I shouted above the din, 'More like Artex, really . . .'

Lightning flared in a huge corona, enveloping both of us in

one gigantic fireball. The floor melted and seeped away beneath and around us, but I didn't feel a thing. More and more of the building was disappearing every second. Prisoners were moaning and collapsing to the ground all round me as the mind-hold gave way.

The Queen's claws stabbed again . . . but all that emerged were a few faint sparks. She stared at her hands in sudden horror.

'Zekar!' she wailed. 'Do something!'

Hezekiah looked around him with the puzzled unfocussed glare of the seriously drunk. 'Whaddya want, m'liddle dove-chick, my pearl, my tiggie-pie?'

She kicked him viciously on the shin. 'Get up, you mindless doughbag! Get rid of her!'

'Forget it,' I told her. 'Your hubby's as drunk as a skunk.'

'You . . . you . . .' Words failed her. 'I'll tear you apart, you – you *dwarf*, you . . .' To my dismay, she jumped down off the dais and came for me. There was murder in her eyes. I backed away hastily. Magic I seemed to be able to cope with – but physical violence was something I definitely didn't feel equipped to handle. I gave up on cautious withdrawal and ran for it.

'I am the *Queen*,' she panted, as she chased me round the ballroom. 'I am *beautiful*! I am *immortal*!'

'Oh, get stuffed,' I snapped over one shoulder. 'You're a disgusting painted old prune with dyed hair and the personality of a cow pat. You're the *pits*!'

I found Ferdinand at last, and gripped his wrist hard. Now was the time to make a rapid getaway. I'd drawn her fire so far, so perhaps if we left, she'd pursue, and the other prisoners would get a chance to escape. I was playing it all by ear: trusting to luck – and Oz.

'Nice to have met you,' I yelled, backing towards the door. 'Thanks for the firework display. Pity most of the squibs were duds.'

'Stop!' she screeched. 'Let go his hand, or he dies!'

'Hurt him,' I warned, 'and this thing gets it.' I held the glass brick high as if to throw it.

For the first time a fearful, panic-stricken look crossed her face.

'No! ' she gasped. 'You dare not destroy it! You must not!'

'Just try me,' I snapped.

'But you cannot . . . The power . . . it won't let you go . . . You can't control it . . .'

But I *was* controlling it – how, I don't know – and at last it seemed to dawn on her exactly what that implied. With that brick I could depose her. I could have anything I wanted. I could rule the world. I could become what she was . . .

Her gasp dopplered up into a howl of sheer terror. 'No! It's mine! Mine! No-o-o-a-w!!'

'Oh, shut up,' I said in disgust. I swung my arm back and hurled the glass brick hard against what was left of the wall. I expected it to shatter – but it didn't. It described a graceful parabola right *through* the wall, and vanished into the darkness beyond. Her scream echoed in the rafters.

I gave Ferdinand's wrist a sharpish tug. 'C'mon, Ferd. Time we went.' He turned like a clockwork toy and followed me obediently towards the door.

There was a deafening roll of thunder – but I'd been half expecting something like that and ignored it. More startling was the fact that immediately afterwards, the entire palace blew up all around us. The ground didn't tremble, and nobody was blasted into oblivion: all the force seemed to be directed upwards. Walls, mirrors, thrones, chandeliers, begonias, robot creatures and plaster dwarfs all went shooting up into the sky in one spectacular flare of light. A few bits and pieces rained down on the trees at the edge of the clearing, and melted into nothing as they touched the ground.

We were left standing in the empty clearing, sporadically lit by burning fragments of wall and floor. The blue searchlight had gone out. Zekar/Hezekiah lay struggling feebly on the ground, swearing suphurously. The Queen had aged another thirty years at least. Her make-up was cracking off, her ridiculous gown had split. She tottered as she glared at me. There was no sign anywhere of the glass brick.

She raised a trembling hand, and hailstones as big as eggs began to pelt down from the sky. As they struck Ferdinand he gave a startled moan. He was coming out of his trance. I tugged him along again.

We'd gone a few more steps – me in front, and Ferdinand stumbling behind – when the hail stopped. Very close behind me I heard a low, menacing growl – the sort of noise which got hot-wired into the human database half a million years ago and filed under Extremely Bad News. The hairs sprang to attention on the back of my neck. I turned round.

112

I was holding the forepaw of an enormous and very crabby-looking lion. Its big yellow fangs were only inches away from my face, and its breath was hot and smelly. The illusion was so convincing that I almost let go out of shock. More by luck than anything else, I held on. The lion vanished, and Ferdinand stood in its place.

I'd been smugly congratulating myself on winning the battle. Now I realised, with a sinking feeling inside, that the skirmish in the ballroom had only been the first round. Between them, Hezekiah and the Queen still had power – and I'd thrown half of mine away. The important thing seemed to be to hold on to Ferdinand. I tightened my grip on his wrist, just in case.

We kept walking. Suddenly I was snatched up into the sky. Ferdinand had become a dragon, eighty feet tall or thereabouts (I was in no state to take measurements) – and I was dangling from its forelimb. It snarled horribly and breathed out fire. This time sheer dread of falling kept me from letting go. (The Queen can't have been thinking too clearly at this point, or she'd have predicted that.) I shut my eyes and held on.

The odd thing was that as soon as my eyes were closed I could feel solid ground under my feet and Ferdinand's human wrist in my grasp. It was only when I opened them that the illusion worked.

Like a fool, I peeped. I was holding a rotting human corpse. It was so disgusting I nearly threw up. I held on.

Nothing seemed to be happening, so a few moments later I opened my eyes again – and this time I almost fainted. The Queen had hit the jackpot. I was holding on to a colossal snake.

I've always loathed snakes. Okay, so I know it's a ridiculous, pathetic phobia; that snakes are actually beautiful and interesting and that very few of them are dangerous if you just leave them alone. I *know* all that – but it doesn't alter the fact that every time I see a snake (or even a picture of one) I want to pass out. When we were kids, Jo had one of those plastic jointed rattle-snakes which wriggle when you hold them by the tail. It used to frighten me into hysterics – so much so that I couldn't bring myself to pick up the plastic sections after it fell to bits.

And here I was, wrapped in the coils of the biggest anaconda I'd ever imagined: a thing thicker than a tree-trunk and glaring at me eye to eye with that wide evil grin snakes have. I was paralysed with terror. I couldn't even shut my eyes to dispel the illusion. Then, if ever, the Queen could have vanquished me.

113

Could have, but didn't. A breathless human voice spoke in my ear. A pair of skinny arms reached past me and clasped the snake in a grip of iron.

'Hang on!' Margaret gasped. 'You're winning! You're winning!'

'What are you *doing* here?' I yelled. 'I told you to go away!'

'Fat chance,' she grinned. 'I followed you. You seemed to be doing okay so I just sat in a corner and watched. But look!' She gestured around the glade.

The prisoners were coming round: blinking, staring at each other in disbelief, helping one another to stagger away into the wood. The Queen and Hezekiah were getting older and older: shrinking, wizening, seemingly held in their shapes only by the Queen's vengeful will. The enchantment was breaking up.

After that, the giant tarantula was child's play. Literally. Margaret and I shed ten years each and started to giggle and jeer.

'Ooh, look, it's a great fat hairy spider!'

'It's got a pot-belly bigger than hers!'

'Only just, though!'

The tarantula turned into a scorpion, and then in rapid succession into a shark, a werewolf, a nettle and a piece of toast. Margaret and I greeted each change with roars of laughter and rude remarks. But we held on. And there at last was Ferdinand, looking groggy and bemused but most definitely himself again.

Margaret clutched my sleeve. 'Oh, my God – look!'

Hezekiah and the Queen were melting like hot wax. Rancid oil was trickling out of their mouths and bursting into blue flame. They writhed and screamed, and as they sizzled a foul smell filled the clearing. They charred into cinders before our eyes, burst into a final flare of blue fire – and vanished.

Ferdinand glared down at the two filthy, dishevelled urchins clutching his arms.

'What on earth . . .?'

'Got to get away from here,' I said. 'Explain later. Come on, Ferdinand – *run!*'

Holding onto his arms, we dragged Ferdinand through the wood and out onto the plain. Dawn was breaking: the landscape shone like a grey pearl. Birds were singing in bushes netted with dew. The dry, dead wasteland was coming alive again. The enchantment had lifted – not just over the wood, but over the whole land.

114

As we ran Ferdinand staggered and groaned and tried ineffectually to shake us off.

'What's wrong with him?' Margaret panted.

'Dunno. All those illusions, perhaps? Come *on*, Ferdinand!'

At last we came to a ditch at the foot of a high, steep bank. Looking up, I could see trees above us – oak trees, which had been there, green and growing, for a long time. This had to be the boundary of the enchantment.

Ferdinand's knees gave way under him and he almost fell.

'He's not going to make it up that bank on his own, is he?'

'Okay. I'll go first.' I said. 'You push, I'll pull.'

We selected a convenient ladder of roots to climb. I was almost at the top, when a hand reached down from nowhere, caught my wrist in a vice-like grip and hauled me unceremoniously onto the grass. A brown hand and a muscular brown arm clad in the scuffed sleeve of a shabby leather jacket. Utterly stunned, I stared up into a plain sunburnt face with a pair of anxious brown eyes and a mouth which widened into a grin like sunshine.

'Jo!' I shrieked, and hurled myself at his chest.

PART TWO

Margaret

9.

Your Stars: CANCER (June 22–July 23)
From now on all aspects of your chart should improve.
Travel is indicated, and friends will give a much-needed
boost to your ego.

He let out a grunt at the impact, and staggered a bit. He hugged me, hard and briefly, then he grabbed my shoulders, pushed me to arm's length and subjected me to a fierce, head-to-foot scan. 'You okay?'

I nodded. His face was thunderous.

'Good,' he said. His grip tightened painfully and he shook me until my teeth rattled. 'Don't *ever* do that kind of thing again. D'you understand? Never, ever!' He released me abruptly, and strode off to help Margaret haul Ferdinand up the bank. I could hear them exchanging names.

I just stood there: shocked, hurt, and feeling as though the floor had dropped from under me. A massive, macho put-down from Jo? Of all people! *Why?*

Ferdinand had finally made it to the top of the bank. He staggered to his feet, pushed Jo violently away, lurched a few steps with a mad glare in his eyes – and crashed head-first into a tussock.

'What's wrong with him?' Jo asked over his shoulder.

'Just dazed and sick,' I said coldly. 'He's had a pretty rough time.'

Margaret came scrambling into view up the ladder of roots. 'Oh, poor Ferdinand!'

'Right,' said Jo, taking charge. 'I've got Jeffrey and the cart back there. Margaret, come and help me clear a space for him. Foss, you stay here.'

116

Ferdinand opened one eye. 'A *cart*? You expect *me* to ride in a *cart*?'

Jo shrugged. He and Margaret disappeared between the trees, leaving me to cope.

'Don't be silly, Ferdinand. You want us to leave you here on your own in the middle of nowhere?'

He groaned, and tried to sit up. 'God, my head hurts,' he said, holding it gingerly between both hands as though he was afraid it would fall off if he didn't. 'Where's my horse?' He didn't remember a thing. 'You've kidnapped me, haven't you? Drugged me, or something . . . Well, you won't get away with it, you know. My father . . .'

'Oh, Ferdinand!' I sat down beside him. 'Listen. You were captured by a powerful sorceress. Margaret and I rescued you. You're safe now. I'm telling you the truth, Ferdinand.'

He was staring at me with a faint puzzled frown on his face. 'I've seen you before somewhere, haven't I?' His face clenched in a painful scowl as recollection struggled to surface. Suddenly his eyes flashed. 'Where's Aurora? What have you done with the Princess Aurora?'

I couldn't look at him. I could feel heat rising up my face. 'She . . . she's not around any more.'

'*What?* If you've hurt her . . . If she's dead . . .'

It was now or never. I gulped. 'Remember the girl by the stones? The girl who changed into Aurora? Something happened . . . and I turned into the princess you were looking for. Now I've changed back. Aurora's *gone*, Ferdinand.'

His gaze sharpened. He drew in a hissing breath. 'You expect me to believe that? You're lying! It's some sort of plot. Who's behind it?'

'Ferdinand, I'm telling you the *truth*! And don't go for your sword again, because that isn't going to solve anything.'

He slumped. I could see by his face that he was replaying the whole incident at the stones . . . and that slowly, he was beginning to accept the truth.

'I *knew* you weren't noble,' he muttered through clenched teeth. 'All those fishwife arguments. Lighting fires like a kitchen maid . . . You tricked me.'

'I'm sorry,' I said.

He glanced at me very briefly, with loathing. 'You make me sick,' he said.

I got up and walked to the edge of the bank. Two men in my life, and I was persona non grata with both of them. It didn't seem fair. I bit my lip to quell the tears, and stared miserably out over the plain.

From here I could see for miles across the wasteland. Smoke was rising in thin spirals from the distant town, and I could just make out tiny red blossoms of fire. As I stared, jolted into full awareness, I could see a moving smudge which glinted oddly in the hazy morning light. It got rapidly bigger and resolved itself into people on horseback, heading our way. I caught the glitter of weapons and a brief flutter of black robes.

Feet came thudding down the slope behind me.

'Come *on*,' Jo said urgently. 'Got to get out of here, fast.'

'Why . . . what . . .?'

'Fighting,' Margaret said tersely. 'The spell's broken.' She shaded her eyes. 'Some of the Specials have cut and run. Looks like they've brought the Brotherhood with them.'

Ferdinand glared savagely at all three of us and refused to budge.

'I'm ill. Just leave me alone.'

'I think you'd better come with us, your Highness.' Jo was being unusually diplomatic. 'They're a nasty bunch of villains.'

'They'll kill you,' Margaret pleaded.

'Then I shall die with honour,' Ferdinand announced.

Tact and common sense were getting us nowhere, as always. 'Ferdinand,' I snapped, 'There's a gang of cut-throats and religious maniacs out there, headed straight for us. If you like your skin the way it is, get your arse off that grass and *move*.'

To everybody's surprise (mine most of all), he moved.

Jo and Margaret had padded the back of the cart with sleeping-bags and blankets. Ferdinand lay down without a word. All traces of belligerence had left him, and he looked sullen and resigned. I guessed his headache had started up again.

Margaret climbed in over the backboard and settled herself amongst the camping gear. (Camping gear? Blankets? What had Jo been doing?) There was no room in the back for me. I hesitated. Jo was perched up in front, gathering up the reins. He tapped the seat impatiently. 'Come on, Foss, don't hang about.'

I climbed up beside him and we drove off.

As we jolted down the rough track out of the wood, I kept sneaking furtive glances at Jo's profile. This new, grim, impatient

118

Jo was a stranger, and I didn't know how to cope with him. I found myself edging surreptitiously away, as though I was afraid to trespass on his personal space. We drove on in silence until I couldn't bear it any more.

'Jo,' I said, 'Why did you . . .?'

'Foss,' he said, at exactly the same moment. 'I'm sor—'

We both stopped in mid-sentence, looked sheepishly at one another, and started to laugh.

'After you,' Jo said politely.

'No, after you.'

'Oh, rats,' Jo said. 'Foss, I behaved like a pig back there. I'm sorry.'

The load of despondency sprouted wings and soared away. 'It's okay, it's okay,' I said.

'No, it isn't. I just overreacted. I'd been wandering about like a spare part for damn near four weeks on the off-chance I'd bump into you somewhere . . . I saw that freak castle go up in sheets of lightning – and then when you turned up . . .'

He'd been *worried* about me. I choked back tears of sheer amazed relief.

'Margaret gave me a quick run-down on what happened out there. I reckon you did us proud, sparrow.' It was nice to be appreciated, however belatedly.

'So what happened to *you*?' I asked. 'The last thing I saw was you and Jeffrey pounding through the gap between the stones . . .'

'You saw us? I didn't see you. Next thing I knew, we were in a strange town in a different century and people were gawping at us as though we'd come from Mars.'

He hadn't had any money that anybody would accept. He'd hired himself and Jeffrey out to a market trader who wanted goods delivered round the villages. Everywhere he went he made enquiries about me, and picked up every scrap of gossip he could about Zones and Gateways so as to get us both home.

I felt terrible. Selfish cow that I was, I hadn't spared a thought for his plight. 'So how . . .?'

'Jeffrey,' Jo said. Apparently one day Jeffrey had decided they were going to a place called Ashwood. He'd been quite stubborn about it.

'I didn't know what the hell was going on,' Jo confessed. 'In the end I just held the reins and told him to get on with it.'

They'd stayed in Ashwood three days, during which time Jo had had a curious compulsion to buy camping equipment. 'Four of everything, don't ask me why. And two tents.'

'So it *was* you!' I told him about Hezekiah. 'And then?'

'Jeffrey brought me to where I met you, and wouldn't budge.'

Jo had tried to climb down onto the plain, but there was a kind of invisible wall in the way. Last night he'd seen the ghostly castle rise up out of the wood, and the various phantom comings and goings. 'Then the whole thing went up like Guy Fawkes night – and the rest you know.'

The track joined a dirt road winding through a grey-green landscape dotted with massive outcrops of bare red rock. Jeffrey broke into a fast trot as though making up for lost time. Dust rose in a white plume behind the wheels.

A few miles further on, the road began to climb a steep ridge with a cutting at the top. Jo, Margaret and I got down and walked alongside Jeffrey, to lighten the load. Ferdinand was still asleep in the back of the cart. We were nearly at the top when a troop of horsemen suddenly appeared in front of us, blocking the road.

We froze. Jo swore under his breath and cautiously inched his farmer's ash-staff from under the seat.

The riders advanced. Ten of them all told – bulky men, overweight, unwashed and unshaven. They struck me as the type of thug who runs at the first sign of real trouble but isn't at all averse to passing the pain down on the unprotected. Behind them rode a gaunt figure in black robes – one of the Brotherhood.

The men were ostentatiously supplied with more knives than you'd expect to see outside a specialist hardware store. I could see guns at their belts, but the leader was the only one holding his. Perhaps they were out of ammunition; if so, that was probably why they'd cut and run.

They dismounted heavily a few feet away, grinning in happy anticipation and fingering their knives. Robbing/murdering us was going to be a piece of cake. The leader's gun was pointing at Jo's head.

'Drop the stick and gimme the reins. Now.' He jerked his head at one of his lieutenants. 'Get the girls, willya?'

The lieutenant advanced on Margaret and me, eyeing us with a lascivious smirk. A large, curved and very shiny knife appeared in his hand. We backed away. I slid my hand over the side of the cart and groped uselessly for a tent-pole.

Next moment the tableau had exploded into mayhem. Ferdinand had erupted from the back of the cart.

I have never seen anyone move faster than he did then. As he leapt his sword flashed briefly and ran the gobsmacked lieutenant through the chest. A karate kick in mid-flight sent a second man sprawling and doubled up with agony at the side of the road. The leader fired at him and missed. Next moment he too was flat on his back in the dirt: Jo had head-butted him and brought him down in a rugby tackle. The gun flew out of his grasp. I dived for it but it went skittering along the ground amongst trampling hooves of the now seriously frightened horses.

'Leave it, Foss! Get Jeffrey out of here!' Jo yelled, whirling his ash-staff like a demented majorette.

I glimpsed a streak of light whizzing towards us, hurled Margaret to one side and ducked. The knife buried itself with a thud in the side of the cart. We scrambled aboard. One man made the stupid mistake of trying to grab on to the backboard and got his fingers mashed by Margaret's furiously-wielded tent-pole. I grabbed the reins and slapped Jeffrey's rump. He shot forwards, only too glad of the encouragement. The robbers' horses reared and bolted as we thundered through. Knives flew, and we ducked. Somebody leapt the wheel and got a whack over the head which tumbled him into the road. The black-robed Brother appeared waving his arms in front of us, but Jeffrey ran him down. As we passed them, Ferdinand's sword was flickering like strobe lighting, and Jo was cracking heads with joyous abandon.

Faced with such deadly ferocity the Specials suddenly lost their bottle. For a few moments there was chaos, everybody tripping over everybody else. By the time I'd pulled Jeffrey to a halt at the far side of the cutting the would-be bandits were lumbering for cover, hotly pursued by Ferdinand and Jo who were bellowing like a couple of bull elephants.

Margaret and I tore back to the fray, armed with our tent-poles – but we weren't needed. The fight was over, and Jo and Ferdinand were swaggering towards us, shoulder to shoulder, thoroughly delighted with themselves and beaming like a couple of idiots.

Ferdinand wiped his bloody sword ostentatiously on a wisp of grass. He turned to Jo and solemnly shook hands.

'Good fight,' he said smugly.

There were no more incidents, which was just as well because we were all far tireder than we'd realised. Throughout the rest of that day I was only vaguely aware of the journey: of Jeffrey stopping at intervals to drink and graze, of the sun burning my sweater, the cart swaying and rumbling beneath me, and Jo's leather-clad shoulder against the side of my face.

I woke up quite suddenly to a cool, bright evening. The cart had stopped on a green verge beside a big lake.

'Everybody out,' said Jo.

We yawned and stretched. 'Where are we?'

'No idea,' Jo said cheerfully. 'Just seemed a good place to camp, that's all.'

I got out stiffly and wandered to the lake's edge. The water looked glorious – clear and blue and above all *clean*.

'Is it okay to swim here?'

Jo shrugged. 'Depends on how strict their anti-pollution laws are. You stink. Or hadn't you noticed?'

I was dismayed. 'That bad?'

'Put it this way: any conscientious public health inspector would've run you and Margaret in as a health hazard.'

'Oh, very funny,' I said, and stalked away to undress behind a convenient bush. Jo tossed a couple of bundles at my retreating back. 'You'll need these.'

One bundle contained soap, shampoo and towels; the other, clean clothes.

'And don't blame me if the gear's a bit naff. I didn't buy it. It just appeared in the cart.'

Margaret followed me rather apprehensively behind the screen of bushes. She stared at the lake, and her eyes dilated to the size of dinner plates.

'He didn't really mean that, did he?' she said in a small, troubled voice.

'He was winding us up. He's right, though – we are a bit iffy.'

'Oh,' she said dubiously, and shivered.

I'd undressed to my bra and pants. 'Come on. Have a good wallow even if you can't swim. Nobody'll see you. You'll feel a lot better.'

'I—I can't . . .' she said, and went white under the filth.

I stared at her – and suddenly realised what the problem was. Margaret couldn't ever have seen so much water before in her whole life. It was entirely possible that she hadn't undressed in ten years, let alone washed. She'd worn the protective layers of grime for so long that the very thought of removing them amounted to a major trauma.

'Take your time,' I said. 'Just paddle if you want.'

She was still sitting there, white and rigid, when I got back from my swim. I dried myself, towelled and combed my hair and opened the bundle of clothes. There were two of everything: one set my size and the other to fit Margaret. Nothing fancy: just underwear, a longish cotton skirt apiece, a plain cotton top, a warm shawl of the type I'd seen country girls wearing in Ashwood, and sandals. Hardly what you'd call stylish, but comfortable, practical – and in this Zone, blessedly inconspicuous.

Margaret fingered the seams and stroked the cloth as though it was pure silk instead of coarse cotton. Her eyes shone. 'For *me*?'

I struck ruthlessly while the iron was hot. 'Yes – but only after you've washed.'

All things considered, introducing Margaret to the rudiments of personal hygiene could have been a lot worse. She might have had hysterics. She could have refused to budge. She could have screamed and fought and run away. Instead, she shivered uncontrollably, like a sick cat at the vet's, while I peeled off layer after layer of disgusting greasy clothing and led her down to the water. While I was scrubbing her she went so white I thought she'd faint.

The big surprise was her hair. The greyish, matted mass extended down her back under her clothes, like a huge lump of dirty felt. Great chunks came away in my hands as I washed it, and combing the rest was a nightmare: I had to cut the worst tangles away with a nail scissors. As it dried, however, it sprang up around her pinched face in gleaming waves of that pure corn-gold colour that's so rarely seen except out of a bottle. What was left after all the emergency surgery rippled to her waist.

She was as taken aback as I was. 'I never knew it was that colour!'

'It's gorgeous! You lucky swine, Mags.'

At last, clean and dry and respectably dressed, we emerged from the bushes and went in search of Jo and food.

Two tents had appeared on the strip of grass overlooking the lake. Jo had a small fire going, and was breaking sticks over his knee.

'Where's Ferdinand?'

Jo jerked his thumb at the lake. 'I can't swim that well, so I came out.'

We started to prepare a meal. Ten minutes later Ferdinand appeared, fully dressed and looking haughty. The warm glow of camaraderie had faded, and we were back to Square One. He sat down some distance away and proceeded to ignore us with a single-minded intensity that was worse than a row. My heart sank.

When the bangers and mash and baked beans were ready I took a plateful across to him.

'Thank you,' he said stiffly, without making eye contact.

'For Heaven's sake, Ferdinand – I've said I'm sorry. Now please come and join us. Please!'

'I'd really prefer it if you addressed me by my title,' he snapped.

'Tough,' I said, and stalked back to the fire.

Jo and Margaret had been watching the exchange with some amusement.

'Is he always like this?' Jo asked, biting into a sausage.

Suddenly I found myself defending him. 'No, he isn't. He's got every right to feel sore. I *cheated* him, Jo. He feels he's been made a fool of, and it rankles. How would you feel if I'd done that to you?'

'Simple. I'd have strangled you.'

'Oh, yeah? You and whose army?'

'Children, children,' Margaret said, waggling a finger at us.

As I grinned at her across the fire it suddenly struck me how utterly *different* she looked. Clean, yes, and decently dressed – but the transformation went a lot deeper than that. Proud and happy in her new clothes, her bright hair framing a face flushed with the heat of the fire, her blue eyes laughing and free from strain, Margaret was extremely pretty. Even the cut over her eye couldn't detract from that.

I woke up next morning in the tent with the sun in my eyes and the smell of bacon in the air. Margaret thrust her arm through the tent-flap and handed me a mug of tea.

'Where's Ferdinand?'

'Stop clucking, Foss. Jo says he spent the night in the cart.'

'Oh.' At least he hadn't tried to go off on his own.

When I emerged, Jo was slapping fried eggs on to plates and spearing rashers of bacon with a fork.

'You'd better ask HRH if he wants any breakfast,' he told me, tight-lipped. 'Personally, I'd be quite happy if he starved.'

'What's he been saying to you, Jo?'

'It's not so much what he *says*, exactly,' Jo admitted. 'It's what his face does when he isn't looking.'

'It's culture shock,' Margaret said with quiet certainty. 'He'll come round eventually.'

She was right. It's difficult to remain aloof and superior when you're crammed into a cart with three other people and piles of camping equipment, especially when the sun is shining, you've just had a long swim in a beautiful lake and everybody's in holiday mood.

Difficult, but not impossible. Ferdinand held out for a whole day – and then, almost imperceptibly, he began to thaw.

'You know what his trouble is?' Margaret said that night, as we were settling down to sleep.

'What?'

'He's terribly insecure.'

'*Ferdinand?* Don't be silly.'

'No, it's true, Foss. He was telling me about his family. He's the youngest son. He hasn't got anything important to do, and he knows it. His two brothers . . .'

'The brainy one and the Genghis Khan lookalike?'

'Right. Between them, they just about cover the field. Ferdinand's surplus to requirements. And he isn't a playboy, or a rich idiot . . . he's really very serious-minded, and he worries a lot. He's terrified of his father . . .'

'I know. And his mother sounds like a werewolf in drag.'

She gave a horrified giggle. 'Does she? Well, that proves my point, doesn't it?'

'Margaret,' I said, 'I'm too tired to argue. Seems to me you're making a big mistake, that's all.'

'What mistake?'

I yawned. 'Treating him as though he's a normal human being. He's an *aristocrat*, for Heaven's sake. Don't trust aristocrats further than you can heave a bus, that's my advice. And don't get involved.'

Three days later we were still trundling along. We hadn't even seen a signpost, let alone a village, and we were getting worried.

'Perhaps we ought to go back to – what was that place again, Jo? Ashwood?'

Jo was dubious. 'I don't think we *can* get back to Ashwood. It took Jeff almost six days to get to the place where I met you, and a couple of very dodgy incidents along the way . . .'

Ferdinand's ears pricked. 'What sort of incidents?'

'Trotting along and suddenly being somewhere else. Very disconcerting, I can tell you.'

'Gateways,' Ferdinand breathed.

I was alarmed. 'So we're in the wrong Zone?'

'Not necessarily,' Ferdinand said. 'But until we reach a town . . .'

Jeffrey, meanwhile, was moving along with the brisk purposeful trot of a horse on a mission. His whole demeanour indicated that he wasn't going to take kindly to alternative suggestions.

Jo shrugged. 'Jeff's the only one of us with any sense. I reckon he knows something we don't.'

Ferdinand was looking a lot happier these days. Puzzled by the banter which went on between Jo, Mags and me; slightly annoyed at not being in charge; facing up to the fact that nobody had any intention of treating him with the deference to which he'd always been accustomed – but happier all the same. He gave the impression of a man who's suddenly discovered that the savages he's despised all his life are actually quite civilised people who can teach him a thing or two.

I was more worried about Jo. Outwardly he was the same placid easygoing bloke I'd known all my life. But something had changed. In repose, when he thought nobody was watching, his face was as grim as when he'd shaken me on that first day out of the late Queen's domain.

'What's eating you, Jo?'

'Good grief, woman, can't a bloke sit down and think for a few minutes without getting fussed over? I'm okay. I'm fine.'

At last we encountered a lone signpost at the top of a hill. Jo reined Jeffrey to a halt. Ferdinand was out of the cart almost before the wheels had stopped turning.

'The coast. Excellent. We can find a ship . . .'

'We?'

Ferdinand looked almost shy. 'Well, I—I thought you might like to come to Boronia with me. Stay at my place for a bit. Um. I'm sure somebody knows about Gateways there . . .'

'That's very sweet of you, Ferdinand.'

Next day we arrived at a large village on the edge of the coastal plain.

'We're not far off the nearest port,' Jo said, counting the kitty. 'How about going out this evening? We can afford to splurge a bit.'

I gazed dubiously at what we could see of the village. 'I shouldn't think the night life's up to much.'

'You never know,' said Jo placidly, 'We might be lucky. There could be a disco at the Over-Sixties Club.'

'Or a bingo session with the WI.'

'You don't seriously want to play bingo, do you?' said Ferdinand, looking puzzled.

'They're joking, Ferdinand,' Margaret said gently.

'Oh.'

'Our best bet,' said Jo, 'is a decent meal at the local pub. It looked pretty sound as we passed.'

Margaret glowed. 'That would be lovely.'

'How about a look round the market first?' Jo suggested.

I hesitated, and glanced at Margaret. 'Don't know about you, Mags, but I need to wash my hair. I don't want to go out looking like a scruff.'

'Me neither,' Margaret said hastily.

Jo shrugged. 'Okay, then. If you two want to indulge in feminine orgies, Ferdinand and I might as well vanish for a couple of hours and leave you to it. ' He looked at Ferdinand. 'Fancy sampling the local hostelry while we're about it?'

'Good idea,' Ferdinand agreed.

When they'd gone Margaret and I heated water and took turns to wash our hair. I was towelling my unruly mop when Margaret said, 'Don't rub it like that. That's why it frizzes up.'

'Mags, I've tried every trick in the book. *Nothing* stops this frizz. It's just something I have to live with.'

'Shut up. Don't be defeatist.' She wrapped the towel tightly round my head. Ten minutes later she undid it and let the mass flop.

'Don't comb it at all. Just run your fingers through like this – right?'

'It won't work,' I grumbled.

'And don't scrape it back like that. It's like you're punishing it for being there.'

'So? I *hate* my hair.'

But, as it dried, it did seem to be – well – curlier. Margaret did some judicious pruning with the nail scissors. 'That's better. Did you know it's going quite red? Must be the sun.'

No chlorine in the water, no petrol fumes, no pollution, I thought. I laughed a bit nervously. 'Now all I need is contact lenses.' And an extra six inches in the leg department. And a bosom. And a face a little less like a squashed prune . . . Oh, Aurora, Aurora.

'Actually, those glasses are kind of cute.'

'*What?*' She dodged the flung hairbrush just in time.

Shortly afterwards we heard voices approaching. As the two figures came towards us down the length of the field it became obvious that something was wrong. Ferdinand was limping and leaning heavily on Jo. Margaret clapped one hand over her mouth.

'Is he drunk?'

'Oh, Lord, I hope not!' We raced up the slope to meet them.

'Ferdinand! Are you all right?' Ferdinand grunted and winced.

'Nothing much,' Jo said easily. 'Just a few bruises, that's all.'

Margaret gave a gasp of horrified concern. 'What happened?'

'Don't ask,' Ferdinand mumbled through a swollen mouth and a cut lip. His left eye was rapidly developing a magnificent blue-black bruise. Margaret assessed the damage and took charge.

'It'll have to be bathed. Come on. Lean on me. That's right.' They moved away towards the camp site.

I turned on Jo. 'Honestly, I can't let you two out of my sight for five minutes . . . How much did he drink?'

'Shut up, Foss. It wasn't my fault.' Jo's normally placid face was angry. 'That stupid mutt. You can't take him anywhere. He needs a nanny, and reins.'

I went cold. 'What did he do?'

'Oh, not a lot. Just wandered about making remarks about everybody and everything in a very loud voice. He seemed to be under the impression that he was walking round his own private zoo . . .'

'Why the black eye?'

'He's got a remarkably colourful turn of phase when he puts his mind to it, has our Ferd. Some of his observations were distinctly pithy.'

'Jo, *what happened?*'

'Had a run-in with a bunch of locals who objected. Very big lads, they were. Gigantic. They were reasonably gentle with me,' he added, examining a scrape on his forearm, 'but they had a field day with His Highness. Didn't even give him a chance to try out his karate.'

I went even colder. 'Thank God he wasn't wearing his sword.'

'Exactly. Anyway, if you were thinking of a trip out to the pub this evening, forget it. The whole village'll know the story by now.'

Two days later we drove over the top of a hill and saw the sea. Inshore, the water was deep green over white sand; further out it was indigo, and glittering in the sun. Margaret gasped.

'That's the *sea*?'

Ferdinand was scanning the empty coastline with a frown on his face. 'We must have taken a wrong turning. There should be a port here somewhere, surely.'

Jeffrey didn't seem concerned. He trotted determinedly down a narrow track leading between the dunes and on to the beach.

'Perhaps he just fancies a paddle,' said Jo.

All at once the sunlight faded. Next moment we were moving through a thick white mist, cool and damp and smelling power-fully of the sea. My glasses steamed up.

'I don't remember seeing any mist pockets from above, do you?'

Ferdinand shrugged. 'Sea fog can roll in anywhere along this coast.'

The beach and the sea were invisible. Jeffrey was plodding between white walls of fog. The silence intensified until we couldn't hear the sound of waves or seagulls any more.

Margaret was shivering. 'I don't like this. What if we fall down a cliff, or something?'

'More likely to be quicksand,' I told her gloomily.

'Shut up, the pair of you,' said Jo.

The light began to fade, as though we'd moved into a tunnel. Jeffrey trudged on undeterred. A few minutes later Ferdinand lifted his head and sniffed like a baffled spaniel. 'I can't smell the sea any more.'

He was right. The fresh, salt pungency had vanished, and in its place our noses registered a richer, danker smell. We all glanced down at the same moment. Jeffrey's hooves were scuffling through deep drifts of pine needles.

'A *forest*?'

The mist thinned and began to lift away in drifting shreds. Shafts of reddish sunlight came slanting low between the tree-trunks. We were on a well-made dirt road cutting through a dense wood.

'It was a Gateway!'

10.

Your Stars: CANCER (June 21–July 22)
Those closest to you look to you for support and guidance
in a sensitive situation. Don't back off: you have more to
offer than you think. Trust your instincts.

In this Zone, it was dawn. The sun rose higher, the mist vanished and to our left we saw a set of large wrought-iron gates standing hospitably open. Jeffrey headed for them with the air of somebody who sees a familiar landmark and is thanking his lucky stars the tedious journey is over at last.

'Hey, hang on a sec,' said Jo, and reined in. 'What is this place? Anybody got any ideas? Ferdinand?'

'Never seen it before in my life.'

'Foss?'

'Why ask me? Jeffrey seems to think it's all right.'

Jeffrey gave an exasperated snort and jerked his head impatiently at the bit.

'Okay then, old son. Off you go.'

A well-kept drive led us out into a wide sweep of parkland glittering white with dew. We crested a gentle rise and saw below us a large, rambling old house of golden-brown stone set amongst rose gardens. As we descended the air got warmer and the scent of the roses wafted up to us like a welcome.

Margaret was gripping the side of the cart so hard her knuckles had gone white. An awful thought struck me. 'You're not allergic to roses, are you?'

'Roses? Is that what they are?' She breathed the air cautiously, like somebody sniffing for a gas leak. 'I've never seen *anything* like this before . . .'

The front of the house came into view, its windows blazing in reflected sunlight.

'I say,' Ferdinand murmured approvingly. 'Rather splendid, don't you think?'

Jeffrey trotted around the corner of the house, under a clipped yew arch and into a stable yard. And there he stopped.

'This is it, I think,' said Jo. 'Everybody out.'

We climbed down, stretched stiff limbs and looked around. The yard was deserted: no signs of life anywhere.

'It's early yet. Perhaps no-one's up.'

Jo began to unbuckle the shafts. 'One thing's for sure. Old Jeff here needs his tucker, and a good long drink.'

Ferdinand had been investigating the stables. 'There's an empty stall just here,' he called. 'Fresh hay, oats, bedding, water . . . it looks as though we're expected, doesn't it?'

He *had* changed. A few weeks ago he'd have gone storming up the steps yelling blue murder for the servants.

Margaret and I unloaded the cart while Jo and Ferdinand made Jeffrey comfortable. In the absence of any instructions to the contrary, we stacked the gear against the wall.

'Somebody'll tell us what to do with it eventually, I expect.'

Margaret was looking decidedly jittery. 'What if it's the wrong place after all? What if nobody's expecting us? What if . . .?'

'We just say we're terribly sorry, and move on, I suppose.'

To our right, a door stood half-open at the top of a short flight of steps. I knocked tentatively, but nobody appeared in the small hall beyond. The only sign of life was the glorious aroma of freshly-brewed coffee.

'Breakfast,' I said with longing. 'Coffee, eggs, bacon, toast, marmalade . . .'

'Oh, stop it, Foss. My insides are complaining enough as it is. It's dinner time where they come from.'

A door suddenly swung open at the far end of the hall, revealing a small, sunlit breakfast-room with a table laid for four. Margaret gave a yelp and clutched me, just as the men came clumping up the steps behind us.

'Breakfast!' Jo said joyfully. 'Let's go get it! I'm starving!'

'But there's nobody here . . .'

Ferdinand thrust his chin over Jo's head. 'Hello? Anyone about?' But no-one answered.

'Come on,' said Jo. 'Eat first, apologise later.'

Margaret grabbed the doorframe and held us all back with unexpected strength. She was trembling violently and her eyes were wild. 'Don't go in there! It's not real! It's like that place Foss told me about . . .'

'Mags, it's okay,' Jo said, detaching limb after limb like somebody unhooking an octopus. 'There's nothing to be scared of.'

She struggled frantically in his grasp. 'You're just like the others,' she gasped. 'We'll be trapped! Kept here for ever and ever! Finish up as ghosts . . .' She was crying now, and her panic was communicating itself to the rest of us.

'Wait,' I said. I gulped down jitters and, holding my pendant, I walked into the hall. Nothing changed. There was no frightening glimpse of any other reality. As I stood there, trying to control my thumping heart, all I could feel was a rush of warm sympathy from somewhere. I blinked.

'Who are you?' I said aloud – but nobody answered.

At the doorway three faces were gazing at me in pop-eyed apprehension. I pulled myself together and went back to join them. Margaret grabbed me and clung.

'Well?' said Jo. 'You look a bit shook up.'

'I think . . . Mags, listen. Remember this pendant?' I held it under her nose, and she nodded. 'It can detect illusions. This place is real, Mags.'

'And another thing,' Jo added, 'Jeffrey's acting under instructions from the good guys. He brought us here. Therefore, the place is safe.'

'That's logical,' Ferdinand approved.

'So,' said Jo, breaking the thoughtful pause. 'Do we get breakfast, or the hell out of here?'

Have you ever noticed that sometimes you can *feel* laughter without being able to hear it? I could feel it now, in the air all round me.

'Breakfast,' I said, and led them across the hall. The atmosphere radiated approval, as though somebody was silently saying, *Well done.* It was unnerving.

There was bacon, of course, and eggs, and toast and marmalade, and a huge bowl of fresh strawberries with chilled cream. There was fruit juice, and coffee in a vast silver pot. To begin with all four of us tackled the repast a bit warily, but caution didn't last beyond the second or third mouthful.

Even so, I found myself keeping tabs on everybody, just in case. I needn't have worried. The conversation was spontaneous and silly and nobody was dictating the script. I felt myself relax. I was aware of the invisible Presence hovering over us, but somehow it wasn't intimidating. All I could sense was warm, motherly delight and hospitable fussing, urging us to eat.

'Now that,' said Jo at last, settling back in his chair, 'was what I *call* a breakfast.'

The air quivered with pleasure. Without thinking, I looked up and said, 'Thank you. It was wonderful.'

There was an uneasy pause in the back-chat.

'Who . . . who are you talking to?' Margaret said, eyeing me as though I'd flipped my lid. I could feel myself going red.

'Uh . . . Somebody's listening. Isn't it obvious?'

'Not to me,' said Ferdinand, looking startled.

'She keeps trying to communicate,' I explained. 'Can't you feel it?'

'I can't feel a thing,' said Jo, 'except full. But why do you say "she"?'

'I don't know. It just fits, somehow.' The giggles. The motherly fussing. Nothing I could put into words. I just knew.

The Presence had disappeared while we were finishing our coffee. Then She was back. I felt a distinct mental pressure to go out into the hall – an urge that was practically a command.

'Our rooms!' I guessed. 'She wants to show us our rooms.' The pressure eased sharply and I knew I'd guessed right.

The others cast odd looks in my direction as I shooed them out of the breakfast-room. I began to wish She'd chosen some-body else as go-between – why me?

Margaret and I had rooms at the front of the house, both opening out onto the balcony, with a shared bathroom between. A towelling bathrobe had been laid out on each bed. Margaret showed signs of renewed catatonia so I hustled her into the bath-room and showed her the shower and the loo, on the principle that nothing dispels panic like a bit of practical plumbing. It didn't work.

'I can't cope with this, Foss. Invisible people around us the whole time . . . What if they won't let us leave? Ever?'

'Mags, I don't *know*, any more than you. For what it's worth, I don't think we've been kidnapped. It *feels* different from the last time, that's all I can say. Have a shower, anyway. You'll feel better.'

When we emerged, Jo was waiting for us on the landing out-side.

'Where's Ferd?'

'Gone off to look at the stables, I think.'

'Oh,' said Margaret.

'But I,' Jo added, extending both elbows, 'am on hand to escort you two ladies round the garden.'

The morning sun was hot and the roses were pouring out great gusts of fragrance from arches, pergolas and hedges. Flagged paths wound in and out of small formal plots, and every so often the view opened out to give a spectacular panorama of a lake and woods behind it.

'Some gardener,' Jo said, prodding the soil appreciatively.

We explored, entranced, until Margaret's feet started to hurt. She sat down on a stone bench, took off her sandal and wincingly inspected the blister on her heel. 'Where did *that* come from? You two go on. I'll just sit here for a while.'

'Will you be all right?'

'I'll be fine. I could do with a rest, to be honest. Just don't be long, though, will you?'

Jo and I strolled away.

'Mags is a bit twitchy, isn't she?' Jo remarked.

'Do you blame her? After what she's been through, anything as lovely as this place has to be bad news.'

Jo shrugged. 'Can't say I'm too happy about it myself. Invisible hostesses, being programmed, manipulated . . .'

A major worry surfaced. 'How do we get home, Jo?'

'Ferd says we have to find a sorcerer to open the Zone gates – whatever that means. I'm as lost as you are.'

We walked on in silence for a while. Then I said suddenly, 'Margaret's in love with Ferdinand.'

Jo winced. 'Poor kid.' He glanced sideways at me. 'How do you feel about that? You still fancy him?'

'Not really. It didn't survive getting to know the guy.' Jo's like Oz. He compels honesty. 'I think it's mostly nostalgia. You know – that wonderful feeling of going all slushy inside. You kind of miss it when it's gone.'

'Yeah.' He grinned, rather ruefully. 'I felt that way about Caren. Still do, I suppose.'

I felt terrible. 'Is that why you've been so touchy? Oh, Jo . . . I've gone and messed up your love-life as well . . .'

'Don't be daft. She finished with me, you see. Went back to a boyfriend in Sweden.'

'But it could still work out?'

He shook his head. 'I don't think so. She made the situation pretty clear.'

135

'I'm sorry,' I said. I didn't know what else to say.

'It's not just Caren, actually,' he confessed. 'Life's been a bit fraught recently, if you want the absolute truth. Dad's got all these plans for expanding the piggery and all of a sudden I'm not sure if that's what *I* want. It's as though they've got my whole life mapped out for me in advance, without even asking me. Oh, I want to take over Meini Hirion eventually, of course. But not right away – you know? I need a bit of head space first.' He gave an embarrassed grin. 'Find out who I am, I suppose.'

'Yes,' I said. I recognised the symptoms.

'What I'd really like to do,' he said thoughtfully, 'is a horticulture degree. Specialise in veg. Dad doesn't see any future in it, though.' He sighed and came to a halt. 'Better go back, I suppose. See how Mags is doing.'

We turned back along the paved walk.

'Why did you say "poor kid" about Mags? Actually, if she and Ferd went off together it would solve a lot of problems.'

'They won't, though, will they?'

I blinked. 'Why ever not? Come on, Jo, you've seen how bloody beautiful she is. If Ferdinand hasn't noticed, he's more of a prat than I thought.'

'It's not that simple, though, is it? I mean, I quite like the man: he's not a bad sort once you get past all that high-and-mightiness . . . but he's hardly the type to run off with an ex-scullery maid, is he?'

'You're saying he's a snob.'

'Well, he is. Not his fault, mind – it's the way he was brought up. As far as I can tell, the one idea that's been hammered into his head since he was born is that he's got to find himself a princess and settle down to rule a kingdom. And he's not the type to kick over the traces, is he? Come to think of it,' Jo added thoughtfully, 'He's not the type to have a bit on the side, either. Very strait-laced, our Ferd.'

'Yes,' I agreed. 'I noticed that.'

'And if—' Jo began, and stopped. We froze. The warm sleepy stillness of the garden had suddenly been shattered by a piercing shriek of sheer terror. We started to run.

Margaret appeared as if catapulted around the corner of the yew hedge. She gave a sob of relief and hurled herself at us.

'Margaret! What happened?'

She collapsed against Jo's chest, gasping for breath. 'I saw . . . I saw . . .'

'What did you see? Mags, what was it?'

She burst into tears. 'I saw something *horrible* in the garden.'

We hurried her back into the house – the Presence hovering, agitated and apologetic overhead – sat her down on a sofa and made her drink the small glass of brandy which materialised on the table beside her. When she'd stopped coughing, the story came out.

She'd sat dozing in the sun for a while; then, feeling a bit nervous on her own, she'd set off in search of Jo and me.

'There's a path between high hedges. I turned the corner and . . .' She shuddered violently. 'This *Thing* was standing there.'

'What sort of thing?'

'Huge! All furry and shaggy . . . I think it had horns.'

'Ah,' said Jo, enlightened. 'Somebody round here keeps Highland cattle . . .'

'No! It was standing on its back legs, like a human. Only – much, much bigger. It was wearing – trousers, I think, and some sort of jacket . . . When it saw me it ducked its head to go under one of the arches . . .'

Jo and I shared startled glances. 'Seven or eight feet,' Jo murmured.

'Mags, are you sure you weren't asleep and dreaming?'

'I was on my feet, Foss, walking – you heard me scream . . .'

The door of the sitting-room burst open and we all jumped. Ferdinand breezed in, looking radiant.

'I say, those stables are superb. There's *the* most magnificent bay stallion. I've never seen such a colossal beast . . .'

'Not now, Ferdinand,' Jo snapped.

Ferdinand's grin faded. 'Why, what's happened? Somebody seen a ghost?'

'Margaret's seen a monster,' I told him curtly.

I should have anticipated the way he'd react, but of course I hadn't. The boyish charm vanished like smoke; all at once he stood at least seven feet tall and positively glittering with bloodlust.

'Right,' he said grimly. 'Wait here. I shan't be long.'

Margaret and I screeched as one voice: *'Ferdinand! No!'*

I'd be prepared to bet quite heavily that our reasons for shrieking were diametrically opposite – but the Presence knew exactly whose side she was on. Suddenly the whole room was jangling and vibrating as if with a thousand protesting voices.

Jo felt it too. He stationed himself firmly against the outer door, blocking Ferdinand's exit. 'Hang on a minute, Ferd. You're being a bit premature, don't you think?'

'I don't see why. Margaret's been attacked by a monster – there's only one thing to do. Get out of the way, Jo.'

'She wasn't *attacked*!' I said vehemently. 'It didn't raise a paw. It was horrible, and shaggy and scary but it didn't even *chase* her! It ran away!'

Margaret raised enormous blue eyes to Ferdinand's face. 'I never thought of that.'

Jo did his elder statesman act. 'I really don't think we should do anything rash until we know a bit more about this thing. I mean, for all we know, it could be some sort of pet. And the last thing we want to do,' he added, with a cunning that took my breath away, 'is to antagonise our host or hostess. Don't you agree?'

Ferdinand's resolve had been wavering, but this last point of Jo's hit him slap in the middle of his sense of propriety. The glitter went out of his eyes. 'I suppose you're right,' he admitted.

'Oh, dear,' said Margaret. 'I'm sorry. I just panicked.'

Ferdinand began to assume his knight-in-shining-armour persona. He sat down beside her on the sofa, and said gravely. 'Now. Tell me exactly what it was you saw.'

Jo winked at me, and tipped his head in the direction of the hall. We slipped out of the room, closing the door behind us.

In the hall Jo was grinning all over his face. 'That ought to throw them together, if that's what you want,' he remarked.

'They deserve each other,' I said hotly. 'Margaret doing Aunt Ada Doom impressions all over the place and Ferdinand switching to seek-and-destroy mode at the drop of a hat . . .'

'Heartless cow,' Jo said. 'Seriously, though, what d'you think?'

'Same as you, I guess. It was real – but we weren't supposed to see it.'

Jo nodded. '*She*' – he pointed upwards – 'was very upset in there. Even I felt it.'

After lunch Margaret followed me into my room.

'D'you really think that Thing was harmless?'

'Positive,' I said. 'It was keeping out of our way.'

She sighed. 'I don't know what came over me. I've been feeling so edgy and strange since we got here – not like me at all.

It's this place . . . I keep expecting everything to disappear –
crumble into dust and ashes – and hideous things to spring out
at me . . . I'm sorry, Foss.'

She wandered off through the connecting door. Seconds later
I heard her gasp.

'Foss! Foss, come here!' I dropped everything and ran.

There were no monsters, shaggy or otherwise, in Margaret's
room. Just a single rose in a silver vase on her dressing table.

The rose was blue. Not the dirty mauve colour of every other
so-called blue rose I've ever seen. This was the true, deep,
bluebell-blue that connoisseurs would kill for, that rose growers
have been trying to achieve for millennia and failing dismally
every time. Propped up against the vase was a gilt-edged card
with her name written on it in an old-fashioned, courtly script
which was at the same time oddly clumsy, as though the writer
had been wearing very stiff leather gardening gloves.

Margaret's eyes were the size of soup tureens. 'For me? B—
but why?'

'Because the monster scared you. They're telling you they're
sorry.'

'*They?*'

'She, it, whatever. Does it matter?'

She drew the rose out of its vase and inhaled the fragrance.
She gave me a shaky smile. 'It was probably as scared of me as I
was of it.'

'Very possibly,' I agreed.

'D'you think, perhaps . . . She's taking care of it? Like She's
looking after us?'

'Maybe.' The Presence was female: the shaggy, shambling
figure Margaret had glimpsed was, as far as we could guess,
male. I didn't point out that there was something about the
handwriting that made me suspect a man's fist. Or even . . . a
monster's? I kept my suspicions to myself.

'What do you want to do this afternoon?' I asked her.

Margaret dragged her eyes away from the rose with some
difficulty. 'What? Oh – I think I'll stay here, if you don't mind,
and have a nap. Time-lag's catching up with me.'

'Fine. In that case, I'll go and find Jo.'

Jo wasn't around, and neither was Ferdinand. I learnt later
that Ferdinand was wandering entranced around the stables,
while Jo had found himself in the vegetable garden with a
fascinating variety of eatables to inspect.

139

As for me – the Presence was waiting on the landing, broadcasting a hospitable flutter of pride and delight on all channels. Before I had time to grasp what was happening I was being propelled on a tour of the house.

Like most of us, I adore being shown round other people's houses. I have to admit, though, that to start with I found it a bit disconcerting to be urged along by an invisible hostess who could only communicate excitement and open doors. The feeling wore off very quickly, however – and pretty soon I forgot to be intimidated and started talking aloud to Her as though She was as visible as I was.

And the house itself was a beauty. Big, rambling, unpredictable – as though it had been added to many times over the centuries without losing any of its charm. Everywhere, the impression I got was of constant, devoted care. The flooring shone with years of polishing; beautiful old rugs were velvet-soft underfoot and the woodwork glowed as if it were alive. The banisters seemed to yearn to be stroked. I stroked them – and the Presence purred with pleasure.

That was when it came crashing in on me that the hospitable, sentient Being I was communicating with was in fact the House itself. The House was *alive*.

In the South Wing I got another shock. Each beautifully-proportioned room was full of the most exquisite art-objects: screens, vases, porcelain; sculptures in wood and ivory and bronze, paintings everywhere. But it wasn't a museum. There were comfortable chairs, newspapers and the odd gardening magazine scattered about, and bookshelves against almost every wall. I caught sight of a familiar-looking painting in one room and went across to investigate. It was signed 'Vincent' – and it wasn't a print.

Somebody must have bought all these lovely things – the voiceless House couldn't have done it all on her own. Somebody not only rich, but knowledgeable, too. This wasn't a mail-order stash – this was a collection.

So who was the collector?

As I wandered about, touching things reverently, pausing to admire, I was aware of a subtle change in the House's attitude. She'd wanted to show these things off to me – but now I was actually here, I could sense a fluttery kind of nervousness, like that of an au pair showing a friend around the master bedrooms while the owners are out.

So . . . there was an owner. A master or mistress. A collector of beautiful things. And where did Margaret's monster fit into the picture?

A House like this couldn't clean itself. Couldn't even wash up. Whose were the hands that did these things? Hands clad in heavy gardening gloves? Margaret's note, written by a man . . . Suddenly I couldn't keep the questions to myself any longer. I had to know.

'Who is he?' I said aloud. 'It's a man, isn't it? The person who wrote Margaret's note?'

The House went very still.

'He's here, isn't he? Why won't he come out and introduce himself?'

No answer. A shuddering sense of anxiety. Not fear – concern.

'Is something wrong? Is he ill?'

Again, a stillness. Then a pleading negation: *Don't ask.*

A person with more tact would probably have backed off at this point. But my curiosity had built up such a head of steam by now that I had to keep probing or explode. Perhaps, too, I sensed in the House's reaction a subconscious desire to give in.

'I don't get scared that easily, you know.'

The House agreed silently: *Yes.*

'So why won't he let us see him? All I want to do is thank him.'

Silence.

'Do you get many visitors like us?'

The negative was forlorn. Then, as though She'd been thinking over what I'd said, I received a surge of loneliness and unhappiness and despair that shook me to the core. I was horrified.

'He's lonely? He's unhappy?'

Yes.

'Then please,' I said, 'Let me see him. Just for a moment. Tell him I won't be scared, whatever he looks like. If he's well enough to talk to me, please show me where he is.'

The silence was profound, cogitative. My heart began to thump and I could feel my palms getting sweaty. This big stupid mouth of mine: what had it got me into this time? What sort of disfigurement did this guy have, for Heaven's sake, that made him so paranoid? Disgusting images from horror movies fast-forwarded inside my brain.

I'd almost given up and was turning to go when finally, and

in complete silence, a bookshelf at the far end of the room started to move. It swung inwards to reveal a large book-lined study. There was no propulsion this time: as far as the House was concerned, I was on my own. She'd gone as far as She dared.

I braced myself and walked in. Sitting at a large mahogany desk in the window, outlined against the light, was a colossal, shaggy, horned figure: Margaret's monster.

We stared at each other, both about equally gobsmacked.

'Well, I'll be . . . Ee, by 'eck,' he said.

11.

Your Stars: CANCER (June 22–July 23)
It's up to you to take the initiative in an unusual social
situation. Your concern over a close friend may put you
in a difficult position.

He was *huge*. A thick pelt of fur covered his entire body, even the backs of his hands, which were black and ape-like. His shoulders, chest and arms were like a gorilla's. But his neck and head were those of a great, ferocious bull.

Suddenly the foolish expression vanished. His bull's nostrils flared and his chest heaved. He brought both fists down on the desk with a crash which made the walls shake, flung back his head and bellowed.

That bellow would have been frightening enough at a distance of a hundred yards in the open air. Here, enclosed within walls, it was deafening. I learnt later that the noise had reached Ferdinand in the stables, and Jo in his vegetable garden; it had jerked Margaret bolt upright in her bed. Me – I just stood there, frozen to the spot in sheer terror.

The monster shouted at the air in a voice like thunderclaps.

'What the bloody 'ell d'ye think you're playing at? Eh? I gave you strict instructions. I won't have it, d'you understand? You've got no right to go disobeying my orders. No right!' I could feel the whole House quivering and sobbing around me. Her terror gave me the shot of bravado I needed.

'Stop that!' I yelled – horribly aware that my voice sounded as feeble as a gnat's compared with his. 'It wasn't Her fault. If you want to shout at somebody, shout at me.'

There was a dreadful, ominous silence. The red glare shifted to me. I shrivelled under it. 'She didn't want to let me in,' I said, breathless now with apprehension, 'I twisted Her arm.'

'You *knew*?' he roared. 'By 'eck, and I thought I could trust that daft cow Ossiana . . .'

Ossiana . . . what the whispering shadow had called Aunt Oz.

I couldn't stop myself. Nobody – but *nobody* – slags off my Aunt Oz in my presence. I heard myself say hotly, 'That's a great epithet, coming from you!'

143

He was on his feet, towering above me, blocking out the light, his massive horned head just brushing the ceiling. I backed against the door-frame.

'I—I just wanted to thank you for all your trouble,' I stammered. 'But now I don't think I'll bother. Oz never said a word about you. I just guessed.' And turned to make a dignified exit, only to bump my glasses against the panelling. The door behind me was shut.

I spun round to face the Beast. I could feel hysteria mounting. Rescue was not on the cards. Nobody knew where I was except the House. I held my breath and waited for Heaven knew what – tossing, trampling, goring . . . it occurred to me in a mad irrelevant flash of thought that the House wouldn't like blood on Her carpets . . .

All at once he seemed to collapse from within, like a punctured beach ball. He slumped back into his chair and covered his face with his huge grotesque hands.

'You shouldn't've done it,' he groaned. 'She's not the one, you fool.' The pain in his voice was dreadful to hear; it sent shudders of empathy down my back. 'Don't you think I've suffered enough? Why d'you do this to me – eh?'

Abruptly, all the terror drained out of me. How can you be afraid of somebody in such bitter distress? I'd got the scenario back to front. It wasn't me who needed rescuing – it was the Beast, from this morass of agonised self-pity.

I took in a few deep breaths to steady my voice. 'There's no need for all that,' I said, as bracingly as I dared. 'I'm not scared of the way you look. I just don't like being shouted at, that's all.'

He stopped rocking himself and sat very still.

'I don't know anything about you,' I went on, 'Except that you've gone to a lot of trouble to make us comfortable here. I just wanted to say Thank you.' I marched up to him without letting myself think of the possible consequences, and held out my hand.

'I'm Francesca Ewins,' I said. 'And I'm very pleased to meet you.'

There was terror in the big solemn eyes he turned towards me. He was actually trembling. I realised with a shock that this great hulking monster was scared stiff. Of *me* – a human – a girl. Slowly, he extended his own hand and shook mine, very gingerly, as though he was convinced that the slightest pressure would crush it into pulp. His black skin was hard, like polished leather. Gardening gloves hadn't been such a bad guess after all.

'How . . . how d'ye do?' he said gruffly. Then, still in shock, 'Er . . . Magnus.'

Magnus. Hadn't Oz been talking to somebody called Magnus on her mobile phone?

I waited. It was quite obvious that the poor Beast hadn't a clue what to do next, and was overcome with embarrassment.

'Er . . . well. I s'pose you'd better sit down,' he said at last.

'Thank you,' I said, and sat.

'You . . . you must be Ossiana's lass,' he said awkwardly. 'Aye. She . . . hrrumph! . . . she mentioned you.'

'Did she?'

'Aye, she did that. Knee-high to a grasshopper, she said.' His eyes began to twinkle with suppressed amusement. 'And every other inch a short fuse.'

I cringed. 'That's about right,' I admitted.

He chuckled – a creaky, half-embarrassed noise deep in his throat. Then he looked anxious. 'That . . . er . . . t'other little lass – t'little fair haired one . . . she's got over her fright now, has she? Eeh,' he added, shaking his huge head, 'I'd no idea. T'last thing I wanted was to upset her like that.'

'She's fine,' I assured him. 'That rose you sent her was fabulous. She was over the moon.'

'Aye,' he said with shy pride, 'One of my best, was that . . . Poor lass,' he went on. 'Terrible place, that. Terrible. Still, I gather Gloria got her come-uppance, thanks to you, eh?'

'*Gloria?*'

'Well, Gloriana was what she called herself. Queen Gloriana. Never heard such a load of rubbish in my life,' he added with a snort of contempt. He was warming to his subject now, and forgetting his shyness. 'Gloria Phipps was what she started out as, and a right little gold-digger she was an' all. And crooked! Dealing wi' Gloria was like slicing bread with a corkscrew. Trust her about as far as you could heave a truck.'

I looked at Magnus and couldn't help reflecting that for him, this might be quite some distance. But I didn't say so.

'Mind you,' he went on, 'She didn't do much harm to start off with. Didn't have the power. Then she took up with that Zekar and the next thing we know, she's got her claws on a PET unit from somewhere. Stole it, I shouldn't wonder . . .'

145

I was lost. 'A *what* unit?'

'PET. Psychic Energy Transformer. Absorbs psychic energy, bumps it up, emits it in any form you want. Sorcerers've been using them for years.'

The glass brick thing. 'But when I threw it out, it vanished.'

'Aye, it would, that. Touched real earth, d'ye see. Trouble with them things is they're unstable. Got to be shielded at all times.'

I was puzzled. 'So . . . she got me transformed into Aurora? She was keeping tabs on Ferdinand and me right from the start?' It didn't make sense. Gloria hadn't struck me as being capable of reasoning from A to B, let alone mastermind a complicated transformation in another Zone. Powerful, yes; bright, no.

He shook his head. 'No, no. Her getting hold of you and your young man was an accident. Strayed into her territory, you did, d'ye see. I lost track of you for a bit there. Ee, I felt bad about that. Ossiana'd have torn me limb from limb if summat'd happened to you.'

I stared at him and cold chills chased themselves up and down my spine. '*You* sent Ferdinand to Tan-y-Fedwen? *You* changed me into Aurora?'

He snorted vigorously. 'Good God, no. Nowt to do wi' me. First thing I knew was a message from Ossiana, urgent. Never known her in such a state. One o' *Them*'d got a hold of you – on her own back doorstep an' all . . . and I was to keep an eye on you both an' see you safely to Arborea, or wherever They'd decided to send you . . .'

'Why? Why get hold of *me*? Who are *They*?'

He shrugged massively. 'Dunno why. They're just agents. Freelance. We'll find out who's paying them, though, never you mind,' he said ominously. 'You were taken over, d'ye see. You and your young man. Under their control. Couldn't do a thing about it except keep tabs. But then Gloria got hold of you, you changed back, and Ossiana managed to get through . . . I was all for barging straight in there and taking the place apart—' He would have, too. '—but Ossiana said no. "There's more to that lass than meets th'eye," she said – and by 'eck she were right.'

I could feel myself going red. 'But couldn't you have done something about Gloria, before things got that bad?'

He shook his head ponderously. 'Trouble with Gloria's sort,

146

they've got no scruples. Sorcerers can detect other sorcerers, d'ye see. She'd a' drained her victims in their thousands to keep me out.'

A sorcerer? Of course he was. My heart thumped: he could get us home . . .

I didn't get a chance to ask him where Oz fitted into all this, because the House interrupted to remind us it was dinner-time. Magnus (I'd stopped thinking of him as the Beast) got up. 'Best be getting along, lass,' he said.

I hung back. 'Aren't you coming too?'

His shyness returned like a shutter slamming down. 'No!'

'Promise me,' I pleaded. 'Promise me you'll come and meet us all soon. Please, Magnus. You don't have to be shy, honestly.'

He backed off, his nostrils flaring in panic. 'We'll see,' he said gruffly. 'Off you go, now.'

When the others saw me there was a concerted rush which nearly knocked me off my feet. 'Foss! Where have you *been*?' 'Are you okay?' 'Was that the monster we heard? We've been worried sick!'

'Yes,' I said, 'He's—'

'Don't *ever* disappear like that again! Honestly, Foss, you need your head read.' This was Jo.

'But—' I said.

'If that monster's laid a finger on you . . .' Ferdinand was striding about and clutching the hilt of his sword.

'How could you *do* that to us?' Margaret said. 'The rest of us rushed back here when we heard the noise, why didn't you?'

'I just—'

'We nearly went crazy when you didn't turn up!'

'Wait a mi—'

'Ferdinand was all set to slaughter the thing on sight – and then all the sitting-room doors shut and we couldn't get out. Jo tried smashing a window but that didn't work either.'

'I knew all along that this place was bad news,' Ferdinand announced. 'Personally, I think we should leave as soon as possible.'

I'd had enough. Decibels at maximum, I shouted 'Why don't you all *shut up*?!'

The babble died abruptly. 'Right. I'm sorry you were worried. I've met the monster. I've been chatting to him all afternoon.'

147

There was a stunned silence. Then Jo said in a strangled voice, 'You went *looking* for that thing? Foss, you're out of your tiny mind. He could have killed you.'

'I didn't go looking for him,' I said crossly. 'The House took me to see him. The House is alive, in case you hadn't realised. '

'*What?* How?'

'Don't ask me, I don't know. Anyway, to get back to the monster, his name's Magnus, he's a sweetie, and the only reason he hasn't introduced himself is that he's terrified of people seeing him. Desperately shy.'

Margaret's face was troubled. 'Shy? Terrified of *us?*'

The meeting took place in the rose arbour next morning. As social events go, it wasn't a raging success. Everybody felt inhibited and awkward and Magnus most of all. My over-eager attempts to get the conversation started went down like a lead balloon. At the first sound of Magnus's voice Ferdinand shied like a colt and became insufferably haughty.

Later, I found Magnus in the kitchen, washing up. The House produced a teatowel, and I dried.

When we'd finished he led me to his study, where coffee was waiting. He sighed. 'It's no good, lass. They don't feel easy with me, and that's all there is to it. I shan't trouble you again.'

'Don't be silly, Magnus.' I was annoyed. 'Give other people the credit for being as shy as you are.'

He picked up a carved ivory puzzle-ball and began to dismantle it, piece by piece, moving his huge fingers with infinite delicacy.

'No,' he said, shaking his horned head mournfully. 'There's no getting away from it, lass. I'm too old to socialise. Old and cursed and past hope of redemption.'

'You're not *old*! Good Heavens, Magnus . . .' His fur was glossy, his head that of a bull in the prime of life: no wrinkles, no grey hairs . . . in human terms, I'd have put him between thirty-five and forty. 'Stop talking as though you've got one foot in the grave!'

He gave a short laugh. 'I was human once, y'know. Like them lads out there. Was a King in them days, even. How long d'you think I've been like this?'

I was stumped. 'A few years? Ten? Fifteen?'

'Eight hundred,' he said.

I went cold with shock. '*Eight hundred years?*'

'Aye. If it hadn't been for your Ossiana, and what she did, I'd 'a' gone crazy long since. Old,' he repeated heavily, 'and tired, lass. Worn out to the marrow.' He went on in a low voice, as though talking to himself. 'If she were to come now – her who's to break t'spell – I doubt if I'd have the heart to go through with it, and that's the truth.'

'She?'

'I don't know who. She's to come here some time – that's all I know.'

'Perhaps it's me, or Margaret.'

'No. You and young Margaret've got a different road to follow.' He sounded very sure of his facts.

'Magnus – what happened to you?'

Slowly, with a lot of prompting from me, the story came out. Eight hundred years earlier, Magnus had been the ruler of a wild Northern kingdom in another Zone. I gathered that his subjects had largely consisted of well-armed larrikins whose idea of a Saturday night out was to descend in force upon some unprotected village outside the borders and beat hell out of the inhabitants. Magnus had kept this dubious rabble loyal and under some sort of central control simply by being bigger, stronger and wilder than anybody else – a sort of yobbo extraordinaire.

Eight hundred years on, Magnus the monster wasn't proud of this phase of his career.

'D'ye know what my nickname was? The Bull. Magnus t'Mad Bull, that's what they used to call me. I never once thought . . . it never crossed my mind that I was doing anything wrong. Aye,' he said, his enormous paws fitting the ivory sections back together with the deft touch of the expert, 'Magnus t'Bleeding Bull.'

'So what went wrong?'

He sighed ruefully. 'I went a bit too far.'

One night, Magnus and a few other joyful souls of like mind had gone out raiding in the far West. They'd come across a nobleman's estate and had proceeded to rape, murder, pillage and burn as custom dictated.

Unfortunately for Magnus and his friends, the estate was under the protection of a powerful sorcerer whose idea of a bit of harmless fun happened to differ rather sharply from Magnus's own. Retribution was, as the books say, swift and terrible. Of the twenty-odd revellers who'd accompanied him, none returned home: all were struck dead. Magnus himself was thrown into a dungeon while the sorcerer tried to think of a suitable punishment.

The one he hit on was ingenious, to say the least.

'Bull by name and bull by nature,' the sorcerer had said. 'From henceforth you shall be half bull, half man, a monster so hideous that neither man nor beast will accept you in their midst. You shall be outcast forever.'

'*Forever?*' I was horrified. 'No escape clause? No remission for good behaviour? That's a bit over the top, isn't it?'

Magnus shifted his bulk about and looked embarrassed. 'Well, no . . . not exactly . . . Y'see . . . the . . . er . . . enchantment comes to an end if a young lady should . . . hrrumph! . . . fall in love wi' me.' He gave a short, bitter laugh. 'Hasn't happened yet and most likely never will.'

'Oh, *Magnus!*' I'd completely forgotten that less than twenty-four hours ago he'd been a total stranger who'd terrified me out of my wits. He was already a friend – somebody to worry about.

'And then he installed you here, to wait?'

'No, no. The House came a lot later. He just let me out to wander.'

And wander he did, for nearly two hundred years. At first he was savage, working out his rage in murderous revenge. Hunters drove him into the wilderness – and at last he began to understand what it was like to live in fear, and feel pain, and be hunted for sport. Again and again he'd tried to kill himself, but the enchantment had kept him alive however terrible his injuries. He became ashamed of his former crimes, and tried to atone for them by helping people – but as the sorcerer had foretold, humankind refused to accept him. Whenever he approached, they screamed and fled.

Another century passed, and now he was a solitary hermit, afraid to show himself to any sentient being. But the wild beasts came meekly to his hand, and flowers flourished under his care: this was one aspect of the spell which hadn't turned out as planned, and he was grateful.

'That's when Ossiana finally caught up wi' me,' he said reminiscently.

'Ossiana?' Something odd here. 'Any relation to my Aunt Oz?'

He peered at me from beneath frowning brows. 'Far as I know, there's only one Ossiana, and allus has been. Thank God,' he added piously.

'B—but . . .' I was getting chills down the spine again. 'When was this, exactly?'

'Let's see, now . . . Five hundred years ago, near as dammit. Mind you,' he said, watching my reaction, 'She's been at t'job a good bit longer than I have.'

He was laughing silently at me, and no wonder. My mouth had dropped open.

'Wh—what job?'

'Gatekeeper,' he said, 'Keeping t'Zones separate. Letting through them as needs to pass, keeping t'rest out. Always has done, your Oz.'

'*Always?*'

'Aye. It's one of the oldest Gates, that. She won't say, mind you, but I reckon three or four thousand years at least.'

I stared at him, but he was perfectly serious. Not a glimmer of a wind-up in those brown solemn eyes. My head refused to take it in. Dear batty Aunt Oz, who'd cleaned her teeth in the same bathroom as me, who wore Marks and Spencers undies and went to pieces at the sight of an income tax form . . .?

'That little place she lives in,' Magnus said, 'Named after your Oz. They had to change it a bit, mind.'

Tan-y-Fedwen? No, of course not. Triddon? Light began to dawn. Triddon Magna. Such a stupid name, we'd always thought as kids, Jo and me. But now . . . De-Anglicise it. Translate it back into its original Welsh. Tre-something. Tre-don? Tre-ddewin? Tre-ddewin Mawr. More accurately, in the feminine, Tref y Ddewines Fawr. The place of the great sorceress . . .

Shivers like needle-stabs were creeping all over me. My head felt perilously close to total overload. I'd have to think this over later, when I was alone, and had time to absorb the shock. In an odd sort of way, it made sense – particularly in view of all that had happened recently. But it was still hard to take in.

I turned with relief to the rest of Magnus's life story.

Oz had taught him to read and write and tutored his dormant talent for sorcery. He'd become a Gatekeeper. It was a little-used Gate but the responsibility had given him a new purpose in life. He'd built this House, stone by stone – and Oz had cast the spell which had released its living spirit to be a companion in his solitude.

151

'Couldn't she break the spell on you?'

He shook his head. 'She had a go, but it didn't work. It's very hard for one sorcerer to undo another one's magic at the best of times – and this fellow of mine,' he added with a kind of rueful pride, 'was top-notch. She went and had a word with him about it, but all he'd say was, he'd done the job and wasn't backing down.'

As he began to take an interest in the world outside, he'd discovered something which astonished him – he was a financial genius when it came to playing the stock markets. As the years passed he found he was becoming rich – rich enough to indulge his love of beautiful things. 'Ten per cent of all I earn,' he said, gesturing at the priceless objects scattered around the study. 'The rest goes to charity. Trouble is,' he added gloomily, 'These days, wherever you put it, it ends up as guns.'

The thought of all this wisdom and courage and gentleness going to waste brought a hard dry lump to my throat.

'Magnus,' I said, choking a bit on the words, 'She's *got* to come along some time. She *must*.'

He shrugged. 'Pigs might fly.'

'If you're going to skulk in your study every time guests turn up you're never going to find her. Put yourself about a bit. People will understand!'

He shook his great head sadly. 'It's a non-starter, lass. Face facts. Young Margaret had hysterics when she saw me, and no wonder. An eight-hundred-year-old freak with a bull's head is no kind of match for a young girl.'

'What can we *do*?' I said to the others over dinner that evening. 'It's so unfair. He's such a lovely person, and so lonely.'

'Have to be a pretty special girl, though,' Jo said cautiously.

'Hmm,' said Ferdinand. 'Couldn't we arrange something?'

'What d'you mean?'

'Well, if what he told you is correct, he's a millionaire. There must be hundreds of eligible girls who'd be willing to take a chance on that sort of basis.'

'It wouldn't work,' Margaret said. 'She has to fall in love with him. That's the one thing which will break the spell.'

'Knowing poor old Magnus's luck,' Jo said, 'What d'you bet that the one girl who does go for him in a big way turns out to be the one person on earth he can't stand?'

'Don't be defeatist,' Margaret said crossly.

'I'm not. Magnus seems to be an ace bloke and I'm all for breaking this damn stupid curse as soon as possible. I'm just pointing out the snags.'

'You don't have to point them out to Magnus,' I said, depressed. 'He knows them all.'

My remarks concerning putting himself about a bit must have had some effect because next morning Magnus appeared again, and this time communication was a lot less strained. After that he turned up with increasing frequency and even Margaret lost her awe of him and yakked away nineteen to the dozen. The only one of us to remain aloof and suspicious was Ferdinand. He was frigidly polite, spoke only when addressed directly, and excused himself from Magnus's company whenever possible without actually being rude.

'What's the matter with him?' I said, exasperated.

'I can tell you what the trouble is,' Jo said with irritating smugness. 'Magnus is a King, isn't he?'

'Was,' Magnus corrected him sadly.

'Once a King, always a King, me old mate. Something to do with all that oil and stuff. Well, in Ferdinand's book kings don't have Lancashire accents. They don't peel potatoes and do the washing up, or spend their days swopping back-chat with swineherds and scullery-maids and other dubious characters.'

'Oh, pardon me for breathing, I'm sure,' said Magnus.

'Ferd's confused. You don't fit into his conceptual framework, and he's terrified of being nice to you in case you turn out to be a con-man, and not his social equal at all.'

'Oh, that's the problem, is it?' Magnus said thoughtfully.

Next time we met he was very much on his dignity: splendidly dressed, and with a narrow golden circlet on his head, between the horns. He collared Ferdinand and led him off towards the stables.

'Isn't he *sweet*,' I said, gazing fondly after the retreating pair.

'Who, Ferdinand?' Margaret said in a rather tense voice.

'No, dimmock. Magnus, of course.'

'Oh,' said Margaret.

When Ferdinand reappeared, some four hours later, he was looking much happier. I bumped into him at the corner of the House and he greeted me with unprecedented enthusiasm. 'I've had an absolutely marvellous afternoon!'

They'd been for a ride together: Magnus on the gigantic bay, and Ferdinand on 'the most superb black. Magnificent creature. Didn't take too kindly to being ridden, though – not at first. But I soon mastered him.'

I envisaged Ferdinand astride a plunging, bucking black whirlwind and shuddered. 'I'll take your word for it. As long as nobody expects me to ride that thing.'

'Magnus wouldn't allow it,' Ferdinand said crisply. 'That fellow is strictly for the expert. But what a ride!' He was radiating satisfaction from every pore. We began to stroll across the terrace and onto the lawn.

After a few moments Ferdinand said almost shyly, 'He's an extraordinarily good sort, isn't he? D'you know he's actually corresponded with my father from time to time?'

'Really?'

'He knew all about Siegfried and Perry and Berenice and me. He keeps in touch with Baron Plome – Berenice's fiancé, you know – and he knows Hortensia's parents quite well – that's Perry's wife . . . Through letters, and so on, of course. He's never actually met any of them, but that's understandable under the circumstances. Gosh,' he added boyishly, 'Won't they be surprised when I tell them!'

I thought it was about time I inserted a word of caution. 'I don't think he'd like that, Ferdinand.'

'Wouldn't he?'

Feeling like a nanny, I said, 'Well, he's not exactly over the moon about this enchantment of his, you know.'

'You think he'd prefer it if people didn't know.'

'I think we ought to respect his wishes, and not indulge in gossip.'

'Oh,' Ferdinand said. 'Absolutely. Of course.'

We'd reached a small paved court with a fountain. Ferdinand fidgeted, looked sideways at me and gave all the indications of bracing himself for something unpleasant. 'Look, Foss. Er. I . . . er . . . I owe you an apology.'

I stared at him. 'Whatever for?'

'Well . . .' He swallowed hard. 'Let's sit down.' He pulled a stray weed out of the cracks in the paving and began to dismember it leaf by leaf. 'The thing is . . . I didn't understand. I was . . . well, to tell you the absolute truth I was furious with you. I thought you'd tricked me.'

'Ferdinand, it doesn't matter now . . .'

'Yes, it does. Magnus explained it all. It wasn't your fault. We were both being . . . manipulated. He doesn't know why, or by whom, yet, but . . . He says there's something rather sinister going on in Arborea, and he's rather glad we're not going there after all . . . But anyway . . .'

'Ferdinand, it's okay, honestly. We're friends, right?'

'Right,' he said gratefully. 'The thing is . . .' He bent his head and subjected the weed to a fierce examination. 'I . . . er . . . I wasn't entirely truthful with you either.'

I started to laugh. 'Don't tell me you're not the Prince of Boronia?'

'Oh, that part's true. What I may have misled you about is . . . well . . . Boronia isn't quite as I described it to you. To put it bluntly, it's in rather a mess.'

Bit by bit the story came out.

Boronia was a large, ancient, proud kingdom, but the Royal Family itself was bankrupt. Ferdinand had decided to do something about the situation. Arborea was wealthy, prosperous and had lost its Princess. He'd decided to find her, marry her and use Arborea's wealth to bale out the royal coffers of Boronia.

'But Ferdinand,' I pointed out as tactfully as I could, 'Don't think I'm criticising – but shouldn't that have been Siegfried's job? He is the Crown Prince, after all.'

'Ah,' said Ferdinand, and proceeded to enlighten me about Siegfried. 'You see – Siegfried isn't actually the type to get married and settle down.'

'What's the matter – is he gay, or something?'

'No . . . At least, I don't think so. The trouble is, he's never *there*.' Siegfried, it transpired, was a full-time, professional Hero.

'He's such a superb single-combat fighter, you see,' Ferdinand said gloomily. 'Absolutely the best there is. At home, they call him the Dragonslayer.'

'I bet that makes him popular.'

'Oh, absolutely. Whenever he's home, the media have a field day. People come out in thousands to cheer.'

But Siegfried hardly ever did come home except when he was broke, to wheedle a few thousand quid from the rapidly emptying pockets of his old man. I gathered that being a Hero was an expensive business.

'But I thought dragons had hoards of gold and precious jewels.'

155

'Not any more, they don't. These days even the most reactionary worm puts it all into bonds.'

'All right, so what about the Kings whose daughters have been rescued? I mean, it's pest control in a way, isn't it? Highly specialised, too. He could charge the earth.'

'Siegfried,' said Ferdinand glumly, 'is far too well-bred to mention anything as sordid as money. Except at home.'

I shuddered. 'I'm glad it was you who came looking for Aurora, and not Siegfried. He'd almost certainly have lopped my head off without a second thought.'

Ferdinand managed a weak grin. 'I suppose he is a bit trigger-happy.'

'Trigger-happy? The man's a raving psychopath. He needs a shrink.'

Ferdinand winced. 'He *is* my brother, you know.'

'So what about Peregrine? I thought he married a million-airess?'

'He did. Unfortunately, though . . . '

Peregrine, the clever one, had been a little too clever for his own good. He'd invested huge sums of his father-in-law's money in an international heroin racket, and was now living very quietly indeed, under an assumed name, in Rio de Janeiro. The scandal had rocked staid, respectable Boronia to its foundations. It had almost toppled King Theodore from his throne. Almost, but not quite. A forgiving lot, the Boronians, I thought.

Which left Ferdinand.

'I'm not bright, like Perry, and not heroic, like Siegfried, and to be perfectly honest I don't think Father rated my chances very highly. But I had to try. And I muffed it, of course, as I always do . . . ' He sounded very young and miserable.

'Oh, *Ferdinand*! You know what your problem is? You're trying to be Perry and Siegfried rolled into one! It doesn't seem to have occurred to you that Siegfried is King Kong in a tin shirt and Perry's so crooked he'd have trouble drawing a straight line with a ruler! You're a lot brighter than Siegfried, and you're an honourable bloke. Try being yourself, for a change.'

'What am I going to do, Foss? I've failed, haven't I?'

'Only in the first round. Let's see if Magnus can help.' He had to find a princess. A wealthy one, with no strings attached.

In the meantime, there was something else I had to do – but I hadn't the faintest idea how to go about it. Telling your best mate that she hasn't a snowball's chance of getting to first base with the bloke she loves is hardly the pleasantest job in the world – but the more I thought about what Ferdinand had told me, the more convinced I was that Margaret, of all people, had the right to know how things stood.

I spent the whole evening agonising about how best to break the news. In the end, of course, I just blurted it all out as she was cleaning her teeth in our shared bathroom.

Margaret went very pale, and rigidly still. After a while she gave a wan smile. 'Seems like I was right all along, doesn't it?'

'Mags,' I said, 'I feel terrible. It's so bloody unfair.'

'Was I that obvious?'

'Only to me.'

'You didn't *tell* him, did you?'

'Of course not, eejit.'

She shrugged, and sighed. 'I suppose I never really expected anything would come of it. Only sometimes you can't help yourself, can you?'

'He's a *prat*,' I said hotly. 'A complete berk! He wouldn't recognise true love if it jumped up in front of his nose waving xylophone sticks and played the Hallelujah Chorus on his front teeth.'

Margaret squared her shoulders and took a deep breath.

'You don't suppose the House keeps a stack of chipped crockery anywhere, do you?' she said. 'I have this sudden urge to smash something.'

'Let's find out,' I said.

12.

Your Stars: CANCER (June 22–July 23)
An unexpected development may force you to change
your plans. Don't be disappointed – just go with the
flow. Events will turn out better than you expected.

The days flowed into one another, each as golden as the last. We swam and sailed and sunbathed, played tennis and croquet, and went riding with Magnus as our instructor. Ferdinand started teaching Jo the elements of swordsmanship and gave Margaret and me lessons in karate.

Every time I thought about the disastrous Aurora episode, I cringed.

'Just be thankful you're well out of it,' Jo said bluntly. We were out riding, and the others had gone on ahead. 'All that rubbish about a Lost Princess . . . It was all a figment of Ferd's imagination, if you ask me. The Zones are real, Foss. Oh, I know you get sorcerers and whatnot – but most of the people I met out there were exactly like the ones at home, and just as sharp. In the real world, heirs to the throne don't get lost under mysterious circumstances. All that wicked-witch-stole-her-away-in-the-cradle stuff belongs in a fairytale.'

I went cold. 'What would have happened when we got to Arborea?' It wasn't hard to imagine. Bureaucrats, interrogations, demands for proof of identity; being arrested for impersonating a royal personage . . .

'Don't even think about it,' Jo said. 'You probably wouldn't have ended up in the real Arborea anyway. Whatever those whispering shadows had in mind for you two – it wasn't good.'

A shiver went down my back. Agents, Magnus had called them. Their boss would not be happy to find his carefully-laid plans shot to pieces. He (or she, or they) had gone to a lot of trouble to secure Ferdinand and me. Why?

One evening Magnus called me into his study.

'Thought you might like summat to remember us by,' he said bashfully. 'Me and Her.' He thrust a small packet into my hands, turned his back and harrumphed noisily.

Inside the wrappings was an antique silver ring with an intricate pattern of twined leaves surrounding a green stone in the middle. I slipped it onto my right hand and it fitted perfectly. 'Magnus – it's gorgeous!'

'It's only small, mind. Thought it'd go with that pendant. I put a Finding on it, so it won't get lost. Nor you neither. Just in case.'

The significance of the gift hit me like a wet sock. 'So we'll be leaving soon.'

'Aye. Tomorrow, most likely.'

My heart plummeted. Home. Back to Birtles Road, and all the tensions I'd left behind. I thought about Ferdinand going home to Boronia, to explain his failure to his father; Jo to wonderful, loving parents who nevertheless had their own agenda and couldn't understand why he didn't want to be part of it . . . And Margaret . . . Margaret's future was the bleakest of all. For all of us, going back to where we belonged would be like turning a page to a chapter headed Problems Start Here.

'No problem wi' Ferdinand, o'course,' Magnus said later, after dinner. 'We're in t'right Zone for Boronia. It's only a day's ride to Garnock port from here.'

Ferdinand was startled. 'We're that close? I had no idea. Garnock's the major port for the Boronian coast,' he told us.

'What about Jo and Mags and me?' I asked.

'Well, it's all to do wi' t'Gateways, and where you want to end up.'

Jo said, 'I suppose Foss and I go back to Triddon, don't we?'

Magnus nodded. 'Margaret?'

She shrugged. 'Home, I suppose.'

'Mags, you can always come to Triddon with us. Oz'll be delighted, I know she will . . .'

Margaret shook her head. 'Thanks for the offer, Foss . . . but no. I've been thinking it over. I ought to go back. It's where I belong, after all. And don't try to argue me out of it,' she added, as we all began to protest. 'My decision, okay?'

Magnus cleared his throat. 'Right. Thing is, we've got to choose t'right Gate at th'right time. It's all to do with the flux, and the concordances.'

Three baffled faces gazed blankly at him and he explained. Time was what kept the Zones separate, he said: one world, one

159

time. Breaking through the time barrier was difficult enough in itself: enormous energies were involved, and only sorcerers had the know-how to discharge them safely. You also had to choose the right Gate so as to end up in the right time line – what the Gatekeepers called a concordance. In the case of Jo and me, the problem was further complicated by the fact that Time in our world moved backwards compared to the other Zones.

'Mind you,' Magnus added thoughtfully, 'some people have no trouble moving across and back again: geniuses, artists, storytellers . . . they pass across in dreams, mostly, or when they're called for. What you call stories in your world – well, more often than not they're real things that have happened in t'Zones. Things that haven't happened yet in this Zone can be stories hundreds of years old in your world.'

It was a hard concept to grasp. Jo stopped trying. 'So how *do* we get back?'

Magnus's Gate was no good for travel against opposite flows. The nearest useful Gate was further up the coast, in a place called Kettleton.

Ferdinand came alert. 'I know Kettleton. It's north of Garnock.'

Magnus was nodding. 'So, what I thought was, what's stopping you all travelling to the coast together, eh? Stay at Garnock a day or two, see Ferdinand off on his boat and then go up to Kettleton. Margaret can transfer first – hers is easy. Then Jo and Foss.'

'Marvellous idea.' Ferdinand's eyes sparkled. 'You'll like Garnock. Everyone who's anyone passes through at some time or another.' The prospect of meeting up with his glitterati friends had clearly cheered him up enormously.

Margaret was relieved. 'A whole lot better than disappearing from here one by one,' she said with a shiver.

'Couldn't agree more,' Jo said fervently.

Magnus had gone to stand at the window, with his back to the other three, so I was the only one who noticed the fleeting, worried frown on his bull's face, and only I was close enough to hear him murmur under his breath, '*And no traffic to Arborea from there, either . . . God help me, I've done all I can for 'em.*'

A shiver prickled the hairs on the back of my neck. What did Magnus, the sorcerer, know that we didn't?

Next morning my clothes had vanished. There was a new dress on my bed: a long-skirted riding-habit in dark green velvet, with a hat to match, and boots. I was trying them on rather dubiously when Margaret tapped on the door. She was wearing a similar outfit in deep blue and looked stunning.

'What's all this about?' she said suspiciously, indicating the clothes.

'Dunno. Maybe Magnus doesn't want to shame us in front of Ferdinand's posh friends.'

When we got downstairs bulging leather holdalls were stacked up in the hall: the House had done our packing for us while we slept. Ferdinand and Jo were already at the toast stage of breakfast. Ferdinand's eyebrows rose appreciatively when he saw us.

'Very nice. Very . . . suitable.'

I nudged Margaret. 'See? I told you so.'

There was no sign of Magnus.

'He's said his goodbyes already, and doesn't want to prolong the agony,' Margaret said, and sighed. 'Can't say I blame him.'

Ferdinand himself was anxious to get going. 'Come on, chaps, hurry up. We've a long ride ahead of us.'

'Where are we staying when we get there, do you know?'

'An inn called the Providence,' Ferdinand said crisply. 'Magnus had a word with me last night. He's arranged it all. They'll bring the horses back when we've left.' It was becoming evident that Ferdinand had been put in charge of this little expedition, and was, predictably, reverting to type.

Three horses were waiting for us in the stable yard, and with them Jeffrey harnessed between the shafts of an elegant light cart. As the others made their way down the steps with the luggage, I loitered behind in the hall.

'I'm going to miss you two horribly,' I said aloud.

The air quivered – and suddenly the Presence enfolded me in warmth, like a brief hug from a friend. Voiceless words brushed the fringes of my mind.

'Thank you for everything,' She said. 'Take care,' and then She pushed me very firmly down the steps and closed the door behind me.

We rode off up the hill, Jo driving the cart with the luggage, Ferdinand's horse prancing regally in front. The House lay below us, golden and serene in its magical hollow. Then the pinewoods closed around us and it disappeared.

Already the warmth was leaching out of the air. When we

reached the highroad there was frost on the grass verges and russet bracken in the copses.

'Must be late October here,' Jo remarked.

I was horrified. 'October?' I couldn't believe it. We'd been away four whole months . . . Mum would be crazy with worry by now . . .

'Stop panicking. It won't be October at home, will it? Different world, different time, remember.'

The chilly air was a nasty shock to the system. We were all shivering, in spite of our warm clothes. Half an hour into the journey, Margaret began to sneeze.

'I don't believe it! I've caught a cold!'

'You must have been incubating it the whole time we were at Magnus's. We'll all go down with it now.'

'Thanks very much,' she said sourly, and buried her nose in her handkerchief preparatory to another massive sneeze.

We rode on in silence. Nobody felt like talking. My own thoughts got gloomier and more panicky as the day wore on. I did my best to snap out of my despondency – it was a lovely, sparkling day and the wooded countryside was a dusky blaze of autumn colours – but the prospect of going back to Birtles Road seemed to smother everything with the grey sludge of despair. I'd tried running away; I'd tried being someone else, somebody with a *future* . . . and it hadn't worked out. I was still me. I'd failed, as signally as Ferdinand had.

More so, in fact. Ferdinand hadn't made a fool of himself. All those vivid little scenes I'd created in my hopeful imagination flashed back one by one and made me want to curl up and die of embarrassment. Me, the star of the show, being adored by an eager populace . . . Strolling along streets lined with enthusiastic flag-wavers . . . opening charity bazaars . . . being charming to disaster victims . . . wearing gorgeous clothes . . . making love with Ferdinand . . . I winced and cringed as each stupid little fantasy replayed itself on my internal viewscreen.

By the time we reached Garnock, dusk had fallen, and hundreds of twinkling lights from ships and boats were reflected in the waters of the harbour. It was a busy little town, its lamplit streets still crowded with shoppers. Carriages rumbled past on the main roads and there were quite a number of parties like ourselves on horseback.

Ferdinand was in the lead, and looking imperiously around

for someone he could bully into giving us directions, when a group of well-dressed young horsemen cantered out of a side-street. The leader reined in abruptly.

'Ferdy? Good God, what brings you here?'

Ferdinand halted and stared. 'Rupert! Well, I'll be damned!' They leaned across and buffeted each other on the shoulder. 'I could ask you the same question, you old ruffian! Why aren't you in Boronia?'

The young man he'd called Rupert shrugged and laughed. 'Teeny bit of trouble at home, old chap. Thought it best to make a discreet departure, know what I mean?'

Ferdinand's face was admiring. 'Gambling again? You'll go too far one of these days, you know.'

'Not me,' the young man said, his eyes glittering mischief. 'I always know when to run. Seriously, though, what *are* you doing here? Thought you were on some Quest or other.'

'I was,' Ferdinand said stiffly.

'Say no more, old chum. Mission accomplished, I gather.' His eyes scanned Margaret with open admiration. 'How about some introductions, eh?'

'Er . . . yes. Of course. Um . . .' I saw the flash of panic in Ferdinand's eyes, and so, I'm sure, did Rupert, because the smile he bestowed upon all three of us was suddenly avid with curiosity.

'Ah. Um. Lady Margaret . . . um . . . Walford,' Ferdinand said. As lies go, it was a creditable first attempt – but it was pretty clear he'd need a lot more practice if he intended to make a habit of it. 'Lady – er – Francesca D'Ewinnes, my – er – a cousin, and . . .' He glanced wildly at Jo, who was grinning openly. Inspiration made an abrupt departure. 'Mr Jo Morgan. A friend. Um . . . Lord Rupert Maskayne.'

'Delighted,' Lord Rupert murmured. 'Walford, eh? Related to the Glasston Walfords?'

'Oh, no,' Ferdinand said quickly. 'Inter-Zone, actually. I'm escorting them back home for a visit.'

'Charming, charming,' Lord Rupert said. His smile skated over me and hooked greedily onto Margaret again. 'Well, don't let me delay you . . . Where are you staying, by the way?'

Ferdinand told him. He nodded, smiled radiantly at us all, murmured polite farewells and rode away with his cronies.

'Friend of mine,' Ferdinand explained brightly. 'We were at school together.'

'Ah,' said Jo, raising his eyebrows. We rode on.

The inn was situated in a quiet street just off the town centre. It was large and looked clean and comfortable.

'Not bad,' Ferdinand announced resonantly as we trotted into the cobbled courtyard. 'Certainly a cut above the usual waterfront dive.'

'When were you last in a waterfront dive, Ferd?' I asked – but Ferdinand pretended not to hear.

We were expected. Grooms and porters erupted from all sides and scurried about to unload the cart and help us dismount. The manager himself appeared, bowing and grinning and rubbing his hands together in such a state of frenzy it was a wonder his palms didn't burst into flame. It was obvious that the Providence was busting a gut to give a good impression.

Between the courtyard and the reception desk Ferdinand's face acquired an expression I hadn't seen there for weeks: lofty, supercilious and faintly amused. His whole demeanour indicated that slumming it in a quaint little hovel like the Providence wasn't at all what he was used to, but given the right conditions (i.e. abject submission to his every whim on the part of the staff) it could be quite fun. Margaret, Jo and I followed meekly in his wake.

Margaret's cold had worsened during the day. Once the signing-in formalities were over she retired thankfully to her luxurious first-floor suite to nurse her sneezes in front of a blazing fire. The manager, gibbering with concern, promised to send up a selection of delicacies plus a hot posset to help vanquish the virus.

When I rejoined them Jo and Ferdinand were perusing the menu in Ferdinand's room.

'Nothing terribly enthralling, I'm afraid,' Ferdinand said. 'Personally, in view of the crowd downstairs, I'm inclined to pig it up here. Care to join me?'

'No thanks,' said Jo. 'Me, I feel like sharing a trough with the hoi polloi in the dining room, if you don't mind. How about you, Foss?'

'The dining-room,' I said, 'and now, this minute. My stomach's beginning to think I'm dead.'

'Okay,' Ferdinand said absently, still scanning the menu. 'See you later. Have fun.'

The dining-room was crowded. I couldn't see a single unoccupied

164

table. A waiter oozed up to us as we hesitated at the door. 'Your Ladyship? Sir? If you'd care to come this way . . . There's a private room at your disposal . . .'

My heart sank. 'Nothing personal, Jo – but if I have to eat in some ghastly mausoleum for two, I'll die. I'd rather join Ferdinand.' Eight hours of gloomy introspection had left me desperate for human company. Lots of it, the rowdier the better. 'What I'd *really* like,' I admitted, 'is a huge noisy party.'

Jo gave me a sympathetic grin. 'Take you out on the town after, if you like.'

I looked round in desperation, and spotted a table by the window where a thin, elderly gentleman with a kind face was sitting alone. Without giving myself time for second thoughts, I marched up to him, gave him a bright apologetic smile and said, 'Sorry to disturb you, but would you mind if we shared your table?'

He got up politely, and beamed a welcome.

'Not at all. Do sit down. It's terribly crowded in here tonight, isn't it?'

We settled down and introduced ourselves while the waiter took our order. Our companion's name was Mr Gilbert. He was on his way home after a business trip to the Southern Archipelago.

'Dangerous journey,' Jo commented, having spent a lot of time looking at maps of the Zones in Magnus's study.

Mr Gilbert nodded. 'Indeed, yes. But this time, I'm glad to say, the voyage was uneventful.'

'This time?'

He shrugged. 'My last venture South was fifteen years ago. It was a disaster. Three ships sank in a hurricane, and by the time I'd paid off the debts and tried to do something for the poor souls who'd lost husbands and fathers in the tragedy I was practically a pauper. I've had to start again from scratch. But,' he smiled suddenly, 'this last voyage has been more successful than I dared hope.'

I hadn't liked what I'd seen of Rupert Maskayne, but I found myself warming to Mr Gilbert.

His business was importing fine silks. 'But it's very much my second love. My real interest is antiques.'

'Really?' Jo's face lit up. 'We've just been staying with a friend whose house is full of them.'

I kicked him under the table to warn him not to get carried away. He glared, and kicked me back.

'A collector?' Mr Gilbert was intrigued. 'What's his main interest?'

A big hearty voice cut across the conversation. 'Mr Gilbert! Nice to see you again, sir. How are you?'

Mr Gilbert glanced up. 'Ralph Carter!' He stood up, and the two men shook hands heartily. 'Ralph's an old friend,' he explained, his thin face flushed with pleasure, 'and the best waggoner this side of Lindrock.'

The carter beamed. 'How's the family these days? How's my Ariana, eh?'

'Fine, thank you. Fine.'

'Didn't bring her with you on this trip, then?'

'No . . . it was a long voyage. Too dangerous.'

The carter nodded cheerfully to Jo and me. 'Lovely girl, Ariana,' he informed us, clapping a gigantic hand on Mr Gilbert's frail shoulder. Mr Gilbert winced, but bore up well. 'M'wife thinks the world of her. The kids, too. See you again, Mr Gilbert. Keep in touch, hey?'

He breezed away, and Mr Gilbert sat down again, looking pleased and embarrassed.

'Nice chap,' said Jo.

'A good man,' Mr Gilbert said. 'Kindness itself.'

'Ariana . . . is that your daughter?' I asked.

His face softened into a warm smile. 'Yes. My youngest. I have three – Katherine, Damaris – and Ariana.' He gave an embarrassed laugh. 'The other two are married now, but they were always a bit – well – scatterbrained. Ariana's always been the one I could rely on. My wife died some years ago,' he explained, 'shortly after my business failed. Ariana kept us all going.'

As he went on talking a picture began to emerge of a quiet, intelligent girl who had the strength of character to become the supportive one of a family stunned by a double tragedy. The one who got a job; the one who stayed cheerful, who chopped wood and mended leaky roofs and made the housekeeping stretch on a tiny budget.

'How old is she?'

'Twenty-eight now. Pretty, too. The success of this voyage will be a godsend to her. Perhaps now she can start enjoying life as a young woman should.'

Jo's foot was prodding mine under the table. I glanced across at him. He was making the most hideous faces at me while pretending to study the dessert menu.

'Something wrong, Jo?' I asked sweetly.

'No, no,' he said, 'Just deciding, that's all.' And took his revenge by aiming another swift kick at my shin. By the end of the meal I'd be black and blue from knee to ankle.

'Now,' said Mr Gilbert, when the dessert debris was being cleared away, 'You must let me buy you coffee in the lounge.'

I opened my mouth to refuse, but Jo got in first. 'Thank you very much. We'd like that.'

Mr Gilbert moved away to talk to the head waiter. I turned on Jo.

'You didn't have to kick so bloody *hard*, did you? Anyway, I thought we were going out on the town!'

Jo's face was alight. 'She sounds ideal! Just what old Magnus has been looking for all these years!'

I stared at him. 'You're joking!'

'No, I'm not. It's perfect. And he's an antiques buff, too.'

'Hang on a minute. How are you going to explain to Mr Gilbert that we want his daughter to meet an eight-hundred-year-old monster with a view to marriage? Jo – you're crazy.'

'No need to tell him anything. Just suggest that he drops in on Magnus on the way home – to talk antiques with him and so on . . . Oh – and you'd better ask him if his heart's okay first.'

'Me? Why me?'

Mr Gilbert was beckoning at us from the doorway. Jo began to follow him into the lounge.

'Jo! We've got to talk about this! Jo . . .'

He'd gone. I stood there fuming, and became aware of glances being cast my way from neighbouring tables. I pulled myself together in a hurry and tried to make a calm, dignified exit. I was succeeding pretty well when my eye was caught by a young woman a few years older than me, sitting near the door. She was staring at me with a look of sheer horrified astonishment on her face.

I stared back in a similar state of shock. Two things struck me like successive thunderbolts. One: we were so alike we could have been sisters – frizz, Pekingese dish-faces, the lot. Two: she was wearing an identical pendant to mine at her throat. And both pendants suddenly flashed brightly at each other for a moment as if saying hello.

I saw her go white, and clutch the pendant. She leant across the table, said something to her companion and got up.

Outside in the foyer we stopped and looked at one another. She had much redder hair than mine, and no glasses.

'I must be dreaming,' she said.

'If you're dreaming, then I am too,' I said nervously.

'The pendant . . . I hardly ever wear mine . . . and suddenly it started to *glow*.'

The glow had faded, but I was still aware of an excited tingling sensation in the hollow of my throat.

People were beginning to file into the foyer, heading for the coffee-lounge.

'Powder-room,' she said, and led the way with a quick, determined stride.

The powder-room was empty. She faced me, bracing herself against the make-up bench. 'Who *are* you?'

'I'm Foss Ewins,' I said. 'Who are *you*?'

She ignored the question. 'Where did you get your pendant?'

'My father gave it to me. It belonged to my great-grandmother Matilda.'

'Sheesh,' she said, still in shock. 'You know where mine came from? My mother gave it to me. It belonged to her grandmother – Matilda.'

I couldn't take it in. 'We . . . we're *related*?'

'It looks like it. But I don't see how!'

I grinned shakily. 'Me neither.' Garnock was certainly living up to its reputation as a place where you met people.

Her face hardened. 'Have you come from Arborea?'

'No! I'm not from this Zone at all. I got here by accident, and now I'm on my way home.'

'Home? Where's that?'

I tried to explain. She cut me short. 'Yes, yes. The Inaccessible Zone.'

Her hostility was getting up my nose. 'Look, I'm sorry if I gave you a shock. You don't want to know me, and that's fine. Let's leave it at that.'

She looked panic-stricken. 'No, no, it's not that.' She bit her lip and ran a distracted hand through her hair. 'You just . . . spooked me so much. Especially the pendant . . .' She gave a weak laugh. 'I wish I could talk to you, I really do. It's like meeting a sister . . . I just daren't.'

168

'Daren't? What d'you mean?'

'Because . . .' Suddenly the words poured out of her in a rush. 'Look, I've got a life of my own now, and it's a good one. I'm going to marry Francis, and next year I'm going to get my PhD. Oh, I know my research project's nothing special, it's not like finding a cure for cancer or anything – but it's important to *me*. I can't stop thinking about it. It makes me wake up in the morning and rush down to the lab and rant and rave and tear out chunks of hair. It makes me *happy*! And I am *not* going to give up all that to be turned into a *puppet* with somebody else pulling the strings!'

Laughter and chatter suddenly swelled as somebody opened the outer door. She caught herself up and looked round swiftly.

'Do yourself a favour. Keep away from Arborea. It's dangerous.'

'But . . .'

'Just go straight home and forget you ever saw me, okay?' She ran out just as a crowd of women entered in a gust of conflicting perfumes.

When I got out into the foyer she was paying her bill at reception. The man she was with was just emerging from the dining-room. He was young and dark and nice-looking, but there was something wrong with his spine – he was shuffling along on two sticks. He glanced from her to me in concern. 'Tilda?' he said. 'What's going on? Is something wrong?'

She gave him a brief, tense smile. 'Sorry, Francis. It's okay. Let's go.'

As they went out I heard the doorman say, 'Good-night, Miss Devine.'

I was still thinking about her as I sipped my coffee in the lounge. Tilda . . . Matilda. Ewins, D'Ewinnes, Devine . . . I'd just met a girl who looked like me, had almost the same name as me – and who'd fled from me like a hunted hare . . . Why?

'Foss?' Jo was nudging me. 'Wasn't there something you wanted to mention to Mr Gilbert?'

I glanced up to find them both looking at me – Jo with exasperation, Mr Gilbert with puzzled politeness. I dragged my wandering wits back to where they belonged.

'What? Oh, yes. Um.' Mercifully, recollection dawned. 'Yes. It's just that our collector friend lives a day's ride from here, on the Lindrock road. I'm sure he'd be delighted if you were to call in. Especially as you share the same interests.'

'Oh, really, I couldn't impose . . .' Mr Gilbert said – but I could tell from his tone that he was tempted. 'Unless, of course, he happens to be interested in a couple of rather fine pieces I happened to pick up the other day . . .'

'Why don't you write Magnus a note, Foss? You know, kind of an introduction.' Jo collared a waiter and asked for notepaper and a pen.

I scribbled a brief line or two, feeling every kind of a fool. 'Magnus – Mr Gilbert is an expert on antiques. He also has a daughter. She sounds perfect. Don't be shy. Give it your best shot. Love, Foss.'

My conscience was needling me. 'I should tell you – he's . . . well, a bit strange. But he's a lovely person, very kind. Just don't be alarmed, that's all.'

Mr Gilbert pocketed the sealed envelope. 'It really is most kind of you.' He leaned back in his chair and smiled at us both. 'The thing is, a good friend of mine has invited me to a party tonight, to celebrate his son's eighteenth birthday. I gather the young people have organised their own – er – thrash, as I believe you call it: bands, and so on. Of course, old fogies like myself will be banished to another room . . . But if you'd care to come along . . .'

We got back to the inn at three in the morning. We said good-night to a yawning Mr Gilbert in the deserted, darkened lobby and danced all the way upstairs. At least, I danced, while Jo stomped along humming a Zone chart-topper and radiating satisfaction.

'Great band, that. How did that last number go again? Ba-ba-ba-di-dah . . .'

'Ba-ba-dah, ba-ba-da-ba-dah,' I carolled, secure in the knowledge that the walls were thick and nobody else was occupying the first floor suites except us. 'Out of my life, baybee . . .'

We were passing Ferdinand's door at this point. It was wrenched open rather suddenly and with considerable force. Ferdinand himself stood revealed in the aperture. He was wearing a purple brocade dressing-gown. His hair was rumpled, his eyes glassy and his expression that of a Senior Prefect with a hangover.

'Cave, chaps, it's the Beak,' murmured Jo. We lurched to a stop.

'For Heaven's sake,' Ferdinand snapped. 'D'you realise what time it is? Why are you making this bloody awful row?'

'Great party, Ferd,' I chirped. 'You should have been there.'

'Sorry, sor,' Jo said, tugging his forelock. 'Didn't know you were asleep, sor. Won't do it again, sor. Scout's honour, sor.'

Ferdinand froze visibly. 'Very funny. I sincerely hope you don't intend to behave like this for the duration of our visit to Garnock. Consider my position even if you have no respect for your own. A little dignity might be in order, don't you think?'

'Ferd . . .' I said.

'And *don't call me Ferd!*' he snapped, and shut the door decisively in our faces.

'How old is that man?' Jo mused. 'Hasn't he ever partied?'

'Of course he has. He's jealous, that's all. Missing out.'

When we got down to breakfast the following morning we learnt that Ferdinand had gone out at some ungodly hour to join Rupert Maskayne at a hunt on one of the local estates. Margaret looked stricken, and I was angry on her behalf.

'Typical,' I fumed. 'Our last day, too.'

Margaret's cold had subsided to a sniffle, so we spent the day exploring Garnock. To take her mind off Ferdinand I introduced her to the concept of window-shopping. It worked like a dream. We bought each other presents – a bit tearfully – and I found a few things to take home for Mum and Bridgie and Geraint.

By seven that evening Ferdinand still hadn't returned. He'd left a message to say that he was dining with Lord Rupert, and that we weren't to wait up.

He got back almost as late as Jo and I had the previous night. We hadn't waited up, so his condition when he appeared at breakfast next morning was a bit of a shock. He was glassy-eyed, and his face was the colour of cheese.

'Can't understand it,' he mumbled. 'Only had a glass or two of wine. I feel as though I've been on a week's continuous binge.'

'Perhaps you're coming down with my cold,' Margaret suggested.

'God, I hope not,' Ferdinand groaned, and leaned his head in his hands. 'When does the ship sail?'

'Ten-thirty,' said Jo. Ferdinand groaned again.

We rode down to the wharf to see him safely aboard. He'd recovered enough to sit his horse with some approximation of

171

his usual panache though he did wince noticeably every time we broke into a trot.

The streets leading to the waterfront were narrow and cobbled. At the end of the last meandering lane there was an archway through which we could see moored ships and bustling activity on the wharf.

The view was suddenly blocked. A dozen large men rode under the arch and reined in to surround us.

'Wha'? What's going on?' Ferdinand demanded muzzily, one hand groping clumsily for the hilt of his sword.

Lord Rupert rode out of the throng to confront us.

'Sorry about this, old chap,' he said pleasantly. 'Nothing personal, you understand. It's just that I'm about to take charge of that charming package of yours. Get the two ladies, will you?' he added over his shoulder.

Freeze-frame erupted into mayhem. As the men rushed us I caught fractured images of Jo being sideswiped by a cudgel and tumbling off his rearing horse; of Ferdinand's mouth open, yelling 'No!' before a large and competent fist slugged him in the jaw. Shouts echoed off the high walls and the cobbles rang with the clatter of hooves and the squeals of frightened horses. I slashed my whip across the face of one would-be captor, jabbed my elbow into the midriff of a second and left a set of tooth-marks in the arm of a third. Beside me Margaret was struggling in the oaken embrace of a bloke built like a Sumo wrestler. Next moment I too was grabbed from behind and immobilised.

The whole thing was over in less than a minute.

'Spirited,' Lord Rupert remarked, eyeing me appreciatively. He turned to Margaret. 'However, Your Highness, if you wish your companions to remain relatively unscathed, you would be wise to desist from any further struggles.'

Margaret gaped at him. 'Your Highness? B—but I'm not . . . You think I'm Ferdinand's princess? That's crazy!'

'Perhaps I didn't make myself clear,' Lord Rupert said apologetically. 'You will accompany me on board my ship, Your Highness, with every appearance of complaisance. One false move, however, and Ferdy here gets his throat cut.'

13.

Your Stars: CANCER (June 22–July 23)
Saturn has moved out of your sign and all those frustrating
restrictions have finally lifted. Now is the time to embark
on a new road to success. Romance comes your way
from an unexpected direction.

They bundled Jo back on his horse, released their stranglehold
on Margaret and me, and conducted us in procession onto the
wharf, with Margaret and Lord Rupert in the lead. Jo had a cut
on his forehead and was swearing sulphurously under his
breath. Further down the line Ferdinand was being guarded by
a cluster of armed men one of whom was holding an unsheathed
dagger just under Ferdinand's chin. There was nothing we could
do except play along and see where it led us.

We rode down the waterfront to where a lean black vessel
was moored against the wharf. We dismounted in silence. The
horses were led away and the four of us were urged aboard. It
was done politely enough, and no-one watching from a distance
would have noticed the knife-points pricking our spines. One
way of achieving perfect posture, I thought. Slump for one
second and you're dead.

Once aboard, Margaret and I were hustled into a small cabin
and the door locked behind us. Very soon the boat began to
move. We were being towed out into the channel. We heard the
thump and creak of spars being hoisted, and finally the flapping
thunder of sails. The boat heeled and shuddered and shot smoothly
forwards.

Margaret was still in shock. 'He wouldn't *listen!* He's kidnapped us for nothing!'

An hour or so later the door was unlocked and two huge
guards frogmarched Margaret and me into a luxurious saloon
where a table was set for lunch. Lord Rupert, Ferdinand and Jo
were already there. Ferdinand was sulkily applying a wet cloth
to a black eye, and beneath his bloodstained bandage Jo's face
was white and furious.

'I'm not a princess of any kind!' Margaret said angrily as she
walked in. 'Neither is Foss! You've made a huge mistake!'

'She's right,' Ferdinand said, moving his swollen jaw with some difficulty. 'She's not Princess Aurora. Neither of them is Princess Aurora.'

Lord Rupert tutted a bit. 'Really,' he said mildly, 'You'll have to do better than that, you know. I do hope we're all going to be civilised about this.'

'Where are you taking us?' said Jo. 'Arborea?'

He smiled. 'Oh, no. I've had a far more lucrative offer. Duke Thorbert of Marant, to be precise. The present Queen's brother.'

Ferdinand went crimson. 'You *bastard*! He's old enough to be her father!'

'No concern of mine, old chap,' Lord Rupert said with a shrug. 'Business is business. The Duke's an impatient man. A legitimate claim to the Arborean throne is what he's after, and that's what I intend to supply. For a price, of course.'

'Her *uncle*?' I was outraged.

'Good Heavens, no. A collateral branch, I understand – but I'm sure Her Highness will enlighten you.'

'I've no idea what you're talking about,' Margaret said icily.

Ferdinand seemed to be having trouble breathing. He said through clenched teeth, 'Why bother? Why not claim the prize yourself?'

Lord Rupert laughed out loud. 'Do I detect sour grapes, Ferdy? Oh, dear. But don't fret, old chap – I do have a moral code, you know, of sorts. I never renege on business agreements – provided they're lucrative enough . . . Besides,' he added thoughtfully, 'Personally – and do forgive me, Your Highness' – with a little bow in Margaret's direction – 'I've never been attracted to tall blondes. Decorative, yes – but a little too obvious, I always think.' He smiled across to where I was sitting. 'This fiery little red-headed cousin of yours is far more to my taste.'

I dropped my fork. Three pairs of eyes swivelled abruptly in my direction and three shocked faces glared at me. I could feel myself going scarlet.

'Stop staring at me! He's winding us up, that's all. He doesn't mean it!'

'Oh, I do, I do.' His air of injured innocence wouldn't have fooled a baby. His smile broadened. 'And we have a whole voyage in which to get acquainted.'

'If ever I get out of this, Rupert, I'll personally wring your bloody neck,' Ferdinand promised.

'Don't be sour, dear boy. Just think of this as the last little adventure in that boring Quest of yours which you described to me in such tedious detail yesterday evening after I'd drugged your wine . . . You've lost, Ferdy. Might as well be gracious about it.'

Margaret's indignation was escalating by the second. As we were conducted back to our cabin she was revving up through the gears. By the time we reached the door she was at full throttle and well up the fast lane to fury. Even our guards looked apprehensive.

'He's barking mad! Totally out of his *tree*! Doesn't he ever *listen*?' Our escort shut us in with every sign of relief.

'That Duke's not going to take Lord Rupert's word for it, is he? He'll want proof! Birth certificates, pictures, a family tree . . . He might as well cut our throats and be done with it!'

I let her rant on. She was going ballistic for both of us, and I wanted to think.

I heard myself saying, 'So there really is a Lost Princess after all!'

'If he thinks he can get away with . . . What? Of *course* there bloody is! What d'you think Rupert kidnapped us for?'

'I know, I know . . . I suppose I never actually *believed* it before, that's all.' And I hadn't – not deep down. The story according to Ferdinand had been too simple, too corny – too *romantic* to be anything but a fairytale. Jo had been right. However deeply buried under layers of wishful thinking and brainwashing, the core of common sense inside me had told me that in the real world princesses do not get lost. It was different for Ferdinand, whose grasp of reality had never been very secure. I was beginning to suspect that for Ferdinand, aristocrat and romanceaholic, reality had always been somebody else's problem.

But Rupert Maskayne was no fool. Cold-blooded, unprincipled, self-serving, double-dealing – yes, all of those (and also quite disturbingly attractive, a sly traitor thought added). Gullible, no. There *was* a lost heir to the Arborean throne – and it wasn't the present King's daughter (and where had Ferdinand got *that* idea from, I wondered. Another old crone? It would be just like him to rush off without making any enquiries first).

This wasn't make-believe. This was politics: real, nasty and dangerous. Lord Rupert wouldn't be the only fortune-hunter eager to get his hands on her.

175

Margaret had given up on me in disgust. She'd climbed onto the table and was thumping the ceiling. 'Ouch! That was *solid*!'

'What are you *doing*?'

'Trying to get out of here, what d'you think?'

The door was a two-inch thick slab of teak. The cabin was below the waterline. Every stick of furniture was bolted to the floor. I watched her efforts to break a chair.

'How far can you swim?' I said.

'What?'

'I don't know a lot about boats, but this one's *fast*. We're well out to sea now. Breaking out of this cabin's not going to solve anything. If you were planning on flattening the whole crew with a chairleg and sailing her yourself, think again.'

The days passed. The ship sailed on. To my intense relief we saw very little of Rupert. He seemed preoccupied, and didn't follow up his promise to get better acquainted with me. I'd never met a man like him before. He scared me and attracted me at the same time, and I knew that if he ever got round to making a pass at me I'd make a fool of myself. I was simply too green to handle the situation.

By the fifth day indignation had faded into apathy, at least on the surface. I was conscious of a thin cold sliver of panic deep in my guts. My stupid Princess fantasy had come home to roost, and we were living out the consequences in a world that was chillingly real. I tried not to think about what might happen when we reached Marant.

Sometime during the afternoon of the sixth day we heard shouts on deck and the noise of thudding feet over our heads. The ship heeled sharply. A few minutes later there was a distant explosion and then a loud splash which rocked the hull. Margaret and I exchanged startled glances and sprang to our feet.

'We're being attacked!'

There was another explosion, right overhead: the crew were firing back. Something hit the deck very hard, with a crunch and a splintering noise.

It was hard to judge how fast we were moving, but from the vibration it seemed that the ship was flying along, every square inch of canvas stretched to the utmost. There was another explosion from a different direction – and then a loud thud to one side. The ship slewed and staggered, throwing Margaret and me across the cabin.

'*Pirates?*'

Guns went on firing. The chase continued. Finally, the ship rammed against something, sending the two of us tumbling. There was the sound of heavy booted feet on deck, a cacophony of shouts and the clash of drawn swords. We'd been boarded.

At last the sounds of fighting died down. There was an uneasy silence. The ship rocked gently and settled to one side. We could hear sloshing noises in the bilges below us.

Margaret turned a white solemn face to mine. 'We're sinking.'

I sat down rather hard on the bunk. Sinking? How long would we survive once the water started rising? How long did it take to drown? Somehow the thought of drowning in this small cabin without ever seeing daylight again was worse than anything I'd ever imagined before.

A key turned in the lock. Margaret and I jumped to our feet. The door opened and a tall white-haired man in black robes stood on the threshold. He was wearing a kind of mayoral chain round his neck and didn't look in the least like a military man.

'Your ladyship. Your Highness. Thank God you're safe.'

'But I'm *not* . . .' Margaret began. He hushed her with one hand raised.

'Follow me, please. This ship is sinking fast, but my vessel is alongside.'

'Where are you taking us?'

I wasn't particularly surprised when he said 'Arborea'. How many people had told me recently that Arborea, and everything connected with the place, was bad news?

Jo and Ferdinand were both aboard the Arborean ship. We all hugged each other in sheer delighted relief.

'God, we were worried,' Jo said. 'And when those damn cannons started firing . . .'

'I thought we'd sink,' I said, and was surprised at the wobble in my voice.

'Well, we're on our way to Arborea now,' Ferdinand said with satisfaction. 'I've explained the situation to Lord Falcon' – Jo winked at me and grinned – 'and I'm sure there won't be any more misunderstandings.'

We reached the island of Arborea at sunset the following day. From the ship's rail I could see a stretch of mountainous coast-line like a grey cardboard cutout against the afterglow in the

177

sky. The city was a mass of twinkling lights at the end of a long inlet.

Our ship didn't dock at the city wharves. Instead, the fleet of tugboats rowed us into another, smaller inlet. By now it was almost dark. There were buildings on the foreshore but no lights anywhere. The whole place looked bleak, deserted and severely unfriendly.

'Naval dockyard, I expect,' said Ferdinand airily.

On the wharf, a carriage was waiting: plain, shabby, undistinguished by any crest or markings. Ferdinand's eyebrows twitched in haughty surprise as we were ushered up the steps; he'd obviously expected a slightly more prestigious conveyance, more in keeping with royalty. There was no sign of Lord Falcon.

Our military escort had barely shut the door on us when the carriage gave a violent lurch forwards, throwing us against each other and almost knocking my glasses off. We groped frantically for the straps attached to the roof and hung on to them while the horses achieved a breakneck gallop.

'Incredible!' Ferdinand gasped, bracing himself against both seats to avoid being thrown again, 'They looked like nags!'

It was a horribly uncomfortable journey. How the horses kept up that speed I have no idea – but they did, for several miles. The carriage bounced and rocked violently from side to side. The single lamp suspended from the roof swung wildly to and fro but somehow, against all the odds, it kept itself alight.

At last, the horses slowed to a sedate trot. Thankfully, we relaxed our grip on the straps and massaged numb fingers.

'Thirty-mile limit?' Jo said with a grin, and rubbed the steamed-up window with his sleeve. He peered through and I saw his smile vanish.

'Try it your side, Ferd.'

Puzzled, Ferdinand did so, and gave a hiss of disbelief. 'The windows are shuttered. I can't see a thing.'

He tried the door handle, but it was locked. So was the other one. By the dim greenish light of the now steady lamp four seriously worried faces stared at one another.

'If ever I saw a Black Maria,' Jo said, 'this is it.'

The word going through my mind was 'tumbril'. I kept it to myself. I had a feeling that sharing it was probably a bad idea.

Eventually the carriage drew to a stop. The door opened and the steps were let down. We were in a small, dimly lit courtyard with a single door standing open at the far end. As we emerged, a posse was waiting to attention: a dozen or so very solid guards with the blank faces of those who are paid to react very fast and not let thinking get in the way.

Ferdinand sprang out of the carriage and strode amongst the soldiery.

'Is this the way the Arbor Palace treats its guests? I am Prince Ferdinand of Boronia. I demand to see His Majesty immediately!'

'All in good time, your Highness.' Lord Falcon had appeared in the doorway. He bowed pleasantly to each of us in turn. 'His Majesty asks me to apologise for any inconvenience you may have suffered during the journey. All I'm authorised to say at present is that we had – and will continue to have – your best interests at heart.'

'In your own best interests' ranks with 'for your own good' as one of the most duplicitous phrases ever to emerge from the human larynx. The last person to tell me he had my best interests at heart had been Scott after a particularly obnoxious row in which he'd axed me a fortnight's pocket money. If Lord Falcon meant to reassure us, he wasn't making a very good job of it as far as I was concerned.

Ferdinand opened his mouth to retort, but Lord Falcon stopped him with one calmly upraised hand. 'No questions, please. This way.'

He led us into a narrow passageway carpeted in very old, worn coconut matting. A large woman with a vast seamless bosom was waiting for us in the hall. Her face was fat and well-supplied with chins but the features crowded together in the middle were sharp and mean and disagreeable. Her grey hair was arranged in stiff corkscrew ringlets poking out from under her mob-cap. She was carrying a lamp.

'Mrs Grice,' Lord Falcon announced. 'Lady Francesca, Lady Margaret.'

She bobbed a curtsey, like a decorous whale, and the ringlets bounced like springs. 'This way please, m'Lady, m'Lady.'

Margaret and I followed meekly in her wake. Two guards fell into step behind us. I looked back. Jo and Ferdinand were proceeding down a different corridor behind Lord Falcon, more guards trailing in the rear. Jo cast me a glance which was every bit as piteously bewildered as my own.

We walked down one dark, deserted corridor after another, meeting no-one, hearing nothing except the sounds of our own feet. I lost my sense of direction completely. The huge round figure of Mrs Grice with its bouncing ringlets went plodding on in front of us like a gigantic toy with inexhaustible batteries. The lamp she carried bobbed up and down and her vast shadow bobbed alongside.

By the time we reached our destination I was asleep on my feet. I was dimly aware of firelight, of concerned voices and of being womanhandled into a warm bed.

When I woke up it was late afternoon. Dusty bands of sunshine were bisecting the bedroom and making the fire look wan. My head felt muzzy and when I sat up everything spun.

Margaret was sitting at the window with a book on her lap. She looked up. 'How're you feeling? Better now?'

'I've been ill?'

'You had a nightmare, that's all. Some sort of panic attack. Mrs Grice gave you something to calm you down.'

'I don't remember a thing.' I could still feel the panic, though, buried deep down inside but fighting its way up through the dissipating clouds of sedative. Recollections of last night surfaced in a rush: armed guards, Jo and Ferdinand being marched away . . . 'Where are we? Where are Jo and Ferdinand?'

'Foss, it's all right. Everybody's being very kind . . .'

'When are we getting out of this place?'

'Soon,' she said. I'd found my clothes and was pulling them on. 'Um . . . Foss, I don't think you'd better . . .'

I rummaged under the bed for shoes. 'Who's in charge round here?'

'You'll have to ask the guards, Foss . . .'

'*Guards?*'

Somebody knocked on the outer door. Margaret jumped up with every sign of relief and ran into the adjoining sitting-room. I heard her say, 'Come in,' and then Ferdinand's voice saying in hushed tones, 'Hi. How is she?'

'I'm fine,' I called. I finished doing up my dress and marched out to join them.

'So what's the message, Ferd? We're prisoners, yes? Being held on a charge of impersonating the lost Princess, am I right?'

'Of course not!'

'Where's your little pal Rupert? What's he being charged with? Kidnapping, extortion, GBH?'

Ferdinand looked away. I saw him swallow hard. 'Actually . . . he's – er – on his way to Boronia. Under armed escort . . .'

'He's been extradited?'

'Not – exactly, no . . . It's the family, you see . . . they're quite –
well – influential and . . .'

'I see. So Margaret and I get the chop in his place, right? One
law for the plebs and another for the aristocracy. You people
make me sick!'

One thing I will say for Ferdinand, he's a much more satis-
factory person to quarrel with than Margaret. Fuses blew instantly,
as I'd known they would.

'Don't be so bloody stupid, woman! You've got it the wrong
way round. . . .'

'So why the Black Maria? Why have we been locked up in
this place, miles away from anywhere? Why the guards?'

'You're not locked up! The guards are there for your own
protection!'

'Because if I'm going to be executed I'd rather be told now . . .'

'Don't talk such absolute bosh! You're *not* a prisoner!'

'. . . rather than have it sprung on me when they arrive with
the axe,' I yelled.

Ferdinand was hopping up and down with frustration. 'If
you'll just SHUT UP for ten seconds!' he shouted, fortissimo.

'Okay, okay!'

There was a brief pause in hostilities. We glared at one
another.

'Right, then,' he said.

'It'd better be good, mind.'

'Shut up!'

Silence fell. Somewhere, a pin dropped.

'Right, then.' He gulped, and braced himself. 'You've got the
whole thing back to front. I've been talking to Lord Falcon. I – er
– I seem to have made a mistake originally. The missing heir is –
um – a distant relative. And . . . It's quite possible that you're
the real princess after all.'

My knees gave way. I backed away from him and sat down
rather suddenly on the nearest chair. 'Me? Don't be ridiculous!
That's the craziest thing I ever heard!'

'I'm . . . I'm sorry, Foss.'

The look of anguish on Margaret's face cut me to the heart. I
jumped up. 'I've got to talk to somebody. The King, Lord Falcon
. . . This is way beyond a joke. This whole stupid mistake's got
to be cleared up. Now. '

Ferdinand moved to block off the door. 'There's another thing you should know, Foss. Queen Honoria the Queen Mother died yesterday morning.'

I was baffled. 'Yes? Well, I'm sorry, of course, but . . .'

'Just listen! As from yesterday, the Court's in mourning. Black gloves. No balls, no parties, no public engagements . . . They're very hot on the formalities here, believe me.'

I was a tad shocked. 'Ferdinand! Somebody dies and you talk about *parties*? Anyway, what's it got to do with us?'

He sighed noisily, and his face acquired the exasperated expression of a maths master trying to explain the basics of algebra to a more than usually dense class. Patiently, he said, 'What I'm trying to get through to you is that normal Palace business is suspended for the time being. On His Majesty's orders. Your case won't be discussed until after the official period of mourning.'

'Which is?'

'Um – three months, usually.'

I exploded. 'Three *months*? That settles it. Just go and order a ship or something . . .'

He had the grace to look ashamed. 'I'm sorry, Foss. You won't be allowed to leave.'

'Why not?'

Ferdinand stiffened. 'Kings aren't required to give reasons, Foss.'

'They are feeding us, I suppose. Not like the Aunts in Gormenghast.'

'Oh, for God's sake, Foss . . . You're guests. Incognito. Nobody saw us arrive. Nobody knows who you and Margaret are . . . Foss, *listen* to me! The whole situation is – well – extremely delicate. Um . . . it appears the King and the Queen are . . . separated. She's gone back to live with her brother, the Duke of Marant. There's a nasty political situation brewing. Even, possibly, a war. Rupert isn't the only person who'd kidnap you given half a chance. So in the meantime . . .'

I gave up. 'We're on ice. We don't officially exist.'

'Correct. For all our sakes, Foss, don't rock the boat. Just play along. Please.'

'Where's Jo?'

Ferdinand froze. 'Ah. He's . . . he's fine.'

'I see. He's done a bunk, has he?' I was in the mood to believe anything of anybody.

182

'Of course he hasn't. He's just . . .' Ferdinand gulped. 'Oh, rats. Actually, he's hired himself out to the head gardener.'

Margaret stared in amazement. 'Why, for Heaven's sake?'

'Don't blame me. His decision.'

I dashed into the bedroom and found a cloak. 'You'd better get us past those personal protectors of ours and take us there, Ferd. Now.'

We found Jo digging manure into an asparagus bed. He'd stripped to his shirt-sleeves and was filthy, sweating profusely and looking happier than he'd done for weeks. He straightened up as we approached, and braced himself on his spade, looking defiant.

'Jo . . . why?'

'I'm not abandoning you two, okay? I've been poking about, asking questions. There's something iffy going on and I want to find out what it is. I'm no good to you inside that mausoleum full of pillocks in fancy dress, but out here, picking up the gossip . . .'

'Yeah. I understand.'

The glare softened. 'I'll be here when you need me, okay?'

'That head gardener,' I said slyly, 'He's good, is he?'

Jo glowed. 'He's a bloody marvel.' And realised, too late, that he'd fallen straight into the trap. 'Okay, I admit it. Ulterior motive. But I'd be a complete berk not to take advantage of a chance like this, wouldn't I?'

We left him to his digging.

As we walked back to our quarters I got my first good look at the Arbor Palace in daylight. Admittedly, all we could see were the back regions, not the splendid public facade – but it was enough to make me realise that the place was immense, more like a small town than a single building. Wings, courtyards, gardens, towers, walkways – it covered acres.

Margaret was looking around with a frown. 'You know something? Half these buildings are empty. Some of them are almost falling down – look.'

'Can't get the staff these days, I suppose.'

'Or the whole system's shrunk for some reason.'

We said goodbye to Ferdinand and proceeded sedately to the isolated wing next to the kitchen block. Our two guards clumped along behind us.

Margaret bit her lip. 'I suppose . . . if you are Princess Aurora . . . you'll marry Ferdinand, won't you?'

'Mags, I don't *want* to marry Ferdinand! Anyway, I *know* who I am, and I'm not this damn princess. I can't imagine where they got that idea from in the first place. It's the silliest thing I've ever heard in my life, okay?'

The guards were a few paces behind us. I turned round. 'Can you take me to see Lord Falcon? Now?'

They shuffled their feet and looked embarassed. 'Um . . . Lord Falcon's office is in the main Palace block, m'Lady. You're not allowed in there. With respect, m'Lady.'

'What?' Margaret stared from one to the other. They went red. 'Why not, for Heaven's sake?'

'Um . . . we had orders, Ma'am. You and m'Lady are to be kept away from the main Palace. Nobody's to see you or speak to you, Ma'am. It's for your own protection, Ma'am, m'Lady,' he added, shrivelling a bit under Margaret's laser glare.

Keeping a tight hold on my temper in case of accidents, I said, 'Can you take him a message, then? I need to talk to him – urgently.'

When the messenger returned he told us that Lord Falcon was, unfortunately, unavailable.

Dinner was served in our apartment at six o'clock precisely. It was excellent, and even took our minds off our troubles for five minutes or so. Mrs Grice arrived in person to clear the plates. Her cold little gossip's eyes darted from Margaret to me and back again.

'I hope your Ladyships enjoyed your meal,' she said.

'It was delicious,' Margaret said warmly. 'Thank you so much.'

I stifled a grin. Without even trying, Margaret was easing her way into the battleship's good books. The woman's hard fat face almost simpered.

'Everything is to Your High . . . to your Ladyship's liking, I hope,' she said.

Margaret was slightly taken aback. 'Oh, yes. Thank you. '

The little eyes gleamed. 'I'm so glad. Anything Your High . . . your Ladyship requires, please don't hesitate to ask.'

We waited until we could hear her footsteps fading away into the distance; then we both burst out laughing.

'She knows something,' Margaret said. 'She's dying to ask us straight out who we are. Her nose was twitching like a rat's.'

'It's not me, though,' I giggled. 'It's you. You're the one she thinks is the princess.'

Margaret went quite pale. 'Me? Oh, no . . .'

Once I'd started laughing I couldn't stop. 'They've probably opened a book on us in the servants' hall. Wonder what the odds are? Maybe Jo could place a bet for us.'

'Oh, for Heaven's sake, Foss . . .'

'If we timed it right, we could clean up.'

'Foss, that's *disgusting*.'

I laughed even harder.

Later that evening, the minder on duty tapped on the sitting-room door.

'The gardener's lad who used to be your groom wants a word with you, m'Lady. Got a letter from your old nurse.'

'What?' I stared at him stupidly. Luckily, the penny dropped. 'Oh. Right. Show him in.' It was Jo.

Once the guard had withdrawn he didn't waste any time. 'Can't stay long, so *listen*, will you? Falcon can't talk to you himself so he asked me to fill you in. Arborea's on the verge of war with Marant. Both sides dusting off their armies and making threatening noises. That's why they're so desperate to find this missing princess of theirs. She's got to be found and married off to an good solid ally before war breaks out.'

'You're working for Lord Falcon?'

'Unofficially.' He grinned boyishly. 'Undercover, as it were. Told you I'd been asking questions, didn't I?'

My jaw dropped. Jo as a latter-day 007 didn't bear thinking about.

'So what's it got to do with us?'

'Thing is, the girl's some sort of distant relative. There aren't any spare heirs knocking around for the simple reason that every royal sprog but one for the last four generations has died in childhood.'

Margaret gasped. 'That's *awful*. What was it, some kind of inherited disease?'

'No. Genetics doesn't work like that.'

I went cold. 'Assassination?'

'It looks like it. Some organisation that doesn't mind waiting a hundred years or so to put their preferred candidate on the throne.'

'So why me? Why not Margaret?'

'I'm coming to that. Falcon knows who this princess is. Mother

185

married a commoner, apparently. His agents have kept tabs on the family. Trouble is, she's disappeared.'

Margaret stared. 'So if Foss had turned up as Princess Aurora with Ferdinand . . .'

'Falcon would've slung her out on her ear. The King's away playing with the fairies a lot of the time in my opinion, but Falcon's *keen*.' Jo paused, and looked puzzled. 'Funny thing, that. Round about the time you'd have arrived with Ferd, Foss – somebody tried to bump him off. Falcon, I mean. Interesting.'

'Okay, fascinating, but why me? It's not because I *was* Aurora, is it?'

'No. Falcon's afraid the princess's identity may have leaked out. Which means she could be in danger – and you, too, Foss. He wants to keep you safe until they locate the real heir.'

I was losing patience fast. 'Jo. Answer the question. *Why me?*'

'Because you look exactly like her.'

14.

Your Stars: CANCER (June 22–July 23)
What you need most just now is time to collect your
thoughts. As new career opportunities become available,
you're finally in a position to discover what you want
out of life, and who you really are.

The days pussyfooted past. Ferdinand didn't appear and we saw no more of Jo.

In the meantime, Margaret and I tried on the new clothes which kept appearing in our wardrobes (old-fashioned clothes with low necks and tight waists and long skirts, like the riding-habits we'd worn in Garnock), went for walks in the derelict courtyards with our two minders in constant attendance, and put in a lot of hard practice at looking out of the window.

At the end of a fortnight I was going stir-crazy. The fact that I alone knew who the Princess really was didn't help one bit.

All I had to do was open my mouth and blab. Once Lord Falcon knew what name she was using, where she lived and what she was doing with herself, Margaret, Jo and I would be on the next boat back to Garnock. But I couldn't bring myself to do it.

The day of Queen Honoria's funeral approached. From the scraps of gossip we gleaned from the servants we gathered that the Palace was rapidly filling up with visiting dignitaries from all over the Zones. Not that it made a blind bit of difference to us. Nothing and no-one disturbed the graveyard silence of our isolated wing.

One morning our breakfast arrived late. It was brought in by a frightened kitchenmaid who'd obviously borrowed a clean cap and apron several sizes too large specially for the occasion.

'Where's Mrs Sidgwick this morning?' Margaret asked. She knew everybody's name.

Mrs Sidgwick, it transpired, was down with flu. As were half the kitchen staff.

Margaret clucked sympathetically. 'I thought she wasn't looking well.'

'Yes'm. And Mrs Hodgson, that's the cook, Ma'am, she's that short-handed she don't know if she's coming or going, what with all them visitors and all.'

When the maid had gone I opened the outer door very cautiously and looked down the corridor. The guard on duty was helping her manoeuvre the loaded tray down the stairs at the end.

'See you later, Mags,' I whispered, and tiptoed down the nearer flight of steps which led to the courtyard. In a few minutes I was in the kitchen.

Mrs Hodgson received me with stony politeness. 'Yes, m'Lady?'

'You're short-handed,' I told her, 'And I can cook.'

She didn't believe me. 'I'm sorry, your Ladyship, but we are extremely busy just now.' Her face said a lot more, none of it encouraging. Any minute now she'd call in the heavy artillery i.e. Lord Falcon or the captain of the guard, and I'd be politely but firmly escorted back to my quarters.

I glanced rapidly round the kitchen. On a table near the window neat rectangles of pastry were lined up on a long marble slab, with a dish of softened butter and a rolling-pin alongside.

'Puff pastry?' I asked casually. She nodded.

'Okay.' I grabbed the spatula and started to slap the butter on the pastry. There was dead silence in the kitchen. People craned to get an uninterrupted view. I folded, dusted, rolled out, slapped on a second coat of butter. A faint sigh emanated from half a dozen open mouths at once.

I looked up. Mrs Hodgson was regarding me with one eyebrow slightly raised in approbation. 'You do know how.'

No 'Your Ladyship' this time. Simple approval, professional to apprentice.

At this point everybody suddenly remembered what they ought to be doing and began frantically to pretend they'd been doing it all along. Discreet hubbub broke out all over the kitchen.

I learnt more in that day than I'd have learnt in ten years of cooking with Bess. We were catering for two hundred and fifty people on the basis of four meals a day. This wasn't an easy-going potter at the pastry board – this was a military operation with Mrs Hodgson as the field marshal in charge of the troops. Having rashly joined up on the spur of the moment I was deployed ruthlessly wherever there was a breach in the assault. I've never worked so hard in my life. I made mountains of puff pastry. I made profiteroles. I made canapés. I chopped and whisked and sieved, I basted joints and filleted fish. By nine o'clock that evening I was trembling with exhaustion, and so was everybody else.

When Mrs Hodgson said, 'Shall we see you again tomorrow, m'Lady?' I felt as though she'd pinned a medal on my chest.

The next two days were practically a re-run except for one disconcerting incident on the third afternoon. Katie, the tweeny, came flying into the kitchen just as I was putting the finishing touches to a row of game pies under Mrs Hodgson's watchful eye.

'It's Lord Falcon, Mrs H! He's on his way down now! Lord Falcon!'

Mrs Hodgson clamped powerful hands on my shoulders, propelled me into the meat pantry and shut the door. A few moments later I heard booted feet stride into the kitchen, accompanied by the swish of long, heavy garments. I heard Lord Falcon say, 'Ah, Mrs Hodgson. A word, if you please . . .'

When he'd gone Mrs Hodgson unbent enough to give me a conspiratorial grimace. 'If he'd caught you here . . .'

After that I wasn't altogether surprised when she told me later in the day that she wouldn't require my help any more. The emergency was over anyway, the flu victims were beginning to report for active duty again and I was obviously a bit of an embarrassment. Meekly clutching a couple of borrowed cookery books, I went back to my prison in the tower.

November heaved itself up on its crutches and limped wearily into December. The weather turned wet and cold: too stormy to venture out, and so dark the lamps stayed lit all day. And still no word from Lord Falcon and the King about my missing double. No indications that they were going to let us go home.

I sat hunched up on the window-seat for hours on end and thought panicky thoughts about assassins and forced marriages and being forgotten. I saw visions of myself and Margaret aged ninety-three and covered with cobwebs like Miss Havisham in *Great Expectations*. The more I brooded, the tetchier I became.

What made things worse from my point of view was that Margaret seemed to be perfectly happy with the situation. The servants adored her and were always popping in for a chat. Grisly Grice was teaching her to embroider.

'I've got to get the shading right, you see, Foss. When I've finished this, Mrs Grice is going to show me petit-point and cut-work. Then I want to learn how to make lace on a frame, like Mrs Johnson does.'

Big deal, I thought sourly – and wondered how much of my bad temper was jealousy.

Things came to a head one bitterly cold afternoon. We'd had one heavy snowfall two days earlier, and now an icy wind was busily sweeping the landscape bare. I couldn't keep still. I twitched and paced and fumed.

'Why don't you read a book or something, Foss?' Even Margaret was running out of patience.

'The books we've got? You must be joking! How many times can you read *Little Blind Ursula* without throwing up?'

'All right, we'll play chess, then. Or Scrabble.'

Why is it that when you're thoroughly fed up with the world the last thing you want to have to deal with is reasonableness? I snarled and said something unprintable.

'What's the matter, is it PMT?'

'No, it's not! I'm not due for another two weeks, if you must know!'

'Okay. Get some wool from Mrs Johnson and knit yourself a cap or something.'

That did it. I *loathe* knitting.

'Don't be so bloody *patronising*!' I yelled. 'Just get on with that stupid cushion-cover of yours and leave me alone!'

'Actually,' she said, going red, 'It's quite hard to concentrate when the other person in the room is thumping around like a constipated elephant.'

'I'm going out,' I said, grabbing my cloak.

'But Foss, it's *raw* out there!'

I erupted. 'Look, stop fussing, will you? You're so bloody *womanly* these days, it makes me *sick*! It's like living with Polyanna!'

'*Who?*'

'Oh, forget it!' I screeched, and stormed out.

For once there were no guards on duty outside the door. They'd probably nipped into the kitchen for half an hour to get warm, and I didn't blame them. No-one in their right minds would have moved more than six inches from a fire that after-noon. I jammed a woolly hat down over my head, pulled the hood of my cloak up over my ears and marched out into the courtyard.

The wind was Arctic. Hard lumps of eroded snow lay scattered about on the empty flowerbeds like a dentist's nightmare. Yellow-grey clouds were rolling in from the north-east across a dead, slaty sky. You didn't have to be a weather expert to know that more snow was on its way.

As I came out of the shelter of the buildings into open park-land, the wind hit me with a vicious blast which rocked me on my feet and made my eyes water. Trees were tossing in the gale and rooks and jackdaws were hurling themselves across the sky like so many black rags torn off scarecrows.

For the first ten minutes or so sheer fury kept me warm. I walked on and on until my face was numb and my ears stinging. I began to think longingly of hot drinks and blazing fires – but I wasn't ready to face Margaret yet. None of this was her fault, I knew that. I just hadn't quite reached the point of being able to apologise.

Instead, I angled downhill and sought shelter in a large thicket of rhododendrons.

Rhododendrons are devious, deceitful creatures. In ducking and scrambling through them I lost my sense of direction and finally emerged into an immaculately manicured formal garden. I was trespassing in the inhabited part of the Palace.

Luckily no-one else was around. To my right was a narrow walkway between tall hedges. Shelter, I thought, and headed that way at a run.

Between the hedges it was quieter, almost warm. My frozen face began to thaw out. Another hedged path led off to the left, and ended abruptly in a small enclosed garden so still and quiet it was hard to believe that an icy gale was raging overhead. In the middle an almond tree was in full bloom. Crocuses and snowdrops were poking up out of the snow, and a winter-flowering viburnum made a fragrant arch over a little niche with a seat in it.

I don't know how long I sat there, chasing thoughts out into the open. I could see, now, why Tilda Devine hadn't wanted to claim her inheritance. *A puppet with somebody else pulling the strings,* she'd said. Wasn't that exactly what they were doing to me? *I've got a life of my own . . . my PhD . . . marry Francis . . .* A princess wouldn't be allowed to do any of those things. Jo had already told us what they had in store for her – an arranged marriage to a reliable ally. No choice in the matter. Never any choice. Being told what to do; having to be charming to people she despised; being a symbol all her life, never a person . . .

Tilda had been careful – she'd fled to Garnock, an obscure little port where Arborean ships never called; hidden herself away in a small, undistinguished provincial University with a thousand identikit scruffy students; changed her name . . . I hoped with all my heart she was being careful enough.

Footsteps were approaching along the main path. A man's booted feet – a tall man, judging from the length of the strides. I shrank back into the little niche under the viburnum arch and waited for him to continue past the junction.

He didn't. The footsteps paused, turned and started down the path leading to my hideout, and stopped. The intruder was Lord Falcon.

We stared at one another for a long moment. His austere face softened. 'Lady Francesca,' he said, 'What on earth are you doing out-of-doors on a day like this?'

'Walking,' I said defensively. 'I needed some fresh air. Rather urgently.'

He was gazing at me with an odd expression on his face: frowning and smiling at the same time. Suddenly he laughed, and flung both hands wide in a gesture of bafflement. 'It's incredible,' he said. 'Utterly astonishing.'

I began to feel a bit nettled. 'I'm sorry?'

'What you're seeing, my dear, is an old man experiencing déjà vu. This was her garden, you see. She used to sit here, in all weathers – just as you are doing now.'

'Who? Whose garden?'

The smile turned to a frown of concern. 'You're shivering. If you'll accompany me to my office, I'll explain.'

'Office?' I said, as we turned in to the main walkway.

'I'm His Majesty's Steward,' he said. 'I deal with the boring day-to-day administration of this archaic pile.'

'Doesn't sound boring to me,' I said. 'Try doing nothing in two rooms for a couple of months – then you'll know what boring is.'

His grin was unexpectedly sympathetic. 'Is that why you came out alone on such a foul afternoon?'

In spite of my suspicions, I began to warm to the man. Perhaps he wasn't as unreasonable as I'd imagined.

'I had a row with Margaret,' I explained. 'My fault, but I had to simmer down.' His chuckle reassured me even further.

Lord Falcon's office turned out to be a suite of big, well-lit rooms on the ground floor of the main Palace block. Huge fires were burning in the hearths – no Scrooges here. And no staff either.

'Saturday afternoon,' he explained. 'I like to catch up on paperwork at the weekends. Interrupted now and then,' he added, 'by a brisk walk to blow away the cobwebs.'

'You wouldn't happen to have a job going, would you?' I asked wistfully.

He gave me an odd look, but didn't comment. 'This way, m'Lady.'

We entered a much smaller office. He unlocked a big safe, and took out a flat object wrapped carefully in several layers of fabric. Having removed the coverings he laid the thing tenderly down on the table and stood back.

'Matilda, Duchess of Magdaria and Queen of Arborea,' he said.

It was a small portrait, not much bigger than Oz's mirror. The girl in the painting was about my age. She was wearing a low-necked sea-green velvet dress. She had curly reddish-brown hair, a wide smiling mouth and grey eyes. Round her neck was a pendant exactly like mine and Tilda's. The portrait was signed De Gas.

The room spun. I wasn't looking at a historical record. I was looking at the reflection I'd seen in Oz's mirror. I was looking at a picture of me.

Back in the main office I sipped hot chocolate in front of the fire and tried to pull my scattered wits together. 'Where – where does she fit in?'

'She was the princess's great-grandmother. She died eight years ago.'

'She must have been very old . . .'

'She was eighty-nine. The generations overlap more than you think.'

I was still in shock. 'But I'm not related to her. She wasn't *my* great-grandmother Matilda, how could she be? I don't even come from this Zone!'

He shrugged. 'The likeness is phenomenal. And you have the pendant.'

'But nobody else has recognised me! The servants all think Margaret's the Princess. They're running a book on it in the servants' hall.'

He grinned. 'I'm aware of that. But I have the advantage of age, a lifetime's close involvement with the Family, and a good long-term memory. Most people's memories are short, you see. They remember her as a terrifying, white-haired old lady, crippled with arthritis. This one small portrait was in a room no-one uses any more. On the night of your arrival I removed it and replaced it with another.'

I could see why. 'I know about the deaths,' I said, 'and the war with the Duke of Marant.'

'Yes.'

He settled back in his chair and explained. Matilda had been the first person to cotton on to the terrifying possibility that all those mysterious deaths were part of a pattern. When three of her five children died in the same way she got frantic.

'The Palace surrounded the Crown Prince and the Princess with the tightest security we could muster. But Matilda wasn't satisfied. She had a theory that magic was involved.' His face expressed distaste. 'I can't say I agreed with her, but . . . She arranged a fake accident, and smuggled her daughter out of Arborea, giving her the pendant which had been in her family for generations.'

'But you know about the real great-granddaughter. You *know* I'm not her.'

'Yes. You, my dear, are something of a mystery. There is one possibility, however. Matilda was betrothed to the future King Brandolph when they were both in their cradles. But when she was seventeen she ran away and married a commoner.'

Good for her, I thought. I was beginning to like this woman.

'The family were frantic, of course, but they were unable to trace her. Five years later she returned home. There had been an epidemic, she said, and her husband and daughter were both dead. She never referred to them again. All she would say was that she had been very happy. Brandolph still loved her and four years after that she married him.'

At twenty-two she'd lost the love of her life and everything she cared about. She'd picked up the pieces, done her duty to her family and carried on. I felt humbled.

'So you think the daughter survived? That Matilda left her

194

with grandparents or something? To protect her? To let her grow up normally?'

'It's possible. One thing I will say to you. You have the pendant – or one exactly like it. You have Matilda's looks, her build, even her gestures . . .' His mouth twitched appreciatively. 'And, dare I say it, her temperament too?'

'Every inch a short fuse?'

'You could say that, yes.' His smile broadened. 'I imagine she would have been proud of you.'

'Oh, dear,' I said.

Margaret greeted me with profound relief when I got back to the apartment. 'Foss, I'm sorry. I was a pig.'

'Me, too,' I said. 'I'm sorry, Mags. I wasn't getting at you. I just got mad because you were handling the situation better than me, that's all.'

I said nothing about my conversation with Lord Falcon. He'd confided in me against the King's instructions, and it struck me that the penalty for disobeying Royalty could involve losing rather more than one's job.

Next morning a package arrived from the Steward's office.

'*Books?*' Margaret was on her knees, flipping them over one after another. '*A Complete History of Arborea . . . Legends and Customs of the Island Kingdom . . . Book-keeping for Small Businesses . . . Elementary Economics* . . . what's all this about, Foss?'

I stared at the books with a sinking feeling inside. Part One of a do-it-yourself Diploma course on How To Run The Arbor Palace. If I wanted the job of Princess, Falcon would back me. The irony of the situation sank in: first fantasy, now reality . . . I didn't know whether to be flattered or run like hell.

February arrived, and the Court was out of mourning at last. The problem of the missing Princess was being discussed, secretly, behind closed doors.

'I suppose when they've talked it out, they'll let us go home,' Margaret said. She sighed. 'You know, I'm going to miss all this. Perhaps they'll let me stay on – as a lady's maid, or something.'

I had a nasty feeling we'd both be staying on, whether we wanted to or not. Falcon hadn't struck me as the kind of man who'd let sentiment stand in the way of what he felt was best for Arborea. If he couldn't locate the real princess, he'd settle for a substitute. Me.

The bad dreams started again – all involving being hunted and trapped and unable to get out. During waking hours I began to plan possible escape routes. All of them ended at the shoreline. How do you get off an island when all the ports are blocked and half the world's out looking for you? Presumably Magnus knew where I was, through my ring. In my present predicament it would have been a lot more useful if he'd wired it for sound . . .

Meanwhile, rumours were buzzing around the Island with the hopeful enthusiasm of wasps outside a jam factory. The papers, delivered faithfully each day with our breakfast, reported variously that the Lost Princess was on her way by sea from Far Mabukoland; that she was, in fact, a milkman's wife residing in Stoke on Trent; that she'd refused to come home; that she was dead. The Palace was keeping its official mouth firmly shut.

Unknown to us, discreet preparations were being set in motion. One morning Grisly Grice appeared to announce the arrival of the hairdresser. She did this in tones of such icy disapproval that I was totally unprepared for the breathtaking vision in pink and silver brocade which floated into the room behind her.

The first shock over, I was able to register the fact that the hairdresser was a plumpish middle-aged man with pink hair to match his suit. He was wearing an open-necked silver shirt, and spats. I had a nagging feeling that I'd seen him somewhere before.

'Mr . . . er . . . Morico,' La Grice said, pursing her mouth as though she'd bitten on a sloe and was too ladylike to spit it out.

I gasped. *Now* I knew where I'd seen him. His picture had been in all my old chat magazines. If you were rich enough and stylish enough to have your hair done by Morico, you'd definitely made the grade as one of the glitterati. You were the crème de la crème. What on earth was he doing in Arborea?

Never having drooled over fashion magazines, Margaret was serenely unaware of our visitor's exalted status, and completely undismayed by the eccentric splendour of his outfit. 'Oh, thank you, Mrs Grice. How very kind. How d'you do, Mr Morico?'

Morico swept past me in a gust of frangipani which all but knocked me over. He seized Margaret's outstretched hand, kissed the tips of the fingers one by one and clamped it dramatically over his heart. His eyes flickered greedily over Margaret's glorious hair.

'Natural blonde,' he breathed. 'Exquisite! Mademoiselle – my genius is wholly at your service!'

I could see Margaret's startled face over his shoulder. Beside me Mrs Grice was emanating great waves of permafrost. I choked back giggles: the man was *outrageous*.

He fixed us all with a glare that could have petrified Gorgons, and snapped his fingers at Mrs Grice.

'Leave us!' he commanded. She jumped like a hare and fled.

I was shaking with the effort of controlling hysteria. He switched his stony glare to me – and suddenly minced across the room in a faultless imitation of La Grice, bosom and all. You could practically see the ringlets bouncing. I burst out laughing, and so, after a moment's polite hesitation, did Margaret.

He beamed conspiratorially at us, and tapped one finger against the side of his nose. 'Oooh, I am wicked. Now, where's yer barfroom, ducks?'

Everything I'd ever read about this amazing little Cockney was perfectly true. Presented with Margaret's unplaited mane, he didn't hesitate. He washed, he towelled; he lifted, he combed, he cut, all the while keeping up a non-stop monologue of outrageous stories and hilarious one-liners until Margaret and I were both helpless with laughter. The final drying over, he made an expansive gesture of triumph and stood back. We both gasped.

Somehow, he'd coaxed waves out of that heavy wheatsheaf of hair. He'd layered it so that it floated in curling tendrils over her shoulders and down her back, like a waterfall with the sun behind it. It was the kind of hairdo that photographers aim wind machines at. It framed her beautiful face in a golden haze. She looked fabulous.

She looked like a princess out of a fairytale.

'Now you,' he said, pointing a stern finger at me.

Released from its grips, my hair crackled like the proverbial burning bush. Margaret had been right – it had gone redder. Morico ran his fingers through the frizz and made hissing noises.

'Now this,' he said thoughtfully, 'is what we artists like to call . . .'

'Yes?' I said hopefully, thinking of Titian, and the Pre-Raphaelites.

'. . . a bloody 'orrible mess,' he concluded. 'Still, not to worry, eh? Chuck us the shampoo, ducks.'

When he started cutting, great chunks of hair began to drop all round me. It was unnerving. I half expected him to get out his razor and shave the back and sides.

I needn't have worried. Half a ton of hair lighter, I listened carefully to his instructions on washing and conditioning. Then he fluffed up the remains of the mop and stood back.

I'm not a great believer in miracles as a rule, but this was a major exception. The frizz had vanished. What was left was a halo of real curls, each of which shone as though individually rubbed-up with a brasso rag. It surrounded my head like a coppery dandelion clock. My neck seemed to have grown two inches. I stared into the mirror and scarcely recognised myself.

'Foss – it's *gorgeous!*' Margaret said.

'All in the cutting, luv, all in the cutting,' Morico said happily. He beamed at us in the mirror and kissed both hands like a star receiving an Oscar. And vanished.

We spun round, startled. The room was empty.

'M—magic?' Margaret said in a scared voice, touching her hair.

'He was definitely here, though, wasn't he? He's the best there is, you know, outside the Zones.'

Margaret stared thoughtfully at herself, and then at me. 'If he's this good, I don't see how the Zones could stop him, do you? Something to do with genius, perhaps?'

Just after lunch we had another visitor: Ferdinand.

I was rummaging in the cupboard behind the door, so when it was flung open with characteristic panache all I could see were Ferdinand's broad back and Margaret's face. I'd been hoping against hope that she'd had time to get over him. One glance at her made it painfully obvious that she hadn't. She went so white I thought she'd faint; then she blushed crimson.

'Hello, Ferd,' I chirped, and leapt out of my hiding-place to give her a chance to recover.

'Foss!' he said happily, and gave me a bone-crushing brotherly hug.

He was looking very fit. He'd been skiing, to judge from the colour of his tan. I was astounded to see that he'd had his fair hair cut in a stylish upper-class version of Jo's spiky No. 4, and . . .

'Ferdinand!' I squealed. 'You've got an *earring!*'

He blushed. 'D'you like it?'

'You look terrific!' I told him. 'It's a big improvement on the Little Lord Fauntleroy look.'

He glowed. 'I thought so too. The Mater had a fit,' he added proudly.

We offered him coffee, but he refused. 'Get your riding-things on. I've three good horses outside.'

It was wonderful to be outside the Palace again, and on horseback. We rode up into the hills with our heavily-armed escort (Lord Falcon was taking no chances), and had a good gallop through miles of pine woodland. It was a beautiful, serene February day, with primroses in the hedgerows and wild daffodils budding in the woods. The only thing missing was Jo. I hadn't caught so much as a passing glimpse of him in three months.

We left the horses at the Palace stables and walked to our quarters the back way, past cottages where the grooms and gardeners lived with their families.

Suddenly a commotion broke out amongst the dustbins in somebody's yard. A woman shrieked, and a man's voice shouted 'Shoo! Get out, you little bugger! G'wan! Scram!' There was a ringing clunk! as though a flung saucepan had missed. Something very small and brownish shot out around the corner and skidded to a halt just in front of us.

It was a puppy. A brown-and-white spaniel puppy with anxious peat-dark eyes. Seeing us there, blocking its escape route, it crouched, and began to shiver.

Margaret was on her knees, coaxing it to come to her.

'The poor little thing! Look, Foss, all its ribs are sticking out. And what's that on its *ears*?'

The puppy was in very bad shape. Its fur was filthy and as dry as parcel string. Its beautiful long ears were a mass of fat purplish ticks, hanging there like grapes.

'*Ticks?*' Margaret repeated in horror.

The puppy regarded us warily, and tentatively wagged its tail.

'You're not thinking of *adopting* the thing, are you?' Ferdinand said disapprovingly. 'Heaven knows what diseases it's got.'

'Well, we can't leave it here,' Margaret said angrily. 'Whoever owns it ought to be shot.' She'd managed to get close enough to stroke the little dog. It licked her finger trustingly.

I looked round. We were within five minutes' walk of the kitchen garden. At last, here was the perfect excuse to check up on Jo.

'One of the gardeners'll know what to do,' I said. 'Will it let you pick it up, Mags?'

The gardens were deserted except for one man at the far end, digging over a raised bed under the peach wall.

'Excuse me,' I called. He stuck his spade in the ground and turned round.

It was Jo.

In three months, he'd changed. He was taller, broader in the shoulders, deeply weather-burnt. His face had lost all its boyish roundness; his hair was a roughly-cropped mane, and he'd finally grown into his hands and feet. The changes must have been going on for some time, but I hadn't noticed before. This wasn't the flippant, wise-cracking boy I'd known for most of my life. I was looking at a man who was almost, but not quite, a stranger.

For some reason I suddenly felt extremely shy. I had trouble breathing.

'Hello, Jo,' I said faintly.

His smile was genuinely pleased – but quieter, more reserved. Things had been happening to him in the interim – important things which I knew nothing about and couldn't share. I felt a stab of jealousy.

'Foss,' he said. 'Margaret. Hallo, Ferdinand.'

'Good Heavens, Jo,' Margaret said. 'You've grown. I hardly recognised you.'

He gave her a quick, rueful grin and turned to me. 'What's the trouble, Foss?' His voice had changed too: it was deeper. I pulled myself together with an effort, and explained.

He examined the puppy with gentle, probing fingers. It whimpered once or twice, and licked his face.

'Mange, a few nasty scrapes, and the ticks, of course. The kennelman'll know what to do. It's round this way.'

The kennelman was a whippet-shaped individual with a long pendulous nose and the sour expression of one who has seen every aspect of human life and has yet to be convinced that any of it is worth the effort. He glared at Jo and me with acute dislike. Then he saw Margaret, and his expression changed to one of startled awe.

Yes, of course he'd see to Her High— . . . her Ladyship's puppy. A stray, huh? Well-bred dog, too. Welsh Springer spaniel. Must have wandered in from one of the neighbouring estates.

'If you find out who the owners are,' Margaret said earnestly, 'tell them I'll buy him, if that's what they want. That'll be all right, won't it, Foss?'

The kennelman disagreed, forcibly and at length. People who neglected their dogs had, in his opinion, forfeited all rights to ownership. Hell, he seemed to feel, was a cushy number compared to the punishments he, personally, would like to inflict on people like that. He reiterated his point several times and his language got quite fruity. We left him tenderly removing ticks and ordering salves for the mange.

The puppy arrived at our apartment a week later. The transformation was startling. Its belly bulged, its fur shone like satin, its ears curled exuberantly on either side of its face. When it saw Margaret it hurled itself at her in an ecstasy of adoration.

It also left a trail of puddles on the carpet.

'What are you going to call him?' I asked, scrubbing the wet patches with disinfectant.

'I don't know! I've been racking my brains, but nothing sounds quite right.'

'He's Welsh, isn't he? How about Ianto?'

While Margaret was house-training Ianto I had time to ponder over the changes in Jo, and the extraordinary effect they were having on me. If you'd told me six months ago that one level glance from Jo's eyes would make my heart pound and my knees go wobbly I'd have told you to go see a shrink. But it was happening – and I couldn't believe it. I felt confused, appalled and a bit frightened. I found myself wanting rather urgently to see him again.

15.

Your Stars: CANCER (June 22–July 23)
Your career plans are maturing rapidly, and you may
find yourself considering relocation. A snap decision
may need to be taken – but don't worry: trust your
instincts.

Once Ianto had settled in, exercising him became a priority. Our daily walks got longer and began to include the parkland and the fields surrounding the Palace, but always with our armed escort trudging along behind us.

'Just a short walk today, though,' Margaret announced one morning. 'We're going riding with Ferdinand this afternoon, remember.'

We were returning to our wing for lunch when all at once Ianto shot off towards the main Palace block. The four of us hared off in pursuit.

'Ianto! Come back here!'

We found him standing in the doorway of a tower adjoining the servants' quarters. He was panting eagerly and wagging his tail as though asking permission to go inside.

The guards were reassuring. 'It's okay, m'Lady. The tower's empty. Quite safe, though. It got done up, didn't it, Bill? – five, six years ago.'

'They was thinking of putting the upstairs staff in there at one time, I heard. Nothing come of it, though.'

Margaret shrugged. 'Might as well let him go up, I suppose. It'll tire him out and it won't take long.'

Both minders were bored and slightly footsore. 'Look,' I said, 'No need to follow us up. I saw a bench in that room back there. Why don't you take a break? We'll scream if we get into trouble.'

They grinned in relief, saluted and wandered off.

Ianto vanished up the stairs. Margaret and I followed more sedately behind him. Suddenly we heard excited barking, far above our heads.

'He's gone right to the top! Ianto, come back!'

The barking continued. Now it had a hysterical, I-can-hear-you-but-I-can't-get-*out* quality. 'He's stuck!'

We scooped up our long skirts and pelted up the steps. The barking got louder as we ascended. Then, abruptly, it stopped.

'Ianto!' Margaret wailed. 'Where is he? Oh, God, what's he done?'

We staggered up the last bend in the spiral and emerged onto a small round landing. Opposite us was a closed door. A sound was emanating from behind it: a regular, muffled clunking noise overlain by a continuous, soothing whirr. It was oddly familiar.

On the other side of the door, Ianto whimpered. Margaret gave a strangled yelp and slammed the latch up. Ianto shot out straight into her arms.

The room was occupied. An old lady was sitting near the window, making curtains on an ancient treadle sewing-machine. Any other furniture the room might have contained was invisible under mountains of heaped chintz. When we burst in she glanced up placidly, and snipped off the thread at the end of her seam.

'Good afternoon to you, ladies.'

'I'm – I'm sorry,' I stammered. 'We didn't know . . . Sorry to have disturbed you.'

'You're welcome, my dears. Nice to see a bit of company now and again.' She smiled at us. 'Gets a bit lonely up here, but the light's good, you see.'

She slid another long piece of material under the needle, clamped it down and began to sew.

I glanced at Margaret – and saw an extraordinary mixture of expressions flicker across her face. Awe . . . stunned enlighten-ment . . . rapture . . . adoration. It was the kind of look blest souls must have when they get to Heaven. Young Stradivarius must have looked like that when he saw his first violin. Raphael must have eyed the poster paints in his playgroup with much the same expression. I traced her rapt gaze to its objective. She was staring at the sewing-machine.

'Wh—what *is* that?' she whispered.

'Sure, lovey,' the old lady said slyly. 'It's only an old sewing-machine.'

'A machine? That does *sewing*?'

I always tended to forget about Margaret's deprived past. She'd never seen one before – of course she hadn't. Her eyes

203

glowed with visions: beautiful clothes, designed and sewn by herself; wardrobes-full of hitherto unobtainable haute couture . . . Her face said it all.

The old lady stopped the machine half-way along the seam. She was chuckling at Margaret's reaction – and there was something not quite nice about that laugh. 'Would you like to have a try yourself, dearie?' she asked.

Margaret put Ianto down and sat in front of the machine. She gazed helplessly at the needle, and down to the treadle at her feet. 'What do I do?'

The old biddy sniggered. She wanted Margaret to make a fool of herself, I could tell.

'Move over, Mags, ' I said. 'I'll show you.'

The woman was making spluttering noises. 'Hey, now, watch what you're doing. I didn't . . .'

'It's okay,' I told her. 'I've used one of these hundreds of times. Look, Mags, it's easy. You just lower this little lever here . . .'

I let the needle down and showed her how to operate the treadle. 'Getting started is the tricky bit. Once it's moving you just have to learn to control your feet. Watch.' I started the machine and sewed the rest of the seam. Then I hunted about for a piece of scrap material.

The old lady was fizzing like a beer bottle at ten thousand feet. I wished she wouldn't jump up and down like that – it was distracting. 'Okay, now you try!'

Margaret sewed a passably straight seam at the third go, and flushed with delight.

'Now I'll show you how to thread the needle,' I said.

The beer bottle exploded. 'Now look here, you! Stop interfering! You're not meant to . . .'

'It's all right,' I urged. 'We're not damaging it.'

Margaret was threading the needle and scowling with concentration. The old lady gave a shriek of frustrated fury. Suddenly she charged with all the finesse of a bull moose in a crockery shop. She cannoned into the machine – and the needle whacked down onto Margaret's unpractised index finger.

'Ow,' she said, laughing and rueful. 'It bit me!' And held up her finger, a drop of blood glistening at its tip.

The next instant all the colour had drained out of her face, leaving it a dead-white, horrified mask. 'Foss,' she whispered.

'Foss . . . Help me . . . I can't . . .' She slumped forwards in a dead faint.

I rushed to lift her – and found myself locked rigid in an unbreakable paralysis. The room went pitch dark. There was a deafening clap of thunder overhead. Somebody burst into peal after peal of cackling laughter.

Out of the blackness a voice spoke – a voice with a nastiness coefficient way up at the top of the Karloff scale. 'Thus is the Prophecy defeated,' it intoned hollowly. 'The Princess is dead. The accursed line of Runcipole perishes forever.'

In the far corner, a glimmering, twinkling cloud began to form, like somebody throwing glitter-dust about at a party, accompanied by the soft chiming of tiny bells. The light grew stronger. The darkness slunk away with every sign of reluctance.

The old lady had vanished. There were two other people in the room, neither of whom I'd ever seen before.

Where the old lady had been standing, there was now a very tall, thin person with a beaky, sour, yellowish face. Long discontented wrinkles pulled the corners of her mouth down to meet a chin like a lavatory brush; mean little black eyes glittered under scowling eyebrows. It was a face which the most charitable of saints wouldn't have been able to look at without an involuntary shudder of dislike.

She was dressed in a black tent-like garment covered in layer upon layer of tongue-shaped floaty bits studded with greenish-yellow sequins like snakes' eyes. Jammed well down on her greasy grey hair was a tall pointed black hat.

The other person – the one who'd arrived in the tinsel cloud – was a stout middle-aged lady with dyed blonde hair in ringlets. She was wearing a frilly, gauzy little number in shrimp pink, with puffed sleeves and a knee-length full skirt. Her rather large feet were clad in ballet slippers, with ankle socks. In her plump hand she carried a wand with a star on top.

For a wild moment I thought I was hallucinating: that I'd somehow strayed into a very bad amateur panto at the first dress rehearsal. I wasn't, and I hadn't. The air crackled and sparked between them.

'Forbear, Necrotica!' the pink lady cried, brandishing her wand. 'Thine evil schemes have come to naught! The Prophecy is fulfilled! The Princess shall sleep for a hundred years, until the Handsome Prince that is foretold in the stars shall waken her with a kiss!'

The black one swore furiously. 'You stupid bitch, Panacea. Trust you to barge in at the last minute and spoil everything! Have you any idea how much trouble I went to, setting this whole thing up?'

'But it's the Prophecy, dear. I'm only doing my job.'

'Prophecy my backside! Damned unsolicited interference, that's what it bloody well is. You and that bunch of slobbering pink wimps, poking your fat fingers into everything! You make me sick!'

I fought against the paralysis – and suddenly it gave way, like a rubber band snapping. The recoil shot me between the two weirdos. I was livid.

'Right,' I snapped. 'I don't know what stupid game you two pillocks think you're playing, but whatever you've done to Margaret, you'd better undo it fast, or the pair of you are in big trouble.'

There was a shocked silence. Even Necrotica was taken aback.

'Who the hell are you?' she snarled.

I drew myself up to my full five-foot nothing, with all the hauteur I could muster. I was opening my mouth to deliver a blistering riposte – when it suddenly occurred to me that *Foss Ewins* didn't, in fact, carry a lot of clout. Necrotica snorted disdainfully.

'Just leave the Princess to us,' she snapped, 'and get back to lady's-maiding or whatever it is you do.'

'But she *isn't* the Princess!'

'Of course she's the Princess. She's got to be the Princess! I mean, just look at her!'

'Wait a minute,' said Panacea. She stared from me to Margaret and back again. Into her plumply foolish face there crept a faint shadow of doubt. The shadow hung on in there, darkened and slowly turned into a look of sheer naked horror.

'Look at *her*, Necrotica,' she whispered. 'The one with the pendant . . . Who does she remind you of?'

Necrotica glared at me. Her beady little eyes widened.

'Matilda, perhaps?' I said icily. 'And while we're playing spot-the-relative, would the name Ossiana happen to ring a few bells?'

It was a random shot, but it went home. Both faces turned a sickly shade of grey.

'Oh, crumbs,' said the pink fairy.

Peculiar gurgling noises were issuing from Necrotica's throat. 'So . . . wh—who's that?' she managed to say.

'Her name's Margaret,' I told them. 'Her mother was a washerwoman, her father mined coal, and when I met her she was working as a kitchen skivvy in a slum. You may as well admit it, ladies. You've clobbered the wrong girl.'

Panacea burst into tears. 'It's all your fault, Necrotica. We said you were going too far! But you wouldn't listen, would you? And what happens? *Ossiana* gets dragged in. *Ossiana!*'

'Stop snivelling, you pink fool,' Necrotica snapped. 'You and your damn garden parties! *"Oh, don't let's kill her, like the others!"* Pinko liberal wets! I *hate* 'em!'

I stepped in to avert imminent bloodshed. 'Just get on with it, will you? Undo the spell!'

There was an uneasy pause. Then Necrotica said sullenly, 'We can't.'

I stared at them both, feeling as though the top of my head had just blown off. 'You *what*?'

'We can't. It's linked to a Prophecy. From now on, it's out of our hands.'

'I think,' I said grimly, 'you'd better explain.'

They did. The explanation involved a lot of mutual recrimination and arguing over details, but in the end I got the gist.

Arborea, it transpired, had formerly possessed its normal quota of supernatural beings i.e. sorcerers, witches, the odd minor deity or two and, of course, fairies, of which these two were the official representatives, Heaven help them.

For centuries, the fairies had been tolerated by the ruling monarchs of the Arborean line. They'd been invited to all the major social events in the Palace calendar – weddings, christenings, garden parties and so on. They hadn't meddled in politics or attempted in any way to rock the royal boat. They were socialites, pure and simple, and they'd adored every minute of it.

All this had come to an abrupt end in King Runcipole's time. (It was a bit hazy, but I gathered he'd been King Brandolph's grandfather.) Fired with misplaced enthusiasm for the Cause of Science and the Triumph of Reason, he'd announced to a startled populace that magic powers did not exist. Never had existed, despite the staggering weight of evidence to the contrary. Anybody found practising witchcraft or sorcery or just plain magic was to be executed or banished.

The fairies, of course, were banned from the Palace for good.

Listening to Panacea and Necrotica it became very clear that Hell hath no fury like a snob deposed. In comparison, a woman scorned is strictly in the peanut class. When roused, even this bunch of thistlebrained nitwits could turn dangerous. For once in their long lives, they'd felt and acted as one. They'd dusted off their mouldering spell books and got down to business.

To everyone's astonishment, including their own, they'd succeeded – the most unlikely bunch of serial killers in history. They'd whittled down the Royal Family to the present King Eldoric and the newly-discovered lost Princess. But just when they were about to administer the coup de grace, one bright spark had belatedly twigged that if they wiped out the Royal Family completely, they were in fact cutting their noses off to spite their faces. No Royals, no Court. No Court, no snob parties, ever again.

Said spark had also reasoned that a young and beautiful Princess might be a little less inclined to regard fairies as personae non grata. That in the general rejoicing etc. the fairies might even be reinstated as welcome (or at least tolerated) guests again.

The fairies had split into two opposing camps at this point. Necrotica's group wanted to finish the job, and to hell with garden parties. Panacea's group felt it was time for the subtler approach. Instead of killing off the Princess, she was to sleep for a hundred years.

However, mitigating a death sentence into one of suspended animation had proved a bit too tricky for them. Panacea's group had been forced to ensnare a stray Prophecy which happened to be floating around at the time. I gathered that while vague Prophecies were fairly formidable things in their own right, a Prophecy aimed at a specific target was the most powerful thing in the Universe. Once triggered, it couldn't be stopped.

'So Margaret is going to sleep for a hundred years! Great. Wonderful. And what did you expect to achieve by that? The King could have married again, had children . . .'

'Oh, no. It's not just her,' Panacea said smugly. 'The whole Kingdom is going to sleep too.'

'*What?*'

'Everybody. From the humblest peasant to the King himself.'

For a few seconds I was speechless. Then the torrent broke. 'You banana-brained twitheads! Duke Thorbert's got an army waiting in Marant! He'll stomp all over Arborea and slaughter everything in sight – and *then* what happens to your precious Prophecy?'

'Who's Duke Thorbert?' said Necrotica.

'No, he won't,' Panacea went on. 'That's the clever bit. The whole island will be cloaked in enchantment and nobody will be able to enter or leave. Until the Prince of Boronia arrives and cuts his way through the briars and discovers the Princess asleep in her bower of roses.' She simpered. 'Romantic, isn't it? Well,' she added uncomfortably, with a sideways glance at Margaret, 'that's how it was meant to happen.'

'Boronia? You mean Siegfried's grandson, or great-grandson?'

Necrotica eyed me pityingly. 'Not Siegfried, you fool. Siegfried's dead. Killed in a duel with a Black Knight, somewhere up North. Didn't you know?'

'Never liked him much anyway,' Panacea said airily. 'Ferdinand's so much better-looking. That's why we chose him.'

I was getting a very bad feeling about this.

'Picked a name out of a hat,' Necrotica was muttering. 'Damn fool Prophecy had to be tied to a name. All your fault, you pink flitterbug.'

. . . Ferdinand . . . The penny dropped with a deafening clunk.

'But Ferdinand's *here*! He's here, in the Palace, now!'

There was a puzzled pause. 'So?' said Panacea.

'So all of us, *including* Ferdinand, are scheduled to sleep for a hundred years, right? No Ferdinand, no great-grandson, no kiss, no reawakening. The spell,' I added, punching out each syllable separately, 'the spell *never gets broken*.'

'Oh, cripes,' said Necrotica. Then she brightened. 'Then I've won, haven't I?'

'Until Ossiana catches up with you,' I said grimly. She winced.

Predictably, Panacea was wringing her hands and snivelling. 'What are we going to *do*?'

I was thinking fast. Margaret was asleep – already too far gone to be woken. The Prophecy would have to run its course. But in the meantime Ferdinand had to be got off the island, before he succumbed to the spell. Got off by me and Jo.

'How long before the complete spell takes effect?'

Panacea shrugged. 'Two, three hours. Why?'

'Right, then. This is what we'll do.'

They listened, blankly at first, and then with reluctant acquiescence.

'You – you won't say anything to Ossiana about this, will you?' Necrotica said quaveringly.

'Not if you keep your side of the bargain, no.'

When they'd gone I raced downstairs to fetch the two guards. 'The Princess! Something terrible's happened!'

While they pounded up the tower steps to investigate, I pelted back along the deserted corridors and into the inhabited part of the Palace, yelling at the full pitch of my lungs. 'The Princess! Princess Aurora! Come quick! Somebody's tried to kill her!'

Doors were flung open. People began to erupt from everywhere, shouting and asking questions and getting in each others' way. I ran into the Council Chamber where a meeting was being chaired by a short, sandy-haired man with gummy eyes and a nervous twitch: King Eldoric himself. Half the Palace staff poured in after me. Shocked Councillors and Ministers of State spun round in their seats to glare at the disturbance.

'The Princess, Majesty,' I yelled. 'There's been a terrible accident!'

The King went white. We'd never met, and I knew that in a hundred years he wouldn't remember me at all. I didn't care. Margaret would be the Princess Aurora and Tilda and I were both free.

I dodged under flailing arms and headed back to the walkway under the empty tower. It was lined with Palace staff murmuring in hushed, shocked voices. Four guards emerged from the tower carrying Margaret's limp body on a stretcher. Ianto ran whimpering alongside.

I fell into step behind them. It was an eerie, sad little procession. People were craning, staring, recognising Margaret, their faces registering horrified dismay. Many of the servants were weeping openly. Any lingering doubts I'd had disappeared like smoke. I was doing the right thing – for Margaret and for Arborea. This was where she belonged. And if Ferdinand's great-grandson turned out to look a bit like Ferdinand himself . . .

Mrs Grice's eyes were streaming with tears and she was mopping her vast face in her apron. 'Oh, the poor sweet lamb . . .'

They carried her to our apartment, where Mrs Grice and the

maids dressed her in a gown of white and silver for her lying-in-state, and combed out her beautiful hair.

It was horrible. Tears kept threatening my own eyes and my throat felt tight and sore. I had to keep reminding myself that she wasn't really dead. I was very aware that time was running out, and that I had preparations of my own to make.

I changed into riding gear and packed a few essentials into a small bag. Nobody was in a state to ask questions. Even when I took my cloak from its peg nobody noticed. I grabbed paper and a pen and scribbled a note.

'Mags – you're the Princess Aurora now. Keep your mouth shut and DON'T BLOW IT, okay? Good luck with your Prince, I hope he takes after the rest of his family. Tons of love, Foss.'

I slipped it into an envelope, sealed it and tied it securely like a label to Ianto's collar. A hundred years from now (assuming the Prophecy did its stuff as per schedule) she'd open the envelope and read the note. A hundred years from now, Jo and Ferdinand and I would all be dead. Shudders went down my spine. I'd never see Margaret again, ever.

In the Great Hall, tall candles were burning and sheaves of white lilies were scenting the air. They laid Margaret on a white satin bed and drew a golden coverlet over her. Ianto jumped up and snuggled down beside his mistress. He yawned and started to lick her hand. All at once I wanted to cry my eyes out.

'Goodbye, Mags,' I whispered, and slipped quietly away to find Ferdinand and Jo.

Once outside, I bunched up my skirts and ran. Already the spell was beginning to take hold. The people I passed were yawning and staggering. Somebody informed me that Ferdinand was in the stables, and that his friend Mr Morgan was with him.

I was running full-pelt, looking every which way but straight ahead, when I slammed into somebody else who had obviously been doing the same thing, but in the opposite direction. Being the smaller and lighter of the two, I was the one who fell over.

My assailant gave a startled grunt and hauled me to my feet. It was Lord Falcon.

'Foss?' he said. 'My God, Foss, are you all right?' He'd never called me Foss before – at least, not to my face. 'They're saying the Princess is dead! What in the name of all that's holy is happening in there?'

Wheezing, I gasped out the salient details. 'It's Margaret.

Those blasted fairies Runcipole banished have put her to sleep for a hundred years. Plus you, the Court and the whole of Arborea.'

He paled. 'So Queen Matilda was right, after all . . . But why Margaret?'

'They made a mistake. Listen, Lord Falcon – this is important. I have to get Ferdinand away from here before the spell takes hold – it's his great-grandson who's supposed to break it. Do you understand? I'm leaving. Margaret's the Princess Aurora from this moment on.'

'Margaret? But she's . . .'

'You wouldn't want a nasty scandal a hundred years from now, would you? And don't worry about Thorbert – no-one will be able to land on the island until the spell's broken.'

His gaunt face softened into a grin. 'You've thought it all out, haven't you, Highness?' The grin faded. 'Forgive the impertinence, my dear – but I shall miss you.'

And suddenly I saw in his face something I should have suspected from the start. He'd been in love with Matilda. Nearly twenty years' difference in their ages – but he'd loved her faithfully without letting on to a soul. When he met me, it must have been like meeting a grand-daughter he'd never had. And now he was losing me, too. Why is it that every decision you make is guaranteed to hurt *somebody*?

But the decision wasn't mine to make, after all. It had been forced on me – and if I didn't find Ferdinand and Jo within the next five minutes or so Arborea would be doomed.

I reached up and gave Lord Falcon a quick hug. 'I'll miss you too. Look after Mags for me, won't you? You're the only one who knows. And she'll be much better at the job than I'd ever be.'

I ran on towards the stables, praying that Jo and Ferdinand were still there. I could have wept with relief when I heard Ferdinand's cathedral tones ringing out across the yard. With him, and looking heart-stoppingly tough and sinewy in black riding gear, was Jo.

They spun to face me as I raced up. 'Foss! What the hell's going on?'

'Magic,' I snapped. 'Get back on your horse, Ferd. You too, Jo. We've got to get away from here, fast.'

Ferdinand didn't budge. 'But Foss – they're telling us that the Princess is dead . . .'

212

'Don't worry about that. I'll explain later.'

Even Jo was standing there dithering.

'Come *on!*' I screeched, grabbing a bridle at random and turning the horse's head so I could mount.

'But if something's happened, shouldn't we consult His Majesty?'

'And where's Margaret?' said Jo.

Why is it that whenever you try to get men to do anything in an emergency, they just stand around arguing?

'There isn't *time!*' I yelled. 'The whole of Arborea is going to sleep for a hundred years and we've got to escape! Come on!'

Ferdinand's face took on its obstinate look, and my heart sank.

Three metres from where we were standing, a flagstone suddenly cracked with a noise like a bullet going through glass. The horses skittered and reared. A green shoot as thick as Ferdinand's arm pushed through the gap, bent double like a giant's croquet hoop. We froze. The shoot lengthened and swelled like something out of a horror movie. Finally the top end burst free of the ground and sprang upright. It was a rose sucker, eight feet high. Another flagstone cracked on our right. Suddenly the entire stable yard started to resound with flags shifting and splintering as more and more gigantic shoots muscled their way from underground. Around the gate briars were growing at the rate of a metre a second; they writhed like tentacles, wrapping themselves round anything they touched.

Jo was the first to recover. He scooped me up and plonked me astride the nearest horse. Ferdinand was still gawping, open-mouthed and glassy-eyed. Jo stuck Ferdinand's foot in the stirrup and lifted him bodily into the saddle, with minimal assistance from Ferdinand himself. Then he sprang up behind me, and leant across to grab Ferdinand's slack rein. 'Let's go!'

We cantered out of the stable yard, ducking to avoid the briars. Jo swung both horses into the main carriage drive. I dug my heels in and urged them into a gallop.

The movement shocked Ferdinand out of his trance. We rode like dervishes down the drive to the main gates. All around us briars were shooting up out of the ground, and writhing their way up the walls of the Palace.

'It's going to look like one bloody big bramble patch,' Jo muttered.

More briars were weaving a net across the gates. We charged through just in time. Another minute or so and an armoured troop carrier would have had difficulty making it through the gap.

At the gatehouse the guards were snoring. Outside on the road, a carter lay peacefully asleep while his horse dragged its harness nearby. People had succumbed faster than animals.

'Where to, Foss?' Jo said.

'The harbour. We've got to steal a boat. This whole island is going to be sealed off and invisible for the next hundred years, so get a move on!'

'Not the main harbour, Ferd,' Jo yelled, as Ferdinand checked his horse. 'Small boats! This way!'

We rode up over a hill and straight across fields to the nearest fishing village. Sheep scattered every which way as we thundered through. In the village, people were already asleep on their doorsteps, in the square and on the wharves. We dismounted. Ferdinand and I stripped off the tack and left both horses free to graze while Jo went scouting along the wharves for a suitable boat. The one he selected was smallish and handy-looking, with a tiny cabin already stocked for a sea trip, and sails furled along the boom. We tumbled aboard. Jo rowed and I steered until we were well out of the tiny harbour. Then we hoisted the sail and headed down the inlet towards the sea.

Half a mile out to sea, we looked back. Arborea was dissolving into mist: first the mountains, then the foothills and the forests, then the city itself. Lastly, the mist crept to cover the hummocks of the shoreline. It hung there for a few minutes, shimmering like a mirage. A gust of wind came from the North, and the mist thinned into shreds and blew away.

The whole island had disappeared. All we could see was a black reef with the breakers foaming over the rocks, and seagulls swooping over. We were alone on the empty sea.

PART THREE

Isobel

16.

Your Stars : CANCER (June 21–July 22)
Unexpected developments will force you to change your
plans. Life will seem to be full of ups and downs for a
while, and romance will take a back seat. Be prepared to
offer a friend reassurance and support.

Nobody spoke for a long time. Jo set the boat heading towards
Garnock. After a while I went into the galley and brewed a pot
of tea.

Ferdinand was still in shock. He accepted his mugful as if he
wasn't at all sure what to do with it. I'd told them the whole
story as we'd sailed up the inlet, but as far as Ferdinand was
concerned the truth didn't seem to have sunk in. He raised
bewildered eyes to mine.

'No Arborea?' he said numbly. 'Nothing? For a hundred years?'

'At least you're not stuck there,' I reminded him.

He shook his head violently. 'Yes, but . . . You were the heir
to the throne . . . There was a contract . . . I was going to marry
you . . .'

I'd guessed as much. Tactfully, Jo turned his head away and
concentrated on steering.

'Did you know this was going to happen?' Ferdinand said
harshly.

'Of course not, dimmock.'

'Word of honour?'

'Word of honour. For Heaven's sake, Ferd – Mags was my
friend.'

Was. Already we were talking of her in the past tense.

'Sorry,' he mumbled.

We sat watching the sun glitter in the boat's wake. Ferdinand
roused himself.

215

'So, what do we do now? I mean – I don't *mind* marrying you, Foss, if that's what you want.' Some proposal, I thought dismally.

'Thanks, but it wouldn't work out, would it? Anyway, you've got to marry the heiress to a going concern, remember?'

The look of relief on his face was like a slap. I winced. Not wanting to marry someone is one thing – finding out just how glad they are not to have to marry you is an altogether more painful jolt to the ego.

'You're a brick,' he said, and gave me a hug. Then his face lengthened. 'But I'm right back where I started. Where will I find a princess now?'

'Magnus'll find you one,' I said confidently. 'Won't he, Jo?'

When night fell we took turns to go below and snatch a few hours' sleep. During our watch Jo and I sat in companionable silence while the sail tugged at the sheets and the rudder sliced rustling through the water. Being with him made me feel weak at the knees and happy and heartsore at the same time. It was very odd.

At midnight Ferdinand took over and I went below to rest. It had been a traumatic day, but all I felt as I lay down on the bunk was a profound sense of relief. We were on our way back to Garnock, and Magnus. The awful edgy helplessness I'd been experiencing in Arborea was over for good. I'd be able to call in on Tilda and lift a load of worry off her shoulders. We'd probably go out with Francis and Jo and celebrate . . .

Magnus would find Ferdinand a princess. I was counting on that.

Around three in the morning I woke up very suddenly to find that the tiny cabin was surging up and plummeting down like a lift gone berserk. Outside, there was a roaring, booming noise interspersed with shuddering thuds. I dragged on my jeans and a set of oilskins from the locker under the bunk and fought my way up on deck.

One step out of the cabin and I had to grab the rail with both hands to avoid being swept overboard. Waves were towering twice as high as the mast. You could see the white crests high above in the darkness, and the gouts and streamers of spray being blown off them in the gale. Water was streaming down the violently canting deck. I had to let go with one hand for a perilous few moments to take my glasses off and stow them in the inside pocket of my oilskins.

216

A human-shaped blur just across the deck from me was Jo, who was struggling to lower the mainsail without getting it in the water. Ferdinand was steering, with both hands locked on the tiller.

'Hang on tight, for God's sake, Foss,' Jo yelled, as I edged my way along the deck to help. 'Got to run before it,' he shouted as we wrestled with the sopping canvas. 'Mainsail's too big . . . Keeping the jib up to give us steerage.'

None of us got any more sleep that night. Wave after wave towered up behind us, snatched us up to a dizzying height, surged us forwards at breathless speed and let us drop with a heart-stopping judder into the trough of the next. It was like being trapped on the biggest roller-coaster in the world – exhilarating at first, and then, as it went on and on, you began to wish from the bottom of your heart that somebody would come along and switch the damn thing off.

Hours went by with no sign of the storm abating. Long before that, all three of us were soaked to the skin, stiff with cold, and exhausted. At last the first grey glimmer of dawn began to appear in the sky.

It was the noise that warned us. A booming sound, so deep-toned it made your bones vibrate. Ahead of us, a thin whitish line gleamed in the half-light.

Jo squinted into the gloom, and swore. 'Breakers! Damn boat's running out of sea!'

The gale bore us inexorably on. The wall of spray approached at horrifying speed. We were within twenty yards of the surf when a gigantic wave picked us up and hurled us on to the shore.

How we survived the impact I'll never know. The boat rode right over the boiling reef and grounded with a shuddering crunch in a maelstrom of dirty yellow foam. The mast snapped and crushed the roof of the galley. Rigging and bits of spar cascaded all round us. Another wave broke over us and dragged us back. The third missed us: tongues of white water surged around the hull, but we didn't move again. The tide was going out.

Slowly, the sea backed away down the beach. We unclamped locked fingers, and slid down the deck onto the wet sand. The wind was subsiding as the sun rose. We looked at the reef of wicked, jagged rocks and marvelled at being alive.

Jo tramped round to inspect the hull.

'Keel's snapped. Garboard strake's stove in, big hole in the bow . . . No more action for this old girl.'

We salvaged what food we could from the wrecked galley and trudged up the beach into the shelter of the dunes. We collected driftwood and lit a fire. I sat huddled close to the blaze feeling as though a boxing club had been using me as a punch bag. Judging from the way Jo and Ferdinand yelped every time they moved a muscle, they felt much the same.

The sky cleared, the sun got hot and we slept in the thin shade of the tamarisks.

When I woke up it was late afternoon. Clothes were spread out to dry in the sun. Below me, on the beach, the two men were sunbathing. I got up and limped stiffly down to join them.

'Where are we, does anybody know?'

Jo shrugged. 'Nowhere near Garnock, I'm afraid. Look at the sun.' It was edging down the sky on the landward side of the beach.

'The gale drove us westwards,' Ferdinand said gloomily.

I tried to remember the maps I'd seen in Lord Falcon's office. 'What's west of Arborea?'

'That's the trouble,' Jo said. 'Nothing. We couldn't possibly have sailed far enough to make a landfall in one night. Not even in that storm.'

I went cold. 'What d'you mean?'

Jo sighed, and gestured up the beach. 'When we left Arborea, it was March, right? Potter about in those sandhills for a few minutes. All the plants are seeding up. Sun's hot. Summer's nearly over.'

'Jo thinks we may have crossed a Zone interface during the night,' Ferdinand explained. 'We could be anywhere.'

'Or any *when*,' said Jo.

I couldn't understand it. 'But how? There's a tremendous concentration of power at a Zone interface point . . .You need a sorcerer to tap it off safely before you can cross – even without the time-flow calculations.'

'We've gone through Gateways before without knowing it.'

'Yes, on the way to Magnus's. And he was tapping off the energy each time.' I was beginning to get a very bad feeling about this.

As dusk fell we cooked a frugal meal.

218

'Full moon,' Jo said thoughtfully, watching it rise over the sea. 'What d'you think? Should we move on now, or wait until daylight?'

'Might as well walk as far as we can tonight,' I said. 'If we keep to the shore, we won't get lost. There might be a fishing village or something.'

We both looked at Ferdinand, who was sunk in the apathy of acute depression.

'I suppose so,' he said, getting up reluctantly. 'Anything's better than sitting here brooding.'

There's something very weird about walking by the light of the moon. You think you can see quite well, but actually you can't. Your sense of distance is scrambled: huge crags a long way off suddenly turn into manageable hummocks close enough to touch. Shadows look solid; the sea is glass and the sand is a pale bank of mist stretching on forever.

We walked and walked. Rocks shimmered, shadows slid and changed shape, horizons opened up and closed again. At first we bunched up close together, needing human reassurance. Then, as the eerie silence deepened, each of us drifted into a trance-like state. The only sound was the faint silken rush and sigh of the sea; the only real object in the whole world was the big round scornful disc of the moon, keeping pace with every step we took.

I was so far out of my head that when I saw a tall, spiky rock move silently down the beach some distance away, it didn't surprise me at all. From it came a sudden stabbing gleam of silver. Then it vanished.

Jo ground to a halt. 'Hang on a minute. Something's happening over there.' His voice was slurred. He, too, had been mesmerised into a state of half-sleep.

We halted and tried to focus our sluggish senses in that treacherous pearly light.

'Fishermen?' I guessed. 'Smugglers?'

Using the rocks as cover, we crept cautiously forwards – until less than ten feet away one of them detached itself from the featureless shadows and walked onto the sand.

It was a knight in full armour, mounted on a massive Shire horse and carrying a lance. Horse and rider stood quite still for a few moments, etched in silver. Then they moved noiselessly down the beach and seemed to float away until they dwindled to a speck in the distance.

I thought I was hallucinating: we all did.

'Was it *real*?' Ferdinand whispered.

Jo uttered a muffled curse and began scraping his boot vigorously against a rock. 'Don't know about the rider, but the horse was real, all right.'

'He was armed for a joust!' Ferdinand said excitedly. 'Come on!' – and set off at a crouching run. Jo and I followed.

Around the next headland the beach opened out into a huge semicircular bay of hard sand, with a river spreading in silver tongues across the middle. On the far side stood a castle, its turrets and battlements gleaming blue-white in the moonlight. On the beach beneath it, knights were jousting in tournament.

The horsemen moved like wraiths, black and silver against the pale sand and the glittering sea, and so far away that no sound of horse or arms carried to where we stood. They advanced, struck splinters of silver from each other's lances, retreated, pranced, wheeled and swung together again, like an intricate, silent ballet. It was an eerie, beautiful, unforgettable sight.

We crossed a wooden footbridge over the river, and climbed up onto a stone embankment that curved away towards the castle. The embankment was crowded with onlookers, all watching in rapt, silent attention. I'd always imagined tournaments as the medieval equivalent of a day at the races – lots of colour and noise and excitement. This was different. There was no shouting. The atmosphere was as tense as a battle.

To our left a platform had been built out over the sand. It was decorated with banners and pennants, all of which were fluttering shades of grey in the moonlight. In the centre of the dais was a throne on which sat a man with long, pale hair and a long beard. He was wearing a crown, and robes that looked as though they'd been drenched in liquid silver. Beside him, similarly dressed, was a slender dark-haired girl.

Jo tapped the nearest spectator on the shoulder. 'Excuse me – can you tell us what's going on down there?'

The whole group turned and stared.

'Don't you *know*?' a woman said in a scandalised voice.

Jo shrugged. 'Sorry, no. Just passing through, you see.'

'Oh,' said the man of the family. 'Well, it's like this, d'ye see . . .'

'It's the Last Challenge, that's what,' his wife said briskly.

'Challenge?'

'That's right,' the man said. 'Like I was saying, it's . . .'

'Happens every seven years,' his wife said. 'King Fergal of the Sea, he reckons the Kingdom of Lermos is his by rights, and our King Romeric, he do say otherwise. So they do challenge: King Fergal's knights against King Romeric's.'

'That's right,' her husband said. 'And, like I was saying, this is . . .'

'The third and last time,' his wife added. (I began to feel quite sorry for the poor man.) 'King Romeric, he won the first Challenge, and King Fergal the second.'

'So who's winning now?'

They shrugged. 'It do look as if King Fergal's got the edge this time,' the husband admitted. 'Mind you, King Romeric, he's had it cried through the Kingdom that the man who defeats King Fergal, hand to hand, be he Prince or peasant, he'll get to wed the Princess and inherit the Kingdom.'

'Can't say fairer than that, can you?' said Jo.

'Sounds like a last-ditch attempt to rustle up some useful muscle,' I muttered.

On the sand, the tournament continued. We were close enough now to hear sounds: hooves pounding, the clank of armour and the shivering clash of lances.

Ferdinand's face was alight with a fierce, keen joy: jousting was something he knew about. He was itching to join in, you could tell.

Two knights were facing each other across the sand. Their horses shifted restlessly and stamped their shaggy hooves. A flag dropped. Armoured legs kicked padded flanks. Encumbered by the weight of ironmongery on their backs, the horses moved ponderously into a trot, then a canter, and finally to an earth-shaking gallop. Two lances dipped with the rhythm of the strides. At the last possible moment both lances clamped rigid. Both knights hit each other's shields with a clash. The bigger of the two – a knight in black armour – toppled slowly from the saddle and fell with a ringing clang onto the sand. A cheer went up from the onlookers. The victor raised his right arm in a formal salute to the dais.

Another black-armoured knight was already galloping towards the victor. The silver-clad knight urged his horse forwards to meet the challenge. He'd barely managed to achieve a gallop when the black knight's lance neatly swiped him off the saddle.

There were indignant yells and boos from the crowd. I gathered one of the rules had been broken.

Nobody was watching the other black knight lying on the ground. I only glanced that way because I was cleaning sand off my glasses. I saw him shimmer briefly, and vanish. I grabbed Jo's arm and pointed, just as the knight rematerialised – complete with horse – a hundred yards away across the bay.

Jo gave a hissing whistle. 'Translocation, huh?'

We both looked back towards the unhorsed silver knight. He was being helped to his feet by a couple of hefty manservants. He limped as they led him tenderly away.

'Did you see that, Ferd?' Jo said. 'They're cheating! The black guys are using sorcery, so they're bound to win . . . Ferd? Ferdinand!'

A figure was climbing the steps of the dais. Even at this distance, and in this light, Ferdinand's gallant grace was unmistakable.

'Oh, my God,' said Jo. We slid to the bottom of the embankment and started to run.

'The stupid, *stupid* idiot!'

'Remember what I said about a nanny, and reins?'

We arrived panting at the enclosure where Romeric's silver knights were arming themselves. They wouldn't let us in. There was no sign of Ferdinand. Fretting with impatience, we watched and waited.

One black-clad knight in particular seemed to be doing most of the unhorsing. He was a massively broad figure on a colossal grey stallion. As he rode past, the moonlight glinted on a crown set into his helm.

'That's your man,' Jo said. 'That'll be King Fergal.'

The unequal contest crept to an end. Silver-clad knights lay groaning on the sand, their horses waiting patiently alongside. At a signal from their King, the knights in black armour advanced in a solid phalanx, their horses stepping proudly, pennons and pennoncelles streaming in the thin breeze.

The crowned knight rode to the foot of the dais. His voice carried like the booming of breakers. 'Your last Challenge has failed, Romeric. I, Fergal, King of the Sea, claim sovereignty over all your lands and the hand of your daughter in marriage.'

Romeric stood up. His shoulders were slumped in resignation. He raised one hand, palm upwards, in a gesture of defeat, and opened his mouth to speak – but at that instant a loud clear trumpet note pierced the stillness. The gates of the enclosure swung open and the King's last Champion galloped out.

It was Ferdinand. I had to hand it to him – his timing was impeccable.

He wasn't dressed like the others. His armour was light and flexible: mostly leather and chain-mail. Instead of a huge cumbersome helm like an upended coal-scuttle, he wore a close-fitting helmet with nose and cheek guards. The horse he'd chosen was unconventional too: it looked slimmer, livelier and a lot faster.

Below the dais he reined it to a fidgeting halt and began shouting a challenge of his own. The words streamed away from us in the freshening breeze, but Fergal evidently got the gist. He raised his visor, and I caught a glimpse of a dark bearded face.

'To the death, then, stripling,' he roared.

They wheeled their horses about and galloped to opposite ends of the course. Lances sank horizontally to armpit height like the grotesquely long horns of unicorns. The horses began to advance on each other.

'He's mad,' Jo was muttering. 'Stark raving bonkers.'

I'd stuffed my knuckles into my mouth and was babbling under my breath. 'Oh, Ferd, for Heaven's sake be careful. You stupid twithead. Please God don't let him get hurt. Please God . . .' But he'd got himself into this particular jam, and there was nothing anybody could do to get him out of it.

The horses were thundering towards the point of contact. Fergal's lance was longer and heavier than Ferdinand's, and both he and his horse were armoured like a tank. Fergal clamped his lance rigid, struck . . . and missed. Ferdinand had ducked. A millisecond later his own lance had struck the front of Fergal's helm. Fergal's horse pounded past us without slackening pace – but Fergal was lying on his back in the sand, with the splinters of Ferdinand's shattered lance scattered all round him. The crowd went hysterical.

Abruptly, the cheering stopped. Fergal rose with translocated grace – no clumsy fumbling and staggering for him. He took off his helm and tossed it away. We all heard the hissing rasp as he drew his sword. Ferdinand dismounted and did the same.

Jo and I squinted tensely across the moonlit sand. Ferdinand was moving lightly, quickly, his sword flickering and flashing. Fergal was using his like a butcher's cleaver: one false move on Ferdinand's part and he'd be split down the middle. I couldn't see how Ferdinand could possibly win. How can you wound a man who's strapped into solid steel from the neck down? Ferdinand feinted, slid to one side. Hampered by his armour, Fergal stumbled slightly as he returned the stroke. Ferdinand darted in – and the next moment his opponent was down on his knees, clutching with mailed hands at his own throat.

The crowd went berserk. Jo and I yelled and hugged each other and swung each other around.

'I knew he was good,' Jo yipped, 'but not *that* good! Wowee! Half a ton of hardware coming at him every which way and he goes straight for the throat. Cool as a bloody cucumber!'

The black King shimmered. 'Look out, Ferd!' I shrieked – although he was too far away to have heard me.

The King became a blur on the sand. The blur lengthened, and became a wolf the size of a small pony. It sprang at Ferdinand's chest. I shut my eyes.

And jerked them open again to the noise of frantic cheering and trumpeting. The wolf was lying on the sand with the hilt of Ferdinand's sword protruding from its gullet. Ferdinand was backing away, nursing his right arm.

The crowd rushed onto the beach, regardless of protocol. The wolf was sprawled in a puddle of blood which was soaking into the sand. Ferdinand was staggering a bit – he'd been quite badly mauled. Just as the leading edge of the crowd converged on their hero, the wolf's body blurred once more, and vanished.

Jo and I pushed and shoved to get through to Ferdinand, but it was like fighting your way onto the pitch after a Cup Final. Over the heads of the crowd we saw Ferdinand being hoisted on to the shoulders of two large men-at-arms and borne away in triumph to the dais. He looked a bit taken aback to begin with: then he got into the spirit of the thing and waved his bloody sword over his head. The crowd roared its appreciation.

My eye was caught by a flurry of movement on the dais. The Princess was standing up, her attendants fussing and fluttering round her. She gave the triumphal procession a long, cool look; then she turned her back and began to walk up the ramp to the open gates of the Castle.

'Seems a bit rude,' I remarked.

'What does? Oh.' Jo turned to look where I was pointing. 'Probably some stupid rule or other.'

We watched as the King greeted his Champion. The procession moved off up the ramp and into the Castle. Horses followed, ridden by the less badly wounded knights. The courtiers came next, chattering and laughing, and finally a forlorn little tail-back of stretcher cases.

The crowd began to disperse. The tide was coming in, smoothing out the hoof-prints and the blood and the marks of battle. The moon was low on the horizon.

Jo gave a short laugh. 'Who'd have thought being shipwrecked would lead to something like this?'

'Well,' I said, 'At least Ferd's okay. That's the main thing.'

'Yeah,' said Jo.

Feeling rather forlorn and surplus to requirements, we began to trudge across the foreshore. A moment later hooves pounded behind us. We turned round.

'Lady Francesca? Mr Morgan?' the messenger said. We nodded.

'His Majesty's compliments, and would you care to join His Highness Prince Ferdinand at the Castle?'

'Would we ever!' I said. 'Come on, Jo!'

17.

Your Stars: CANCER (June 22–July 23)
Nothing much seems to have been happening recently,
and you crave excitement. Try to curb your impatience:
a situation is developing in which you'll need all your
energy. You will find a way to resolve a personal problem.

Ferdinand was waiting for us in the main reception-room of what the messenger called the Visitors' Suite. His wounds had been bandaged up, and he looked dazed but happy. He greeted us with relief.

'I didn't know where you were. I thought you'd disappeared.'

I hugged him warmly. 'Ferd, you were *magnificent*! But don't ever give me heart failure like that again, d'you hear?'

Jo gripped his good shoulder. 'Brilliant, man. Just brilliant.' Ferdinand blushed and beamed.

'And you've won yourself a Princess!' I crowed. 'And now it's Happy Ever After!' There was a lump in my throat and my eyes were going misty.

His face glowed. 'I hope so! Isn't she *beautiful*? What an extraordinary stroke of luck, don't you think?'

'Rubbish, man. You deserve it,' said Jo.

I swept downstairs next morning dressed in a flame-coloured gown (courtesy of the Castle) and feeling like a million dollars, specs and all. Jo and Ferdinand were waiting for me. Jo was wearing a sober wine-coloured tunic belted over black trousers, but Ferdinand looked every inch the Handsome Prince in blue trimmed with silver, like a bridegroom. He was also looking pale and a bit strained.

'Nervous?' I asked sympathetically.

'Just a bit, yes.'

'Don't worry,' Jo said briskly. 'She won't turn you down! You're the Champion of Champions, remember.'

A liveried equerry appeared to escort us to the King's apartment.

The Visitor's Suite had been relatively modern, but the rest of the Castle was dark, crumbling and Gothic. We were halfway across the Great Hall when something small and hard whizzed from above and struck me painfully just below the cheekbone. I yelped and looked up.

Two little girls with white-blonde hair in fat plaits were leaning over the balcony of the musicians' gallery, and grinning evilly. From one child's hand there dangled a lethal-looking catapult.

'Gotcha!' she yelled, and disappeared. I heard the noise of scuttling feet on invisible stairs. The older child turned her head. 'Daddy,' she shouted in chainsaw tones, 'There are some frightfully common-looking people downstairs. What do they want?'

Jo and Ferdinand were clustering round me in concern.

'Are you all right, Foss?' Ferdinand asked anxiously.

I rubbed my cheek and winced. It was swelling already. 'Who are those appalling brats?'

The equerry coughed delicately. 'Their Royal Highnesses Princess Sasha and Princess Masha, m'Lady.'

'Oh, really,' I said.

King Romeric was waiting to receive us in a tall gloomy room hung with crumbling banners and cluttered with strange, faintly obscene objects which I dimly recognised as occult paraphernalia of the type you see in low-budget horror movies. Romeric himself was a lot older than I'd realised. In daylight, his long hair and beard were white. His eyes had a switched-off, mildly harassed look, and he blinked incessantly.

He was not alone. The brats were already there, and behind them stood his Queen.

My first impression was of a very large lady with far too much of everything, including jewels and temper. She wasn't actually fat: just very big-boned, and put together in a way which suggested that the individual parts had been rather hastily assembled from a random selection of features intended for an even larger model which had been discontinued due to lack of popular support. She had a jawline like a barracuda and huge, bony-knuckled hands.

Romeric greeted us with the forced nervous smile of the terminally shy. He had overlong teeth, stained yellow, and chipped at the edges.

'My dear chap ... dear lady ... Mr ... er ... You slept well, I hope? Everything to your liking? hey? what?'

Ferdinand bowed. 'Oh, absolutely, sir. Perfectly splendid.'

'So glad,' the King murmured, beaming nervously. 'So glad . . . Er . . . my dear, I don't believe you've met His Highness Prince Ferdinand of Boronia, have you?'

She stared at us down her big blunt nose. 'How d'ye do?' she said distantly.

'Prince Ferdinand is the Champion as foretold in the oracle, dear,' the King said proudly.

'Oh, really.' Her tone conveyed the impression that in her view Champions as a species were perhaps slightly less obnoxious than back-street muggers, but not much. Abruptly, she turned her back on us and clumped awkwardly out of the room. From somewhere deep inside my genetic code, Matilda's hackles rose.

The two little girls remained. The younger one was looking me up and down.

'You're awfully small,' she said in the raucous tones I'd come to associate with the whole family except Romeric. 'Are you a midget? I saw a midget in a fair once. They tied him up and set fire to his feet.' She and her sister burst into snorting giggles. 'It was funny!'

Beside me Jo was rigid with outrage. I glanced at Ferdinand and saw nothing but polite acquiescence in his face. I was a bit shocked. If this was how the aristocracy normally behaved *en famille*, I thought, thank God I'm not one of them . . .

Romeric was saying, 'I . . . er . . . I expect you'd like to get acquainted with my daughter Clarissa.' He cast a longing glance at his magical impedimenta. 'I have . . . a few, er, things to do now, so . . . um . . . Masha, darling, show His Highness to Clarissa's room, will you?'

As Ferdinand turned in my direction I saw his eyes. They were blank and spaced-out, the eyes of a sleepwalker. My heart missed a beat. I trod on Jo's foot. The glance he gave me was as seriously alarmed as my own.

I hadn't been included in the invitation to visit Clarissa, but I followed Ferdinand anyway. Jo strode along close behind me.

Princess Clarissa was lounging on the window-seat of her room, idly turning the pages of a magazine and biting into a chocolate. She was extremely beautiful. Long black hair, rose-petal skin and deep blue-violet eyes under thick dark lashes. As we entered she turned her head languidly and stared at us without betraying a flicker of interest. I saw with a shiver of dismay that her glorious eyes were as switched-off as her father's.

Nobody suggested that we should sit down. I looked round, found a chair and settled myself, and after a moment's polite hesitation Ferdinand and Jo did the same. Clarissa shifted slightly so as to turn her back to us and continued to munch chocolates with the steady, relentless dedication you associate with cows chewing grass.

'Are you going to marry her?' Sasha demanded in a voice like sheet metal being cut.

'Er . . . well,' Ferdinand said with a gallant bow, 'That rather depends on Her Royal Highness.'

'You won the fight, so you'll *have* to marry her,' Masha announced. Her unpleasant little face twisted into a sneer. 'Mummy says she hopes you realise how lucky you are.'

I stepped hastily into the breach. 'What a lovely view you have from up here,' I said brightly. 'Those sands must be wonderful for exercising horses. Do you ride, Clarissa?'

'She doesn't *do* anything,' Sasha declared. ' Servants *do* things.'

'Anyway,' Masha said viciously, 'she's not "Clarissa" to commoners like you, you know.' She and Sasha began to snigger.

'She called her "Clarissa",' Sasha giggled. '"Clarissa"! Just like that!'

It was the most dismally awful half-hour I'd spent for years. Clarissa ignored us completely. The two little girls monopolised the conversation and were breathtakingly rude. I was keeping my temper on a tight rein, while Jo sat beside me like a chapel deacon at a gay bar – outrage emanating in waves.

Ferdinand didn't seem to be reacting at all. He was just gazing at Clarissa with a soppy, dazed expression on his face.

'Did you really kill King Fergal?' Sasha demanded.

'Yes, actually, I did,' Ferdinand admitted.

'Gosh,' said Masha enviously. 'I wish I could have seen that. Was it really *bloody*? Did it come spouting out in big jets all over everybody, like a fountain?'

This time even Ferdinand looked slightly shocked. 'It was fairly messy, yes,' he said primly.

'I told you it would be, didn't I?' Sasha said. Her fat face darkened. 'It's not fair. They won't let us watch beheadings, or hangings, or *anything*.'

My temper jerked free for a moment. 'Perhaps they should,' I snapped. 'Perhaps then you'd realise that watching someone die is not fun.'

Two pairs of round blue eyes fixed me with a penetrating stare.

'You're wet,' Masha said in disgust. 'You're as wet as he is. Mummy said he wasn't up to scratch.'

Up to that point I'd been trying hard to be polite for Ferdinand's sake. That last remark was too much. Matilda erupted in a shower of sparks.

'Not up to scratch?' I said furiously. 'You're a disgustingly rude little brat, and your mother should have known better. Prince Ferdinand risked his life on your family's behalf! How *dare* any of you insult him like that?'

Masha was purple with rage. 'You can't speak to me like that! Daddy will chop your head off. Mummy says you're nothing but a common tart and no better than you should be.'

Jo and Ferdinand jerked upright simultaneously. Ferdinand's hand clenched around the hilt of his dagger – an instinctive reflex, because the next moment he'd remembered where he was and had subsided, seething.

I doubt if anything could have persuaded me to subside at that point.

'Frankly, dear child,' I said icily, 'I couldn't care less what you or your vulgar, obscure, ill-bred little family think of me. Your attitude to Prince Ferdinand is thoroughly obnoxious and utterly unforgivable.' I stood up. 'I'm sorry, Ferdinand, but I'm getting rather bored of hearing my friends being insulted by a couple of dirty-minded little guttersnipes and a mother too ignorant to know which side her bread's buttered.' I headed for the door. 'Goodbye, Clarissa. Do remember to clean your teeth tonight, won't you? Rotten teeth are so unattractive, don't you think?'

Jo and Ferdinand were on their feet.

'Jo?' I said grandly, and indicated the outer door. He opened it with alacrity, and I swept magnificently out. Sky-high on the powerful stimulant the Edwardians used to call Umbrage (taken, you may like to note, in sniffs through the nose) I sailed down the first flight of stairs with Jo close behind me. I was so furious I couldn't trust myself to speak.

I heard a door open and close, and clattering footsteps on the stairs: Ferdinand was demonstrating his solidarity with the cause. I stormed through the Great Hall, ignoring the servants who appeared out of every nook and cranny. Jo and Ferdinand marched behind me, looking dangerous. Nobody tried to stop us, which given the mood I was in, was probably just as well.

Safely back in the Visitors' Suite, I deflated like a pricked balloon.

'Oh, Ferdinand . . . I'm so sorry! I've blown the whole thing sky-high. I shouldn't have let those two little monsters get under my skin like that! I just couldn't help myself!'

Jo was seething. 'Don't be so bloody stupid, woman! You did exactly the right thing.'

Ferdinand was pacing the floor. The glazed look had vanished from his eyes, and he was grim-faced. 'It was unforgivable,' he fumed. 'Absolutely intolerable.' He turned on me, and I cringed. 'How *dare* she slander you like that?'

I felt shaky with relief. He was talking about the Queen, not me.

'Filling those children's heads with poisonous gossip . . .'

'Free-range kids,' Jo said with disgust. 'They get right up my nose.'

I felt terrible. 'But if I hadn't been there, it might have turned out differently . . .'

'No!' Ferdinand was pacing round the room again. 'I'm very glad you were there. You . . . brought me to my senses. It was all . . . washing over me. As though I wasn't really *there*. And then you blazed out like that, and suddenly – it all snapped into focus, somehow . . . That awful zombie of a girl, those dreadful children . . .'

If you want to know what parents are really like, watch the kids. These people were *monsters*.

Ferdinand had flung himself into a chair and was staring bleakly out of the window. Suddenly speech burst out of him. 'I *can't* marry that girl! Obligation or no obligation – I absolutely can't!' He let out a huge, baffled sigh, and clutched his hair. 'It was all so *perfect*,' he mourned. 'A Princess . . . a Kingdom . . . As though it was meant to be. Fate, or Destiny, or something . . .' Pangs of anguish distorted his handsome features. 'I mean . . . it's not as though I wasn't *eligible*, is it?' Ferdinand, the man with everything, facing rejection for the first time in his life. And from a family who should have been gibbering with gratitude.

231

'If you want to stay sane, get out of this place,' Jo said bluntly. 'Something very iffy's going on. Cut your losses and scarper, Ferd. Now. Tell Romeric you're terribly sorry, but you have a pressing engagement elsewhere, thank you very much.'

'Right,' I said. 'The Zones are huge, Ferdinand. There's bound to be another Princess somewhere. A Princess who really needs *you*.'

'If Clarissa carries on chomping choccies at that rate,' Jo said thoughtfully, 'she'll be gross in a year or two. A right barrel of lard. Toothless, too. False noshers in a glass on the dressing-table every night . . .'

'We're not trying to influence you in any way, Ferd,' I told him. 'Just expressing a personal opinion, that's all.'

He began, reluctantly, to grin. 'Thanks very much.' Then he laughed. 'Actually, just at this moment, I wouldn't *mind* marrying a barrel of lard. As long as she was a nice warm barrel, with a sense of humour.'

'And a Kingdom in tow,' I reminded him.

'That, too, of course . . . All I'm saying is, I'm getting a bit wary when it comes to beauty. I mean, other things are just as important, aren't they?'

Jo and I exchanged bemused glances. Ferdinand thinking deep thoughts was something of a shock to the system.

He stood up and squared his shoulders. 'Right. I'm going to tell Romeric the deal's off.' He paused with one hand on the doorknob. 'Hang on a minute, though . . .'

'Second thoughts?' I asked with trepidation.

'Not exactly, no . . . I mean, dash it, though – I *did* save his kingdom for him, didn't I? One hates to be mercenary about that sort of thing . . . but under the circumstances wouldn't you say he owes me something?'

'Brilliant, Ferd,' I breathed. 'What did you have in mind?'

'Horses,' he said promptly. 'Camping gear. Provisions. Decent clothing.'

'Another boat?'

Ferdinand shuddered slightly. 'I've rather gone off boats, if you want the absolute truth.'

'I wouldn't mind some sort of weapon,' Jo said. 'A bit of ready cash would come in handy, too.'

Ferdinand measured him by eye, squinting like an undertaker. 'I'll get you a sword. Me, too, come to think of it.' He turned the doorknob purposefully.

'What about me?' I said.

He stopped. 'You?'

'Don't you think I should have a weapon of some sort too?'

Ferdinand blinked. 'Don't be silly, Foss. Ladies don't rush about clobbering people with swords.'

'Oops,' said Jo. I shot him an annihilating look.

'Fine,' I said. 'Right. I understand. I'm not supposed to defend myself, am I? I'm supposed to sit there and file my nails while you two get cut to ribbons by bandits, yes?'

'Actually,' Jo murmured, 'I think you're supposed to faint.'

'*What?*'

'Loud voices. Blood . . . Oh, never mind.'

I ignored him. 'And when it's all over, it doesn't matter what happens to me once my men are dead. I'm only a girl, after all. Is that what you're trying to say?'

'Don't talk such absolute bosh, Foss. If we were ambushed by bandits, you'd be no use anyway. You couldn't even lift a full-sized sword even if you knew how to use one.'

'So what do boys use when they're learning?'

Jo coughed tactfully. 'Actually, Ferd, it wouldn't be a bad idea.'

Ferdinand glared frostily at us both. 'I don't see it. Enlighten me.'

Jo shrugged. 'Seems to me that a high-born lady travelling with two men might attract a lot of attention from the wrong sort of people on this trip. Whereas two blokes with a young lad tagging along . . .'

Ferdinand opened his mouth to argue (mostly out of habit, I felt), thought better of it and expressed his disapproval in a grunt. 'Okay. Your decision. I'll see what I can do.'

As it happened, Romeric didn't need much persuasion to cough up. Apparently he'd been gazing raptly into some sort of crystal ball when Ferdinand and the Steward had walked in. His acquiescence had been along the lines of, 'Yes, yes, give His Highness anything he wants, just leave me alone.'

Ferdinand wasted no time. When we left Castle Lermos an hour later we were mounted on three good horses. Ferdinand was carrying a fat leather pouch of gold coins at his belt and a hefty sword dangled at his side, a twin to the one Jo was wearing. As an additional discouragement to would-be marauders, three crossbows glinted evilly at our saddle-bows.

Out of deference to Ferdinand's sense of propriety I was wearing a dark-blue riding-habit, but the bundle strapped to my horse's rump contained boys' clothes and a short, light sword. I'd extracted a promise from Ferdinand that he'd teach me how to use it and I vowed privately that he wasn't going to be allowed to wriggle out of that commitment, no matter what.

As we rode out of the courtyard Ferdinand jerked upright and swore. A slug from Sasha's catapult had hit him in the small of the back. I had to admit she was an excellent shot.

'The sooner we get out of this Zone, the happier I'll be,' Jo announced as we cantered off down the road. 'Where's the nearest Gateway, Ferd?'

'The Steward said we'd have to cross the mountains. There's a town, apparently, on the other side.'

At first we passed villages, a small fishing-port and scattered crofts in the hills, but by the second day there were no signs of human habitation anywhere. On the third day the road swung in towards the mountains and began to climb.

Each day Ferdinand drilled Jo and me in swordsmanship. At the end of the first day, muscles I never knew I had were screaming in agony. After four days Ferdinand remarked, 'You know, if you were a boy, I'd say you were doing pretty well,' – a backhanded compliment if ever I heard one. Between times, we practised shooting with the crossbows.

I also had time, finally, to come to grips with my feelings towards Jo.

It couldn't be love – that was too ridiculous. Me – falling in love with the boy next door? My self-respect was outraged. There was a perfectly reasonable explanation for it – Ferdinand, the disquieting episode with Rupert, all those months of purdah in Arborea – I came to the conclusion that my hormones had suddenly decided enough was enough, and hurled themselves at the first attractive male who'd happened to come along. By sheer bad luck it had been Jo.

Which left me with a major problem. I was too fond of Jo to risk wrecking a lifetime's friendship for the sake of a brief flirtation. There's only one thing to do about rampant urges which have got out of hand, I told myself. Ignore them. Sooner or later, they'll get bored and start looking around for a more appropriate object to lose their collective rag over. In the meantime, I'd just have to act as though nothing was happening.

As we climbed, the road dwindled to a rough track. Finally we reached a shallow upland pass between craggy peaks. One or two tumbledown walls straggled out across the moor, and . . .

'I say, there's a village!' Ferdinand cried. We urged our tired horses into a canter.

As we got closer the cluster of stone huts began to look less and less welcoming. No stock in the weed-infested paddocks, no people anywhere.

We walked the horses slowly along the one street. Shutters creaked in the wind. Front doors gaped open. Inside we could see crockery on tables, mouldy food, ashes in hearths . . .

'They must have left in one hell of a hurry,' Jo remarked.

Cold shivers were chasing each other up and down my spine. The place was like a violated tomb. Something horrible had happened in this lonely, silent village, and left no record behind. I didn't want to know what – I just wanted out. Fast.

The track continued across the open moor. It meandered amongst boulders shattered into bizarre shapes by millennia of frost and thaw. I saw a ship, a castle, a man's head . . . and in the distance two immense, thin spars leaning drunkenly against each other like gateposts into nowhere.

Suddenly, out of the corner of my eye, I saw one of the boulders move. It shambled forwards. Reared up. Lunged towards the horses . . . I fought back a scream.

It was huge, grey, naked; vaguely (but only vaguely) man-shaped. Its hide hung in wrinkled folds from its scrawny limbs and enormous pot-belly. It had claws, and fangs a foot long – and it was hungry. Spittle poured out of its gaping maw as it reached out to take a swipe at me.

The horses reared in terror and took off. All around us, more and more of the boulders were coming to life: their sunken eyes gleamed red. We drew our swords while desperately trying to keep our frantic horses under control.

'Run for it!' Ferdinand yelled, swiping with his blade.

We gave the horses their heads. But the creatures were all around us now. Clawed forearms reached out, slashed at us and narrowly missed. Jo hacked at a groping arm and severed it. The arm, still twitching, was snatched up and devoured by another of the creatures. The wounded one went down, shrieking, under a barrage of eager claws and teeth.

As the rest closed in, all those endless sword-arm exercises clicked into place. I stabbed and slashed and hacked. Behind me, Jo was grunting with effort. Ferdinand's own sword was flickering like summer lightning. Maimed bodies were littering the track behind us. And still more creatures were converging on us from the front.

I looked up, breathless and blurry-eyed, my heart pounding and the blood singing in my ears. We were nearing the two gatepost rocks. I felt a sudden, overwhelming compulsion to ride through the gap – a compulsion that was like an urgent command. I swung my horse off the track and galloped off towards them.

Pounding hooves sounded close behind me, but I dared not look round. Stone-creatures rose up to bar my way. I pelted on.

In close-up, the two spars were gigantic. As I galloped through the gap, the entire sky seemed to explode into blinding light. I could hear screams in the distance, and a noise like far-off thunder. Milliseconds later Jo came pounding through after me, looking a bit wild about the eyes. After him came Ferdinand, dishevelled and with singed hair.

Abruptly, there was silence.

18.

Your Stars: CANCER (June 23–July 23)
More options are available than you thought. This is a
good time to remind other people that you are still around.
An unexpected encounter has surprising consequences.
Trust your own judgement and your sense of timing.

We were in a different place. Lowlands, heavily wooded, the trees leafless and the ground stippled with snow. A different season: a different Zone. The spars had shrunk to a couple of gateposts in a crude stone wall. The stone-creatures had vanished.

I got a fit of the cold shudders. 'What *happened*?'

Jo swallowed hard. 'When you rode towards those rocks . . . That pendant of yours – it was like a force-field, or something – white fire all round you. It just frizzled those creatures as if they were gnats. And when you rode through . . .'

'The whole valley exploded,' Ferdinand said with a gulp. 'One gigantic fireball.'

Jo let out an unsteady breath. 'If we'd been more than a yard or two behind you . . .'

'*Nothing* could have survived that blast,' Ferdinand said with certainty. 'Not those – creatures – nothing.'

I had the shakes again and couldn't stop. 'Those poor people . . .'

Jo gave me a reassuring hug. 'Think of it this way, Foss. Romeric's Kingdom has been saved for him. Again.'

'What?'

'Those creatures were resting, I guess. Getting hungry again. They'd have moved on: down the moor towards the coast. How much of Lermos would've been left, do you think? Everything in it would've been eaten alive.'

'Oh, my God,' I said. I could feel the blood draining away from my face and lips. 'I was right. A sorcerer set the whole thing up. The storm, the duel, everything.' Those blank eyes, Ferdinand's zombie-like acquiescence . . . A sorcerer – *the* sorcerer? – the one Oz had called the boss? The boss who'd gone to so much trouble setting up Ferdinand's quest? 'Romeric let us go, and he wasn't supposed to . . .' The stone-creatures had been close to a Gateway. That sorcerer had put them there to wipe us *all* out. As a punishment for disobedience.

I slid down off the horse in a hurry, scuttled behind a tree and threw up.

We walked the sweating horses into the woods and onto a track trampled clear of snow.

'More horses,' Ferdinand said, squinting like a detective. 'A fair-sized troop, at a guess. Well-shod, too – not your average peasant cob. '

'Maybe there's a town nearby.'

'Make a nice change after all this emptiness,' Jo remarked. 'I could murder a pint of bitter.'

The horses broke into a trot as though they, too, couldn't wait to get back to civilisation again. Hay, oats, a nice warm stall, grooms to fuss over them, reassuring smells . . . you could practically read their minds from the way their ears pricked up and their heads tossed. To hell with Nature in the raw, they seemed to be saying. Give us the smoke and the fleshpots and the teeming hordes every time. Nature's no place for a decent horse.

Ferdinand halted and sniffed. 'Can you smell burning?'

The trees ended and there, ahead of us, was a sizeable town. Or what, until very recently, had been a town. We stared in horrified dismay, all our dreams of comfort shattered.

There was smoke, certainly – pouring out of dozens of gutted buildings inside the boundary wall. Teeming hordes there were none – unless you included the neat rows of tents parked in a semicircle outside the shattered gates. And as for fleshpots (whatever *they* are) – one glance made it abundantly clear that anything of that nature which had survived the day's massacre was earmarked for the exclusive use of the troops patrolling the streets.

'It's a bloody war zone,' said Jo.

Suspicious guards were already making pointed advances towards us. Pointed, as in wicked-looking pikes.

'We'd better have a word with their commanding officer, don't you think?' said Ferdinand, and rode confidently to meet the welcoming committee.

I had a strong feeling we'd have been invited to meet the boss anyway, whether we wanted to or not, but I didn't say so. Jo and I trailed meekly in Ferdinand's wake.

He looked round as we approached.

'We seem to have arrived at a rather inopportune moment, I'm afraid. There's been a fairly serious insurrection in these parts – a rebel Earl, I gather. But it's all over now. His Majesty led the assault in person.' He was being every inch the gracious scion of Royalty.

'Oh,' I said. 'Good.'

'We'll pay our respects to His Majesty, of course,' Ferdinand added – somehow managing to convey the impression that he and the King had been bosom buddies since kindergarten. 'Lead on, Captain.'

'Do you know this king?' I hissed, as we trotted in the midst of our escort.

'Never heard of him before in my life. His name's Haglund. Does it matter?'

King Haglund's tent was marginally bigger and very slightly smarter than the rest. His banner – a black stag on a red background – was prominently displayed outside. A warrior King, I deduced, doing some Sherlocking of my own, and possibly more at home on the battlefield than at Court. Perhaps he really had led the assault on the town.

Haglund was a tall, lean, big-boned man in his forties, with a scarred face and one sleeve empty from the elbow down. Warrior King was right; he looked as though he'd spent most of his life fighting.

Ferdinand introduced us, and explained that we were just passing through. The King listened courteously enough, but in complete, unnerving silence. Evidently, he wasn't the chatty type. My heart sank. Everything about this man emanated power – the way he stood, his silence, his immaculately-drilled aides standing rigidly to attention all round him. Even Ferdinand started to stammer a bit.

Haglund looked all three of us up and down. Finally one eyebrow rose in faint, sardonic amusement. It took a lot more than a regal manner to impress this man.

'My country is at war, Your Highness. I take it you want a safe-conduct as far as the border.'

Ferdinand gulped. 'That's correct, sir. Had we known about your campaign,' he added, 'we'd have avoided the area completely, of course.'

The king gave a curt nod. 'Those swords you're wearing,' he said abruptly. 'Can you use them?'

239

'Of course, sir.' Ferdinand looked stung, as well he might. Me – I was having terrifying visions of being conscripted into the army.

'Good. This is what you will do. Five miles outside this town you will reach a crossroads. You will take the left fork. Ten miles further on you will come to a town where I imagine you will be able to purchase a lodging for the night.'

'Thank you very much, sir,' said Ferdinand.

'Wait. Tomorrow there is to be a muster of noble Lords at my Court in Stourlin Town. You will present yourselves there. If you do not, the safe-conduct becomes invalid, and you will be shot on sight. Do you understand?'

Ferdinand bowed. 'Perfectly, sir.'

The audience was over. A wooden-faced aide showed us out. We mounted our horses and started breathing again.

The horses weren't at all impressed with the change in plan. They sulked, ears flat and heads down.

'Another fifteen miles . . . D'you think we'll make it before dark?' The prospect of being benighted in the middle of a war zone in winter didn't appeal one bit.

We began to pass straggling groups of refugees from the battle: townsfolk and peasants, some with all their possessions stacked into carts, others trudging wearily along with nothing but the clothes they stood up in. Their faces looked shocked and hopeless.

Further on we began to see other, grislier mementoes of war. Every hundred metres or so along the road a group of gibbets had been set up. Bodies dangled from them like clusters of obscene fruit. We averted our eyes and rode on.

Jo reined in. 'Isn't that the crossroads just ahead?'

The sign said Melwhiddan. Ferdinand glowered at it. 'Melwhiddan? Stourlin?'

Hope dawned. 'Ferd! You've been here before?'

He frowned, and shook his head. 'No – but the names sound familiar, somehow.'

'So – we're back in the right Zone?'

'I honestly don't know,' he said fretfully. 'If only I could remember . . .'

'It'll come to you,' Jo said comfortably. 'Meanwhile, Melwhiddan next stop.'

The road was a narrow country lane between high hedgerows.

It crossed the brow of the hill and plunged almost immediately into thick woodland. Something glinted amongst the trees, and the next moment . . .

'Look out, Foss!' Ferdinand yelled.

I ducked instinctively as the crossbow bolt whizzed past my ear, making a noise like an angry wasp. Ferdinand was already firing back.

Jo grabbed my reins and hustled us both behind a holly bush. All three of us fired at once. In the thickets on the far side of the road somebody screamed. There was a scuffle, and the noise of several pairs of feet running away.

Rather shaken, we restrung our crossbows and rode on.

'Could Haglund have . . .?'

'No,' Jo said decisively. 'No time. No point. Gangs of bandits, hanging round the fringes of the battle zone, waiting for easy pickings. That's my guess, anyway.'

'He knew they were here, though.'

Ferdinand's face was grim. 'Right. If that's the way he wants to play it . . . Keep a sharp lookout from now on, okay?'

We urged the tired horses into a canter.

The second attack came five miles further on, as we were riding down a steep hill towards a T-junction at the bottom. About twenty ragged men armed with everything from pitchforks to cutlasses came charging through the woods on both sides of the road, yelling blue murder.

The attack was savage and brutal. If we and the horses had been fresh and rested, we might have routed them, in spite of being outnumbered. But it had been a long, gruelling day, and as we hacked and thrust and slashed even Ferdinand was showing signs of strain. I blessed his merciless drilling – without it, I wouldn't have lasted two minutes.

Suddenly a shrill whistle sounded from within the wood. Our attackers froze. Then, as one man, they fled into the shelter of the trees.

Horses were approaching – a large troop of them, along the road at the bottom of the hill. We backed behind some thick bushes, feeling desperate. Three close brushes with death are quite enough for one day – four, if you include the encounter with Haglund. Melwhiddan and somewhere warm to sleep seemed like a million miles away.

The troop of horsemen emerged into the thin winter sunlight:

241

fifteen heavily-armed men in helmets and mail shirts, all riding with the kind of relaxed alertness which distinguishes the professional from the enthusiastic amateur. My heart sank.

The leader of the troop was a young man of about Ferdinand's age. One glance at him and your eyes were riveted. He literally shone like the sun. His long cloak was dazzlingly white, thrown back from a breastplate polished like a mirror. His snow-white horse displayed enough gold on its harness to stock a dozen High Street jewellers' shops. The young man's head was bare, and glossy black curls tumbled over his broad shoulders.

Ferdinand stared, shaded his eyes – and gave a strangled squawk. The next moment he'd urged his horse out of the thicket and was galloping down the hill, yelling like a maniac.

The troop reined in. Fifteen crossbows levelled themselves at Ferdinand's heart.

'For God's sake, George,' Ferdinand shouted. 'It's me! Don't you recognise me, you idiot? Tell your chaps to put those things away!'

Jo and I exchanged resigned glances. 'Another old mate of his, d'you reckon?'

'I think that's a fair assumption, yes. Remember the last old mate we bumped into?'

Jo winced. 'Rupert. How could I ever forget?'

'At least it proves we're back in the right Zone,' I said.

We edged our horses back onto the road and made our way down the hill. When we reached the junction Ferdinand and his friend were clouting each other on the back in that painfully hearty way men have of greeting one another. Ferdinand turned a shining face towards us.

'Foss . . . Jo . . . Come and meet George. George Waters. Not in the least like Rupert, I promise you . . . George, old chap, I want you to meet my – er – cousin, Lady Foss . . . and another friend, Jo Morgan. George and I were at school together,' he added, beaming fatuously.

In close-up, Ferdinand's friend wasn't just handsome. He was breathtakingly beautiful. Huge violet eyes, lashes a yard long, blue-black hair in long ringlets, cheekbones faintly flushed with ripe apricot, exquisitely modelled nose and jawline . . . I gawped, dumbfounded – and then had an almost overwhelming urge to giggle. George's luscious feminine beauty was the biggest turn-off in a man that I've ever experienced.

Masterfully suppressing hysteria, I rode forwards and shook hands.

'Gosh,' he said idiotically. 'I say. Jolly pleased to make your acquaintance, what?' He squeezed my hand in a bruising grip. 'Ferdy, you rat, you never told me you had a demmed pretty cousin.'

'I must have done,' Ferdinand lied glibly. 'You weren't paying attention, George – you never did.'

Jo and I waited while Ferdinand told George about our skirmishes with the bandits. George's lovely face took on a look of concern.

'Oh, I say. Bad show.' He went on to explain that he and his men were on a routine patrol of the area for the express purpose of discouraging such attacks. 'Mean to say, we're not in the war zone here, are we? Thank God,' he added piously. 'Dashed if I'm going to allow a bunch of desperadoes to terrorise my tenants. Enough problems as it is, dammit. Had to ship up wagonloads of food from Melhuish last week. Poor souls'd have had nothin' to celebrate Christmas with if I hadn't.' So George was a landlord, and a conscientious one at that.

'*Your* tenants, George?' Ferdinand enquired.

'Ah, yes,' said George, looking ludicrously mournful. 'The pater, y'know. Popped off. Three years last Michaelmas.'

'Sorry to hear that, old chap,' Ferdinand said with genuine sympathy.

'Thanks,' George said simply. 'Miss him, y'know.' He squared his broad shoulders. 'Still, life goes on, what?'

He insisted on us accompanying him back to his Border castle. 'Won't take no for an answer. Pretty basic up here at Castle Craig, mind you,' he added. 'Not like Melhuish, of course. Comfortable, though. Saw to that myself. My guests – for as long as you care to stay.'

We reached Castle Craig in half an hour. Dogs came pouring out of the hall door, barking joyously as we rode into the courtyard.

'Bachelor establishment, I'm afraid,' George apologised, as well-trained servants homed in from all directions and he himself gallantly helped me to dismount. 'Eleanor's at Melhuish at the moment. Baby, y'know,' he explained self-consciously.

Ferdinand's eyes widened in stunned astonishment.

'You're *married*, George?'

243

I could see his point. It did seem a little improbable.

George blushed. 'Eighteen months ago. Eddie Corvannis's sister. Remember Eddie?'

'Good God,' Ferdinand said. 'Well done, George! Congratulations!' – and thumped him between the shoulder blades. 'You swine, you never asked me to the wedding!'

'Wanted you to be best man, old chap, but nobody seemed to know where you were. Very quiet wedding, of course – Pater not there, y'know.'

'And the baby?' I asked.

George beamed with paternal pride. 'Boy. Healthy little monster. Month old. Best set of lungs I ever heard.' He was leading us up the steps and into the entrance hall as he spoke. 'Convenient, that. Get the old heir business out of the way, y'know. Bit early yet, of course – but next time I rather fancy having a daughter. Little gels dashing about the place,' he said wistfully. 'Never had sisters meself. Only child, and all that. Always felt I was missing out.'

'Oh, George,' I said, 'You are sweet.'

If George considered Castle Craig's facilities basic, I couldn't help wondering what his main seat, Melhuish, must be like. Castle Craig seemed awesomely luxurious to me.

'Is he very rich?' I asked Ferdinand privately, as George bustled off to organise hot baths, clean clothes and dinner.

'Rather. Wealthiest family I know. Oodles of the stuff.'

'And you didn't remember he was here?'

Ferdinand looked chagrined. 'Didn't connect Melhuish with Haglund. Or Stourlin either, for that matter. Old Lord Waters was pretty much a law to himself – ran the place like a petty kingdom. Well, they all did – all the big estates, I mean. Apparently this Haglund hasn't been King for very long – a first cousin, or something – and it looks as though he's decided to assert his authority. Can't say I blame him, even if his methods are a bit brutal. You can't rule a country if every minor squire with a few acres of land thinks he can thumb his nose at you with impunity.'

'H'mm,' Jo said thoughtfully. 'Tell you what, though – if I were George, I'd be very, very careful.'

'I'm sure he is,' Ferdinand said loftily.

'What I mean is, I wouldn't flaunt my wealth about in that ostentatious way if I were him.'

I got his drift. 'You think Haglund might get greedy?'

Jo shrugged. 'He's got a war to pay for, hasn't he? Allies to keep sweet. Things like that don't come cheap.'

George, however, seemed blissfully unaware of any potential unpleasantness between himself and his monarch. He was full of praise for his king's abilities.

'Brilliant general. Superb tactician. Exactly what this country needs – a strong King to weld us all together, y'know.'

We discovered that the Lermos episode had lost us nine months in this Zone. We'd left Arborea in March and it was now late December. Ferdinand didn't turn a hair but Jo and I were stunned.

'Oz or Magnus must have sent us here, so it must be okay,' Jo said, but dubiously.

'I don't think it was them,' I said. 'The pendant just burst us back into the right Zone, with a massive energy discharge. And we lost nine months, remember. I can't see Oz or Magnus being that sloppy.'

'Well, we're here now, so it doesn't matter, does it?' Ferdinand said.

Over dinner Ferdinand filled George in on the details of our flight from Arborea and the downfall of his hopes. George was suitably shocked.

'So I still have to find a suitable princess,' Ferdinand concluded. 'Got any ideas, George?'

George pondered. 'Haglund's got a couple of daughters. First marriage. Wife died about ten years back.'

Ferdinand's eyes brightened. 'No heir?'

'Not yet,' George said cautiously. 'Point is, he's married again. Young gel. Nobody we know,' he added with unconscious snobbery. 'Nothing wrong with her, mind you. Good blood and all that. But practically a pauper – or so I've heard, anyway.' George, as I'd already gleefully suspected, was a dedicated gossip.

'The way I heard it,' he went on, leaning cosily across the table, 'Haglund spotted this gel in some God-forsaken croft at the back-end of nowhere and fell in love with her at first sight.'

I suppressed a shudder. 'Sounds a bit out of character, if you ask me. He didn't strike me as the romantic type.'

'Deep, though,' said Jo. 'That's the type that falls the hardest.'

'Absolutely,' George agreed. 'And God help the feller that gets in his way.'

'She must be an absolute scorcher,' Ferdinand said enviously.

During coffee the conversation got round to Ferdinand's safe-conduct, and his promise to the King.

'Personally,' Jo said, 'I don't think much of that man's sense of humour. He knew we were going to be attacked; he sent us straight into an ambush situation without so much as a word of warning.'

'I'd trust him about as far as I could heave a truck,' I agreed.

'Look, why don't we just let him assume we're dead, and ooze away out of his ambit?' Jo said. 'George'll have maps of the borders, won't you, George?'

George was examining his fingernails and looking unhappy.

We all looked at Ferdinand, who was chewing his lower lip. Suddenly he thumped the table.

'No! I'm damned if I'll give him the satisfaction of thinking we couldn't handle his beastly little brigands. I think we ought to turn up at Stourlin just to show him what we're capable of.'

George was nodding agreement.

'And after all,' Ferdinand added, 'I did give my word.'

'Know what I think?' George said. 'Play it by the book, old chap. Absolutely. He's not a man you want to take risks with. I've fought in his army, and I *know*.'

The muster at the King's court in Stourlin was a more important occasion than we'd realised. George explained that it took place every year, just after Christmas, and lasted three days. Attendance was compulsory for all the nobility, from Great Lords to petty squires, and wives and families had to make an appearance as well – Haglund's way of keeping tabs on his subjects. As an added incentive to good behaviour, everyone had to swear an Oath of Allegiance – which must have stuck in a good many gold-plated throats.

We set out for Stourlin the following morning. This first day was reserved for visiting dignitaries, civil servants and other minor officials. The Great Lords – which included George – weren't due to show up until the third and most important day.

George rode with us as far as Melwhiddan.

'Magistrates' Court,' he explained. 'Open house once a quarter. Same thing in Melhuish. Pretty informal, y'know. People just tip up there if they've got a grievance. Usually manage to sort something out.'

246

'What a brilliant idea, George. Sort of Citizen's Advice Bureau, with muscle.'

He beamed. 'Exactly. Pater's idea. Get to know your people that way – they get to know you, and everybody sees justice being done. Personal touch, d'ye see. Spend the whole day here – gives me plenty of time to ride on to Melhuish and pick up the family.'

As we rode through the little town, people crowded around George to call out greetings and ask after Lady Waters and the baby. George chatted and joked and seemed to know almost everybody by name.

'Popular bloke,' Jo murmured.

Ferdinand nodded. 'They respect him, too.' The look he gave George was unusually thoughtful.

At the Courthouse George shook hands and said good-bye. 'See you all at Stourlin. Take care, what?'

Jo moved alongside me as we trotted off with the armed escort George had insisted on providing for us. 'What d'you reckon to old George, then?' he said quietly.

'He's a sweetie,' I said. 'A big soft cuddly teddy-bear.'

Jo scowled impatiently. 'No . . . *you* know.' His voice sounded a bit edgy; if I hadn't known better I'd have said he was jealous.

'You want the truth?'

'Yes.'

'Okay. Every time I look at that incredible face of his, I want to laugh.'

He blinked. 'You're kidding.'

'I'm not. Cross my heart. He's just too good-looking. I don't understand why, but he isn't sexy *at all*.'

'I'll never understand women,' Jo said, looking baffled. But relieved, nevertheless.

Melwhiddan had been a market town: cheerful, clean, unpretentious, with wide streets to accommodate wagons. Stourlin was a walled city out of a different age. Narrow, cramped streets rose tier upon tier to the Castle at the top of the hill. The upper storeys of the houses overhung the streets, making them gloomy even in the noon sunshine. Slush and yellow-stained foam of dubious origin filled the gutters: the stench indicated all too plainly that the sanitation was as ancient as the buildings and nowhere near as functional.

'If it's like this in December, remind me not to visit in the middle of a heat wave,' Jo said, holding his nose.

Our escort left us at the Castle gates. The Castle was formidable: massively thick walls bristling at the top with armed soldiers. As we passed through the gate arch with the portcullis poised above our heads I felt as though we were entering a prison. The echoing clang as the outer gate shut behind us didn't do a thing to correct the impression.

Not for the first time, I wondered what in the Zones we'd got ourselves into now . . .

Haglund received us in a gloomy, firelit cave of a room, its bare stone walls hung all over with weapons, presumably as a dire warning against flippancy. For a millisecond his face betrayed a glimmer of surprise, even respect – he hadn't expected us to make it this far.

He was as laconic as ever, and three minutes later we were being dismissed and directed to our quarters.

In the adjoining hallway we were met by a vast haddock-faced female accompanied by a wizened stringy one like an anchovy well past its sell-by date.

'This way, Your Ladyship,' they chorused, and detached me neatly from Ferdinand and Jo. Emanating disapproval on all wavelengths they bore me away to a tiny garret bedroom in the Queen's Tower, where they unpacked for me and stood by glaring as I changed out of my riding habit. George had lent me a couple of Eleanor's dresses which, in the absence of a sewing machine and any female assistance at Castle Craig, I'd laboriously shortened and taken in to fit. I got the strong feeling that both haddock and anchovy were mentally ticking-off every bodged stitch, and filing the list away to be used in evidence whenever they felt like it.

Their silence, like Haglund's, was unnerving. The significant looks they exchanged said plainer than words that a young lady who arrived at the King's Court in the company of two men, unescorted by a maid and in second-hand clothes, was hardly the sort of person they were used to, and probably No Better Than She Should Be. Once again, I could feel Matilda's hackles rising.

They rose even further when Hilda (the haddock) marched me down to a large, sunny room on the first floor of the Tower. It was crammed with colourfully-dressed ladies all accompanied

248

by their maids and all twittering away in high-pitched artificial voices.

There wasn't a single male in sight. I wasn't introduced to anyone. I caught a glimpse of a tall, handsomely-dressed young woman in the midst of a throng of adoring hangers-on, but whether she was the Queen George had told us about, or one of the Princesses, I had no idea. Hilda sat beside me like Mount Everest, ice from the waist up, and I dared not ask her.

Every now and again somebody would glance my way and whisper something to her neighbour, and they'd both hide their mouths and giggle. It was the kind of situation in which you begin to wonder if you've got BO. I sat there and seethed in silence until dinner was announced. Everyone got up, fussing and simpering, and we all trooped down to the Great Hall like a bunch of schoolgirls invited to a Rotary Club lunch.

The Great Hall was huge and gloomy and torchlit. There was a blazing firepit in the middle, and the air was acrid with smoke. The men had already started on their meal: they sprawled at the round tables swigging ale out of enormous tankards and shovelling the food in with their fists. The noise was overpowering. Haglund and a few favoured noblemen sat at a table on a raised platform at one end of the Hall; the ladies of the Queen's Household took their places next to them, and the rest of us were led to another table shoved inconspicuously up against the wall.

The meal arrived. There were no forks: just knives, and hunks of bread to sop up the gravy. The ladies' tables were supplied with bowls of scented water and napkins, but the men seemed to be expected to wipe their fingers on their clothing. I couldn't help wondering how fastidious Ferdinand was making out. I squinted hopefully through the murk but I couldn't see him or Jo anywhere. Perhaps they'd had the sense to opt out.

The men at Haglund's table were a strangely assorted lot. A few military types with dour faces, a grossly fat man in purple with a magenta complexion, a skeletal hatchet-faced man in black, and a skinny little man in outrageously flamboyant clothes who seemed to be telling a string of dirty jokes. Not one face I'd trust further than I could spit.

The same went for the hoi polloi at floor level. Perhaps hoi polloi is the wrong term, because a fair number of them were richly dressed even if they did look as though they took a sniff at a bath once a year and then thought better of it. There was lots of noise, lots of steady scoffing and quaffing and quite a bit of horseplay – but nobody showed any signs of mellowing-out under the influence of all that alcohol. You got the distinct impression that any moment a knife-fight might break out – and that if it did, nobody would take any notice.

I suddenly began to feel very nervous and very much alone. Officially, of course, Ferdinand and Jo and I were under the protection of the King – but Haglund had already shown a fairly casual attitude to human life. In this place, strangers had better watch out.

The decibel count soared. The stench and the fug were indescribable. I glanced cautiously around. Haglund's place at the High Table was empty. The maids, including Hilda, were gossiping in a corner, and at my table the ladies were squealing over a sugary pudding. Nobody was looking my way. I slid off the bench and slipped quietly through the nearest door.

Five minutes later I found myself at a door that opened into a walled garden. The flood of cold air made me gasp. I unhitched a cloak from a peg and shrugged it round me. It was far too big, and smelt like the dining hall (garlic, ten-days-old sweat and last night's beer), but the fleece lining was warm.

Outside in the garden it was blissfully quiet. No-one else was about. The sun was a dull red disc on the horizon and the air had that thick blueish look which heralds a hard frost. I walked briskly to the far end and leaned over the parapet.

There was a magnificent view over the city, but after a minute or so I stopped looking and succumbed to gloomy thoughts. Two more days in this gruesome dump, segregated away from Jo and Ferdinand, surrounded by drunken oiks and catty women and hostile servants . . . George must have been out of his mind to have sent us here. The thought of George – sweet, kind, and above all *civilised* – made me want to cry.

Dusk fell. Torchlight and candlelight appeared in the windows behind and above me and cast dapples of colour on the snowy lawn. The frost began to sharpen its teeth and get down to business as though it had decided that tonight was the night to go for the all-time record. I was shivering. Images of a roaring fire and a scalding hot drink were suddenly very attractive. On the other hand, I knew that if I had to put up with another session amongst the hens something serious would blow and I wouldn't be responsible for my actions. I couldn't go indoors just yet.

The garden was cleverly sectioned off with fences and trellises to make you think it was bigger than it actually was. Pulling the cloak around me I chose a path at random and started walking.

The cold was intense. I was just starting to face up to the fact that whatever social horrors might be awaiting me inside the castle, an unscheduled dose of pneumonia might possibly be a lot worse, when I heard a faint sound from the other side of the withy fence.

Somebody quite close by me was sobbing her heart out.

19.

Your Stars: CANCER (June 22–July 23)
The situation you find yourself in is delicate and needs
tactful handling if you're to succeed. Much will depend
on the support of colleagues and friends. Honesty is the
best policy.

She wasn't having a tantrum. She hadn't stormed out of the Castle in a fit of rage or jealousy or any of the violent emotions you'd normally associate with a bout of tears. This was the quiet, pitiful, helpless sobbing you do in absolute privacy, when you simply can't cope any more and you know there's nothing on earth anybody can do to help.

The noise homed straight in at levels of my subconscious I didn't even know existed. It made my heart gallop and goose-flesh crawl all over my skin. It reminded me of Mum . . .

My first impulse was to barge straight in there and make her *stop*. Hug her, comfort her, offer her a shoulder to cry on – *anything* to spare me the horror of that awful, soul destroying sound. Then I hesitated. How I felt wasn't important. In her place the last thing I'd want was the embarrassment of being overheard. My best bet, I decided, was to tiptoe away and then make a tactfully noisy approach. That way, she could slip away and hide if she really wanted to. Or, hopefully, stay and talk to me.

I was about to put Plan B into operation when words, high and tremulous, suddenly emerged out of the sobs.

'S—sorry . . . Oh, Mama . . . please forgive me . . . Never w—wanted to do this . . . Wicked . . . B—burn in Hell . . .'

A faint light flickered between the withies of the fence. She gave a gasp of pain – and I heard the clink of steel falling to the ground.

So much for Plan B. I've never moved faster in my life. I catapulted around the end of the fence. And jerked to a horrified stop.

Everything registered in a couple of heartbeats. The lantern with its stump of candle-end casting a circle of dim light on the snow. The crouching girl, even younger than me, her eyes glaring up at me through a dishevelled mass of dark hair. The fact that all she was wearing in this murderous cold was a thin sleeveless shift. And the blood pouring down between her fingers and dripping in slow heavy gouts onto the silvering flagstones . . .

I can't say I *thought* at all at this point: I just reacted out of instinct. I remember lunging for the dagger she'd dropped, and fumbling frantically with cold fingers to slit the seam of my underskirt. I remember tearing off a long strip of fabric and wrapping it tightly around her slashed wrist. She didn't resist: she seemed stunned.

Thank God, she'd bodged the job. The blood was streaming, not spurting – she'd missed the artery, probably because her right hand had been too numb to grip the dagger properly. I was pulling off my cloak to wrap round her when I saw her clothes lying in a neatly-folded heap just outside the circle of lantern-light. Folded as though they'd been precious to her – too good to be stained and spoilt by what she'd intended to do to herself.

I shook them out, garment by garment, and dressed her hastily and not very gently. Halfway through the process she came out of her trance and tried to push me away with an inarticulate cry. But her heart wasn't in it, and after a moment or two she gave up the struggle and went limp, like a rag doll.

She was a tall girl – nearly as tall as Aurora – and well-built to match, but the outer garments were too big for her. The over-dress had been patiently stitched to fit. Another second-hand person, I thought, in this place where such things mattered.

As I was wrapping her cloak around her she started to shiver violently. Then she buried her face in her hands and began to cry.

'Right,' I said harshly. 'Now you and I are going to move around. Walk. Skip. Jump about. Act like a couple of lunatics. And nobody's going to see us, or be any the wiser afterwards – understand?'

Getting her to her feet almost pulled my arms out of their sockets and seriously threatened to fracture my spine. She was a big girl. But I did it somehow. I had no idea if I was doing the right thing – all I had to go on was a vague memory of Mrs McAllister telling us about hypothermia and that muscles made heat. If she'd lost more blood, I wouldn't have dared – but I figured I'd got there just in time.

Right or wrong, it worked. She was young and healthy and the deathly chill hadn't gone deep. Once she'd started to walk on her own – crying out with the pain in her numbed feet and cramped legs – the colour began to return to her pale lips.

'Is there anywhere I can take you to clean you up, get you properly warm?'

Until then all I'd got out of her were moans of protest through chattering teeth. Now she pulled away from me and shook her head violently.

'No! I c—can't! They'd all see me . . . They'd know!'

If by 'they' she meant sour-faced old bags like Hilda and those twittering bitches in the Queen's solar, I couldn't have sympathised more. I remembered noticing a little wooden tool shed in the far corner of the garden. I steered her there, hoping to Heaven it wasn't locked.

Heaven was on our side. The shed was open. I settled her on a pile of sacks and slipped outside to fill a tin scoop with snow, which I melted over the lantern. Then, with the door shut and a fragile warmth beginning to percolate, I tore off another strip of underskirt and began to clean the blood off her hands.

It was then that I saw the wedding ring. It gave me quite a shock. Perhaps she was older than I'd thought, after all.

She was shivering less violently now, and the colour was coming back to her cheeks. I was aware of her huge brown eyes watching me warily amidst the cloud of curling dark hair. 'Who . . . who are you?' she said at last.

I told her. 'I only arrived this afternoon. With Prince Ferdinand. We're just passing through. What's your name?'

For a second she looked startled, and defensive. Then she smiled shyly.

'Isobel,' she said. A pair of dimples appeared for an instant, and vanished. With a bit of colour in her face, and those dimples, she was quite astonishingly pretty. And so young I couldn't help being nosy. 'How old are you, Isobel?'

'Thirteen,' she said. 'I'll be fourteen in February.'

I was thunderstruck. Thirteen, and already married? What about the husband? One of those lager louts in the Great Hall, probably. A bloke with about as much warmth and tenderness and sensitivity as a charging rhino . . . Poor scared kid. My heart ached for her.

The bleeding had almost stopped. In a few days' time all she'd have to remind her of tonight would be a thin scar.

254

'You were lucky,' I told her. 'Another half-hour out there in that cold, and nobody could have saved you.'

Her mouth lengthened in a bitter sneer. 'So?'

'You didn't really want to die, did you?'

'N—no,' she whispered, and turned her head away. I waited. She took a deep breath and straightened her shoulders with a kind of weary dignity. 'It doesn't really matter. I think . . . I'm probably going to die pretty soon anyway . . . so . . .'

I was horrified. 'Why, for Heavens' sake? Does your husband beat you up? Because if so . . .'

'No, no. It's something else. I just . . .'

The shed was dim and warm and quiet. I retied her bandage and waited.

'There's – something wrong with me,' she said at last. 'Some sort of . . . disease.' She shuddered. 'Something – dirty. Horrible.'

'What kind of a disease, Isobel? Have you seen a doctor about it?' She looked perfectly healthy to me – even a bit on the heavy side. Things like cancer or TB would have made her thin and wasted-looking – wouldn't they? I was floundering in ignorance.

She'd gone white. 'No . . . I daren't. I don't *know*, you see. I—I keep bleeding . . . down here.' She laid a hand quickly on her belly. 'My friend Annie – she was a lot older than me – she bled and bled, she couldn't stop it. They said she'd been with the Devil . . . and then she died . . .'

Miscarriage? I was horribly conscious of not just floundering here, but of being right out of my depth. I didn't know a blind thing about gynaecology. And yet, when I'd dressed Isobel earlier, I was prepared to swear there hadn't been a spot of blood on her shift.

'How long has this been going on?'

'About a year. Just before I got married.'

I stared at her white, miserable, frightened-little-girl face and a horrible suspicion began to dawn. It couldn't be. Could it?

I began to feel like Grandma. 'This bleeding. Is it all the time, or just now and again?'

She shrugged. 'Every few weeks, I suppose.'

Suspicion was hardening into certainty – but I still couldn't believe that a girl her age could be so ignorant of her own body. 'And it lasts four, five days, right? And then it stops? And starts again about four weeks later?'

She made a little startled movement. Her huge brown eyes were wide and horrified. 'How did you know?'

'And you didn't tell anybody? Didn't your mother ever have that little chat with you about the Facts of Life?'

She shook her head in bafflement. 'Mama died when I was eight.'

I made a conscious effort not to sound like a police officer interrogating a suspect. It wasn't easy. 'Weren't there any other women about at home? Older sisters? A nanny? Friends?'

She didn't know what I was getting at. 'No. It was such a small croft, you see. Miles away from anywhere. We didn't have maidservants, like they do here. We're an ancient family,' she said, with a sudden spark of hauteur, 'but . . . we lost our lands, a long time ago, so . . .'

'No servants at all? Just you?'

'Me, my father and my six brothers. And old Christy to do the scrubbing. And when . . . when it started, I didn't dare tell anybody because . . .' She gulped. 'Christy used to say such terrible things.'

'Like what, for instance?'

'Like . . . some women are born of the devil, and full of sin and wickedness, and God's curse is on them. And when they bleed it's the wickedness coming out . . .'

I listened, appalled, and so furious I could barely keep still. What sort of a father would leave a half-insane old witch to bring up a young girl? And what sort of society was this at Stourlin, where a kid of thirteen could be married off in total ignorance of physiology?

'What about when you came here? Didn't your maid . . .?'

'I was so ashamed,' she whispered. 'Brigid and Marie caught me burning the . . . the rags . . . one day, and – they laughed at me.' Her eyes filled with tears of mortification. 'They said the same things as Christy, only worse.' She paled. 'They said I'd be better dead.'

I went cold. Servant-girls deliberately taunting their young mistress to suicide? What the hell was going on here? I got a chilling picture of Isobel's plight. Month after month, the panic-stricken search for clean rags. Not daring to ask for any help. Stomach cramps. The disposal problem . . . Good God, if I'd believed half the stories going round the girls' loos when I was thirteen I'd have ended up in the local loony bin.

And nobody had made it their job to enlighten her. She must have been out of her mind with terror.

I got a grip on myself. 'Right. Now you listen to me, Isobel. All girls bleed once a month. It's called a period, and it's *normal*. Got that? I do, those little sluts that laughed at you do, the Queen, your mother, the Princesses – everybody. It's not wickedness or a punishment or the Devil's work or anything like that. It's not dirty. It's clean and perfectly natural and normal and *good*. Understand?'

Her eyes were wide with shock. 'But . . .'

'They lied to you,' I said brutally. 'Christy because she's old and off her trolley – and your maids . . . well, they're a poisonous pair of bitches and I'd get rid of them if I were you.'

'They *lied* to me? They made me feel like a–a freak! They . . .' She was on the verge of another flood of tears.

'Well, you're not. You're normal.'

Tactful enquiry elicited the fact that she did know where babies came from, which was a great relief. Earlier on that evening (it seemed like a million years ago, but it was only an hour at most) I'd been racking my brains to envisage all the unpleasant surprises that this place might have in store for Jo and Ferdinand and me over the next couple of days. Oddly enough, rescuing a would-be suicide and giving a thirteen-year-old kid a crash course in human reproduction hadn't been on my list, I couldn't think why.

The candle-stump was at its last gasp. Isobel got to her feet, shakily, but with a fragile dignity that wrung my heart. Nobody would have taken her for thirteen now. Her height and her figure were those of an eighteen-year-old.

'They'll be looking for me. I'd better go back.'

'Will you be all right now?'

She nodded, and squared her shoulders like a lone soldier going wearily back to the battlefield. She had a lot of courage, this kid. 'You don't have to go back through the Great Hall. I'll show you a short cut.'

Two pairs of cold fish eyes turned to glare at me as I walked into my room. The haddock and the anchovy had waited up. Their expressions indicated all too clearly what they thought of young women who disappeared for hours on end and turned up frozen to the marrow, their clothing torn and wearing a borrowed cloak stinking of yesterday's beer. The word trollop would feature pretty prominently, I was sure, along with slut, harlot and, once again, Being-No-Better-Than-She-Should-Be.

'We were expecting you to arrive with the other ladies, your Ladyship,' Hilda said. Her voice was steel-tipped and had a lot of weight behind it, like a Doctor Marten's being tested on a dustbin lid. A lifetime ago – last night, for instance – I'd have stammered out some sort of explanation. Not now, though.

'I left the Hall early,' I snapped. 'Where I come from, men don't behave in that unseemly manner when there are ladies present.'

She flinched. I'd hit her with her own prejudices, straight between the eyes.

'I borrowed a cloak and went for a walk,' I told them icily.

'What, *alone*, m'Lady?' To give her credit, the haddock rallied fast.

'No, of course not. A little servant girl came with me, and showed me the garden.' I took the cloak off and brushed myself down distastefully. 'And now I'd like a bath.'

'A *bath*, m'Lady?' Their jaws dropped. Thirty-fifteen to me. My serve.

'Yes, a bath. You know – a tub, hot water, towels, soap . . . you do have soap in this place, I suppose?' Matilda speaking – I grinned inwardly.

'Well, yes, m'Lady, but . . .' Baths, I gathered, were not on the regular agenda. Thirty all, after a very shaky rally on the part of the dragons. My advantage.

It couldn't have been any later than eight o'clock, but all at once I felt weak with tiredness. I relented.

'Tomorrow morning, then. And now I think I'll go to bed. I hope the sheets are clean?' If they wanted hauteur, they'd get it.

My body was out for the count, but my brain had gone into hyperdrive. Isobel. The cold, grim King. The tension I could sense everywhere. The drunken diners. High-born ladies segregated and guarded like so much priceless porcelain. Coarse, brutish menfolk. Servants with cold fish eyes, servants who deliberately drove their young mistress to suicide . . .

I went to sleep, and dreamt about blood.

When I woke up next morning a large tub was steaming in front of the bedroom fire and clean towels had been draped over a rail. I wallowed for a blissful few minutes and was just getting down to some serious scrubbing when the bedroom door opened, and Isobel walked in. I was so startled I dropped the soap. It skidded across the floor and she dived to intercept it.

'Isobel!' I gurgled.

The dimples vanished. 'What's wrong? Aren't you pleased to see me?'

'Of course I am! – but I'm in the bath, for Heaven's sake!'

She giggled, and looked me up and down in the fascinated way people inspect bearded ladies in funfairs. 'That's all right. I don't mind.'

Nobody would have taken her for thirteen this morning. I suppressed a sneaky little twinge of envy. Bartenders will be asking me for proof of age when I'm twenty-seven.

In one respect, however, we were still sisters in misfortune. Today she was wearing a faded purple undergown (and no other colour fades as spitefully as purple) and a very ugly sage-green overdress which was three sizes too big for her and tied in the middle like a sack. Both garments had been good quality once – about twenty years ago, for a guess – but by now age was taking its toll and the fabric looked distinctly geriatric.

She grabbed my can of talc and sprinkled some on to her hand. 'Oh, this is lovely. No wonder you smell so nice. Can I have some?'

'Isobel,' I said crossly, 'Do you make a habit of walking into everyone's bedrooms when they're having baths?'

She blinked at me. 'Of course not. I can, though. I can go anywhere I like, in the Queen's Tower.'

'Oh, really. And why's that?'

She looked puzzled. 'Because I'm the Queen,' she said.

Everything spun. If the bath had been bigger and the water deeper I'd have slid under in shock. 'You're the *what*?'

'The Queen. Didn't you know? Oh, dear,' she said, and burst into horrified giggles.

I pulled myself together, using considerable force, and groped for a towel so as to hide my face. My brain was reeling. This . . . *kid* . . . (and however mature she looked, she was still, technically, a kid) was the girl Haglund had fallen in love with? *Haglund?* What was he, some kind of pervert?

I climbed out of the tub – horribly conscious of her bright, interested eyes on me – and was drying myself with unnecessary vigour when another thought struck me like a thunderbolt. Last night I'd rescued the Queen of the realm from a suicide attempt. The Queen . . . in ill-fitting, second-hand clothes . . . whose servants treated her like something the cat threw up. What in hell was going on here?

She was poking through my underwear like an inquisitive squirrel.

'What's this?'

'A bra.' I yanked it out of her grasp and put it on.

'It's pretty, isn't it?' she said wistfully, 'It wouldn't fit me, though. You're as skinny as a boy.' I had to laugh.

She perched herself on the armchair and watched me while I cleaned my teeth. The bubbly mood had evaporated and her face was tense.

'Foss . . . About last night . . .'

I went cold. 'I'm going to wash my hair,' I said loudly. 'Since you're here, you can help.'

I opened the door quickly – and sure enough, there was Hilda against the doorpost, trying to look as though she hadn't been listening.

I sent her for more hot water, and breakfast for two. Hilda's eyes were popping out of her head. Huge jugs of water and a clean bowl arrived in record time. Then she bustled away to organise breakfast.

A moment after she'd gone Isobel had covered her face with her hands and was shuddering with sobs.

'Isobel . . .'

'It's no good,' she wept. 'I'll n—never be a proper Queen. How could I be? I'm only a poor laird's daughter, I don't know anything about Courts and s—servants and p—protocol . . . Everybody laughs at me. I never asked to be Queen! I never wanted any of this! And oh, Foss – I'm so scared!'

I tried, awkwardly, to comfort her. 'But Isobel, everybody makes a few mistakes to start with . . .'

'No! You don't understand!' She scrubbed her face with her knuckles. I offered her the box of tissues and she blew her nose. 'It's different for you! Everybody can see you're used to all this . . . Being important . . . bossing people about . . .'

I gawped at her. 'Me?'

'It's true, isn't it?'

'No! Of course not! Where I come from, I'm just ordinary! I

260

hate being rude to people. I *loathe* being haughty and insolent. But sometimes you have to be. Because the people who sneer and snigger and look down their noses at you are snobs – and the only way to deal with snobs is to stamp on them – hard.'

She sighed. 'It sounds so easy, when you say it.'

'You won't know until you try.'

'Well, you didn't know who I was, did you?' she said.

'No, but . . .' I gave her a severe look. 'To be honest, Isobel, those clothes don't help.'

'I know,' she breathed. 'I have got clothes . . . lovely, new clothes . . . but they've put them away somewhere, and I can't find them. These are all they let me have.'

I couldn't believe what I was hearing. 'His Majesty's orders?'

She shuddered, and went white. 'No! He doesn't know. And I daren't say a word! He – he scares me more than anybody.'

Oh, Lord. I could feel myself going hot all over. I didn't know what to say. Mercifully for me, she didn't go into details.

'I don't know what to do. Everybody hates me . . . they treat me like dirt . . .'

'Who are *they*, exactly?'

'Oh, everybody. The Lords, the Council, the two Princesses, all the servants . . .'

Feeling like a middle-aged agony aunt, I said awkwardly, 'But the King loves you. Doesn't he?'

She shook her head. 'I don't know. Look at me. How could he love me, like this? They say,' she added miserably, 'I don't please him any more. When we were first married, he was so gentle and kind – I didn't mind being married then. But we came here, and he went away to the war . . . and now he's not kind any more. I hardly see him.'

I was struggling to readjust my thinking, get rid of my prejudices. Because that's all my feelings were – just prejudices. Older men fell in love with pretty young girls in my culture, too, I reminded myself. A few eyebrows got raised – but nobody thought it particularly shocking. And here, like it or not, at thirteen Isobel had been of marriageable age. Mature in looks and in the way she behaved: I reminded myself that she'd been the lady of her father's household since her mother died, she'd had to grow up fast. If she could accept the situation as normal, then so could I.

Hilda arrived with the breakfast trays, followed at a discreet distance by two manservants to remove the bath. She hovered reverently while we ate. Her grim unlovely face was noticeably softer and her whole attitude towards her young Queen was respectful and deferential. She thawed visibly even with me.

Later, Isobel took me to the Queen's apartments on the first floor.

Even after what she'd told me, the state of the place was a shock. I wasn't prepared for the bunch of servants lounging about drinking and gossiping and casting not a single glance in their mistress's direction, or for the shabby, much-mended furniture, the unswept hearths and the piles of dirty crockery lying everywhere. I began to seethe with fury.

Isobel flushed miserably. 'I . . . I'm sorry it's such a tip,' she said. 'I try to clean up, but . . .'

With the servants all looking on and sniggering, no doubt. I wouldn't have put it past them to mess everything up again the moment she'd finished, just for a laugh.

'What does His Majesty say?'

'He . . . he gets angry . . . but not with them. You see, it's my job to make them do things . . . And most of the time he's in his study, or away, so . . .'

Later that morning, a visitor was announced: the skinny, outrageously dressed man I'd seen at the King's table the previous afternoon. Isobel's eyes lit up.

'Lord Vorgan. You'll like him, Foss. He's so *funny*. He's the only friend I have here.'

Lord Vorgan was on his best behaviour, and oozing charm. Having watched his antics at the High Table I was on the defensive at first, but after a few minutes I thawed – I couldn't help myself. It wasn't hard to see why Isobel liked him so much: he *was* funny. Great Lord he might be, but within moments of his arrival you could tell he'd missed out on his true vocation by the sad accident of noble birth. The man was a born comedian – jester, wit and compulsive exhibitionist. He performed for our amusement, capped every quip I made with a better one, told us some hilarious stories about the Castle and its inhabitants and then departed, leaving us in fits of laughter.

'He *is* nice,' I said. 'I wonder why George didn't mention him to us?' George had given us the low-down on most of the prominent figures at Court, but Vorgan's name hadn't come up.

'George?' Isobel said, tilting her head enquiringly. Her dimples flashed. 'Not young Lord Waters? The one who's so pretty he makes you giggle?'

I was delighted to discover a kindred spirit. 'You, too?'

'I can't stop myself,' she confessed. 'I saw him at Court when I first arrived. If he'd been presented to me I'd have *died*.' Her eyes went distant for a moment, and her cheeks flushed pink. 'I wish Lord Vorgan had brought young Lord Carrickburn along this time, though. Now he *is* good-looking.' She pouted and giggled. 'I think he's in love with me. Just a little bit.'

Somewhere inside my head tiny, shrill alarm bells began to ring. 'Does your husband know?'

Now she was all of twenty-five – pert, worldly, patronising. 'Oh, really, Foss! I can't think why you're looking so stuffy! There's no harm in it. All the ladies have paramours. Lord Vorgan said so.'

The alarms in my head were ringing loud enough to wake up a corpse. It was a wonder Isobel couldn't hear them. I went cold all over. 'You haven't . . .?'

Abruptly, she was thirteen again, and petulant. 'No, of course not! But I don't see . . .'

She didn't – that was obvious. I had a sudden, hideous mental image of a lamb skipping merrily about on a butcher's chopping block. Sermon time was well overdue.

'Isobel, listen to me. You're the *Queen*. If His Majesty hears *one whisper* that you've been unfaithful to him, you are *dead*. Young Lord Whatever-his-name-is will be next in line for the chop. It's High Treason, Isobel. Got that?'

She stared, white-faced. 'B—but I never meant any harm! Lord Vorgan said . . .'

I felt sick. 'You've got more enemies here than I thought, and Vorgan's one of them. Isobel, you've got to start talking to His Majesty. He's got to know what's going on. He's the only one who can protect you!'

When I got back to my room that evening I was astounded to discover that Hilda had organised another bath for me without even being asked. She brushed my thanks aside, but she was still hovering, fidgeting with towels, as I got ready for bed.

'Um . . . m'Lady . . .?' Her face was troubled.

'Yes, Hilda?'

The words burst out of her in a rush. 'Pardon me, m'Lady, I

know it's not for me to say, but . . . it did me good to see Her Majesty with you this morning, a respectable young lady like yourself.'

I wanted to laugh. In spite of my unorthodox arrival, I'd finally made the grade as A1 respectable.

She went on. 'It's about time she had a friend in this place. Maybe you can help her to see what's what, m'Lady.'

I stared at her and saw nothing but concern and transparent honesty in her eyes. I remembered how she'd behaved around Isobel: not obsequious, but deferential, respectful – everything the other servants weren't.

'Hilda – what exactly is going on round here?'

'Danger, m'Lady, that's what. This is no place for an innocent young girl, and that's the truth. There's many here that'll stop at nothing to see her disgraced and dead.'

I went cold. 'I know.' I didn't tell her how nearly they'd succeeded.

She hissed in exasperation. 'He should never have brought that sweet young thing here. But that's men for you! I was in His Majesty's household, when he was Duke of Strathlone,' she explained. 'Personal maid to the Duchess. And a kind sweet lady she was, too. His Majesty grieved for her, as was right and proper. And what I say is, he's got a right to look to the future now, and his own happiness. But there's too many here who want him grieved all over again.'

It made sense. Haglund had made a lot of enemies in his attempts to wrest power from the Great Lords. He'd fallen in love with Isobel, just as George had told us. Then, like a fool, man-like, he'd dumped her here, an innocent stranger in a corrupt and hostile Court, and rushed off to set his Kingdom in order. It hadn't even occurred to him that she might need sympathy, kindness, time to adjust. Or that the knives would be out the moment his back was turned.

I began to feel quite sorry for Haglund. Fortyish, battle-scarred, all too aware, perhaps, of his deficiencies in the sweetness and light department – his enemies could crucify him through Isobel. Was that why he'd been so cold to her recently? Because the whispers had already started?

I woke up next morning knowing that after today we'd be free to go; that George and Eleanor were on their way and that the nightmare was nearly over. Just one more day . . .

Isobel was dubious when I proposed Hilda as resident dragon.

'But I've got enough servants, Foss. I don't need more.'

'Did you know they're all being paid by Princess Lutetia? That she and Lord Vorgan are in this together?'

She paled. 'No, I didn't, but . . .'

'Hilda's ultra-respectable and fanatically loyal. She'll spoil you rotten, but she won't stand any nonsense from you or anyone else. She's a godsend, Isobel, believe me.'

Hilda arrived looking flustered, and nervously smoothing her apron over her massive hips. Isobel was just as tongue-tied. Hilda's eyes flickered round the room and focussed abruptly on the pile of unwashed crockery, the rumpled rugs and the dirty floor. They pinpointed the duster Isobel was holding (which I hadn't noticed until that moment) and the broom she'd left leaning against the wall. Isobel went scarlet. But the face Hilda turned to me was shocked and ferocious.

'Excuse me, m'Lady, Ma'am,' she said grimly. She surged like a battleship under full power into the next room where a manservant and two maids were lounging with their feet up, gossiping. 'You! Young man! On your feet this instant!'

'Who, me?' he said, and all three sniggered. I'd seen the girls yesterday – brash, mouthy types that made your fists itch. Hilda fixed them with a glare like a thermionic lance, and the grins faded.

'Are you on duty just now,' she demanded, 'or just using Her Majesty's apartments as a social club?'

'Aw, get stuffed,' one of the girls said.

'I see,' Hilda said. 'You. Get in there and take those dirty dishes downstairs. You – start cleaning the hearth. Or do I have to trouble His Majesty the King with a trivial complaint like this?'

They got to their feet. Hilda's voice could have levitated concrete. I was mildly surprised that the furniture wasn't standing to attention as well.

'B—but . . .'

'Do it,' she snapped, in tones marginally above absolute zero. Isobel and I both flinched. The servants fled.

'Thank you,' Isobel said when she'd got her breath back. She dimpled at Hilda. 'I think Lady Foss was quite right. I do need somebody like you.'

I remembered something. 'Her Majesty's clothes, Hilda. They've hidden them somewhere . . .'

'I'll find them, m'Lady, don't you fret,' she said grimly. We left her to survey her new domain, and went out into the garden.

'Would she really have gone to His Majesty?' Isobel said, round-eyed.

'You bet. And he'd have listened, too. She should have been put in charge of you from the start.'

Sudden as winter sunshine, the dimples came and went. 'Would you do me a favour, Foss? It's just that . . . well . . . I have to be there on the dais this afternoon, when the great Lords ride in for the muster. Would you be my lady-in-waiting?' She saw me hesitate and went on hastily, 'I did what you said, Foss. I asked His Majesty. And he said yes.'

I was impressed. It was only a small favour – but she'd made an attempt at communication. It was a start.

I watched her as she wandered a little way ahead of me. And suddenly I saw what Haglund must have seen. Beauty, yes, youth and freshness. But also dignity. Honesty. A loving heart. She'd been too young for this particular burden: she'd wilted under the strain. But by the grace of Hilda, in a few more years she'd be a Queen to be proud of.

I wanted so much for her. I wanted her confident, secure, surrounded by a clutch of hopeful sons and daughters. I wanted the royal apartments to ring with the words, 'Yes, dear,' uttered in suitably deferential male tones. I wanted Haglund humanised. My heart ached for them both.

20.

Your Stars CANCER (June 22–July 23)
You are involved in a conflict of interests. You'd be wise
to back down until you know what's going on. Now is
not a good time to maintain a high profile.

When we got back to the apartment Hilda was unpacking a large wooden trunk. Two more stood unopened on the dressing-room floor.

'Your Majesty's wardrobe,' Hilda said with grim triumph.

'Where . . .?'

'In a basement,' she said, and shut her mouth like a rat-trap. 'The muster starts at noon, Ma'am. If her Ladyship's agreeable, we'll get Your Majesty bathed and dressed.'

With Isobel wrapped in towels we got down to the serious business of selecting a suitable outfit.

'No more Grandma's cast-offs,' I warned. 'This has got to knock them in the aisles.'

'Young, but not too young,' Hilda agreed. 'Regal.'

'Nothing flashy,' I added, sternly removing Isobel's hand from the diamond collar she'd been fingering wistfully as we talked. 'No, Isobel, not the cloth of gold.'

In the end we decided on a high-waisted gown of white satin worked all over with silver rosebuds, with a silver underskirt. Over it we draped a long white cloak with a crimson lining, the one splash of colour the outfit needed for maximum impact. We piled her cloud of dark hair into a smooth coil; then, reverently, Hilda set a silver coronet on Isobel's head. We stood back to judge the effect. She looked stunning: tall, beautiful, every inch a young queen.

The gown Hilda had chosen for me was pale lilac. Predictably, it hung on me like a sack and was six inches too long. Hilda squinted ferociously at me, produced pins, a scissors and thread, and proceeded to sew me into it. A wide belt and a deeper lilac cloak covered the altered waistline and the tucks at the back of the bodice. Hilda herself disappeared for a few minutes and came back looking demure in dark blue, and minus her apron.

Gorgeously attired, and nervous as hell, we issued forth to face the muster.

Haglund and his noble Lords were waiting in the courtyard. The conversation died as we approached – a spontaneous tribute to Isobel's magnificence. A number of noble faces looked as though their owners had swallowed vinegar, and I didn't bother to hide my glee. If they'd expected Isobel to disgrace her Lord on this most public occasion, they were horribly disappointed. Lord Vorgan's face alone expressed unconditional approval. I wondered, fleetingly, what he was up to.

Haglund moved towards Isobel, his eyes full of wonder and a flush colouring his granite cheekbones. She smiled shyly up at him and for a second his heart was in his face. I felt choked. All unbidden, I heard George's voice in my memory: '. . . *and God help the feller who gets in his way*.'

The moment passed. Haglund offered Isobel his good arm, and they moved in slow, stately procession through the inner gates, me carrying Isobel's long train, the rest of the nobles falling into step behind us.

It was a perfect winter's day. Cold, of course, with patches of snow in the shaded corners of the bailey, but the sun shone bravely in a sparkling blue sky. The keep was bright with banners and crowded with people in their best clothes: all the townsfolk had arrived to witness the muster. The two thrones were set on a high dais on the wall overlooking the outer bailey.

I spotted the two Princesses sitting with their hangers-on in a kind of covered balcony to one side. I fervently hoped they were choking on bile.

The crowd was cheering the royal dais. Haglund lifted a hand in greeting, but Isobel sat rigid, gripping the arms of her chair. She was experiencing a late attack of stage fright.

'Smile!' I hissed in her ear. 'Relax! You look fabulous! Haglund's bursting with pride. The Princesses are *livid*! Smile!'

She bared her teeth obediently. It wasn't much of an improvement.

One by one the noble families rode into the bailey to take the Oath of Allegiance, each family heralded by a fanfare and announced in a loud voice by a sergeant-major type with medals on his chest. As the ceremony progressed Isobel began to relax. The sight of all these high-born Lords and Ladies bowing the knee before her was boosting her ego no end. As her confidence grew, her natural dignity was blossoming. She was giving a faultless performance. I hoped Haglund had noticed.

My own jitters were subsiding. Nothing could go wrong now.

I had to admit, the ceremony was impressive. Judging from the cheers, and the sudden, profound silences every time the Oath of Allegiance was repeated, the crowd felt the same way.

George appeared towards the end of the muster. As always, he was hard to miss.

'Here he comes,' I whispered to Isobel. 'Shade your eyes.'

Isobel gave a horrified giggle. 'Oh, for Heaven's sake! What on earth is he *wearing*?'

Not content with mere silk and velvet, George, predictably, had gone the whole hog and opted for cloth of gold. Not just one cloth, either – in fact, as many cloths as you'd need to construct a doublet fantastically puffed and slashed and scalloped, breeches ditto and a cloak which almost reached the ground. (I remembered, dimly, that cloth of gold was woven from the sticky threads of an exotic mussel; George's outfit must have brought the entire species perilously close to extinction.) His broad chest was lavishly bespattered with the family diamonds.

His horse was similarly adorned: saddle and harness ablaze with gems and dripping with gold. Even the hooves had been lovingly covered in gold leaf in front and silver behind. As he rode out from beneath the arch he blazed in the sun like Phoebus personified. It was an entrance to make a rock star swoon with envy.

It dawned on me quite suddenly that none of this was vanity, or playing to the audience. George was as simple as a child. He loved bright colours and glitter and beautiful fabrics; he loved dressing up – and like an eager little boy, he'd put on his very best clothes to honour his King. I doubted if he'd even looked in a mirror.

I wondered how many of the wily Lords behind the throne would see it that way.

There was an approving murmur from the crowd as he rode out into the open space, then a spontaneous burst of applause.

On the dais, nobody made a sound. The silence was tense and somehow heavily significant. I glanced quickly at the Lords of the Council: their faces were completely expressionless. Except for Lord Vorgan, who was gazing at George with a faint smile on his lips. Out of the corner of my eye I saw him stoop to murmur something in Haglund's ear.

George dismounted, knelt before his Sovereign and repeated the Oath in tones of ringing sincerity. He moved on to honour his Queen. I could feel Isobel shaking with suppressed hysteria. I gripped her arm hard, and probably left bruises to the elbow, but she sobered up enough to greet him with propriety. As he rose from his knees his huge violet eyes lifted to where I was standing. The rosebud mouth opened.

'Oh, I say – hullo, Foss,' he said.

After George, Eleanor – through no fault of her own – was a bit of an anticlimax. The peculiar jangling tension faded out of the air, leaving me wondering if I'd imagined the whole thing. Eleanor herself had a sweet humorous face, full of character. She gave Isobel and me a warm smile, but her eyes never strayed far from her astounding husband.

The remaining noble families made their obeisances, and all at once the muster was over. Haglund got abruptly to his feet, pulling Isobel with him. The move caught everybody on the hop, including me – I had to scramble awkwardly between the crowding Lords in order to dive for the hem of Isobel's train.

I caught a glimpse of Haglund's face: it was thunderous. Something was wrong. It couldn't be Isobel: she'd behaved impeccably.

In the courtyard he released her hand and moved aside to speak to a group of noblemen. Isobel didn't seem to have noticed the grimness: she was still sky-high on adulation. She looked radiant: so beautiful it made you catch your breath.

Lord Vorgan homed in on one side of her, the Chancellor on the other.

'A triumph, Your Majesty,' Lord Vorgan purred. 'A goddess dressed all in white and silver, like the moon. After today, there's not one young Lord in all the land who wouldn't die for one smile from those lips, one glance from those divine eyes! How can you break so many hearts and be so heartless?' Ridiculous, extravagant, smiling his manic clown's smile . . . but subtly – *different*. I stared at him, trying to pin the impression down.

'I'll wager ten gold sovereigns there was not one face in all that throng that moved you to admiration! Not one!'

Isobel was laughing and shaking her head – a bit embarrassed, not quite sure how to respond to the teasing attentions of these two senior Lords, but flattered, nevertheless.

The Chancellor bared yellowing teeth in a greasy forced smile. The effect was ghastly. 'Oh, come now, my Lord Vorgan. Your wager must fail! Her Majesty is not cold, nor is she blind.' He bent confidingly to Isobel's shoulder, like a dirty old dutch uncle. 'Settle the wager, Your Majesty. Whose was the fairest face amongst all that throng today? Eh?'

Haglund turned. Isobel's laugh rang out into a sudden, deathly hush.

'Why, young Lord Waters's, of *course*!'

Haglund had gone white. A pulse throbbed violently at the side of his mouth. His eyes burned like coals. All around us courtiers were laughing, chattering, moving around, unaware of the crisis. But amongst this one small group of people there was a silence so profound that everything else seemed to have receded into the far distance. My heart was beating loud enough to march to.

Haglund spoke. Stiffly, harshly, as though the muscles of his throat had gone into spasm. 'I'm neither young nor fair of face, my lady. Yet it would have eased my heart if you had named me – and not that young lordling for whom you decked yourself in such splendour, whose name comes so smoothly off your tongue.'

In that frozen second everything clicked. We hadn't won. We'd played straight into our enemies' hands. I could have moaned aloud when I saw how stupid I'd been. Preachifying, fusspotting about . . . when all the time they'd been whispering poison in Haglund's ear. This young Lord . . . that young Lord . . . young Lord Waters.

Hilda and I had decked Isobel for sacrifice.

For a moment I thought Isobel was going to faint. But she had more inner strength than I suspected. The sheer unfairness of the accusation stung her into a desperate show of courage.

'My Lord, you are the *King*! Before whom every Lord in this land must bow down! I wouldn't speak your name lightly, as a wager! That young Lord means nothing to me, nothing at all . . .!'

'Be silent!' Everyone was hushed now. Haglund directed a look of bitter hatred at his young Queen. 'You have betrayed me, Lady.' He jerked around to where his men-at-arms stood to attention. 'Arrest him,' he snapped. And began to stride furiously away.

Isobel ran after him, pulled at his swinging cloak. He slapped her hand away.

She clutched at him, falling to her knees, almost hysterical. 'My Lord – I dressed myself for you, not for him . . . they stole my clothes . . . they hid them . . . They were only found this morning . . .'

He dragged himself free and strode off without a backward glance. I saw the Chancellor's face as he hurried after his King. It wore an expression of such malign glee that if I'd been wearing a sword I swear I'd have run him through.

George? Arrest *George* on a trumped-up charge like this – a mere domestic tiff? It was *insane*.

I *had* to see Haglund: had to explain. Too late, I saw that I should have gone to him yesterday, laid all the evidence in front of him then. Perhaps I still could.

But first there was Isobel to see to, pale as marble, staring blindly at her liege Lord's retreating back, the knuckles of her clenched hands showing blue-white. Hilda put her arms around her, but she didn't respond.

I was suddenly shaking with shock. Somebody put steadying hands on my shoulders. It was Jo. I couldn't help myself, I clutched him and buried my face in his chest. 'George, Jo . . . they're arresting George!'

He hugged me. 'I know. Ferd's dashed off to do what he can.'

'Did you see what happened?'

'Enough. I gather His Majesty's convinced himself that old George has been having it off with his missus.'

'It's *crazy*, Jo! It's a plot. It's all a put-up job!'

'Doesn't take a genius to work that one out,' Jo said grimly.

Isobel got as far as the steps, then she collapsed. Jo caught her as she fell and carried her into the Castle. Courtiers and guards alike drew away from us as we approached and stared in silence, as though we'd suddenly become lepers. Untouchables, contaminated with treason.

At the door to the Queen's apartments, guards with pikes barred our way. One of them took the limp Queen out of Jo's arms, and the pikes parted to let Hilda and the soldier through. I tried to follow and got half a yard of steel thrust flat against my chest.

'Go back, your Ladyship.'

'B—but I'm her lady-in-waiting . . . '

'His Majesty's orders, m'Lady. The Queen and her maid. No-one else.'

I started to bluster. 'But she's ill! In shock! The whole thing's a huge mistake! You've got to let me in!' The pikes didn't budge.

'They're only doing their job, Foss,' Jo said gently. 'Come on. I'm escorting you back to your room. And if anybody tries to stop me,' he added loudly, 'it'll take a damn sight more than a couple of pikes and a fancy hat.'

I hung back. 'Jo, you don't know what's been going on! I do. I've got to talk to that man, make him listen to me . . .'

I picked up my trailing skirts and pelted downstairs, towards the cave-like study where Haglund had received us that first morning. That was where he'd be, I was positive. His own private retreat. Seething; pacing up and down; slamming his fist into the furniture and never noticing the pain . . . The picture in my head was so vivid I shuddered mid-flight. But somebody had to tell him the truth. Hilda and I were the only people who would, or could. And Hilda didn't know about the suicide attempt.

I skidded to a halt at the study door. It was guarded even more ostentatiously than the Queen's apartment upstairs. Panting a bit, I made my request.

'No-one to be admitted, m'Lady,' they told me. 'His Majesty's orders.'

'But I must see him! Tell him this whole ridiculous mess could be straightened out in about thirty seconds if only he'd listen to me! I have information no-one else has!' My voice was getting shrill with hysteria. I controlled it with an effort.

Pikes and mailed feet clattered uneasily. 'Sorry, m'Lady . . .'

The old jobsworth argument. Stalemate. I could have screamed with frustration.

The commotion had an effect – though not the one I was hoping for. The door opened and a senior officer came out, closing it quietly behind him. The guards snapped to attention.

'His Majesty will see no-one, m'Lady.'

'He doesn't know it yet, but he needs to see *me*.'

I'd seen this man before – in the King's tent on the battlefield. Not a courtier, this: a heavyset, grizzled man who wore his uniform like a second skin, as though he'd slept in it many times and expected to do so again. Somebody who knew Haglund – had fought with him, respected him. Somebody he might, perhaps, listen to.

273

He shook his head and started another disclaimer. I lost my temper.

'You're all fools! I'm talking about high treason, for God's sake. I'm talking about a long-standing plot to discredit your *Queen*. I'm talking about an innocent young girl who was driven to a suicide attempt the night before last. An innocent man arrested. Let me see His Majesty – please!'

His eyes flickered surprise, but he just repeated what the pikeman had said.

'Okay,' I snapped. 'Get me paper and a pen. One is allowed to communicate by letter, presumably?'

His eyebrows shot up, but he did as I asked. Writing materials were produced. I scratched out a brief note, ink-splattered but explicit, and handed it to the officer.

'I want witnesses to all this,' I told him. 'You'd better read it.'

He'd barely started to read when the narrow bright crack of the study door suddenly broadened into a wide shaft of lamp-light. I looked up, my heart lifting with hope. The hope died. It wasn't Haglund. It was Lord Vorgan.

His eyes were like flint. No humour in them now, no easy charm. He took the letter from the officer's hand, read it and then, very slowly and deliberately, he tore the paper into tiny pieces and scattered them like confetti on the stone floor.

'Let me give you a word of advice, my child,' he said. 'Don't try to meddle in affairs of State. I can assure you that His Majesty is quite capable of ruling his Kingdom without taking advice from an ignorant, hysterical young girl.'

There was an outside chance that Haglund was within hearing range. I took it.

'You mean, I tell the truth?' I said loudly. 'That's something of a rarity around here, isn't it? You're a traitor, Vorgan, a lying, treasonous toad, and I hope you fry in Hell.'

That did it. The slight sneering smile vanished. The look on his face was pure hatred.

'A curse,' he said. 'You all heard how the witch cursed me!' He took one step towards me. 'In this land witches are burnt at the stake, my lady. Conjure up your spells, witch, summon your demons and your familiars. They won't help you when you're dragged screaming to the fire. As you will be.'

I backed off, horrified. He bowed flamboyantly. 'Goodbye, your sometime ladyship. I doubt if we'll meet again.' And shut the door.

We fled, Jo and I both. Back to my room, where I crumpled like wet Kleenex. Jo held me close, stroked my hair, kissed me and rested his face against the top of my head while I sobbed and shook.

'Crazy,' he kept muttering. 'They're all stark raving bonkers. The whole damn lot of them. '

When my sobs subsided he gave me a quick kiss and released me.

'Stay here. Bolt the door. Don't let anybody in unless it's Ferd or me.'

'Where are you going?'

'To find Ferd. To get us out of this loony-bin. Stay put, okay?'

He disappeared. I huddled up close to the fire, and waited.

An hour went by. Two. It got dark. I lit the candles, but without Jo there the room itself seemed to threaten: executioners lurked in every flickering shadow. I built up the fire, but that didn't help; the flames reminded me of the stake, and capering devils, and Lord Vorgan's smile . . .

I clenched both hands together and prayed. I prayed for Isobel; I prayed for George. I prayed for Ferdinand and Jo and me. I touched Oz's pendant and Magnus's ring, but both were cold and unresponsive. Perhaps we were all beyond help, from sorcerers or anyone. We were all trapped and doomed. It was the blackest hour of my life.

When the soft, furtive knock came at the door I nearly jumped out of my skin.

'Who is it?'

'Jo,' he said, very quietly. And then, '*Agor y drws*, sparrow *bach*. I've brought a couple of friends.'

I unbolted the door with fingers that fumbled and refused to grip. Hilda came in; her face was glistening with tears. She held out her arms to me and I ran into them.

'I am not a witch, Hilda! I'm not!'

'I know it, lovey. And so does her Majesty, the poor sweet lamb.'

Behind Jo a taller figure loomed. I stared at him, flummoxed. It was the officer from Haglund's room.

'He's going to help us get away,' Jo said. 'You, me, Ferd.'

'George?'

Jo shook his head and swallowed visibly. Hilda crossed herself. 'God rest his poor soul.'

Chill fear settled in my guts. 'Why – what's happened?'

'High treason, m'Lady,' the officer said grimly. 'He's to be put to death by the sword, on the Heading Hill, at noon tomorrow.'

Disbelief choked me. '*George?* But he's innocent! No trial? No reprieve? '

'Him and his wife and child, m'Lady. It's the custom.'

'*What?* But that's *barbarous*!' The officer looked away.

I remembered thinking that George was a fool to flaunt his wealth so blatantly. How many greedy eyes would be glittering tonight, at the thought of Melhuish? I felt sick.

'It's not your fault, Foss.' Jo was reading my expression, and sounded savage. 'They fixed the whole thing. Sooner or later it would have happened anyway.'

'But I could have stopped it – if only I'd gone to the King yesterday!'

'That letter, m'Lady,' the officer reminded me gently. 'I'd be obliged if you'd write a replacement. Names, what was done, what was said – all the evidence you've got.'

'Will it save George too?'

Regretfully, he shook his head. 'I know His Majesty. In this mood . . .' He shrugged helplessly. 'He listens to no-one. But God willing, the Queen will be spared, and her accusers brought to justice.'

I nodded. It was all we could hope for.

Jo was getting anxious. 'Get that letter written, sparrow. Grab your gear. Let's go.'

I wrote the letter as directed. I put in every single thing I'd heard or witnessed, and I read it aloud so that all three people with me in that shadowed room would know the truth. The officer pocketed the letter and bowed.

I packed in frantic haste. There was no time to change out of the lilac dress. I threw my warm travelling cloak over the top and stuffed my feet into riding boots. We crept out into the deserted corridor.

'Quiet,' Jo murmured. 'This whole place is crawling with troops.'

And Haglund's senior officer was sticking his neck out on our behalf. For us, and for Isobel, and for his King's sanity.

The escape route was tortuous and very, very dark. We left Hilda behind and plunged into a low-roofed tunnel which emerged via a locked gate into an alley. Another tunnel under the city walls . . . and finally, blessed clean air to breathe, and turf underfoot.

Horses shifted and snorted in the shadow of a clump of bushes. The officer withdrew, leaving Jo and me to go cautiously on alone, praying that it really was Ferdinand out there.

It was. I felt weak with relief. Jo and I mounted and the three of us rode away, towards the coast, and freedom.

We rode all night. Morning broke, heavily overcast, with spatters of cold rain. We reined in on a hilltop to take stock.

Below us was a small town which I recognised with a lurch of the heart. Without realising it we'd veered southwards in the dark. We were looking down on Melwhiddan.

Five days ago it had been a peaceful, sleepy little place. Now the broad streets and the squares were packed solid with people. More were converging purposefully on the town from every direction.

'Market day?' Ferdinand said dubiously.

'Stay there,' Jo said. 'I'll go and find out.'

When he'd gone Ferdinand reached across and squeezed my hand.

'You all right, Foss? Sure?'

I nodded and gulped. 'George, Ferd. Did you . . .?'

He shook his head and stared unseeing into the distance. 'I couldn't get to him, Foss. Not even to speak.' He shuddered. 'Locked up, chained . . . I swear there were a hundred armed men all round that gaol. They wouldn't let me within twenty yards of the place. Haglund wouldn't see me. I talked to everybody I could. Even tried bribery . . .' His voice broke. 'I tried, Foss. I swear I tried every way I possibly could. Gaolers, the Governor, the Chancellor – right to the top. I even pleaded with the Princesses . . . It was like bashing my head against a stone wall. You do believe me, don't you?'

'Of course I believe you! I was there, remember?'

He swallowed hard. 'My best friend,' he said thickly. 'Used to do prep together. Cheat like hell. Visit each other in the hols . . .' All at once he cracked. His shoulders gave a convulsive heave and he began to weep – noisy, racking sobs, painful to watch. All I could do was sit there and hug him fiercely while the horses shifted and sidestepped under us.

'How could such a thing be allowed to *happen*?' Ferdinand

277

blurted out between gasps. 'It's so . . . bloody . . . awful. Eleanor . . . the baby . . . George, who never hurt anybody in his . . . entire . . . life. Not once.'

I could believe it. Tears were pouring down my own face.

I handed him a hankie. He blew his nose gratefully, and took a grip on himself. 'I'm sorry, Foss.'

'For Heaven's sake, Ferdinand. Don't apologise for grief!'

He swallowed. 'Perhaps there'll be a reprieve,' he said, and blew his nose again.

Jo was on his way back. His face was sombre.

'What's happening, Jo?'

'George's town, remember?' He gulped. 'I've never seen anything like it. People are trekking in from ten, twenty miles away. More arriving every minute. Massive silent protest outside the courthouse. Everybody in shock – just standing there, waiting. But when that wears off . . . A few hotheads are already talking about marching on Stourlin.'

I remembered the zone around the war-blasted town, the gibbets along the road, the refugees . . . I went cold. If Melwhiddan rebelled, Haglund wouldn't leave a soul alive. He'd slaughter the lot without a moment's compunction.

'They need you there, Ferd,' Jo said. 'You knew George better than anybody. Go and talk to them. Get them to see sense . . . He must have been one hell of a guy,' he added quietly.

Was. The past tense. As though the event had already happened. Which, in a sense, it had. George, condemned and in chains, was as good as dead. With his sweet innocent Eleanor and their baby son. All that was left of the Melhuish dynasty.

We rode soberly down into the town to share the prayers and the awful waiting.

All three of us were numb when we finally rode out of Melwhiddan in the mid-afternoon. The crowds around us were dispersing quietly, as Ferdinand had asked them to. I looked at him with a new respect. He'd stood on the courthouse steps, in George's place, and he'd spoken very simply, from the heart. And if he'd choked up once or twice in speaking of his friend, nobody had thought any the worse of him.

'*You* are George's family now,' he told them. 'You are Melhuish. He lives through you. Don't let him down. You have a choice – to rise up in anger and be slaughtered and forgotten

278

forever . . . or to stay calm, go back to your homes, and keep his memory alive. I know what he'd want. He'd want you all to survive, in spite of his enemies.'

When the noon bell began to toll I knew I'd remember the sound for the rest of my life. That, and the absolute silence which followed, in a square packed with a thousand people. It would haunt my dreams.

The crowd parted to let us through. Hands reached up warmly to grasp ours. Voices murmured their farewells. The cannon that had been fired at the moment of his execution in Stourlin thirty miles away had set bells tolling in every town and village between there and the coast. By now every soul in the Melhuish lands would know that their lord and protector was dead. Would mourn and tremble, and wonder what was in store for them, when the lands were divided up and the new landlords moved in.

'I suppose in ten years' time they won't even remember his name,' Ferdinand said bitterly.

He was wrong. The country people, unlettered, untaught, have their own ways of remembering. As we rode past the sad little groups of pilgrims returning to their homes, snatches of a haunting tune kept floating up to us. Every now and again words seemed to condense out of the melody, a phrase or two at a time. Slowly, mysteriously, the song was taking shape. By the time we reached the next village, whole verses were emerging.

> *'Oft have I ridden through Stourlin Town*
> *Through the snow, aye, and the sleet,*
> *But never have I ridden through Stourlin Town*
> *With chains upon my feet . . .*
> *And oft have I ridden through Stourlin Town*
> *In the wind, aye, and the rain,*
> *But never have I ridden through Stourlin Town*
> *Never to return again . . .'*

The song followed us down through the barley fields and into the lush pastureland of the coast. The boy leading his herd in for milking was humming it; women sitting on doorsteps in the winter sun were crooning it to their babies.

In a wild, sandy croft on the southern border, a shepherd leaning on a gate sang us the last verse.

> *'And they have taken to the Heading Hill*
> *His horse, aye, and his saddle,*
> *And they have taken to the Heading Hill*
> *His young son in his cradle.*
> *And they have taken to the Heading Hill*
> *His young wife fair to see,*
> *And for the words the Queen hath spoken*
> *Young Waters he did die.'*

PART FOUR

Odette

21.

The end of a long, hot, exhausting day.

'Just run it past us one more time, Ferd.' Jo's tone was heavily patient. 'The village. You're sure it was the right village?'

'I told you.' Ferdinand was getting fretful. 'We saw that hunting lodge.'

'Okay. The pass between those two peaks.'

'Yes!'

'So how did we end up here?'

'I tell you I don't *know*! It was all coming back to me so clearly – everything was so familiar – and suddenly I don't recognise a thing!'

'You can't have forgotten a lake this big,' I said gloomily.

It stretched away in front of us for miles: a vast sheet of glassy water reflecting the sunset. Hills rose steeply on either side, covered in dense pine forest. Above the tree-line we could see the snow-covered tips of distant mountains. It was the loneliest place I'd ever seen – lonelier even, and more utterly silent, than the mountains behind Lermos.

We'd been on the road for six months since leaving Stourlin, and it was now June. We were lean, fit, tanned to the colour of cork (even me). And lost.

Melhuish port had been crawling with Haglund's soldiers. We'd had to beat a hasty retreat. On the Southern border we'd got bogged down (literally) in a vast peninsula of swamplands flooded in the spring thaw. After six weeks of dismally slow going (hiding by day, riding at night) we'd finally crossed Haglund's Northern border and had ended up staying with another friend of Ferdinand's at Perramar, two hundred miles inland.

Edward was a shy, bespectacled young man with a stammer and a study full of maps. Jo and I had stared at them in dismay. There was a huge slab of empty continent between us and the Garnock coastline. I'd never seen that much blank white space on a map before: it was like the Antarctic.

'It l—looks f—f—flat,' Edward had explained apologetically. 'B—but actually it's the b—b—biggest m—mountain range in the no—northern hemisphere. And to—totally uncharted. The l—lo—locals know the p—passes, of course, b—but . . .'

'And Garnock's way South on the far side! How the heck do we get there?'

'Hang on a minute.' Ferdinand's finger was tracing a route into the whiteness. 'Didn't we go skiing up here one hols?'

It had sounded so easy, the way Ferdinand had suggested it. Once the passes were clear we'd make our way to the ski resort, hire a guide and cross the massif.

'Remember that birdwatcher chap we met, Edward? There's a major migration route right through the passes to the headwaters of the Garnock river . . . He'd done it a number of times. It'll be a long trip, but perfectly feasible.'

And now, weeks later, we were inexplicably lost. Somehow, we'd missed the ski resort completely.

Jo sighed. 'We'll just have to back-track. Again.'

We'd set up camp for the night at the lake's edge. We hadn't cooked a meal for the simple reason that the only eatables left in our packs were sardines, biscuits and jam. Earlier on, we'd tried fishing for an hour or two, but hadn't caught anything. The food situation was getting critical.

As the sun went down the midges came out in their trillions. Jo scratched and swore.

'Huddle up to the fire,' I said. 'It helps.'

'If I get any closer I'll roast.'

Ferdinand reached for his crossbow and stood up, tucking a handful of bolts into his belt. 'I'm going for a walk. Might see something worth shooting at.'

'As long as it's edible,' I pleaded. 'And please, Ferdinand – no otters.'

'Oh, all right,' he snapped, and strode away into the dusk.

The crunching noise of his feet on the gravel shore faded away into the distance and ceased, swallowed up in the immense silence.

'You know,' Jo said thoughtfully, 'I don't think there *are* any fish in this lake. With all those midges around you'd expect to see a few noses coming up for a nibble. But there's nothing.'

He was right. The lake was like a mirror. Not a single ripple as far as the eye could see. The silence deepened. The midges disappeared and the moon rose. It glared down at its perfect reflection in the water: not a breath of a breeze to scatter the twinned brilliance. A dead lake in the middle of nowhere. The thought made me shiver.

'What's wrong?' said Jo.

'Nothing, really. Just what your mother would call a goose walking over my grave.'

'By the pricking of my thumbs, something evil this way comes?'

'No!' I tried to laugh. 'Not this time. At least I don't think so. It's just so . . . inhuman. You can see why people go batty wandering around alone in the wild – like after a plane crash, or something.'

'Planes,' Jo murmured. 'Seven-four-sevens. Concorde. Heathrow. Package holidays . . .'

'"Will Mr Jones travelling to Barcelona report to the information desk immediately, please?"'

'Hard to imagine, isn't it? A different life.'

I was watching his face in the firelight. The bones showed up sharply above shadows that hadn't been there a year ago. I wanted, desperately, to reach out and stroke my finger along his cheekbone and the line of his jaw – but I didn't dare. Since that night at Stourlin when we'd clung together, he seemed to have retreated from me emotionally. He'd shut off that moment of closeness as though it had never happened.

Suddenly I couldn't bear it any longer. I heard myself say viciously, 'I wish I was tall and blonde and Swedish, with hockey-player's legs.'

At least I'd got his attention. He swivelled and stared at me in blank incomprehension. 'You *what*?'

'It's Caren, isn't it?' I'd never met her, but I *hated* her.

'Caren? What are you on about? I haven't thought of her for months.'

'What, then?'

He pulled both knees up against his chin and clasped them tightly. Closing himself up against me. 'Look, Foss . . . I . . . If you want the truth . . . I – I just can't commit myself right now. Understand?'

'No. I don't.'

He winced. 'What I'm trying to say is – I care about you. I care about you a lot. But . . . I don't feel *real* in this world. Never have. A bit kind of – well – two-dimensional. As though most of me is somewhere else. Back home at Meini Hirion, for a guess, probably fast asleep.'

'You're saying this is a dream? But it's real, Jo. It's as real as home is.'

'To you, yes. You seem to belong here. Because of your grandmother, perhaps. You're real in both places. Maybe if Ferd and Mags came into our world, they'd feel the same as I do here. And it makes a bloke – well . . . cautious.'

'I don't see why.'

He looked embarrassed. 'This is not *me*, Foss. In this world I've become what they call a hard guy. I'm – well, a formidable sort of bloke. The kind of feller who might be attractive to . . . a girl like you, for instance.'

I caught my breath. 'But Jo . . .'

He gave me a crooked, sideways smile. 'What scares me, Foss, is . . . Okay, supposing we did get involved with each other. What happens when we get back home and I wake up as plain ordinary Jo the pig farmer again? No edge, no glamour – just a country hick? How long d'you think we'd last?'

'But now is now, Jo.'

He shook his head. 'It all comes down to being *real*, Foss. I feel as though I'm some sort of dream projection. A fantasy figure. And I . . . I care too much about you, Foss. Even in a dream, you're not a casual affair, understand? I'm scared of hurting myself, and I'm scared of hurting you.'

I nodded, and couldn't trust myself to speak. He felt the same way I did. Part of me soared and did cartwheels for joy, the rest of me ached like hell.

Jo leaned over and gave my hand a brief squeeze. 'Let's see this thing through first, huh?'

A flock of swans flew up the lake towards us, their necks outstretched, their powerful wings creaking. As they landed, the moon's reflection splintered into a million tiny dazzling shards of light and then slowly coalesced again.

Jo frowned. 'Ferd's been gone a long time.'

I jumped guiltily. I'd forgotten Ferdinand existed. 'He can't have got lost, surely? He's only got to follow the lakeshore.'

'Unless he dashed off into the forest after a stag or something.'

'In the dark? He wouldn't be that stupid!' Or would he? With Ferdinand, you could never be absolutely sure. Even after months of living rough and travelling in the wild, he still seemed to harbour the conviction that every move he made was shadowed by invisible servants, and that there'd be a civilised place with baths and well-heeled acquaintances just around the corner.

We waited uneasily, straining our ears for the noise of footsteps on the pebbles.

'I suppose we'd better go and look for him,' Jo said with a sigh. 'Come on.'

'Damn Ferdinand,' I said. 'Why can't he grow up? Other people manage it. It's not that difficult.'

Our feet crunched loudly on the pebble shore as we set off. At first the fire glowed brightly behind us; then we rounded a small promontory and it vanished. The lake was motionless under the white sneering moon. The forest was primeval blackness. Between the two, the pale strip of shoreline beckoned like a causeway.

We'd trudged a good two miles when – at last – a solitary figure stood revealed on the moonlit shore. We broke into a run, waving and yelling.

Ferdinand showed no sign of having heard us. He was standing like a statue, his head tilted up to gaze at the sky. We put on a burst of speed and skidded to a halt alongside him. He turned, blinking and unsteady, like somebody waking up from a dream.

'Ferdinand? Are you okay?'

His eyes came slowly into focus. 'Foss? Jo?'

'Who else did you think it was? You've been gone for ages. We were worried sick!'

'Oh,' he said, still bemused. 'Really?' He looked at us both and his face suddenly broke into a wide, soppy, radiant grin. I tugged at his arm, but he just stood there, glowing all over like a neon sign.

'Oh, Foss,' he said huskily. 'I'm the happiest man in the world. It's happened, Foss – just as you said it would.'

'Sorry?'

'I . . .' Again, that gormless radiance. He swallowed noisily. 'I'm in love, Foss.'

'What, *again*?'

He came back to the present with a jolt, looking hurt.

'What d'you mean, *again*? I've never felt this way before. There's never been a girl like this before . . . The only girl in the world . . . and the amazing thing is, she feels the same way about me. She's The One, Foss. The girl I've been waiting for all my life. And I never knew it till now.'

Jo and I looked hastily around in the dappling moonlight, and exchanged concerned glances. 'Ferd,' Jo said cautiously, 'What girl?'

'She flew away,' said Ferdinand, as though that explained everything.

He'd flipped his lid. The stress of the last few months had finally got to him. The curse of the inbred had struck. Something to do with the full moon, perhaps?

I took him gently by the arm. 'Come on, Ferd. Let's get you back to the campsite. You've had a dream, that's all.'

He shook off my hand as though it had bitten him. 'You don't *understand*!' The aristocrat at his haughtiest. 'I'm not dreaming. As a matter of fact I've never been wider awake in my entire life.'

Jo sighed. 'Okay. Tell us exactly what happened.'

As we walked him back to the camp site the story emerged, in randomly-assorted chunks, like a toddler's jigsaw puzzle. In his present state rationality was a bit too much to expect.

He'd wandered along the beach, slinging the odd rock into the trees in an attempt to rouse some game. There'd been no response. He'd been on the point of giving up and turning back, when a flock of swans had circled above his head. He'd slipped a bolt into his crossbow and taken aim.

'*Swan?*' I said, revolted.

'Well, you did say we needed meat. Any meat.'

'Not *that* badly.'

'Anyway, as it happens I didn't shoot. Because the leading swan was wearing a crown.'

'A *crown*?'

'Well, not a crown, exactly, more a little gold circlet thing with diamonds in it.'

'Oh.' I felt he was missing an important point here. Personally,

I'd have been fairly flummoxed to see a swan wearing *anything* on its head. But for Ferdinand, the crown had been the salient feature, obviously.

'And then what?'

The crowned swan had alighted on the water and floated to the shore, where she'd turned into 'the most beautiful girl I've ever seen in my entire life.'

Ferdinand was silent for a while, solemnly reliving the moment.

'What happened then?'

'Well,' he said with a trace of embarrassment. 'We . . . er . . . talked. Her name's Odette,' he added dreamily.

'What about the other swans?'

'Oh, they changed too.'

'Into princesses?'

'No, of course not. Into ladies-in-waiting.' Another pause for a mental replay.

I didn't quite know how to put my next question. 'Ferdinand . . . How did you know she was real? A real princess?'

He glanced at me pityingly. 'The crown, of course.'

'Yes, but . . .' I took a deep breath and started again. 'Look – the last thing I want to do is shatter the idyll . . . but . . . could it have been an illusion? Or even a hallucination of some kind?' Or even, I added to myself, a trap, baited with magic?

'Even if she's real, marrying a swan could pose a few technical problems,' Jo said bluntly.

'Oh, that's all right,' Ferdinand said, his brow clearing. 'She's not a swan who turns into a girl now and then. She's a girl who's turned into a swan. She's under an enchantment,' he explained. 'She told me all about it. A wicked sorcerer called Kostchei wiped out her entire family about two hundred years ago, and transformed her into a swan. He lives in what used to be the family castle, a bit further along the lakeshore.'

I became aware that he was looking at me the way a puppy does when it wants to be taken for a walk: eager, beseeching, trusting. If he'd had a tail it would have been wagging pitifully.

'Foss . . . Would you . . . He's a sorcerer, Foss, like the Witch-Queen . . . You rescued Margaret. Couldn't you . . .? For me? Please?' He shivered suddenly. 'If I lose her, I'll die.'

'I can't guarantee this is going to work, you know,' I said, as we set off early the following morning for a preliminary snoop around the alleged sorcerer's domain.

'You've still got the pendant, though,' Ferdinand pointed out.

'Yes, but . . .' I'd had plenty of time for second thoughts, and was well into a pre-emptive fit of the jitters. 'There was that glass brick thing . . . I'm not sure if the pendant helped at all, really . . .'

Ferdinand reined in. 'This must be the place.'

From the lakeshore a narrow gully led steeply upwards between pinewoods. We tethered the horses and set off on foot. After half a mile the trees parted, the gully widened out, and above us was a castle, perched high on a rocky spur.

'That's it,' Ferdinand said with suppressed excitement. 'Kostchei's stronghold.'

I'd been expecting something grim and forbidding, to match the dead lake and the sombre pines. What I saw was a castle as delicate as a dream: all slender turrets and spires and glittering white in the morning sun. Rhododendrons in full bloom smothered the sides of the crag in a riot of colour. I touched my pendant, just in case. Nothing happened.

'Rhododendrons,' Jo said belligerently. 'I *loathe* rhododendrons.'

'Why, for Heaven's sake?'

'Dunno. I just do, that's all.'

'That's the back,' Ferdinand said. 'Odette says that on the other side of that spur, the valley flattens out, and there are farms and a village.'

Jo's eyes brightened. 'Where there's a village, there's a shop.'

I was having serious doubts. 'Are you *sure* this is the right place, Ferd? It all looks so . . . *normal*.'

We trudged upwards until we reached the base of the crag. A rough track crossed the stream bed via a worn stone bridge, and emerged in front of a half-ruined gatehouse, behind which a path zig-zagged steeply upwards through the rhododendrons to the back of the castle.

In front of the open gates stood a little man with a bald patch surrounded by a bush of wiry, greying hair. His tattered gown was hitched up around his middle with string, exposing a pair of skinny legs which didn't appear to have encountered soap and water for some considerable time e.g. several years. Both his ankles were surrounded by a woolly mass through which heels and toes poked more or less at random, and which – at a stretch of the imagination – might possibly have begun life as a pair of socks. Strapped to each foot was a sandal mended with orange nylon cord. He was playing hopscotch.

Fascinated, we moved closer. An elaborate spiral of squares had been chalked out on the paving-stones. Every time the little man kicked his pebble, it squeaked and did its best to slide the wrong way, and the chalk marks did a quick wriggle to compensate. We watched open-mouthed.

When he'd finally got to the middle the filthy little man let out a yell of triumph and began jumping up and down like a maniac.

'I won! I won! I'm the King of the Castle, and you're a dirty rascal! Nyah-nyah-ni-nyah-nyah! I'm the K . . .' He stopped. A half-turn in the course of a jump had brought him face to face with his unsolicited audience. There was a moment's shocked silence.

Then, 'I won!' he said to us, in the sharp barking voice you associate with terriers. 'Pesky thing thought it could beat me! Hah! Me! I won, though. D'ye see? I won!' He began rubbing both hands together, very fast, grinning savagely as he did so.

'But you were cheating,' Ferdinand pointed out.

The manic grin vanished. 'Cheating? Me? How dare you, sir! How dare you!' He made a flicking gesture with an indescribably filthy forefinger – and Ferdinand and Jo both vanished. At my feet lay a couple of large and slimy slugs.

The little man and I stared at one another. His face went through a whole gamut of expressions, from slack-jawed astonishment via wariness to extreme suspicion. I stood there feeling helpless. He raised his forefinger again. This time I felt a mild jolt. I did a quick check, but nothing seemed to have happened.

It looked very much as though the pendant was doing its job after all. And if this was the famed and feared Kostchei – then, maybe, twisting his arm about Odette mightn't be such a daunting proposition as I'd thought.

First I had to get him to normalise Ferdinand and Jo. And something was telling me that blowing my top in this particular situation wouldn't get me very far at all.

'Nice one,' I said politely, and gave him a cheerful smile. 'Very smooth. Very . . . er . . . professional.'

His attitude changed in a flash. He smirked and strutted.

'Thank you. Thank you. Takes a lot of practice. But of course – one needs considerable natural talent to start with.'

'Oh, yes. Yes, I can see that.'

He gave me a quick, feral grin. The next instant his eyebrows had snapped together.

'Who are you, anyway?'

'Me? Oh – sorry. I didn't introduce myself, did I? My name's Foss. How d'you do?'

We shook hands.

'You're . . . er . . . a sorcerer?' he asked warily.

'Oh, no. I've just been around a bit, that's all. You wouldn't be the sorcerer Kostchei, by any chance, would you?'

His chest swelled. 'Well, as a matter of fact,' he began grandly, 'Yes, I . . .' All at once he writhed and crumpled. 'Ouch! No! No, I'm not! *Stop it!*' he screeched, squirming under some agony whose source I couldn't see. The writhing stopped, and he faced me dejectedly. 'I'm his brother Borschei,' he said. 'I'm a sorcerer too, you know.'

'So I see,' I said pleasantly. 'Now, how about reversing the spell on these two friends of mine?'

He eyed me slyly. 'You say you're not a sorcerer?'

'No, just immune.'

'Well, I won't then,' he snapped, and strutted off into the house.

I picked up both slugs – not without a shudder – and placed them carefully in the pockets of my shirt. Then I followed him inside.

'Kostchei won't like it, you know.'

'Hah! Fat lot *you* know! Kostchei doesn't care. He lets me do whatever I want.'

I glanced around. We were standing in an unbelievably filthy, cluttered main room. The windows were so caked in grime they might just as well have been shuttered for all the light they let in. Cobwebs draped the walls and the ceiling like grey mosquito netting. In the gloom you could just make out the humped shapes of objects which might or might not have been furniture. Between the humps, the floor was a death-trap of broken bottles, crockery, torn books and clumsily-opened tin cans. The smell was nauseating.

'Actually,' the little man boasted. 'I'm a very good sorcerer. Much better than people think. Hah! Haha!' Again, that mirthless, manic grin, and the hands rubbing together. 'Kostchei doesn't know half the things I've taught myself over the years. He thinks I'm a complete washout. Well, I'm not. One of these days, I'll show him! Haha! I'll make him squirm! He's . . .'

'Careful,' I warned, 'What if he's listening?'

All the bounce went out of him. He sighed, and flopped down onto one of the humps. Dust rose in clouds as he landed. 'Oh, he stopped doing that years ago.'

'But when you mentioned his name out there . . .'

'Oh, that. Stupid little misunderstanding we had about a hundred years ago. I mean, all I did was sign his name on a few things. Nothing important. Just saving him the bother, really. What's a brother for, when you come down to it? Hey?'

'And he objected?'

He nodded, and began rubbing his scalp as ferociously as he'd sanded his hands. 'Ridiculous. Ridiculous. But that's Kostchei all over. One little mistake and he's down on you like a ton of bricks.'

'Bossy sort of bloke,' I suggested.

'I hate him,' Borschei snapped. 'Take a look at this place, for example. Dreadful, isn't it?'

'Moderately awful, yes.'

'Correct. And what's he got? A bloody great palace up there on the hill. Cooks, maids, butlers, you name it. But d'you think he ever invites me up there? Oh, no. Little brother's got to slum it in a hovel by the back gate. I haven't had a decent meal in five hundred years, and that's the truth.'

'But you're a sorcerer. Can't you . . . you know . . . magic whatever you want?'

His snort set the cobwebs vibrating. Dust showered down and made me sneeze.

'Shows how much *you* know. Magic food – hah! Looks wonderful, smells wonderful – tastes like nothing on earth. No texture,' he added wistfully, 'No flavour. Fills you up but that's about all. Translocation doesn't work either. Molecules don't reconstitute properly, or something. Roast beef moos, soufflés end up as biscuit . . .'

I suppressed rising excitement, took a deep breath and exposed my trump card.

'I'm a cook. Fully trained,' I lied glibly, crossing my fingers behind my back.

Borschei was goggling at me, as at a being from another planet. 'A *cook*? You mean – *real food*?'

I nodded. His jaw dropped. 'Gosh,' he said. He was nibbling at the baited hook – you could see it in his face.

'Steak au poivre?' he whispered reverently. 'Crepes Suzettes? Sirloin of beef?'

'With all the trimmings,' I assured him. 'Crown roast of lamb, duchesse potatoes, chocolate pudding, pears Hélène, paprikash, stroganoff, lobscause like you've never tasted before . . .'

Somewhere along the line I'd struck a deep, resonant chord. His entire being quivered. '*Chocolate pudding?* No lumps? No hard bits?'

'Light as a feather,' I said. 'Melts in the mouth. Practically floats off the plate. With a really thick sauce. Made with eggs and real chocolate and brandy and lashings of cream.' He swallowed noisily.

'So,' I said, 'Why don't we make a deal? Let's say I cook you a week's meals in exchange for normalising my two friends here?'

'M'mm,' he said, and glowered at me from under his eyebrows. 'Make it six months.'

'Six months? You've got to be joking! In six months I can find a dozen sorcerers who'll do the job for free!'

'All right, all right – two months, then.'

'Make it a month,' I said generously. 'Four weeks exactly. Change Jo and Ferdinand back into their proper forms *now*, and I'll throw in a bit of general housework as well. How's that?' A month should give us more than enough time to suss out Kostchei's weaknesses. *If he had any*, I found myself thinking.

He grunted. 'How do I know you won't walk out on me?'

'You don't. Except that I'm a professional, and I keep my word.'

He hesitated. 'Chocolate pudding for dinner tonight?'

'If you get the ingredients, yes.'

'Oh, all right then. Put the blasted creatures down on the floor.'

Two seconds later I was being squashed between the newly reconstituted bodies of Ferdinand and Jo. Borschei eyed them with acute dislike.

'Well, are they going to hang about here all day?'

Ferdinand went stiff with outrage. 'Now look here, my man . . .'

I stamped on his foot, hard. He yelped.

'It's all right,' I told them. 'Mr Borschei and I have done a deal. I'm going to cook for him in return for changing you back. Of course, we haven't discussed the details yet, but . . .'

Borschei's head jerked up. 'What details?'

'Oh, nothing important. Like finishing at nine each evening, one day off a week plus Sundays, that kind of thing . . .'

'You never mentioned days off,' Borschei wailed.

'Don't complain,' I said severely. 'You don't know how lucky you are. Your brother Kostchei' – I emphasised the name for the men's benefit – 'would give his eye-teeth to employ me.'

Jo had caught on, and was grinning appreciatively. Ferdinand still looked puzzled.

'I agree, I agree,' Borschei snapped. 'Just get them out of here.'

'Meet you at nine, Foss,' Jo said. 'C'mon, Ferd.'

They left.

'About time, too,' Borschei growled. 'Well, get started, girl. What are you waiting for?' – and flung the kitchen door open.

The rush of foetid air made me gag. The stink in the main room was lavender water compared with the overpowering garbage stench of that kitchen. There wasn't a square inch of unlittered surface – and that included the floor. Even the range had disappeared under a heap of miscellaneous rubbish. Unwashed crockery and empty pans were strewn everywhere, sticky yellow ooze dribbled out of overturned milk cartons and every single item was encrusted with greenish-black mould. The microflora in one saucepan alone would have kept a botanist happy for a hundred years. I reeled under the impact.

'You expect me to cook in *that*?'

'That was the deal, take it or leave it,' he growled.

I surveyed the disaster area with a sinking heart. 'Okay. I'll need a couple of buckets, a scrubbing-brush, clean cloths, about a gallon of grease-remover, and half a dozen bottles of household bleach. Oh, and some washing-up liquid, a roll of those big plastic bin bags, and loads and loads of hot water. You do have hot water, don't you?'

'In the tap, idiot,' he snapped. 'Anything else?'

'Half a dozen packets of those soapy steel pads would be nice,' I said sweetly.

Where he got them all from, I dared not ask. But in a few minutes everything I'd asked for was neatly lined up on the sitting-room floor.

Cleaning the kitchen took most of the day. I'd carted out the garbage, disinfected the sink, unblocked the drains, scrubbed the floor and the worktops and washed the dishes, and was beginning to scrape the grease of centuries off the range when I heard voices in the main room. I identified Borschei's quick barking tones – a bit subdued for once – and a mellifluous, beautifully-pitched male voice which had to belong to his brother, the sorcerer Kostchei.

A truly enterprising mole would have abandoned the job in hand at this point and crept to the door to listen. I was frankly too busy to waste that much time. In agreeing to clean up the kitchen I'd set myself a near-impossible task, and if Borschei was to have his lamb cutlets and chocolate pudding at 7.30 as promised, the range would have to be spotless – and roaring – by five. I scrubbed fiercely, and one of the grids fell off with a heart-stopping clatter.

The voices ceased abruptly. Footsteps approached across the sitting-room floor – one set swift and purposeful, the other scuttering behind. The kitchen door was flung wide. I kept my head down and my elbows moving.

'What in the name of Hecate's going on here? Borschei – who is this woman?'

Thank God, I was covered in cobwebs and grime. I'd tied a cloth round my head and swathed myself in an outsize wrap-around apron and looked the very archetype of the downtrodden kitchen drudge.

Borschei was gibbering. 'J—just a servant, Kostchei. She came here looking for work.'

'Well, send her away again. I don't need any more servants.'

Borschei's voice was querulous. 'But I do, Kostchei. Look at the state of this place. She won't cost you a penny – I'll pay for her myself.'

I risked a quick peek in Kostchei's direction. And got a shock which made every hair on my head do its best to stand on end.

Miraculously, he wasn't looking at me, but over his shoulder at Borschei. Miraculously, because one direct glance from him and I knew I'd have been utterly lost: every single thought in my head would have unrolled itself for him to read at leisure. Power emanated from him like a force-field and made me feel giddy and faint.

This was a sorcerer of the first rank. A superstar. Way up at the pinnacle of whatever league table sorcerers go in for. Compared with him, Magnus was a clumsy amateur. And Oz . . . As yet, I didn't know enough about Oz to judge.

Physically Kostchei was impressive enough: tall, lean, broad-shouldered, with black hair lightly touched with silver. A handsome, bony, fastidious face which reminded me, disconcertingly, of Oz herself. They could have been brother and sister.

This man was the ultimate bad news.

I dropped my gaze hastily and cowered against the range. I felt his glance flicker over me like an electric discharge, from head to feet and back again. Scanning – but finding nothing of importance.

'What's her name?'

'I forget,' Borschei said. 'Moss, or Mary, or something.'

'H'mm,' Kostchei said shortly, and turned away. My heart began to pound with relief. 'Well, if she cleans you up too, I shan't object. Now listen carefully, Borschei . . .' They were in the main room now, and moving towards the outer door. 'Odile tells me you've been pestering her again. I won't tolerate that kind of thing. Keep your silly tricks for the villagers. They stop at the Castle gates. Is that clear?'

Borschei's agitated denials were too faint to make out. Both voices faded off into the distance, leaving me wobbly at the knees.

Ferdinand was expecting *me* to tackle *that*? Single-handed? No Oz to help? I faced facts squarely. Unless I could find some chink in that formidable armour, I might as well forget the whole thing right away.

Soberly, I resumed the scrubbing of the range.

22.

Your Stars: CANCER (June 22–July 23)
Your home-making talents are appreciated, and you
find yourself playing a central role in a major social
event. Friends are depending on you for support and
encouragement.

When I emerged from the gatehouse at nine, Jo was waiting with Bonny the mare. I was so tired I couldn't even climb into the saddle without his help.

'I gather the dinner was a success,' he said.

'You wouldn't believe it,' I said wearily.

Owing to the state of the living-room, Borschei had had to eat in the kitchen. Even so, I'd done my best to present the meal as well as I knew how. He'd gasped, goggled – and proceeded to stuff himself so fast it was a wonder he had time to draw breath. Two helpings of everything and four of chocolate pudding. Where he'd found room to put it all had been a mystery.

'It's real food!' he'd kept saying. 'Dammit – it's *real*!'

Back at the camp site I stayed awake long enough to give Jo and Ferdinand an update on the situation. Ferdinand's face was ludicrous with disappointment. 'You mean you can't do anything?'

'Look, Ferd, give me a break, okay? I've got a foot in the door and a month to work out some way of saving your Princess. It's not bad for starters.'

To my intense relief, Kostchei didn't show up again at the gatehouse. Borschei seemed to think he'd gone away.

On the second day, I turned out Borschei's living-room. Turned out is the correct, literal term: every single thing in it got slung out onto the lawn. Borschei hovered anxiously about, twitching and hopping and complaining and getting in my way. I made a bonfire in the back yard and ruthlessly burnt the lot.

Borschei's reaction was predictable.

'But you can't burn *that*! I've had it for three hundred years!' *That* being a scrap of carpet so rotten it disintegrated at a touch.

I found eight nests of baby rats in the furniture. The cushions were a seething mass of maggots. In the corners of the room there was compost a foot deep. I held my breath and used a shovel.

We had an argument about Borschei's favourite chair. It quite literally fell apart when I tried to carry it outside.

'But I want it!' he squeaked, hopping about and rubbing his scalp in a frenzy. 'I want it! You've got no right to barge in like this and turn my house into a battle zone!'

'Borschei, there isn't any wood left any more. It won't even stand up!'

'Ridiculous! Ridiculous!' he fumed. 'What am I going to sit on? Eh? Hadn't thought of that, had you? What am I going to sit on?'

He couldn't have timed it better.

'That,' I said, and pointed up the lane, where a little procession was wending its burdened way towards the gatehouse. Two men were carrying a red plush sofa. Behind them came a boy bent double under the weight of an old easy-chair in brown uncut moquette, and then a cluster of grinning women bearing a rolled-up carpet. I'd sneaked up to the village before reporting for duty, enlisted the astonished sympathy of the lady in charge of the shop, and hinted that if anybody had any reasonably decent furniture they wanted to get rid of, the gatehouse might be the perfect dumping-off place.

I'd relied on natural curiosity to do the rest, and it looked very much as if I'd hit the jackpot. They dropped their burdens on the lawn and retreated to a safe distance to goggle in horrified fascination at the sight of Borschei being bossed about rotten by a girl even smaller than himself; then they scurried away to spread the news.

In between cleaning sessions, I cooked. The ingredients kept arriving as specified, and again I didn't dare ask where he was getting them from.

'You're stark raving mad,' Jo said when he collected me two nights later. 'All he wanted was a few decent meals. What are you doing all this extra work for?'

I hadn't thought of that. Feeling like a fool, I said lamely, 'I don't know . . . Borschei's . . . just . . . so pathetic.'

Which he was. Obnoxious, filthy, boastful, cowardly, sly – but somehow, in spite of all that, I'd got quite fond of the horrible little man. What he wanted – and I mean wanted, not needed – was a Mum to boss him about. For the time being, I was it.

'Borschei, you stink. Go and have a shower.'

'What, now?'

'Yes, now. And change your clothes. Underwear, socks, the lot. Put your dirty ones in the basket – don't kick them under the bed.'

'You're so infernally *bossy*,' he grumbled. 'I don't know why I put up with you.'

He was also addicted to practical jokes. I flopped exhausted onto the sofa one afternoon only to have it turn into a monstrous bear-like Thing which trapped me in a vicious hug and clashed its jaws in my ear. I struggled out of the writhing embrace with considerable difficulty. Borschei was laughing like a drain.

'Very funny,' I said coldly. 'Next time that happens, it's fish pie and tapioca for three days running, okay?'

'Stupid woman,' he grumbled. 'Can't take a joke. No sense of humour.'

Half an hour later, I walked into the kitchen and found the sink full of live tarantulas.

'Borschei!' I yelled.

There was no sign of him anywhere. I pictured him hiding somewhere – up a tree in the Castle grounds, probably – twitching and giggling and rubbing his hands together, half-gleeful, half-terrified. I swore.

Meanwhile there was a rather urgent disposal problem. Already, one or two of the more athletic ones were climbing onto the draining board.

I remembered hearing somewhere – a zoo programme on TV, probably – that tarantulas are actually very placid and hardly ever bite unless you hurt them. Okay in theory – but actually getting to grips with the hairy seething mass in the sink took all the nerve I could muster. In the end I transferred them one by one into a large bucket, using gloves and a couple of thick tea-cloths, took them upstairs and deposited them between the clean sheets of Borschei's bed.

I never found out what happened when he hopped into bed that night. Borschei himself never said a single word on the subject. But he didn't play tricks on me again.

I took Saturday and Sunday off, despite vigorous protests from Borschei. I felt as though I'd earned every minute.

Saturday was another gloriously hot day.

'We thought we'd go for a swim, and a barbecue,' Ferdinand said. 'Jo's found a marvellous swimming hole. You'll love it, Foss. And no cooking. I promise. '

As we started off along the lakeshore I noticed a large black bird hopping from branch to branch alongside. I threw a stone at it, and it flapped off, squawking indignantly. Minutes later it was back. It settled on a tree nearby. Its beady little black eyes glittered down at us.

'Oh, go away, Borschei,' I said wearily. 'I'm off duty, remember?'

The branch gave a sudden downward lurch, there was a sharp crack and a muffled curse – and next moment Borschei himself was plummeting earthwards through the mass of thinner branches. He hit the dirt with a shuddering thud.

'You spoke my *name*,' he complained.

'Serves you right for snooping,' I told him callously. 'Now push off.'

'You're mean,' he whined. 'I like barbecues. Can't I come too?'

'No, you can't. It's my day off, Borschei. I need a break. Just leave me alone!'

'Oh, all right,' he said sulkily. He shimmered into bird-shape and flapped heavily away.

'Will he follow us, d'you think?' Ferdinand was worried.

'Probably.' The day had suddenly lost some of its carefree glitter. 'I should have expected something like this.'

'He wouldn't blab on us to Kostchei, would he?' Jo said.

'Don't bet on it. I wouldn't put anything past that disgusting little man.'

Whether he followed us or not, we saw no more of Borschei that day. My own view is that he did sneak along behind us for a while, and then got bored. One thing I'd learnt about Borschei was that he had the attention span of a two-year-old. A grasshopper brain if ever I met one.

The swimming hole was fabulous. Jo and Ferdinand had organised the barbecue between them and I didn't have to do a thing except eat, drink and wallow. It was wonderful.

Ferdinand had shaken off his despondency and was almost manically happy. Later that evening, I found out why.

'You must meet her, both of you. You'll like her tremendously, I promise you. She's – oh, not like anyone else. So fragile, and so brave . . .'

On the dot of midnight we were waiting tensely at the lakeside just below the camp site. The flock of swans glided gracefully into view on the water, and paddled ashore. As she touched the pebbles the leading swan (Ferdinand was quite right: she was wearing a coronet) shimmered and changed into a slender girl in a white dress. She and Ferdinand fled wordlessly into each other's arms.

The other swans paddled tactfully away to eat duckweed. Jo and I stood around, shifting awkwardly from one foot to another and trying unsuccessfully to look elsewhere. Finally the absorbed couple suddenly remembered what this meeting was all about and reluctantly released each other. Ferdinand took Odette's hand possessively in his and led her with exaggerated tenderness to where Jo and I were waiting.

She wasn't at all as I'd expected. She was *tiny* – smaller even than me. Ferdinand had described her as ethereal – but the word which jumped into my mind was *scrawny*. Bones stuck out everywhere – collar-bones, knuckles, wrists, ankles – and I found myself wondering wildly if this was what a diet of snails and duckweed did to a person, and how she'd look fattened up. She also had what I tend to think of – perhaps unfairly – as a Home Counties jaw: not fitting very well, and with too many teeth.

He'd been right about her fragility: everything about her was as insubstantial as thistledown. Baby-fine hair wispy as gossamer and pale as moonlight; pale translucent skin and a voice scarcely above a whisper. I held my breath instinctively in case I blew her away. Her handshake was like grasping a wad of dandelion fluff. She made me – five-foot nothing and size eight – feel like a huge fat strident cow: not a feeling one relishes.

'Oh, hello,' she said breathlessly. 'Ferdinand's told me so much about you.'

'Has he?' I said feebly.

'Yes, and he says you're going to get Kostchei to welease me fwom this dweadful spell. You must be incwedibly bwave.'

After a while Jo and I excused ourselves and wandered off, leaving the lovers gazing fatuously into each other's eyes and murmuring idiotic endearments. Once out of earshot, Jo let out a long, whooshing breath.

'Fancy old Ferd falling for a girl like *that*!'

It was a mystery, profoundly and eternally puzzling. Why do

the most unlikely people fall in love with each other? I did a quick mental review of Ferdinand's previous attachments – the ones I knew about, anyway. Aurora. Clarissa. The infamous Princess Lutetia (who'd gone for him in a big way, according to Jo). If there were others, it was a fair bet they'd all have been of the same type. Glamorous, stunningly beautiful, well-endowed where it mattered most i.e. chest and pocket. And *tall*.

'Up to now he's always gone for the type that'll impress the folks back home, I suppose. This is different.'

'It looks like the real thing this time,' Jo agreed. He added thoughtfully, 'Makes sense, if you think about it. Aurora never actually *needed* him, did she?'

'You're saying he fell for Odette because she's so helpless and pathetic and dependent? Quite apart from being so fwightfully well-bwed?'

The more I thought about it, the more I agreed with Jo's analysis. It tied in with what I knew of Ferdinand's insecurity, his sense of inferiority. He'd needed somebody to protect and cherish, somebody who adored him and would be helpless without him. The tragic, cursed figure of the Swan Princess fitted the bill as though she'd been designed specifically with him in mind. And vice versa.

Which is perhaps, I mused, what true love is all about. Not glamour. Not romance. Mutual dependence. Mutual needs . . .

Jo's hand was rock-steady under my elbow. 'Wake up, sparrow. You're asleep on your feet. Want me to carry you?'

'No!' I blazed.

Jo chuckled. 'Didn't think you would. Thank God you're not Odette.'

I didn't altogether like the sound of that.

Borschei was gibbering when I arrived at the gatehouse on Monday morning. As I walked in, he burst into an ear-numbing tirade of accusations. He was so agitated that although words like 'bastard', 'swine', 'rotten lousy spoilsport' and 'that'll teach you who's boss' came through loud and clear and at frequent intervals, I was completely at a loss to understand the gist.

'Borschei, calm down! What's the matter?'

The gibbering rose to a crescendo, accompanied by frenetic hopping and scalp massage. I marched to the sink, filled the kettle and plonked it on the range.

'Right. You and I are going to sit down and have a nice quiet cup of tea, during which time you're going to tell me exactly what all this fuss is about, okay?'

Mug in hand, he subsided. To my horror, he began to snivel.

'It's Kostchei. He's stealing you away from me. He wants you up at the Castle.'

Everything spun. I gulped a mouthful of scalding tea to steady myself.

'K—Kostchei? What d'you mean?'

'Oh, really,' he snapped, his irascibility coefficient restored to normal, 'Can't you understand plain English, girl? Watch my lips. Kostchei wants you to cook for him up at the Castle. Got that?'

'Yes, but why? When?'

'Questions, questions – how do I know what his motives are? I'm only his brother. His cook's walked out on him and there's a big party planned for tomorrow, that's all I know. Not that I've been invited, mind you,' he sniffed. 'And you'd better keep a civil tongue in your head from now on, my girl. Kostchei won't stand the kind of back-chat I've been tolerating from you this past week, I can tell you.'

It could be a lucky break. It could be the ultimate disaster. Borschei had no integrity whatsoever – not even where his own best interests lay. One word from Kostchei over the weekend, and he'd have spilt every bean in his possession, regardless of the consequences.

'When, Borschei?'

'As soon as you've fixed my lunch,' he said grandly, strutting a bit. Then a spasm doubled him up and he squealed. 'No! Now! Immediately! Stop it! Stop it, I tell you!'

Ruthless as his methods were, I couldn't help admiring Kostchei's tactics regarding his brother. It was probably the only way you'd ever get Borschei to tell the truth.

Since I was going as a cook and not as a drudge, I tidied myself up before setting out for the Castle. I walked up the steep, winding path beneath gargantuan rhododendrons dripping obscenely with flowers the colour of arterial blood, and felt sick with apprehension. Borschei was no help. The last thing he'd said to me was something rude about my glasses.

At the servants' entrance, a grossly overweight butler ushered me into the kitchen, which was large and well-lit and very clean.

Three nervous scullery-maids bobbed curtseys at me as I walked in, and an elderly woman in a wraparound pinny glowered at me from the hearth.

The butler made the introductions. 'Sophie, Katie and Victoria, from the village,' he said. 'And Mrs Briggs, who comes in daily to clean. And you are . . .?'

'Mrs Ewins,' I said firmly. Cooks, I knew, are always granted the courtesy title of Mrs. The tradition goes back a long way.

Mr Boscombe looked me up and down with intense suspicion. 'You're rather young to be a qualified cook, er . . . Mrs Ewins,' he said.

'Oh, I'm very experienced,' I lied. 'I've worked with some of the best chefs in the world. My last job was temporary assistant cook at the Royal Palace in Arborea.'

He thawed slightly. 'May I ask how you happened to be in the area?'

'A camping holiday with some friends. Lord Kostchei heard that I was in the vicinity and asked me if I'd help out for a few days.' Kostchei hadn't struck me as the type who'd gossip with the servants, and Mr Boscombe's reaction told me I'd guessed right. All at once he was falling over himself to be friendly.

Tactful enquiries elicited the fact that Kostchei himself was out, and not expected back until late evening. I began to breathe normally again.

It was a peculiar sort of day – mainly because everything was so *ordinary*. In a way, it was a big let-down. It seemed bizarre that someone like Kostchei – arguably one of the greatest sorcerers in the Zones – should live such a correct, blameless life, waited on by such unremarkable people as Mr Boscombe and Mrs Briggs. But then, why shouldn't he?

The guests, I was told, weren't arriving until tomorrow. There was to be a dinner party for twelve in the early evening; then a grand ball for which a buffet was required. In the course of the morning the girls and I prepared the vegetables and made a start on the savouries for tomorrow's buffet. We did the ground-work on some fairly spectacular chilled desserts; then I cooked lunch for the staff.

In the afternoon, Mr Boscombe took me on a tour of the Castle. It was beautiful. Not in the least like Magnus's House, of course – no squashy armchairs, no books, no magazines. Here, each room was austere to the point of being monastic. Minimal furniture, each priceless piece individually chosen to complement the few exquisite artefacts and hangings and paintings displayed with enormous care against smooth white walls. Flowers in sculptured vases were arranged with meticulous precision. This was a house where people came to admire, but never to relax.

As we left the drawing-room my eye was caught by a movement in the garden outside. A girl was walking away from the house. All I saw before she vanished round the corner was a straight slender back – but I had the weird feeling I'd met her somewhere before.

'Lord Kostchei's niece,' Mr Boscombe informed me. 'Lady Odile.'

The name rang no bells. I was mystified.

We completed the tour and strolled back to the green baize door via the dining-room. And there she was again, standing with her back to us, gazing out of the window with one hand lightly braced against the curtain. This time recognition flooded over me like a cold shower.

'Hello, Xenia,' I said.

She spun round, letting the curtain drop. Her eyes widened as though she'd seen a ghost.

'Foss? Foss Ewins?' Mr Boscombe made a hasty bow and disappeared tactfully down the corridor.

Xenia had gone quite white. 'What on earth are you doing here?'

'I'm the new cook,' I explained cheerfully. 'More to the point, what are *you* doing here? You're not really Kostchei's niece, are you?'

Her eyes flashed. Colour came back into her face with a rush.

'It's hardly any business of yours, is it? If you must know, I have certain . . . talents, and he's adopted me. He . . . keeps an eye open for that sort of thing. But you wouldn't understand.'

She'd altered. She looked older, somehow – as though years had passed since that day in the Biology lab at school. And perhaps they had. Here in the Zones, time seemed to be a pretty arbitrary thing. The haughty, fine-boned face was still the same, and so was the shining ash-blonde hair. But something had happened to take the radiance out of her beauty. The lustre and sheen I'd envied so much had vanished. She'd lost weight, and it didn't suit her. In repose her mouth was a hard bitter line, and her eyes looked haunted. I stared, and instead of gloating, which is what I'd have expected, my heart was suddenly wrung with pity.

She'd been staring at me, too, taking in every detail. 'Well,' she said grudgingly, 'I must say, you've improved quite a lot since I saw you last. Your hair looks different. Who cut it for you?'

I couldn't resist it. 'Morico,' I said casually, hoping she'd read the same fashion mags as I had.

Her eyes widened. '*Morico?* Not *the* Morico?' It was a squeak of pure envy. 'Don't tell me he's opened a salon in Birtles Road?'

I laughed. 'Of course not. No – I had a job in the Arbor Palace for a while. He saw me there, and decided to cut my hair.'

Her jaw dropped. 'Just like that?'

'More or less, yes.'

All at once she became quite animated. 'Is he really as outrageous as they say?'

I remembered the plump little Cockney in his pink suit and spats, and laughed out loud. 'He's completely and utterly OTT.'

'Gosh,' she said. 'Do tell. I mean – you don't have to go back to the kitchen this instant, do you?' She was offering a temporary truce. She was asking a favour. That, if nothing else, told me how desperately lonely she was.

I groaned inwardly. The last thing I could afford right now was to get emotionally involved in Xenia's problems. Pitiable or not, she was still bad news.

I looked at my watch. 'I can spare half an hour,' I conceded.

Chatting in her room was actually quite pleasant. We talked about people we'd known at school (again, I got the weird feeling that she was looking back over a period of years, not months). I gave her a plausible but strictly fictional account of what I'd been doing in the meantime. At last I got up to go.

'Thanks for the chat, Xenia. It's been lovely.'

Her face was almost wistful. She hadn't nattered with a girl-friend for ages, you could tell. 'Perhaps we could talk again some time.'

I felt I ought to insert a word of caution – for my sake if not for hers. 'I get the impression Lord Kostchei mightn't approve of you hobnobbing with servants. But you know him better than I do, of course.'

All the light drained out of her face. 'Yes,' she said distantly, 'Well, goodbye, then, Foss.'

'You're late,' Jo said. 'What happened? Borschei cut up rough?'

'You won't believe this,' I assured him, and gave him a precis of my day.

'In the *Castle*? My God, Foss . . . you're in! You've done it!'

'Not yet, I haven't. It's a step in the right direction, that's all.'

We approached the camp site. Ferdinand and his horse were conspicuously absent.

'Sneaked off to meet his Ugly Duckling, I expect,' Jo said cattily. 'Damn. And I told him to light the fire so you could have your cuppa before turning in . . .'

'Why would he take Jupiter?'

Jo shrugged. 'How should I know? Anyway – this Kostchei. Are you sure Ferd's got the right end of the stick? The whole outfit sounds squeaky clean to me.'

'He's a sorcerer, Jo.'

'Okay, but perhaps he's a good guy. Perhaps he's retired.'

I hadn't thought of that. 'It's possible, I suppose.' Then I told him about meeting Xenia. He blinked. 'How the hell did she get here?'

'Same way as we did, I suppose,' I said – and stopped. But that couldn't be true, could it? All of a sudden I was thinking in hyperdrive. What, exactly, had she said? That Kostchei had picked her because she had 'certain talents'. What sort of talents? Sorcery? Witchcraft? The only talent I was sure she possessed was for pure, unmitigated, conscienceless evil . . . And Kostchei – Jo's retired 'good guy' – 'kept an eye open for that kind of thing'. In our world? How? The answer popped up, chilling my blood. Talent-spotters. *Agents*.

It couldn't be a coincidence. There *had* to be a connection.

Jo was shaking my shoulder. 'Foss? Are you okay? You've gone white.'

I elbowed him aside and plunged into Ferdinand's tent. My heart hit my sandals. 'Jo! His gear's gone!'

'*What?*' He leapt to his feet. 'All of it?'

The only thing he'd left behind was his sleeping bag.

It was only then that we saw the note. It was pinned to the tent-pole, but facing inwards, so of course we'd missed it.

'*Foss, Jo . . .*' Ferdinand had been in a hurry: the writing was a scrawl. '*By the time you read this I shall probably be up at the Castle. You'll never guess who paid us a visit earlier this evening! Lord Kostchei himself!*'

I couldn't hold the paper steady. The writing swam and blurred. Jo snatched the letter from my limp grasp and began to read aloud.

'*We were quite wrong about him, you know. He's absolutely charming . . .*'

'I bet,' I said grimly.

'*. . . and knows my father quite well. In fact Siegfried was here a couple of months ago! What a coincidence! He explained about Odette, too. Actually none of it's his fault. The enchantment was laid on her by a Black Knight who has recently returned to terrorise the district. He's scheduled to issue a challenge the day after tomorrow. I intend to destroy him if I can, and break the spell. Odette is staying at the castle too. Apparently Kostchei has a limited influence on the spell that binds her – but I've promised to keep my distance. I hope to see you both soon. Yours, Ferdinand.*'

'He fell for it,' I breathed. 'The stupid well-meaning blockhead actually fell for it.' I felt sick with sheer terror.

Something else was nudging my memory circuits, just short of data retrieval. Something vitally important. About Siegfried . . . I punched mental replay buttons frantically. The missing line hit the screen and I gasped.

'Necrotica!' That nasal, whining voice in the little garret room, with Margaret lying in a dead faint across the sewing-machine – a lifetime ago. '*Oh, Siegfried's dead. Killed in a duel with a Black Knight, somewhere up North.*'

Jo's eyes widened. 'Siegfried? But Ferdinand never said . . .'

'Of course he didn't!' My knees gave way and I sat down rather suddenly on the grass. 'Because I never actually got round to telling him that Siegfried was dead! He was so shocked that day, remember? I was going to break the news gently, later on. Except I never got the chance. There was the storm, and the shipwreck, and Lermos . . . and I forgot.'

Jo was silent.

I felt terrible. 'Kostchei's lying his socks off, Jo.' My voice didn't sound like me at all. 'He masterminded the whole thing from the start. Ferdinand's Quest, me as Aurora . . .' It all fitted. Arborea . . . The attempt on Lord Falcon's life . . . a bunch of fluff-brained fairies who suddenly got staggeringly good at magic . . . the feeling I'd had all along that there was a single brain and a single purpose behind it all . . . 'Lermos, the storm, the stone-creatures . . .'

Jo was wagging his hands frantically in the effort to slow me down. 'You can't prove any of that!'

'Xenia's here. A girl from the same town as me. He had agents there – we know that . . . He lied about Siegfried. It's too much of a coincidence, Jo. And now he's got Ferd.'

'But Foss . . .'

'And don't say it's not my fault, Jo. If Ferdinand had known about Siegfried, Kostchei wouldn't have been able to sweet-talk him. He'd have been on his guard. He'd have . . .'

'He'd have what? Run the old man through?' Jo snorted. 'Pull the other one, Foss. Kostchei wanted him, he's got him. As I see it, the immediate problem is this Black Knight.'

'The one who killed Siegfried! *Siegfried!*' My voice went up in a wail.

'If it's the same one.'

'Of course it's the same one! It all slots together too well!'

Jo swore. 'We've got to warn him. I know he's good – but . . . Siegfried? The ultimate hard guy?'

All at once I felt drained. 'I'm going to bed. I'm on duty from seven-thirty tomorrow.'

'You don't think Kostchei's connected you with Ferdinand yet?'

'Of course he has. He's been on to us from the word go. But I've got to warn Ferd, Jo. He's got to know. Anyway, if I don't go, he'll get suspicious.' Kostchei couldn't have known I'd bump into Xenia like that; he couldn't have expected Necrotica to spill the beans . . . Perhpas he didn't even know I'd been Aurora – why should he? His agents had handled all that. We had a day to get Ferdinand out of his clutches.

'Okay. Then I'm coming with you.'

23.

Your Stars: CANCER (June 22–July 23)
Your suspicions regarding a colleague are well-founded.
A confrontation is imminent, but don't do anything rash.
When the moment is right, have the courage to take the
initiative.

I woke up at dawn with a headache and a profound sense of foreboding.

Up at the Castle, all trace of yesterday's leisurely routine had vanished. Below-stairs, panic reigned. Mr Boscombe was in a flat spin and bewildered footmen were dashing about every which way in response to the stream of conflicting commands issuing from the butler's pantry. I hardly had time to put on my clean cap and apron before being deluged with requests, queries and demands from all points of the compass.

Thank God for Mrs Hodgson, who'd taught me the absolute authority a cook needs to project (and whose menus I'd pinched). I bolted the connecting door on the inside and told Mr Boscombe firmly but politely that the kitchen was out of bounds until I decided otherwise.

Thank God for the preparations we'd made the day before. Thank God for Katie and Sophie and Victoria and Mrs Briggs, who eased off the panic the moment Mr Boscombe was off their backs, and who took orders like troopers. It didn't occur to me until much later just how weird it must have been for them to be bossed around by someone no older than Katie. The fact that they took it all on the chin and didn't flinch says a lot for their basic integrity. And I did know what I was doing.

We worked flat out all day. There wasn't a hope of taking time off to search for Ferdinand. By five-thirty we were all flagging, but everything was ready bar a few last-minute touches. At six the three girls and I took platters of cold meat and pitchers of beer out to the stables for the grooms. Jo was there, merging effortlessly with his surroundings as always. We managed to exchange a few words while the rest of the stable hands were scoffing the nosh and flirting with the girls.

'I had a quick chat with Ferd on the quiet,' Jo said. 'He didn't believe me, though.'

'He's not going to blow it, is he?'

'No. Thinks we're a couple of raving nut cases, but he'll keep his mouth shut.'

Dinner was at seven, and the ball guests were arriving for nine-thirty. We'd sent up the last course for dinner, and were taking a well-earned break when the two upstairs maids appeared, giggling and looking smug.

'Guess where we've been! Up on the balcony, watching the ladies and gentlemen!'

Hubbub broke out. 'You lucky things!' 'What about us?' 'It's not fair, we do all the work and never get the chance to see anything.' 'Did you see Prince Ferdinand? Is he really as good-looking as they say?'

Quelling the uproar, I said, 'Won't Mr Boscombe give you a rocket if he catches you peeking at the guests?'

'He doesn't know,' Sophie said. 'It's dark up there. Nobody can see us if we're quiet.'

Three pairs of eyes switched beseechingly to me. 'Oh, please, Mrs Ewins, can we go and watch the ladies come out of the dining-room? Just till the plates are sent down?'

'We'll be back in plenty of time to wash up,' Katie added.

I struggled with the weird feeling of being middle-aged, and a killjoy. Sophie was a year or two older than me, for Heaven's sake.

'Dead right you will,' I said, abandoning pretence, ''Cos I'm coming with you.'

The tiny balcony was high up under the ballroom ceiling, above the chandeliers. We had a superb view of the ballroom floor and the grand staircase at the far end. The girls had been right – nobody below us would dream of squinting up into the darkness past the dazzle of so many lights.

I had to pinch myself. This was Kostchei's house: a sorcerer's den. And here we were – six little serving girls doing what downstairs maids have done in great houses since the beginning of time: sneaking a peek at the gentry.

The dining-room door opened and the ladies emerged, chattering like parakeets in their flamboyant gowns and over-elaborate hairdos. Alongside me the other girls sniggered and made catty remarks. I scarcely heard them. I was waiting tensely for a glimpse of Ferdinand – and possibly of Kostchei himself.

Two minutes later the men appeared and strolled across to the drawing-room. They hadn't lingered over the port and cigars this evening. Ferdinand wasn't amongst them, and neither was Kostchei.

When the hall was empty again a small slender girl in white appeared on the upper landing and leant over the banisters. My heart gave a jump – it was Odette.

Ferdinand emerged alone from the dining-room. He stopped at the foot of the stairs and looked up. Odette leaned over the banister-rail. They reached out their hands to one another, Ferdinand gazing raptly upwards, Odette leaning down: Romeo and Juliet. A small white slip of paper passed from her hand to his; he kissed it and pocketed it above his heart. She straightened with a sigh, mimed a last lingering kiss, turned her back and drifted away.

I touched my pendant briefly, and my worst fears were confirmed. Xenia was impersonating Odette.

All the scattered jigsaw pieces suddenly swam together and clicked into place in one flash of illumination. Ferdinand was the key. Not Jo, not me – I was just a bit-player who'd left the stage at the end of the first act, and Jo wasn't even in the script. We weren't part of Kostchei's schemes at all. Ferdinand was.

Because we knew him so well, we'd tended to forget that Ferdinand was a lot more than just another aristocrat on the lookout for a wealthy heiress. He was now the heir to a large, powerful kingdom. Perhaps meeting Odette had been an accident Kostchei hadn't foreseen; perhaps she'd been introduced as bait. But that didn't matter now. Ferdinand was caught in the trap. He'd succumb to Kostchei's mind-hold, marry Xenia, and their children would rule huge areas of the Zones – all under Kostchei's iron control. And in a hundred years' time, the sorcerer would get his claws on Arborea . . . and Margaret.

I opened my mouth to scream at Ferdinand, to tell him to get out, now, fast, while he was still in charge of his own head. The shout died in my throat. Kostchei had entered the ballroom.

I watched him place a fatherly arm around Ferdinand's shoulders and steer his victim towards the drawing-room. I was trembling. Perhaps there was a way to defeat this man – but direct confrontation wasn't it. Shaking, I shepherded the girls together and went back to the kitchen.

By the time we'd washed up the dinner dishes, the ball guests were arriving. It was a warm evening; doors and windows were wide open and even in the kitchen we could hear the buzz of chatter, the usher announcing the guests, the musicians tuning up in their gallery. As we put the finishing touches to the buffet, the dancing began.

Darkness fell – and subtly, the atmosphere of the Castle began to change. Outside in the yard everything was normal: grooms and coachmen talking amicably to each other. But indoors, something sinister was happening. The noise from the ballroom got louder, the music wilder; we could hear screams, and cackling, inhuman laughter.

The three girls were looking frightened. On an impulse, I shut and bolted the inner kitchen door. 'Time you all went home,' I said. 'I can deal with anything else that crops up. You've all been megastars. Thanks a million.'

As the girls collected shawls and cardigans we heard Mr Boscombe's voice in the corridor. He sounded drunk. I was positive he couldn't be – there hadn't been time. It takes a lot more than the odd nip of brandy to make a person of Mr Boscombe's weight and girth slur his words and trail off into high-pitched giggles, which is what he was doing.

'Whe's th' party?' he was saying. ''S party time. Go'n gether girls'n bringum to th'party.'

Nobody laughed. Somehow we all understood that on this occasion Mr Boscombe being squiffy wasn't funny at all.

The door knob turned. Rattled impatiently. Somebody began to thump on the panels. 'C'mon, girls. Le's in! C'mon, c'mon, open th'door!'

'Home,' I said, breaking the tension. 'All of you. As fast as you can run.'

They hurried to the outer door. One step over the threshold and they staggered back as though they'd bumped into an invisible wall.

'We can't get out! Something's stopping us getting out!'

Something heavy hit the inner kitchen door. A panel burst. A hand pushed through the gap and groped for the bolt. Vicky screamed. The hand was scaly, with ragged flaps of skin, and claws.

I grabbed my pendant. 'Katie, hold my hand. Vicky, Sophie, hang on to Katie. Don't let go.'

I felt the barrier across the opening, like a sheet of plate glass, like the barrier at the Meini Hirion Gate. I gathered up my will, and pushed. The pendant blazed in my fingers – and I was through, dragging the three girls behind me. We stood trembling in the cool lamplit courtyard.

The head groom was approaching, looking anxious. 'Getting a bit wild in there, are they?' He couldn't have known what was really going on, of course, but he'd heard enough gossip about aristocratic high jinks to be concerned. 'Don't you worry, ladies. Me and a couple of steady lads'll see you all safe home.'

When they'd gone I slipped back inside. The empty kitchen was a shambles of broken crockery and furniture. The door was splintered like a greengrocer's lettuce box. I dived through the wreckage and headed for the little dark stairs leading to the hidden balcony above the chandeliers.

I had to hold on to every scrap of self-control I possessed in order not to run back downstairs again screaming. The ballroom was seething with creatures out of a nightmare. All hideously disfigured in different ways: bat snouts, tentacles, scales, claws; hair like snakes, leering gargoyle faces. Here and there I caught a glimpse of someone who was almost a complete, recognisable animal. They looked a bit lost and bewildered, as though they'd got sucked into this debauch by accident and wanted out. The most revolting creatures were the ones with multiple disfigurements, and those, strangely enough, were the most obscenely human. The ball guests weren't just letting their hair down: all the individual personal nastinesses they'd brought with them were being let out and given shape . . .

I couldn't see Ferdinand anywhere. He'd be an animal, I was sure – one of the bewildered ones. Mentally I classed him as a potential dog: one of the bigger, classier breeds, noble and faithful and soppy at heart.

There was no visible sign of Kostchei either. Perhaps he didn't care to watch while his demons were unleashed. He'd struck me as a fastidious man.

There was one more place to check before I stuck some sort of disguise on my head and started searching the adjoining rooms and the terraces.

Xenia was alone in her room, sitting pensively at the dressing-table. She was Odette again. When I opened the door she turned, smiling shyly, one hand modestly on her bosom. When she saw me, however, her entire act disintegrated.

'What the hell are you doing here?' she hissed. 'Get out, you fool! Get out *now*!'

Enlightenment struck. I started to laugh. 'You're waiting for Ferdinand! The big seduction number, huh?'

Her reply was unprintable. Every hint of the Swan Princess had vanished. She was a hundred per cent Xenia, and hopping mad. She thrust her hand out at me, palm uppermost. I felt a mild jolt, but nothing more.

'I'm immune, Xenia, so don't waste your energy. Where's Ferd?'

Her face was livid. 'Get *out* of here! Or do I have to throw you out?'

I looked at my watch. 'He's a bit behind schedule, isn't he? How long have you been waiting, Xene? Ever since you made that assignation on the stairs after dinner?'

Her eyes blazed. 'How did you know about that?'

'Never mind.' I sat down on her bed. 'Well, if Ferd's got an appointment with you, I might as well wait. I need to see him fairly urgently myself.'

She was controlling her temper, but only just. 'Listen, pug-face. I don't know what you think you're doing here, but let's get one thing clear, shall we? Ferdinand's *mine*. He's going to come up here, insane with longing for his scrawny little goose-girl – and I'm not going to let a scabby little kitchen drudge like you interfere. Got that?'

I'd suspected as much. 'Make a habit of it, do you?' I said. 'Is that what Kostchei pays you for?'

Her laugh was like fingernails on glass. 'What in hell would *you* know about sex, Little Miss Goody-goody-po-face?'

I faced her steadily. 'What makes you so sure he'll turn up, Xenia? He's not here now, is he? There's enough going on down in that ballroom to send anybody's inhibitions into a flat spin – but he's not here.'

'Don't be ridiculous. He's got hormones, hasn't he? Not like that great oaf Siegfried.' She bared her teeth at me. 'What's the matter, fishbreath? Jealous? Tried your luck with him and blew it, did you?'

I felt sickened. 'What happened to Siegfried?'

'Oh, the usual thing. He challenged Kostchei's Black Knight to a duel, and that was that. Quite entertaining, really, while it lasted.' She laughed. 'What was left of him was hardly worth

314

feeding to the animals.' She saw the look of horrified disgust on my face. 'Squeamish, prawn? You won't last long around here . . . Anyway, why have you got this fixed idea that your precious Princeling isn't going to arrive?'

I found myself pitying her. 'I doubt if you'll ever understand, Xenia. You or Kostchei. You're both dead where it matters. Ferdinand actually *loves* Odette. It's much more than just a gonad thing. He wouldn't do anything to harm her or put her in danger. Ferd's all the things you and Kostchei know nothing about. He's brave, he's honourable, and he plays by the rules. He promised to keep his distance – and he will.'

'Sez you,' she spat.

'I'd start worrying if I were you, Xene baby. You've blown it. Kostchei's not going to be too chuffed with you, is he? Not happy at all.'

That did it. Blazing with fury, she sprang to her feet, palm outstretched, screaming incantations. When magic didn't work she hurled herself straight at me. I dodged, grabbed a vase at random and smashed it across her shoulders. She spun round and raked my face with her nails.

She was taller than me, heavier, and with a longer reach, but not as strong or as fit. I punched her in the jaw. A wild swipe caught me across the face and my nose began to bleed. I kicked her shins, grabbed a handful of her hair and slammed her head into the bedstead.

It wasn't an elegant fight. It was messy and vicious. 'Puke-faced git!' she screamed, and I yelled things like 'Slag!' and 'Sorcerer's tart!' We went for each other's faces, hair and bellies. Small tables fell over, priceless china and crystal crashed in shards to the floor. Very shortly Xenia was developing a magnificent black eye and I was bleeding from umpteen scratches. Chunks of our hair littered the carpet. Intent as we were on mutual disfigurement, neither of us was aware of the window being rattled, and frantic male shouts from outside . . .

Finally I got in a hard punch to the diaphragm, and she doubled up, wheezing. In the relative silence that followed, the noise of the window being shaken fell like a tin tray on concrete. Both of us jerked around to look. And froze, thunderstruck.

Ferdinand's appalled face was pressed to the glass – all squashed-up and white in patches, like a clown's. 'Open the window, Foss!' he was shouting. 'Quick! The ledge . . . Open it!'

I dived for the catch. Xenia staggered to her feet, making noises like the *Lusitania* in fog. She lurched against me and the heavy casement swung outwards, knocking Ferdinand off-balance. He scrabbled frantically at the pane, his face registering ludicrous dismay – and the next moment he'd fallen out of sight.

We stood there frozen with shock. All we could hear was a series of diminishing crashes as Ferdinand bounced helplessly through the branches of the giant wisteria on which he'd been perched. There was one last, sustained brushwood crackle in the distance – and silence.

'You bloody *fool*!' she screeched, and came at me again. But she was tired now, and I held her off easily.

'Stop it, Xenia! This is serious!'

She gaped at me. All at once the fight went out of her and she slumped. 'He's killed himself! He's dead! What am I going to *do*?' She'd gone white.

I pushed her into a chair, and went to lean out of the window. Xenia's room was high up in one of the round towers of the castle. Over to my left, about thirty feet below, I could see the end wall of one of the terraces, clearly visible in the light pouring out of the ground-floor windows. But where Ferdinand had fallen there was only darkness. Perhaps forty feet down, the tops of trees were faintly outlined in the reflected glow.

'What's down there? The garden?'

She'd put her head between her knees. 'Kostchei's Zoo,' she said bleakly.

'His what?'

'His private zoo. He keeps these . . . creatures . . .' Her voice broke and she began to sob hysterically. She wasn't thinking of Ferdinand at that point, she was anticipating Kostchei's reaction, and I didn't blame her one bit for freaking out. 'If he's dead . . .'

I'd heard the way the big, knotted branches of the wisteria had broken his fall. 'Xenia. Pull yourself together. He's an athlete, his reactions are fast. Injured, maybe. Killed, no.'

'You don't understand. Those creatures down there . . .'

'He's a superb swordsman. Offhand, I can't think of anything he couldn't handle.' And remembered, too late, that tonight he wouldn't have been wearing his sword.

316

'There's a force-field. He won't be able to get out. They'll kill him . . .' I heard a rattling noise and realised that her teeth were chattering. 'Oh, Hecate, what am I going to *do*?' She started to cry again.

I gripped her shoulders and shook her. 'Stop it, Xenia! Listen. I can get through Kostchei's force-field. I've done it twice already.'

'*You?*' From which I gathered she couldn't.

'Shut up. We've got to co-operate. We both want him alive, don't we?'

She nodded fearfully.

'So this is what we'll do. You'll get me Ferdinand's sword. Then you'll tell me exactly how to get into this zoo, at the closest point to where he landed. And no tricks, Xenia. The way I see it, you're in deep trouble.'

'But if you escape with him . . .'

'You won't be implicated. This whole accident never happened. But if you leave him there, Kostchei'll know.'

She got up, clenching and twisting her hands. 'All right. Beneath the terraces there's a path. Keep heading towards this tower. You'll come to a high wall, and a gate.'

'Locked?'

'Yes, but . . .' She grabbed a face tissue and a lipstick, and scrawled one word: *Joranokabikil*.

'Don't say it aloud,' she mouthed. 'It opens the gate. Both ways. He'll have landed about twenty yards from there . . . Hurry, Foss.'

Ferdinand's sword was hanging on the wall of his room; I snatched it down and made for the door. There, with the heavy weight in my arms, I paused. Xenia looked so lost and so desperate that I felt choked.

'Xenia – you don't have to stay here. Come with us.'

She spun away from me. 'Just get the hell out of here, will you? I never want to set eyes on you again. Go!'

I went.

I pelted down the back stairs and shot through the kitchen. The force-field gave way like bubble gum. As I emerged Jo erupted from the shadows of the stable-yard.

'Foss! What the hell happened to you?'

I'd forgotten about the bloody nose and the scratches. 'Had a fight with Xenia. Tell you later. Here – get this thing strapped on and follow me.'

317

Blessings on Jo – he never asks silly questions in emergencies. He caught the sword and buckled it around his waist. As we ran down the dark, twisting path I panted out the gist of what had happened. Jo just grunted and loosened the sword in its scabbard.

We reached the gate. I crouched over the lock and whispered the opening word: *Joranokabikil*. The gate swung silently open. We slipped through, and it shut again with a click. I heard Jo unsheathe Ferdinand's sword with a slick, rasping noise.

The Zoo was thickly overgrown with trees and bushes. There was no path. The light shining from the terraces high above lay in faint dapples on the ground, making the shadows even blacker. Hearts pounding and every nerve on red alert, we began to search for the place where Ferdinand had fallen.

'What sort of creatures?' Jo muttered.

'She didn't say. They scared her, though.'

Looking up, we could see the trail of broken branches vanishing towards the tiny lighted square which was Xenia's window. The gigantic wisteria – I'd never seen one so big – grew out of one of the terraces high above and some distance to our right. It extended around a corner and then branched out to cover the upper storeys of Xenia's tower. A nerve-racking climb, but perfectly possible for somebody as athletic as Ferdinand.

'He seems to have a thing about climbing towers, doesn't he?' Jo murmured.

The zoo was in a deep gully. Above the trees a sheer over-hanging cliff rose to the base of the tower. Nothing could get out that way.

We searched the ground, calling softly. There was no reply.

Jo knelt abruptly over a patch of trampled earth. Our eyes were getting used to the dim light by now. 'Got it,' he said with a satisfied grunt. 'This is where he dropped. Must have grabbed branches all the way down. Swung down through that tree and landed in this bush.'

'Then he gets up,' I said, peering intently, 'and strolls off . . . *away* from the gate?'

'You can't see the gate from here. And he wasn't strolling. Staggering. Hurt himself in the fall, probably.'

We followed the erratic trail. A few yards further along I tripped over something warm and softish and nearly fell. My heart turned over. We knelt, squinting so as to make out details in the gloom.

It wasn't Ferdinand. It was a creature like a jaguar, but with sabre fangs and claws four inches long. The grass where it lay was glutinous with blood. Its throat had been cut.

'He had his dagger, then,' Jo said grimly.

We hurried on. Ferdinand's trail skirted the cliff and continued at the foot of a high, smooth wall. The Zoo was bigger than I'd thought.

We began to hear faint bestial growling noises ahead. Abandoning caution, we broke into a run. The volume increased sharply – and suddenly it erupted into a full-scale fight: a deafening cacophony of snarls, barks, howls and high-pitched squealing. We dashed through the undergrowth and skidded to a stop.

Something huge and grotesque was lying on the ground in a patch of moonlight. We couldn't make out the details because the body was completely covered in a mass of nightmarish animals. They were tearing the carcass apart and fighting over the entrails.

'Ferdinand did *that*?' There was awe in Jo's voice. 'And he didn't even have his *sword*!' I was as shaken as he was.

We backed cautiously away and found ourselves gazing down a trail of wreckage the width of a bulldozer. Small bushes had been trodden down and crushed; the grass was trampled flat, and sizeable bits of branch hung limply from the trees on either side. The trail led straight to the glade where the slaughter had taken place.

All signs of Ferdinand's unsteady progress had been wiped out.

Ferdinand hadn't enjoyed the dinner-party much, he told us later. Odette wasn't there, and although the food was superb (his words, not mine), and his host continued to be charming, witty and considerate, Ferdinand himself had begun to feel more and more uneasy.

That afternoon he'd met Jo, posing as a gardener. The dire warnings Jo had passed on to him were all nonsense, of course. Siegfried, dead? Impossible. Killed in a duel with this same Black Knight, a year ago? Absolute bosh. Siegfried had passed this way only two months ago – Kostchei himself had said so. And as for that ridiculous story about Kostchei being responsible for every other near-disaster that had come their way . . . it was nothing short of slander.

But as the meal progressed he'd begun to wonder if there was something in what Jo'd said, after all. Supposing – just supposing – Siegfried really had found his match in this Black Knight. All right – absurd, impossible . . . but supposing he had?

All at once Ferdinand had begun to feel nervous about tomorrow's duel. The toasts, the congratulations and the speeches in his honour had suddenly seemed to indicate a rather heartless lack of tact on everybody's part.

When dinner was over he'd managed to have a brief word with Odette. She was looking particularly lovely tonight. She'd asked him to join her in her room – but that was out of the question, of course. He'd promised Kostchei that he'd keep his distance, for Odette's sake, and he had no intention of breaking his word. Enchantments were damned dangerous things, he knew – you had to play it by the book or Lord knew what might happen. If he slew the Black Knight tomorrow, Odette's terrible ordeal would be over, and she'd be his forever.

Or so Kostchei had told him. But Foss and Jo didn't trust Kostchei: they were convinced he was lying.

Ferdinand didn't know what to believe. He was confused. He liked things to be straightforward and simple and clear-cut – and when they weren't, he got morose and irritable.

The guests began to fill the ballroom; musicians struck up a waltz. Suddenly Ferdinand knew he couldn't face any more jollification that night. He filched a flagon of excellent wine from the dining room and wandered out onto the terrace. After a while he found a little niche around the corner, well away from the French windows, and settled down to get drunk all by himself.

He wasn't aware of the change that came over the Castle as dusk fell. Nobody saw him sitting there, and nothing interrupted his solitary musings.

From his hiding place he could see Odette's window, high up in the tower opposite. He wondered what she was thinking about up there. Whether she was worrying as much about him as he was about her. And all at once he knew that he simply had to see her again before he went out to do battle on her behalf. Just one last glimpse – and if Fate decreed that he should lose his life to the infamous Black Knight, then he'd die happy.

Well, perhaps not happy, exactly – in agony, more likely – but at least he'd have a last image of her adorable face to carry with him to the grave.

Ferdinand gazed longingly at the lighted window – and spotted the wisteria.

He was just drunk enough not to think twice about the awful drop beneath him as he started his climb. He was brimful of confidence and as skilful as a cat. He reached the window, and cautiously – so as not to startle his beloved – he raised himself onto the narrow ledge and looked in.

She was sitting at her dressing-table, alone, brushing her beautiful hair. He lifted one hand to tap on the pane – but then something about her made him pause. Something wasn't right. Her movements were different, somehow; they didn't raise echoes in the very fibre of his being as they normally did.

It was a case of true love seeing through superficial illusions. Puzzled and confused, Ferdinand shrank back into the shadows.

Then Foss burst into the room – and in an instant the girl at the dressing-table had changed. She wasn't his Odette after all. Appalled, Ferdinand heard every word of the angry exchange between the two girls. The awful truth dawned. Foss and Jo had been right all along. He'd been tricked.

Then the girls started brawling like a couple of angry cats, and he knew he had to help Foss. The window was locked. He hammered on it to attract Foss's attention. He saw her deliver a telling punch to her opponent's solar plexus – and then part of the ledge he was standing on gave way. The window opened, slammed him in the face, and to his horror he found himself falling . . .

His highly-trained physical reflexes took over. He grabbed at lintels and swung from branches as he plummeted earthwards. Branch after branch broke, but he managed to slow his fall. He crashed into the upper branches of a tree and hung on. Giddy, sore, bleeding from scores of scrapes and scratches, he dropped heavily into a clump of bushes and landed on the ground.

Almost immediately something large and cat-like and snarling came leaping at his throat. He punched its jaw and deflected it away, but the long claws ripped his left arm. It sprang at him again, but this time he was able to draw his dagger and slit its throat. The cat fell, and didn't get up again. Ferdinand wiped his blade on a tuft of grass, breathing heavily and feeling sick.

It was horribly dark down here in this part of the garden. As he straightened up he heard growls and rustling noises in the undergrowth. Eyes glowed green in the faint light from above:

more cats, a whole pack of the creatures. What was this place – some sort of zoo?

It had to be an enclosure of some sort; he was pretty sure the cats didn't roam the valley at will. He began to look for a gate, or a wall he could climb. It didn't occur to him that he was walking in the wrong direction.

The cats followed him warily, at a safe distance: he could hear their padding footsteps and occasional furtive growls. His arm was bleeding heavily, and soaking his shirt. He began to hurry. Being savaged by a pack of deformed moggies seemed such an ignominious way to die . . .

He had grim thoughts about Kostchei.

Suddenly something which he thought was a bush just ahead reared up with a terrifying roar. The moonlight shone full on a gigantic bear-like creature – a monstrous chimaera with a long scaly tail and ferocious teeth. Snarling horribly, the creature attacked.

Against something this big and this savage, Ferdinand's short dagger was practically useless, and he knew it. His left arm throbbed, his right hand was slippery with blood. With the last of his strength, he dodged and stabbed and dodged again. Part of his conscious mind was watching the creature, calculating which way it was likely to swipe next, how far he was from the nearest climbable tree and whether he'd make it in time. The rest of him was in a fog of weariness and didn't care much anyway.

He heard himself shouting for help, and was dimly surprised at how desperate his voice sounded.

Something was happening behind him, where he dared not look. Something huge was crashing through the undergrowth with a creaking, clanking noise, like machinery in need of oiling. A voice was shouting back – a vast echo of his own.

And then the gigantic Being swept between him and the beast like a natural disaster. Dimly, he heard the roar of fury, saw the creature rear up and go tumbling backwards end-over-end. Registered, but didn't see, the final fatal blow which crushed the huge rib-cage into pulp.

For a long breathless moment, there was silence.

The creaking noise approached him gingerly. An immense dark shadow came between him and the moonlight. From high above, a rather squeaky tenor voice issued out of the blackness.

322

'I say, old chap. Lorst a bit of the old vital fluid there, I see. Better get you out of here pronto, what?' A huge mailed hand cupped his elbow and lifted him tenderly to his feet.

There was a wall, and a gate. And then Ferdinand found himself standing outside the enclosure, on a slope of close-cropped turf. The giant steadied him with a protective arm.

'Name's Brian, by the way,' the giant said diffidently, and extended a hand the size of a haunch of beef. Ferdinand shook it tentatively, and introduced himself.

'I say, what ho, what?' The giant was gratified. 'Jolly pleased to make your acquaintance, don'tjerknow, what?' He brushed Ferdinand's stammered thanks away like a horse flicking off flies. 'Don't mention it. Just happened to be passin', y'know. Heard the noise. Thought I'd take a swift dekko.' He peered down at Ferdinand with concern. 'Um – don't mean to shove my oar in, old chap, but – seems to me those leaks of yours could do with pluggin'. Take you back to the Castle, if you like. If not – got a little shack up there. Pretty basic, don'tjerknow. Hot water, bandages . . .'

'I think I'd prefer your place, if you don't mind,' Ferdinand said.

As they walked slowly up the slope in the moonlight – Ferdinand limping, and the giant shuffling with small steps in an effort to keep pace – Ferdinand had time to observe his rescuer. He wasn't quite as colossal as he'd seemed in the wood. He was about seven feet tall, and broad in proportion. He was clean-shaven; his hair appeared to be fair, and he was dressed in a one-piece leather garment like a jumpsuit. The creaking and clanking came from inside the suit, which struck Ferdinand as being extremely odd.

'Pardon me askin',' the giant said curiously, 'But was it a bet?'

'What?'

'Gettin' into the zoo like that. I mean to say. Dangerous. Very,' he added disapprovingly.

Ferdinand explained that he'd fallen. And then, because Brian was clearly such a kindly, helpful, sympathetic sort of chap and he desperately needed to talk to somebody just then, Ferdinand told him about Odette.

'Love,' Brian said wistfully. 'Was in love meself once. Dreadful business. Dreadful.'

Safely ensconced in Brian's hut at the top of the slope, Ferdinand began to relax and pay some attention to his surroundings. There was quite a lot of jet-black armour hanging up, he noticed, and an immense black jousting-helm reposing on a crocheted mat on the window-sill, with a bunch of fresh flowers stuck through the visor. An impressive display of weapons hung in tasteful patterns on the walls, each with a neat white card stating a time and place.

Brian was bustling hospitably about, producing hot water, dettol and bandages as promised. And little by little it began to dawn on Ferdinand – muzzy as he was with the after-effects of shock, blood-loss, alcohol and emotional upheaval – that this extraordinarily well-disposed, pleasant, understanding, thoroughly splendid chap . . . was none other than the Black Knight himself . . .

24.

Your Stars: CANCER (June 21–July 22)
Prompt action is called for if you are to hang on to the
gains you've made. Colleagues will prove helpful in a
crisis, but watch your back. There's more going on than
meets the eye.

Jo and I followed the wreckage trail. It ended in a heavy steel gate set into a twenty-foot-high wall. The gate was shut. I muttered the word and nothing happened. I tried again. Still nothing.

I was close to panic. 'He's come back! Kostchei's cancelled the Word! We can't get out!'

Resorting to brute force, Jo gave the gate a violent shaking. 'No good. We'll have to climb over.'

'But it fits like a glove, Jo, and the wall's like glass – who're you kidding?'

Jo attacked the gate like an infuriated gorilla. It didn't budge.

It was at that point – Jo sweating from his exertions, and me gibbering with frustration – that we both suddenly noticed the spring-handle of a Yale lock. We dived for it at the same moment, cracked our heads together and saw stars.

Jo tugged the gate open. There was no force-field. Feeling very silly, we marched through and slammed it behind us.

There was a light at the top of the slope: a warm, friendly sort of light. We homed in as on a beacon in a stormy sea.

We peered apprehensively through the half-open door. Ferdinand and the Black Knight were sitting one on each side of the hearth with their feet on the fender. Ferdinand had stripped off his shirt and was wincingly dabbing his wounds with antiseptic. A pan of soup was simmering on the hob, and a whisky bottle stood hospitably uncorked on the table between them. They turned round and saw us.

'Er . . . I hope we're not intruding,' Jo said politely.

The Black Knight got clankily to his feet. 'Good Lord, no. Come in, come in, take a pew. Well, I must say,' he beamed. 'Three visitors in one evening, by Jove. What a turn-up for the book, what?'

Half an hour later Brian was still glowing all over with delighted hospitality. Ferdinand had fallen asleep before we'd had a chance to broach the subject of tomorrow's duel. We lifted him onto Brian's bed, took his boots off and tenderly covered him with the duvet. He was out like a light.

'Best thing for the poor fellow,' Brian murmured. 'Sleep it off. Right as rain by mornin'.'

By now it was getting on for one a.m. I was yawning, and struggling to keep my eyes open. It had been a long and stressful day; blissful oblivion was just around the corner. Jo dug me in the ribs. 'Oi. Wake up. There are one or two things we need to get sorted, right?'

I roused myself with an effort. 'Um, Brian . . . d'you mind if we ask you a few questions?'

His ham-like face registered mild surprise. 'Good Lord, no. Fire away. Can't guarantee I'll be much help, though. Do me best, of course.'

Getting straight to the point, Jo said, 'About tomorrow. You and Ferdinand and this duel.'

Brian's face was a blank. 'Sorry?'

'The duel,' I said. 'You and Ferdinand are scheduled to fight a duel to the death, tomorrow morning, straight after breakfast.'

Brian's jaw dropped. He looked thoroughly upset. 'Oh, no! Must've made a mistake. Must have. I meantersay, His Highness there? Chap who's drunk m'whisky, slept in me own bed? Shockin' bad form, don'tjerknow.'

'Good,' Jo said with immense satisfaction. 'I thought you'd see it that way.'

'Hang about,' I said. 'Are you telling us you didn't know about this duel? You didn't issue a challenge, or anything?'

'Good Lord, no,' said Brian.

It didn't add up. Jo and I exchanged baffled looks.

'You are the famous Black Knight, though, aren't you?' Jo said.

Brian gave a modest little cough. 'Was, old chap. Was. Long time ago, though. Well, fancy you knowin' that. Small world, isn't it? Retired,' he explained. 'Took this Zoo-keepin' job. Just as well for His Highness, don'tjerknow. What?'

I stared at Jo with a sinking heart. 'You know what this means, don't you? There must be another one. Another Black Knight.'

All traces of diffidence vanished from Brian's face. His eyes bulged dangerously and his neck went red. 'Another Black Knight? In my own back yard? By Jove! Meantersay! Good Lord.' He clanked to his feet and began creaking agitatedly round the room. Powerful emotions were raging within his jumpsuited chest. 'Y'mean some cad, some unspeakable *bounder*, is mollockin' about pretendin' to be *me*?' His face had gone from ham-coloured to purple. 'D—disgraceful! Utterly beyond the d—dashed pale! Who is this obnoxious pustule? Hey?'

Patiently, we told him all we knew. He calmed down as suddenly as he'd erupted, and sat down heavily.

'This demmed charlatan, this Black Whatsisname, has killed His Highness's brother and turned his ladylove into a swan?'

'That's what Kostchei told Ferdinand. That's why Ferdinand agreed to fight the duel. If he wins, the spell breaks and Odette's free.'

Brian grunted. 'Well, good luck to him, by Jove. Deserves to win. Plucky young feller. Did the same sort of thing meself at his age.'

'But,' I said, 'there's a snag. We think Kostchei's lying his socks off.'

'Get away,' said Brian, blinking owlishly.

'You see the mess we're in, Brian. Ferdinand won't leave the area without Odette. He'll go in there tomorrow and fight this Black Knight, whatever happens. But, what we're afraid of is *(a)* if he wins, Kostchei'll rat on the deal, or *(b)* that Kostchei'll rig the duel so that Ferdinand can't possibly win anyway.'

I was quite pleased with that statement. Neat, I felt: succinct and to the point. Mentally, I awarded myself a little tick in red biro.

Brian was shaking his head. 'Don't understand it,' he muttered. 'Don't understand it at all.'

'Seems fairly clear to me,' Jo said impatiently, 'Look, Brian, it's . . .'

'Shush!' I said. 'Hang on a minute.'

Brian wasn't telling us everything. In his eyes there was a haunted, worried look – as though he suspected something dreadful and was trying not to think about it too hard. I tried a shot in the dark.

'Why did you stop being the Black Knight, Brian?'

'Eh? Oh, that. Avalanche,' he explained. 'Rocks, not snow. In the mountains not far from here. Joggin' along on dear old Boswell one mornin' . . . That's Boswell up there,' he added sadly, pointing to a highly-coloured picture of a horse above the mantelpiece. 'Gone to a better place, poor chap. Where was I?'

'Jogging along.'

'Oh, yes. Mindin' me own business, when all of a sudden crash, rumble, down it all comes, out of the blue. Shockin' thing. Thought I'd handed in the old dinner pail, don'tjerknow. Like m'poor old Boswell. Buried, poor feller . . . Still, mustn't grumble, what? Act of God,' he added piously.

'Who dug you out?'

'Why, m'Lord Kostchei's men, from the Castle, don'tjerknow. Smashed to splinters,' he said soberly. 'Arms, legs, chest, hip-bones . . . Lucky to be alive.'

I held my breath. 'Yes?'

'Clever feller, m'Lord Kostchei. Marvellous job. 'Strornary. New arms, new legs, steel plates on m'chest, nifty little artificial ticker . . . Which is why,' he added severely, 'I can't bring meself to slander the chap. See your point of view, mind you. Don't agree, that's all.'

'So you're bionic,' Jo said faintly.

Bionic Brian the Black Knight. A Being capable of heaving a ton and a half of mutant bear into the wild blue yonder and crushing its ribs in the process . . .

'Programmable?'

'Definitely, I'd say.'

I let out pent-up breath in a long sigh. 'Brian – I hate to disillusion you – but we think Lord Kostchei's been using you in a very bad way.'

'Without your knowing, of course,' Jo added hastily.

'It's the only explanation which fits. You must have a remote-control thingy somewhere . . .'

'Right. And when the big K switches on . . .'

'You're a killing machine.'

'The ultimate warrior.'

Brian was looking more and more unhappy. 'Now see here . . .'

'Do you ever have dreams about fighting people?' I asked him. 'Lose half a day and don't know where it's gone?' Brian's face was a frozen, horrified mask. 'Recognise the names of people you don't ever remember meeting? Like Siegfried, for instance?'

Brian moaned.

'That's it, Foss. We've cracked it,' Jo said quietly.

'Now, wait a jiff,' said Brian. 'Lost me there. Never was much good at all this Science and whatnot.'

'It's quite simple, Brian, honestly. When he was rebuilding you, Kostchei slipped in a very small computer.'

'A kind of second brain,' Jo explained. 'I'd like to have seen how he did it, though,' he added wistfully.

'And at the same time,' I went on, 'he incorporated some sort of remote-control device. So whenever he needs a hit man, all he has to do is switch off your conscious mind and operate you like a machine.'

Brian sat down heavily. An expression of deep horror came over his face. 'Oh, I say. Meantersay I could have slain young Prince Ferdinand there, and not known a demmed thing about it?' I knew, then, that he believed us.

'Problem is,' I said, 'how do we scramble that without scrambling you?'

'Fairly simple, actually,' Jo said, getting to his feet. 'No need to touch the wiring, just blank off the receiver somehow.'

'Open up, Brian,' I urged. 'Let's have a butchers at your control box. If it's somewhere personal, I promise I won't look.'

Reluctantly, the giant unzipped the top half of his jumpsuit. Underneath it he wore a string vest. Beneath the vest was the steel plate he'd mentioned, cleverly jointed to allow him to breathe. In the centre was the outline of a panel.

'I'm not going to do anything,' Jo told the trembling knight. 'Just taking a look, okay?'

Brian pulled up the string vest and very delicately, Jo slid the panel open.

A gust of icy air blew through the doorway, which a second ago had been shut and barred and was now, bewilderingly, wide open. All three of us whirled to look.

'Congratulations,' Kostchei said smoothly. 'An impeccable display of inductive logic. What a pity you arrived at your conclusions too late to put them to the test.'

The cold was intense. It froze us immobile, numbed us to the bone so we couldn't even shiver.

Kostchei strolled into the room. Behind him, crowding the doorway, were his semi-human mobsters. They drooled and giggled, rat-ears, bat-snouts and tentacles a-twitch.

He was holding something between his long, graceful hands. It was a Chinese puzzle of carved ivory. He spun the puzzle, it clicked, and Brian's chest panel slid shut. Brian's face was like a waxwork, totally blank. The puzzle clicked again, and Brian stood up, his arms dangling limply at his sides.

'Arm him,' Kostchei said. The creatures darted in from the doorway and led Brian through to an inner room.

Kostchei turned to watch. For a few seconds the outer doorway was empty – a hole into darkness. Jo was looking at me. He couldn't move or speak, but his eyes glared messages. Suddenly I found the cold ebbing out of me. I lunged for the door and dashed through.

Exactly what I thought I'd be able to accomplish on my own, I've no idea. In any case, it didn't matter – freedom lasted rather less than ten seconds. I ran straight into Mr Boscombe's waistcoat. We impacted with a thud. Clawed mole-hands tried to grab me, but I seemed to be slippery, and when he touched me, he squealed.

Then Kostchei was close behind me, and the power the pendant had given me was annihilated.

Kostchei moved his hands in front of my face. The fingers emanated a deathly chill. 'Ah,' he said. His hand dipped – and came away holding the pendant. I hadn't even felt the pain as the chain snapped.

'Who gave you this?'

'My father,' I said.

He shook his head. 'No. The power . . . whose is the power?'

A force I couldn't resist dragged my chin up and made me look for the first time at his eyes. They were an intense turquoise blue, like shadows within a glacier. I had an overwhelming compulsion to speak. I struggled against it until I could feel sweat trickling down the sides of my nose and beading my upper lip. The voice which eventually emerged from my mouth didn't seem to belong to me at all.

'Ossiana,' I whispered.

Kostchei's mouth curved down in a cruel, sneering grin.

'Indeed.' He closed his fist. When he opened his hand again, a few tiny, shattered scraps of silver lay in his palm.

Tears of loss and despair welled up in my eyes. Where they trickled onto my skin, they froze into ice.

'What is her Name?' he said softly. 'Her Name, child. The Name of Power. Speak.'

The pain in my head was incredible. Five minutes of that, and I'd have gone insane. Abruptly, it stopped, leaving me doubled up on the floor and shuddering. I hadn't even known I was falling.

'You don't know,' Kostchei said, and turned his back.

Then his creatures surrounded Jo and me and bore us away into darkness and oblivion.

It was morning. Jo and I were standing behind Kostchei's ornate gilded chair and looking out on a green lawn in bright sunlight. Crowds were filling the white-painted stands above the lawn: real people, dressed in bright holiday finery and bearing no outward resemblance to the creatures they'd metamorphosed into the night before. Flags and banners were flying from gilded poles.

We ourselves were in a kind of pavilion, carpeted in red and canopied in white and gold. Xenia was sitting with her back to me in a smaller chair on Kostchei's left. I wondered if she still had her black eye.

I could see, I could hear, think and feel – but I couldn't move a muscle. I caught a glimpse of Jo out of the corner of my eye: he was as immobile as I was.

The crowd settled. People leaned forward in anticipation. Cheers broke out, flags waved . . . and Ferdinand walked out into the arena. The duel was about to begin.

Ferdinand was wearing dark-blue leather, but no steel. His head was bare. He unsheathed his sword and bowed gravely to the dais.

From the other end of the arena Brian emerged, dressed, like Ferdinand, in regulation leather duelling gear, except that his was black. The two combatants bowed to one another and then stood back, their raised swords glinting in the hot morning sunlight. Kostchei lifted his right hand, and dropped it. The duel began.

Jo and I watched with hardly a blink as the two men struck, parried, feinted and dodged. We had no choice. Kostchei wasn't going to let us miss a thing.

Ferdinand was doing the attacking. He was lithe and quick on his feet, and at first Brian's axe-like swordplay couldn't touch him. But then Brian's tactics changed, and suddenly Ferdinand was having to work hard to maintain his advantage. I realised that I'd been expecting Brian to fight like a machine, in some predictable pattern. He didn't. His thrusts and parries were as cunning as Ferdinand's own. Every few minutes a near-miss brought a sigh or a roar of approval from the avid crowd.

I'd got so involved in the duel that it was quite a shock when I found myself leaning up against the back of Kostchei's chair and looking over his right shoulder. I'd been creeping slowly forwards without realising it. Cautiously I turned my head towards Jo. He was still locked rigid, but his eyes glowed encouragement.

Kostchei was holding the little Chinese puzzle in his hands, and moving the spheres with infinitely delicate touches of his fingers. Kostchei himself was fighting Ferdinand, through Brian – and he was operating the controls with the tunnel-like concentration of a computer geek at a playstation.

I was too short to reach the puzzle over the high back of the chair. Very cautiously, I began to edge round to the side. The snatch would have to be instant and unerring, I knew. Fumble just once and we'd all be dead.

My right arm was throbbing. I looked down. The green stone in Magnus's ring was pulsating, pin-points of ruby light flashing on and off in the depths. I closed my eyes and uttered a silent prayer of thanks. Finally, Magnus knew where we were. Magnus – and Oz.

The crowd roared, jerking my attention to the arena. Ferdinand was down, and rolling like a cat from under the killing stroke of Brian's huge sword. But he'd been gashed; his sleeve was torn and a dark stain was spreading over the blue.

Kostchei chuckled. The two men fought on.

I became aware that the bright sunlight was fading. A huge bank of black cloud was rolling up over the horizon, and moving swiftly in our direction, its leading edges suffused with gold. The weather had been too hot, too sultry – and here at last was the inevitable, the long-awaited storm.

The blackness spread. Now people in the stands were glancing anxiously up at the sky. Some were even beginning to pull their cloaks about them and hurry away.

Ferdinand and the Black Knight fought on. Ferdinand was beginning to tire now: his feints were clumsier, his thrusts less sure. There was blood on the grass.

And Kostchei's Chinese puzzle was still out of my reach.

I cast my eyes up in despair . . . and saw a sight I'll never forget as long as I live.

Out of the massing clouds ahead, a huge flock of swans came flying, dazzling white against the blue-black sky, necks and pinions stroked with gold. There were hundreds of them, phalanx after phalanx, flying in spearhead formation, disciplined as an army. They flew towards us until they filled the whole sky, and the valley echoed with the thunder of wings. Tears jumped to my eyes: it was the most incredible, heart-stoppingly beautiful sight. And much, much more than beautiful – *dangerous.*

The spearhead fanned out. One after another the squadrons wheeled and began their descent in attack formation, heading straight for the duelling arena.

In seconds the arena was like a battlefield. Everywhere people were screaming and scattering and huddling to protect their heads from vicious beaks and outstretched necks and wings which can break a human thigh-bone without even trying.

In the pavilion, Kostchei was on his feet, swearing, his concentration scattered to the four winds. On the field, Brian was stamping round and round like an automaton, stabbing his sword mechanically at the air. Ferdinand was invisible behind a wall of protective wings.

Five of the squadrons converged on the pavilion. An arrowhead of necks like steel swooped out of the melee and dived straight for Kostchei's head. The pavilion was suddenly full of thundering wings and thrashing necks. Feathers were clogging the air like snow. Kostchei was shrieking incantations and hurling bolts of deadly fire at his attackers. Swan after swan reeled back after striking the nimbus of force protecting his body. To my left, Xenia was screaming and trying ineffectually to beat off the onslaught. I saw her arm snap and dangle, and then her head slump brokenly against the chair-back. The leading swan veered off, wheeled and swooped back to deliver a killing blow to Kostchei's neck. She fell with a gout of flame in the chest – and crumpled to the grass as a fair-haired girl. It was Odette.

More swans hurtled to the attack, and at last Kostchei lost his grip on the Chinese puzzle. I grabbed it just as it hit the floor and jumped on it, hard, with both feet. It crushed into a million powdery bits. In the middle of the arena, Brian fell over and lay still.

Kostchei whirled. His terrible gaze locked mine. There was death in his face: my death, and Jo's, and Ferdinand's, and Odette's. He raised his hand . . .

. . . And suddenly I wasn't there any more. Jo and I were standing in the middle of the arena next to Ferdinand and Brian and the limp body of Odette. Brian was sitting up, looking bewildered. But Ferdinand stooped over Odette with a cry of anguish and gathered her up into his arms.

Milliseconds later, the pavilion exploded.

The shock wave tumbled us to the ground. The field shook like custard. Splinters of wood and burning cloth showered down all round us. A huge cloud of black dust rose up from where the pavilion had been. Out of the cloud there emerged two gigantic figures: Kostchei . . . and my aunt Oz.

No trace of vagueness or diffidence about Oz now. She strode like a Colossus above the wreckage of the dais. The woolly cardigan was a robe of light; the neat grey hair was a swirling cloud in which lightning flickered and crackled. Her face was stern enough to frighten even me.

Vast bolts of raw energy flashed between her and Kostchei. The air sizzled with static: I could feel the hairs rising on my arms and legs. Incandescence leapt the gap between the combatants, enclosing them both in a nimbus of fire.

This was the real battle. Everything and everyone stopped to watch. The swans settled on the grass and were still.

They began to shout at one another in voices huge as thunder: spells, names, incantations, while lightning arced and spat from one immense pulsating aura to the other. The light seared our eyeballs. We huddled together on the grass, afraid to move and quite unable to look away.

'What are they *doing*?' Jo muttered. 'Why don't they get to grips? Calling each other names . . .'

Something clicked. Names. That was what they were striving for, out of the perfectly balanced impasse of equal powers. Each other's secret, innermost Name of Power. Like Rumpelstiltskin . . . Out of nowhere I remembered the word Xenia hadn't dared utter aloud. The Word she'd scribbled on a scrap of tissue. Her hands had been shaking as though she was committing the ultimate act of blasphemy . . .

Could Kostchei have felt so utterly secure and unassailable in this remote Northern manor that he'd amused himself by using his innermost Name as an opening-spell?

I scrambled to my feet, pushed Jo away and ran across the wildly bucking arena until I was perilously close to the colossal cloud-girded figure that was Oz. I flapped my arms frantically to get her attention.

'Oz!' I screeched. 'Joranokabikil! Joranokabikil!'

She was too intently focussed to hear me – but Kostchei did. His aura of power faltered visibly – just long enough for Oz to deliver a blow which knocked him sprawling.

'Joranokabikil!' I shouted – and at last she heard, and took up the cry. With her voice uttering his Name, Kostchei began to diminish. It wasn't a gradual process: it happened in sudden abrupt steps and spasmodic jerks, as though his power was plummeting down from one energy level to the next, like electron shells round a collapsing nucleus. With each quantum step, enormous concussions rocked the valley. He shrank and shrank, screaming obscenities, writhing, raging . . . shrank to man-size, then to child-size, then to the size of a doll . . . smaller and smaller, one jerky step after another until he was no bigger than a ladybird. And finally, to nothing.

The last, most violent explosion seemed to blast my head apart.

I'd gone deaf. The silence was like a thick wad of cotton-wool in both ears. Cautiously, I opened my eyes. I was crouched in foetal position just below the burnt-out dais. I uncurled, and looked up.

Oz was standing just in front of me. Normal-sized now – but her robes hadn't changed: she wore them like regalia. She held out her arms to me, and I dived into them. She smelt of lavender and old roses – and *humanity*.

'What took you so long?' I raged – and burst into tears. She even had the tissues handy.

We walked back to where the others were waiting in the middle of the arena. Jo and Brian stood up when they saw us coming. But Ferdinand was kneeling beside Odette, her limp hand held against his heart. Tears were pouring down his face.

Oz put him gently aside. Her face registered pain.

'So *unnecessary*,' she murmured – and if there'd been enough left of Kostchei to rate a tombstone, that would have been the only fitting epitaph.

She knelt down and laid one hand on Odette's chest and the other on her forehead, murmuring words that no-one else could hear. At last Odette stirred a little, and opened her eyes.

'Ferdinand?' she whispered. Ferdinand gave a choking sob and gathered her up in his arms.

The arena was littered with concussed swans and injured girls in white dresses. Most of the swans had been real ones, come to help their enchanted sisters in distress. Oz went to and fro, healing burns and contusions and broken wings and limbs. Those of us who weren't hurt gazed around, feeling shocked and utterly disoriented. For everything had changed. It wasn't just the pavilion which had disappeared: with it had gone the zoo, the gardens, the terraces . . . 'and every single bloody rhododendron,' Jo said with enormous satisfaction. The stands had vanished, and all the onlookers. Everything created or distorted by Kostchei's magic had followed him into extinction. The only exception was Brian. Maybe because although Kostchei had wired up his computer to Brian's body, he'd never been invited inside Brian's head.

The Castle itself was even more of a shock. In place of Kostchei's gleaming fairy-tale concoction of turrets and spires there stood a grey, square-towered building which looked as though it had grown out of the crag millennia ago: Odette's ancestral home.

The swans took wing, circled the field in ceremonious farewell, and departed. We pulled ourselves together and shepherded everybody else up the grassy slope and into the Castle. At the main door we were met by a clutch of stunned grooms and gardeners and a hysterical Mrs Briggs, who'd arrived as scheduled to help with the clearing-up. Villagers were homing in from all points of the compass, urgently demanding to know what the hell had been going on. We left Jo to deal with the enquiries. Not one of the live-in servants had survived. Just as we got inside, the storm broke overhead.

'There are some important decisions to be made,' said Oz, 'and the sooner, the better.'

It was a lot later, and we were sitting in what had been Kostchei's drawing-room. The retinue of ladies-in-waiting had been packed off upstairs to rest – but judging from the giggles and the pattering feet on the stairs, they were recovering fast.

Odette was still very weak. She was lying on the sofa next to the fire. Ferdinand sat beside her, holding her hand. Neither of them seemed to want to talk much.

'What sort of decisions?' Jo said.

'Well, this Castle, for instance. I assume you and Ferdinand are going to get married, Odette – so what do you intend to do with your Castle?'

Odette blushed. 'I hadn't thought quite so far ahead,' she confessed.

'We'll go to Boronia first, of course,' Ferdinand said. 'I do have certain responsibilities now, after all. I'm afraid you'll have to resign yourself to a big wedding, darling – they'll rather expect it, you know.'

'I don't mind,' Odette said. 'But afterwards, we'll need a home, won't we? Our own home. So – I think we should westore the Castle.' She looked round contentedly. 'Make it a happy place again, as it was when I gwew up here.'

'It'll take a horrendous amount of money,' I said dubiously. With Kostchei's demise the place was looking decidedly dilapidated. He'd been too stingy to get the builders in, and without the cloaking of magic, all sorts of major problems were coming to light – like half-collapsed chimneys, gaping holes in the roof and dry rot. 'Ferdinand's broke,' I added. 'We all know that.'

'I don't think money'll be a problem, somehow,' Oz said. 'Kostchei owned a lot of property across the Zones. Get a good lawyer, and you may be able to claim reparation. And who knows what he may have stashed away in this place in case of emergencies?'

Ferdinand laughed out loud. 'Treasure hunts?' He hadn't looked so relaxed and happy in months. 'You told me once you didn't believe in Happy Ever After, Foss. I think you're wrong.'

Jo cleared his throat. 'Well, actually . . . I hate to say this, but . . . you do have a minor, permanent problem on your hands.'

'What's that?'

'Borschei's still at the gatehouse.'

Oz burst into peals of laughter. Everybody else glared accusingly at me.

'Oh, Foss, *really*,' said Ferdinand in disgusted tones.

'It's not my fault!'

'I'm afraid it is, dear,' Oz said. 'You wished him well – and he survived. Not that he'll be grateful, mind you.'

'But what if he turns everybody into slugs?'

'I'll just have to make sure he doesn't, won't I?' said Oz.

'The other thing,' Ferdinand said thoughtfully, 'is . . . what about Brian?'

Brian jumped, and gave a tactful cough. 'Really, old chap. No need to worry about me. Want the shack back – happy to leave any time. Get on famously on my own, don'tcherknow.'

'Brian!' I said, shocked – but Ferdinand got in first.

'Don't be an idiot, old man. You saved my life last night. Of course you must stay. Mustn't he, Odette?'

Odette was nodding. 'Do you know what I think, darling?'

Ferdinand was all attention. 'Yes, dear?'

'We'll be away a lot of the time, won't we? Visiting pawents and so on. I'd like Bwian to be in charge here. Organise the wepairs, look after our best intewests genewally.'

'Chief Steward? That,' said Ferdinand warmly, 'is a bloody good idea. What d'you think, Brian?'

Brian was so overcome he couldn't answer.

Odette's thin face was flushed, and her eyes were sparkling. 'Then this is what we'll do. Tomowwow,' she said – and I was stunned to notice how decisive she'd suddenly become – 'the thwee of us – Bwian, you and me – will make a complete tour of the estate. I want to find out exactly what's been going on in my family's absence. And after that . . .'

Jo looked at me, and tipped his head towards the door. We got up quietly and slipped out into the corridor.

'And I thought she was a wimp!' I gasped. 'She's as tough as old boots! She's got Ferdinand twisted round her little finger. Brian, too.'

Jo chuckled. 'Didn't you tell me you thought Kostchei's transformations fitted people's personalities? That you were expecting Ferdinand to turn into a big soppy dog? Well – Odette turned into a *swan*, for Heaven's sake. You don't mess about with swans!'

Point taken, I thought. And a personality strong enough to make sure all nine ladies-in-waiting got turned into swans too.

We wandered off across the empty ballroom, dingy now and dimly lit, with worn flagstones underfoot instead of parquet, and chunks of plaster missing from the walls. Suddenly I felt shy – and very aware of Jo beside me.

Outside, the rain had stopped and everything was fresh-smelling and glittering in the evening sun.

'Foss,' Jo said. His expression was serious, and very vulnerable. He didn't have to say anything else, he just reached out.

A long time later there was a polite cough behind us. We released each other and looked round. Oz was standing in the doorway.

Jo grinned at her. 'Decisions?'

Oz nodded. 'Now it's your turn. What do you want to do? Go to Boronia with Ferdinand's wedding party? See all the places you didn't get the chance to visit? Or – we can go home.'

An unexpected wave of homesickness rushed up my throat and threatened to choke me. Triddon – and Oz and Jo. Mum and Bridgie and Geraint. I had to go back. We both did. To sort out our real lives, our real futures. And all at once I knew that from now on, I could cope. I didn't need illusion any more.

'Let's go home, Foss,' said Jo.

Dusk was falling as we made our way down the path to the lake, and the moon winked in and out of scudding clouds. The stream bubbled and chuckled over its pebbles. That unearthly silence had lifted, and the forest was full of stealthy, living sounds. Waves were rippling the surface of the lake and lapping the shore. At our feet an otter slipped out of the undergrowth and slid into the water.

On the lakeshore Oz raised both hands to the sky, and called.

Out of the twilight came a flock of swans, silver in the fitful moonlight. They settled on the water and came gliding majestically to the shore. Somehow Jo and Oz and I were lifted up and deposited on a raft of soft feathers and outstretched wings. The flock broke the water and rose in powerful flight, carrying the three of us up into the cloud-wracked, starry sky.

Lands blurred beneath us as we flew. After a while the movement and the steady beat of wings hypnotised me into a half-doze. I was only dimly aware of Oz talking to Jo.

'Kostchei was behind it all,' Oz was saying. 'He was the ultimate control freak: obsessed with power. He worked by selecting key figures and taking over their minds. He had his whole strategy planned out in advance. He helped the fairies whittle down the Arborean succession to one lost candidate. Sorcerers can afford to wait hundreds of years, if necessary, you see. His next big coup was going to be Boronia. Siegfried didn't come up to scratch so he sent Ferdinand off on his Quest for the Lost Princess, expecting to scoop up Arborea and Boronia in one move. One of Kostchei's minions selected Foss at random to be another puppet. And then he lost you both.'

I roused myself. 'So the Witch-Queen and Hezekiah weren't working for him?'

'No. Gloria and Zekar had their own agenda. They were opportunists – they grabbed you when you strayed accidentally into their territory. Kostchei must have been furious. He arranged for Arborea to be put out of circulation for a while.'

'What about Lermos?'

'Oh, he netted Romeric a long time ago. So many rulers were under his thumb without realising it – Kings, Presidents, Generals, tycoons . . . and he'd done it all so cleverly that it seemed natural. Until you saw the whole picture and started to get suspicious.'

'Like you and Magnus?'

She nodded. 'But we couldn't pin him down. Until you two got tangled up in the whole thing by accident. I think he felt that under his rule the Zones would be orderly, logical places, everything and everybody ticking along like clockwork. No more messy human emotions. No mistakes, no surprises. A machine state. Pathetic, really.'

'Scientific, though,' said Jo.

'No! Technological, perhaps. Not scientific. Ask any biologist. Any top-rate physicist, for that matter. It's change which keeps the Universe going. Randomness. Diversity. Potential for change. Kostchei wasn't nearly as intelligent as he thought he was. He had the arrogance to believe that he knew all the answers.'

'He didn't understand about Ferd and Odette,' Jo said.

'Right. And you two kept popping up and disrupting his plans, and he didn't even notice. He simply couldn't grasp what real people are capable of. He knew about greed, and selfishness and so on – but the fact that somebody might risk their life to save a friend was completely outside his experience.'

'Big mistake,' I agreed.

'No emotions,' Jo said thoughtfully, meaning Kostchei. 'No imagination.'

Something occurred to me. 'What about Arborea now? Did that spell break like the others?'

'No,' Oz said. 'Kostchei was careful. He supplied the know-how but he didn't actually cast the spell or ensnare the Prophecy. So I'm afraid the hundred-years schedule is still in operation.'

'So it's all down to Ferdinand and Odette,' I said.

'We'll set Foss onto them if they don't come up to scratch,' Jo grinned.

Our flight was slowing. Woods, fields and little folded hills came up to meet us as we descended. Finally the great swans backwinged and came to rest in the front yard of Tan-y-Fedwen.

Inside, nothing had changed. The fire was lit. After months of lamplight and candlelight, the electric bulbs seemed far too harsh – they made my eyes water. On the kitchen table was a long brown envelope addressed to me – my GCSE results. But the envelope looked shiny and crisp, the stamp looked new, the postmark wasn't even faded.

'Oz . . .?'

'Look at the calendar,' she grinned.

The picture at the top was the same as when I'd spent that day at Tan-y-Fedwen. It was the same year. I flipped the pages in disbelief. It was the end of August, just over two months since I'd ridden off into the Zones with Ferdinand.

Oz looked from one stunned face to the other, and broke up laughing. She was still giggling helplessly half an hour later when I said good-night and stomped off to bed.

25.

Everything is different now. Perhaps it's me: perhaps it's just that since the Zones I'm looking at the world with eyes that don't take anything for granted any more.

Scott has gone: disappeared out of all our lives forever. Mum has changed, too: she's a bit more assertive, a little less fearful and not so inclined to look on the black side. It must have taken a lot of courage to get rid of Scott, but she did it.

A few weeks after I got back, Martin appeared out of the blue: fit and suntanned and bearded, with presents for everybody. The kids rushed at him with hugs and shrieks of delight. He'd spent the year on an island in the Indian Ocean, helping with a bird survey.

'The expedition's got a base camp there, with chalets for visiting scientists. Next summer, why don't we all go out there for a few weeks? Air travel's not that expensive any more . . .'

A real holiday, on a tropical island . . . it sounded heavenly.

One evening Mum and Martin dragged me along to their folk music session at a local pub. Okay, not my scene – but I had to admit it was fun. The place was poky and dimly-lit and jam-packed with people playing instruments: Martin sawing away at his fiddle and Mum with her bodhran alongside a whole clutch of concertinas and penny-whistles and mandolins and guitars playing an endless flow of jigs, reels and polkas with such gusto you couldn't help tapping your feet along with everybody else.

There was a lull in the music, and somebody said, 'Give us a song, Mairhi.' And to my utter astonishment my mother – my shy, elegant, reserved mother – sat up straight in front of all those people and sang in a clear, sweet voice one of the songs her grandfather had taught her in Ireland when she was a kid. You could have heard a pin drop. Martin was bursting with pride, and I was choked.

I suppose I've changed too. I've noticed the difference in

people's attitude towards me. I'm more assertive than I was, but the funny thing is, I'm calmer, too. I don't lose my rag as much as I used to. I can look into the mirror now without wishing I was somebody else. Okay, there are still quite a few things I'd change if I had the chance – but I've learnt the hard way that the way I look is right for *me*.

What Jo feared hasn't happened. He's still, as he jokingly said, a formidable sort of bloke. You can't imagine anyone pushing Jo around. I can't think of him without going weak at the knees. In less than two months real time, Jo and I have done a whole two years of very rigorous growing-up, and it shows.

Jo's doing his Horticulture degree, as he's always wanted, and I'm doing A levels in Business Studies because, as Martin points out, a qualification like that is never wasted. Afterwards, I'm going to catering college. And after that . . . who knows what might happen? Not me. I've cured myself of trying to anticipate too far ahead. Set your future in stone, and that's how it turns out.

I know so much now – and sometimes it's a bit hard to handle.

Margaret is/was asleep in her briar-choked palace, waiting for her Prince to wake her up with a kiss . . . Ferdinand and Odette are, were or will be, happily married. Isobel, Haglund, Tilda Devine . . .

Was, is, will be . . . What happened in the Zones was quite literally outside Time: a thousand years ago, today, tomorrow. It was quite a shock to discover that I knew the stories already – had known them since I was knee-high to Mother Goose. When you're in the Zones, memories like that somehow get blotted out.

Which is just as well – because the stories themselves are nothing like the truth. Most of the important details have either been embroidered out of recognition, or have vanished completely. Ferdinand and his Swan Queen, for instance – funny how it's his dumb brother Siegfried who gets landed with the starring role in the version we all know: pink tights and tutus and a romantically tragic ending.

Nowadays, when I hear fairy tales being read to little kids, I have an overwhelming urge to say, No, it wasn't like that at all, you've got it wrong . . . But I keep my mouth shut.

One legend doesn't seem to have changed much at all. Last Saturday Mum started humming a tune which was so hauntingly familiar it chilled my blood.

'What – what's that?'

She flushed, and gave a slightly embarrassed laugh. 'Oh, just a song I've learned. For the session next week. It's a Scottish border ballad. Very improbable story, I suppose, but . . .'

And she sang it for me:

> '*Upon the Yule, when the winds blew chill*
> *And the round tables began*
> *Ah, then there came to our King's High Court*
> *Many a well-favoured man . . .*'

Shivers were crawling up and down my spine.

> '*The Queen stood up on the Castle wall*
> *To view both dale and down*
> *And she espied Young Waters*
> *Come riding through the town . . .*'

She broke off. 'Why, Foss, darling, whatever's the matter?'
I was crying.

Martin and Mum decided to get married at Easter. Plans for a sneaky ten minutes or so at a registry office were effectively demolished by Bridgie, who announced that nothing on earth was going to stop her being a bridesmaid in a frilly dress and bouquet, and insisted on including me in the scenario. It was going to be a proper wedding after all, in church, with both families present.

I went to Triddon for the Spring half-term. Money being short as always, Oz and I got down to some serious dressmaking. I was crawling about on the floor of my tower room with the scissors, cutting out, and Oz was clunking away at the old treadle sewing-machine, when suddenly she swore.

'Damn! I've put this sleeve in back to front! And I thought I was being so careful . . . Have you got the seam ripper there?'

I hadn't. 'It's probably in the workbox in the little front bedroom.'

Oz sighed. 'Run and get it for me, will you, love?'

As I was rummaging in the workbox I saw a car glide up the lane and pull to a stop just outside the front gate. An enormous, gleaming, dark-green limo with an unmistakable cachet. I shouted along the landing. 'Oz, who do we know with a Rolls?'

'A what?'

'A Rolls-Royce.'

'Good Lord,' she said.

The driver was a very tall, broad-shouldered man in his forties, with a neatly-trimmed black beard, dark eyes and bushy eyebrows. He looked vaguely familiar, somehow – perhaps I'd seen his face on the telly, or something . . .

He walked round and opened the passenger door. A girl got out – a young woman of maybe twenty-eight or so: one of these tall well-proportioned women, with lovely legs. The big man took her arm, and the smile they exchanged made me feel ashamed of myself for watching. He guided her through the gate, and strode ahead to knock on the front door.

Wheels were clicking round in my mind, like a rusty fruit machine. A huge man, built like a tank . . . No: a bull. Big kind brown eyes. Shaggy dark hair. A millionaire . . .

Click! went the machine, and suddenly bells rang and the jackpot came clattering out. I hurtled down the stairs and wrenched the door open.

'*Magnus!*' I screeched, and hurled myself into his arms.

He caught me up in a crushing bear hug. 'Foss! Ee, lass, it's good t'see you!'

It was too much: tears of joy were pouring down my face.

'Oh, Magnus!' I sniffed. 'You look terrific! I'm so *happy* for you!'

'Ee,' he said, all concern. 'No need to take on, lass. Won't do at all.' He fished out a clean hankie. 'Blow your nose. Come and meet Ariana.'

Ariana Gilbert! I was gobsmacked. So much had happened since that night at Garnock that I'd completely forgotten poor Mr Gilbert and the sneaky trick Jo and I had played on him.

Oz was behind me on the doorstep, radiating smugness.

'You knew!' I accused her.

'I didn't want to spoil it for you,' she said. 'Ariana, dear, it's lovely to see you. Magnus . . .'

'Ossiana,' Magnus said with enormous affection. He bowed formally, and kissed her hand as though she'd been a queen.

'You wouldn't like to do that again some time, would you?' she said wistfully. 'In front of Jo, and Emlyn, and Mr Thomas the builder, and one or two others?'

Magnus laughed.

Ariana was gorgeous. She had the kind of face you don't forget: not strictly pretty, but fine-boned and humorous and intelligent – and a throaty voice with a rich chuckle. I warmed to her immediately. Magnus was so proud of her it hurt.

After a hastily-assembled tea of hot scones and jam, I took Ariana up to my tower room so that Oz and Magnus could talk business.

Ariana deposited herself on the rug in front of the fire and said shyly, 'You know – Ossiana isn't at all as I imagined. I was expecting somebody – well – fierce and mysterious and dramatic.'

'Black flowing robes and masses of combat jewellery?'

'Right. But she's so – ordinary. A real sweetie.'

'You should see her in action,' I warned.

'Fearsome, huh?'

'Biblical,' I said. 'The human vocabulary doesn't stretch that far. You have to be there. Speaking of fearsome,' I added tentatively, 'How on earth did you manage to winkle Magnus out of his shell for long enough to find out what he's really like?'

Ariana laughed. 'The House helped, of course. She approves of me, I'm glad to say. But what really tipped the scales was when you and Jo and Ferdinand went missing. He was so worried he forgot to be shy.'

I was startled. 'Did we? Go missing?'

'You were okay as far as Arborea. But when you left the island, you vanished completely. Just a tantalising flash now and again . . . He almost went out of his mind.' She leant forwards, her face serious. 'I owe you such a lot, Foss. If you hadn't persuaded my father to call in on Magnus . . . '

'It was Jo's idea. I hope he didn't get too much of a shock, though.'

Ariana's expressive face was brimful of mischief. 'Well, actually, he didn't meet Magnus at all – until he picked one of his blue roses.'

I stared at her in consternation. 'Oh, no . . .!'

She nodded. 'Magnus blew his top. You know what he's like. Then, of course, when he'd finished blustering, he couldn't bring himself to mention a daughter – so he went into some ridiculous mumbo-jumbo about my father having to send him the first living thing he met when he crossed his own threshold.

I ask you! He could have ended up with our cat! But as it happened, it was me.'

As she told me the rest of the story, I realised that I knew it already. Mr Gilbert, frantic with worry about Magnus's ultimatum. Ariana/Beauty, calmly arguing that six months wasn't long and that she'd soon be home again safe and sound . . .

'Weren't you scared?' I said. 'I'd have been terrified.'

'I was, yes . . . but somehow – don't ask me how – I knew it was going to be all right.'

Magnus hadn't shown up for weeks after she'd arrived. Ashamed of his outburst, I suspected, deeply embarrassed, convinced that he'd blown the whole thing sky-high. And it had taken her several months after that to realise that she loved him.

'He let me go home for a while. He thought I'd left him for good.' Ariana's face was sombre. 'He tried to kill himself, but of course that didn't work. The awful thing was, I knew something was wrong. I *knew* – but I let the family persuade me that I was just imagining things. I missed him terribly, and in the end I went back. He was in a dreadful state. He hadn't eaten for weeks and he couldn't even stand. The House was frantic. I had to do some fast talking afterwards, to calm Her down.'

Ariana had nursed the transformed Magnus back to health and then they'd got married. Now they were on their way to London, to sort out Magnus's financial affairs in person. His stockbrokers, I felt, were in for a fairly considerable shock.

'And you must come and visit us, Foss. We'll go shopping, you can show us the sights, we'll go to the theatre . . . Get our hair done at Morico's . . . ' It sounded wonderful.

When they'd gone, Oz and I sat peacefully in front of the living-room fire. Oz was reading the paper, her glasses on the end of her nose, her fine-boned intelligent face frowning a little as she scanned the headlines. And suddenly I wondered what it was must be like to have lived so long, to have experienced so much that was beyond my understanding. As I watched her I seemed to see the centuries swirl and dissipate around her, like frail mists in a great void.

She turned and smiled at me over the top of her glasses. She knew what I'd been thinking, but the expression on her face warned me not to ask.

Instead, I said, 'Was my pendant very old? Where did it come from, originally?' The pendant had begun to feel like part of me, and I missed it terribly.

'I made yours for one of Matilda's ancestors, centuries ago. She was a dear friend, very supportive when I needed it. It was my way of thanking her. When Matilda gave her pendant to your grandmother, I made her another one.'

'The little girl who disappeared? What happened to her?'

'She grew up here, with me, of course. I was the only person Matilda trusted enough.'

'But . . .' I faltered. 'She died, didn't she? Like . . . the others . . .'

'Yes.' Oz's face was sombre. 'She and her husband found their own way into the Zones, without asking me. They weren't careful enough.' She gave a sad smile. 'They were a wild couple. Adventurous. Always taking risks . . . I loved them both very much. They must have asked too many questions, alerted Kostchei's minions – and they died. I rescued your father and adopted him and gave him my name, to keep him safe.'

'But . . .' I couldn't bring myself to say it.

'Tom's death was a genuine, tragic accident,' Oz said firmly. 'And now, Kostchei himself is dead. Thanks mainly to you. The nightmare is *over*.'

She made a rueful face. 'I suppose I'll have to make another pendant for you now, won't I?'

We smiled at one another. 'Thanks, Oz,' I said.

The next moment, Jo was knocking at the door.

THE END

ABOUT HONNO

Honno Welsh Women's Press was set up in 1986 by a group of women who felt strongly that women in Wales needed wider opportunities to see their writing in print and to become involved in the publishing process. Our aim is to publish books by, and for, women of Wales, and our brief encompasses fiction, poetry, children's books, autobiographical writing and reprints of classic titles in English and Welsh.

Honno is registered as a community co-operative and so far we have raised capital by selling shares at £5 a time to over 400 interested women all over the world. Any profit we make goes towards the cost of future publications. We hope that many more women will be able to help us in this way. Shareholders' liability is limited to the amount invested, and each shareholder, regardless of the number of shares held, will have her say in the company and a vote at the AGM. To buy shares, to buy books directly, to be added to our database of authors or to receive further information about forthcoming publications, please e-mail:

information@honno.co.uk

or write to Honno:

'Ailsa Craig',
Heol y Cawl,
Dinas Powys,
Bro Morgannwg
CF64 4AH.

www.honno.co.uk